Also by MJ Duncan

Second Chances

Veritas

Spectrum

ATRAMENTUM

MJ DUNCAN

Prologue

A knock on Joss Perrault's office door after six o'clock at night always spelled trouble, after seven meant possible disaster, and after eight guaranteed some kind of catastrophe, so when a distinctive triple-knock hit her door at a few minutes before nine, she cringed and just prayed for the best.

"Joss, I need you to fly to New York to meet with Niall Reynolds."

You have got to be fucking kidding me. Joss closed her eyes and took a deep breath. It was career suicide to argue with Charles Rand, the founding partner of Rand, Royal, & Wilkes, and after nine years at the firm with a partnership lurking somewhere in the not too distant future, it would do her no good to lose her temper now. "Christmas is in two days, Charles. Surely this can wait until next week?"

He shook his head. "Sorry," he said, looking entirely unrepentant, "but Niall is concerned about his company's end-of-year accounts and you're the only one I trust to make sure this is handled correctly."

Yeah, because there's no way in hell you're going to screw up your trip to Kauai to deal with his obsessive-compulsive bullshit. "Charles…"

"I've had Ashley book you a seat on the red-eye out of LAX. You'll be in New York by morning, and if you can talk him off the ledge fast enough, you'll still get to Vail for the holiday."

"Sky," Joss corrected, shaking her head.

"Right. Of course…"

1

Joss ran a hand through her hair and sighed. *Why do I keep dealing with this shit?* she thought, even as she asked, "What time's the flight?"

"Twelve-thirty," he said, tossing a printed boarding pass onto her desk.

The paper landed on top of the files she had been trying to finish so that she could leave for Colorado the next evening for a day of some much-needed rest and relaxation, and she bit the inside of her cheek as she picked it up. *At least they got me a seat in first class.* "I'll let you know when I've gotten this taken care of."

"I know you will." Charles smiled and nodded. "Good luck."

"Yeah…thanks," Joss muttered.

Once he was gone, she opened the bottom drawer of her desk, pulled out the bottle of Aberfeldy 21 she kept on hand for occasions such as this, and poured herself a generous couple of fingers of the smooth, amber alcohol. She capped the bottle and set it back in the drawer, and sipped at her drink as she spun around in her chair to look out the window. The public accounting firm of Rand, Royal, & Wilkes occupied the top four floors of a towering twenty-story building overlooking Marina Del Ray, and her corner office on the nineteenth floor provided a spectacular view of the marina below.

Joss rarely had time to appreciate the view her office location provided, but she did so now. The airport was thirty minutes from her condo, which was only two blocks away from the office, so she selfishly took this time for herself. She could not sleep on a plane to save her life—which was unfortunate, considering the number of red-eyes she flew—so she felt zero remorse about ignoring her work for a handful of minutes since she now had an extra five hours to finish the reports she had been working on when Charles shot her holiday plans to shit.

Sometimes I really hate this fucking job.

It was almost hard to believe that she had worked her ass off for so many years to climb to this exact position in the company. She had thought that building a successful career would make her happy, but as she watched a thirty-foot sailboat maneuver into a slip at the end of a crowded dock, the thought that she had been doing her best to ignore for the last few months floated across her mind.

What the hell am I doing?

Joss shook her head, dispelling the thought as she downed what was left of her whiskey. She set the dirty glass on her desk and grabbed the leather satchel her Aunt Helen had given her for Christmas two years ago—yet another holiday she missed because of work obligations—and began shoving the files she had been working on into it. She pulled the small file of notes she kept on Niall Reynolds' company from the bottom drawer of the lateral cabinet beside her desk and added it to the pile. Any other documents she might need, she would be able to access remotely since the firm kept digital copies of all records.

"What else...?" she wondered softly as she scanned her desk. There was always something she could work on, but instead of grabbing any other files, she just shook her head and zipped up her satchel. Everything else could wait until after Christmas. Assuming she even actually made it to Sky, she would be back in her office on the twenty-sixth because the firm was only closed for Christmas Day—though, with this trip, it was looking like she would not even get those twenty-four hours to herself—so there was no reason to kill herself over it all.

Joss shouldered her satchel and shook her head as she glanced over her shoulder at the marina below. The view was as magnificent as it ever was, but she had never appreciated it less than she did in that moment. She flipped off the lights as she walked out of her office and made her way toward the elevators. A handful of tired eyes that looked up at her from the cubicles that anchored the center of the floor as she passed, and she silently offered up a small prayer that they would at least get to enjoy their holiday. The elevator doors slipped open as soon as she pushed the call button, and she shook her head as she stepped inside.

God, I hate this fucking job sometimes...

One

Of all the places Joss Perrault might have reasonably expected a life-changing conversation to happen, it was certainly not at the reception following her Aunt Helen's funeral.

The resort town of Sky, Colorado was home to about five thousand residents, and though she knew it was impossible, it seemed like every one of them was packed into Atramentum—the bookstore Helen had owned and operated for over forty years. Joss had only been back to visit a handful of times in the last decade, and she regretted that distance as she struggled to put names to the familiar faces that offered her their condolences. It was nice, though, to see how many people cared enough to take time out of their own lives to celebrate Helen's. Conversations were hushed, though laughter would occasionally ring out, adding a slice of levity to the otherwise subdued atmosphere, and Joss was certain that if Helen were somehow able to see them all now, she would be pleased. Helen had loved this bookstore more than anything in the world, and there was no more fitting a place for them all to gather in her honor.

Helen would have been happy with the proceedings, but Joss was feeling overwhelmed and exhausted, and she took advantage of a lull in the tide of sympathetic well-wishers to sit down for a moment on the stool behind the front counter. Guilt that she had not managed to make it to Sky for Christmas four months earlier settled heavily in her stomach as she smoothed her hands over the lacquered pine, and she smiled sadly when one of Atramentum's permanent residents hopped up onto the counter to look at her.

"Hey, Mister Shakes," Joss cooed, petting the slightly overweight calico. Willy Shakes was the friendlier of the two cats that lived in the bookstore, and though he had been lapping up the attention from everybody who had stopped by the pay their respects, she could tell from the way that he kept looking at the door that he was waiting for Helen. "Sorry, bud," she whispered, shaking her head. "She's not coming."

A light brush against her ankle drew her gaze down, and she sighed as she locked eyes with Dickens, Atramentum's other permanent resident. The fact that Dickens was anywhere near her spoke volumes to how upsetting the situation was for the cats because the beautiful black tuxedo had never liked her, and had always avoided her like the plague. Of course, he did not really like anyone. He had been a standoffish kitten that had grown into a surly old man over the years, and if he had a voice, Joss had no doubt he would use it to yell at everybody gathered to "Get out of my bookstore!"

The phone in the front pocket of her pinstripe slacks buzzed with her thirty-eighth notification in the last four hours. Joss shook her head in disbelief, knowing without even having to look that it was her office.

She had not taken a single day off in the nine years she had been working at Rand, Royal, and Wilkes, but that loyalty and dedication was apparently not enough to earn her even one day of respite from frantic clients and demanding partners. She had spent the morning at the small desk in her hotel room with her MacBook powered up, tearing through files her bosses were convinced could not wait twenty-four hours for her to get back to the office. And as she typed out what should have been common sense answers to their questions, she was also on the phone, trying to reassure overanxious clients that the tax returns they submitted the week before were most likely not going to get audited because she was damn good at her job.

Atramentum

She had known when she signed with the public accounting firm that it was a field that took great pride in burning through the best and the brightest. She was the only one from her hiring class to make it past year three at the firm, but she was beginning to wonder if the promise of making partner was enough to justify working sixteen hours a day, six days a week—or longer, if a pressing matter came up—which left her no time for any kind of a life beyond the office. She had missed more events and holidays than she cared to think about because the firm had "needed her expertise" and, truth be told, she had been pushing herself through her growing feeling of burnout for the last seven months, hoping that it was just a phase and that it would eventually pass.

Her phone buzzed again, and she just barely resisted the urge to hurl it across the room.

From the moment she answered her phone Monday morning to learn that Helen had died after suffering a hemorrhagic stroke, she had denied herself any opportunity to mourn the passing of her only living relative. She had kept to her routine, staying even later than usual at the office every night because of the time she spent on the phone during the day arranging her Aunt's funeral. She had given the firm everything she had over the last nine years, only asking how high when told to jump, and all she had ever asked for in return was that she be allowed this day to grieve.

And they could not even allow her that.

"Excuse me, Jocelyn?"

Joss forced a small smile as she looked up at a man who appeared to be in his mid-sixties, with wire-rim glasses and a salt-and-pepper beard that matched the thick mop of hair on his head. "Yes?"

He smiled and held out his hand. "Robert Harding. I recognized you from the pictures Helen's shown me. I was her attorney."

"Oh. Yes. Hello." Joss got to her feet as she shook his hand. "Thank you for coming today."

"It was my honor," he assured her with a kind smile. "May I speak to you for a moment? Perhaps in the office?"

Joss nodded and led him through the stacks of books to the small office at the back of the store. She pushed the door open slowly, the hinges creaking softly as she stood in the doorway for a moment, looking. The desk was a jumbled mess of order slips and printouts and books that she had no doubt Helen had been in the middle of reading, and Joss felt a tug at her heart as she took it all in. She would have lingered longer, and was fairly confident that Helen's attorney would have allowed her all the time she needed, but she had learned long ago that staring at the possessions of those she had lost and wishing they were still with her did nothing to bring them back. She cleared her throat softly and shook her head as she stepped into the office and leaned against the edge of the desk. Robert closed the door as he followed her inside, and she crossed her arms over her chest as she turned to face him. "What can I help you with, Mr. Harding?"

He set his briefcase onto the edge of the desk, pulled out a thin manila file folder, and turned to Joss. "I'm not sure if you're aware or not, but you are the sole beneficiary of Helen's estate."

Joss sighed and nodded as she ran a hand through her hair. She had known, but she had been too preoccupied with balancing planning the funeral from a distance and her work to give her Aunt's estate too much thought. "Yeah. She had me sign the paperwork a few years ago when she redid her will, but I've pretty much forgotten everything that was in it." She shrugged sheepishly. "Can you just tell me what I need to do?"

"Well," Robert said, flipping the file folder open. "For starters, there are Atramentum and her cottage out by Pine Lake. There are also various investment accounts that you will need to decide what to do with."

"Right…" Joss groaned as her phone buzzed again. "I'm sorry." She pulled it out of her pocket and powered it off—something she should have done hours ago. She tossed it onto the desk and shook her head. "My work is…" She grit her teeth and swallowed back the burst of rage that flashed through her. "Rather demanding."

"Yes, Helen always worried about you putting in such long hours," Robert confided.

"Yeah. I know." Joss smiled sadly. "She was always telling me that, too."

Robert nodded. "As for things here, basically, if it was hers, it is now yours. Helen owned both the cottage and this property free-and-clear, and while there's no real rush to decide what you want to do with the cottage—you can always choose to keep it as a vacation house or use it as a rental property—the business is another matter. I know you're busy and undoubtedly overwhelmed at this point, but you do need to decide what you want to do with Atramentum."

"Right..." Joss massaged the back of her neck as she weighed her options. A soft scratch at the door drew her eyes up, and she brushed past Robert to open the door for Willy Shakes, who had followed them.

Dickens was perched atop the nearest shelf staring at her, and she waited for a moment to see if he was going to join them, but when he laid his head down to make himself comfortable, she groaned under her breath as she closed the door again.

Forget the properties—what was she going to do with the cats? Her condo building in Los Angeles had a strict no-pets policy, never mind the fact that she worked too damn much to properly care for Willy Shakes and Dickens.

Hell, as it was, she barely had time to take care of herself.

She could always try to re-home them. She was sure that there were plenty of people who would be willing to adopt Willy Shakes, and that there might even be a few brave souls who would also adopt Dickens so the brothers would not be separated.

Willy jumped onto the desk, his front paws connecting with her phone and sending it sliding toward the edge, and Joss just watched it tumble to the floor, not really caring what happened to it.

Even though she knew the plush rug under the desk would have more than sufficiently cushioned the phone's fall, a part of her hoped the stupid thing shattered on impact. She had no doubt that it would come screaming to life with a barrage of alerts when she powered it up again, and just thinking about everything she would have to deal with made her cringe. Honestly, in that moment, if she had a choice, she would never turn the damn thing back on at all. She had tried to work through her burnout, but she felt its suffocating presence even more strongly now than she ever had before.

I can't even get twenty-four hours to myself for my aunt's fucking funeral...

Her gaze drifted to a framed photograph beside Helen's open laptop, and she bit her lip as she picked it up.

Though she could not remember when the picture was taken, she knew by the shaggy pixie style of her hair that it was taken the summer before she graduated from UCLA because she had begun growing her hair out during her senior year. Her and Helen were laughing at the front counter here at the store, the floor around them littered with open boxes of books waiting to be shelved, and Joss swallowed back a pang of guilt that she had not visited more often after she graduated. Helen had understood, of course, and had come out to California during the off-seasons to visit, but she should have made more of an effort to get back here. Joss sighed as she smoothed her thumb over the glass, sorry that she could physically touch the happy moment that had been captured on film.

She had been so eager to escape Sky and make her life somewhere else that she had honestly forgotten how much she enjoyed helping Helen with the store. Had forgotten how much Atramentum had given back to her after she had lost everything. Yes, she had built a life for herself in Los Angeles—a successful, stressful, lonely life—but as she looked down at the messy desk and the fat cat watching her, she knew that the life she had built for herself was not the one she wanted any more. She had been edging closer and closer to this point for a while, and the opportunity to come back to Sky was just too sweet to resist. "And if I decide to move here and take over Atramentum?"

Robert smiled and nodded. "I could certainly help you with that."

"Good." Joss swallowed hard and blinked back tears she would not allow to fall until she was alone later as she set the picture gently back in its place beside the laptop. "So, what do we do next?"

"I will draw up the paperwork that you will need to sign regarding the transfer of titles on the properties as well as the investment accounts and such, and then"—Robert looked around the small office—"I am pretty confident that Scott, Helen's only regular employee, would be willing to help you with getting things here organized."

Joss nodded. She had gone to high school with Scott Heitz, and they had worked at the store together during the summer holidays when they had been in college. From what Helen had told her, he was writing now—short stories, or something like that, she wanted to say—and used the busy seasons as his time to plot and outline, and his time off during the off-seasons to write full-time.

She frowned and stared thoughtfully at the door. She had been so frustrated with work and overwhelmed with the funeral that she had not even noticed that he had been absent from the events of the day.

Why wasn't he here?

As if reading her mind, Robert said, "Scott and his wife are in Paris for their anniversary right now."

"Oh. Okay."

"It's the off-season, you know, which means—"

"There's not a lot of business," Joss finished for him, nodding slowly as she considered the logistics of her decision. She needed to give notice at the firm, pack up her condo, put it on the market, and figure out how to physically go about relocating her entire life. The idea of walking away from everything she had worked so hard for over the last decade or so was exciting and more than a little terrifying, but as she looked around Helen's office, she knew that it was something she needed to do. "Right, so, let's just close up shop for a couple weeks until I can get everything taken care of back in

LA and move out here. It should only be two-, maybe three-weeks tops, and I'm sure everybody in town would understand."

"Of course they will," Robert assured her kindly. "Are you sure about this, though?"

"Yeah." Joss took a deep breath and let it go slowly. "I am. One question though…"

"Anything."

Joss looked down at Willy Shakes and then back at Robert. She hated to put him on the spot like this, but she had nobody else to turn to. And, if she had to guess, she would wager that he had already been doing what she was about to ask anyway. "Can you take care of the cats for me until I get back?"

"I can certainly take care of these rascals for a few more weeks," Robert agreed with a smile as he gave Willy's head a little scratch. "I think Dickens is even starting to like me."

"Really?" Joss arched brow in surprise. "That's impressive."

Robert nodded as he slipped the manila folder he had been reading from back into his briefcase. "I know." He snapped the leather case shut and sighed. "Shall we go back out there?"

Joss would have much preferred to just stay where she was, but she knew that was not really an option. "Yeah. Sure." She pulled open the door and waved him through. "Thanks for all your help, Robert. Really."

He gave her arm a light squeeze and smiled. "It's been my pleasure."

Once he had gone, she looked back at Willy and shook her head. She was really going to move back to Sky. "You gonna help me keep this place running smoothly, big man?"

Willy stood up, stretched, and jumped off the desk. He brushed against her shins as if to say "Of course. Follow me." as he walked out the door, and she smiled to herself as she closed the door behind them. *Good. Because I'm going to need all the help I can get…*

Two

Considering the fact that Rand, Royal, and Wilkes had been her entire life for over nine years, it was remarkably easy for Joss to give her two-weeks notice as soon as she returned to Los Angeles the day after Helen's funeral. Her phone blowing up at her with missed calls, texts, and emails as soon as she turned it back on that afternoon in Atramentum had been a more than adequate reminder of what her life had become; and as she settled in to try to triage the mess that had accrued during her few-hours of unavailability, she became more and more convinced that she had made the right decision.

The senior partners had tried to talk her into staying—offering her everything but the moon to change her mind—but the allure of the Rockies and a small, independent bookshop was too tempting to pass up. She wanted a life outside of an office. Wanted to do more than glance at the world through a window. She wanted a life that had friends instead of colleagues, and a part of her hoped that she might even someday manage to find somebody special to share it all with.

The last two weeks had been an exhausting cycle of packing and preparing the accounts she oversaw to be reassigned to those hardy souls who were not yet weary of a five-to-nine workday. And with every file she handed off, she felt lighter and more excited she became for her new adventure.

She did not look back as she left the Pacific Ocean in her rear view mirror and joined the throng of cars clogging the 110 through downtown Los Angeles, and she cranked the radio when she merged onto the 210 headed toward Vegas, doing an energetically terrible job singing backup for Sheryl Crow. She had made the fourteen-hour drive in one-go more times than she could count in the past, but she broke the trip into two legs because the trailer she was towing behind her Jeep dictated she travel at a more lawful speed. St. George, Utah was the perfect stopping point for the night, and though the hotel was nothing special, she still slept better than she had in years. She woke up early the next morning energized and excited to get to Sky—a fact that was especially ironic considering how eager she had been to leave the town years before—and after taking advantage of the hotel's complementary breakfast, she hit the road.

The sanity-restoring idle of the off-season greeted her as she drove through downtown Sky. The mountain was quiet for now, the swaths of ski slopes blooming with wild grasses that swayed in the breeze, and the chair-lifts above them rocked ever-so-slightly, abandoned for the moment but not forgotten. Locals lingered on the sidewalks chatting, enjoying this time to rest and recharge before the frenetic pace of yet another tourist season was upon them, and it seemed like every-other business she drove past had a "Closed" sign hung in the window. In a few short weeks hikers and bikers would descend on to town to take advantage of everything the Rockies had to offer during the warmer months, but for now the town fully embraced its more laid-back persona.

It only took a few minutes to drive through town, and five minutes after the last brick building disappeared from view, she turned off the main highway and onto a narrow gravel road. The knobby tires on her Rubicon bit into the loose surface as she drove slowly down the path. She gripped the steering wheel tightly and kept one eye trained on the trailer that was bouncing in her rear view mirror, and hoped that nobody would be coming the other direction. The gravel road served as a driveway for both the cottage she had inherited from Helen and a large mountain retreat further up by the small lake, and though she knew that her Jeep could handle going into the brush just fine, she was pretty sure the trailer she was towing would not fare as well.

She cast one last look up the main drive as she turned onto the offshoot that would lead to her cottage and idly wondered who owned the mansion now. Helen had mentioned that it had been up for sale the year before, but she could not remember if she told her who had bought it. Winters could be dangerous when large storms rolled through, dumping crippling amounts of snow, and one of the first things Helen had taught her when she came to live in Sky following her parents' deaths was that one should always be at least acquainted with their neighbors in case something happened.

It was something she would need check on eventually, but Joss pushed all those thoughts aside as she pulled to a stop in front of the small cottage at the end of the lane. The exterior façade was covered with stacked stone in varying hues of gray, and the gabled steel roof was painted a dark green to match the canopy of trees surrounding it. It looked just like it had the last time Joss had visited, and there was a part of her that half-expected Helen to come out the front door, arms extended in greeting with a wide smile lighting her face.

"Right, not gonna happen," she reminded herself as she killed the engine and opened her door.

She stood beside the car and stretched her arms up over her head, leaning left and then right, working some of the stiffness from her spine as she took a moment to take in her old home. The one-bedroom loft had been crowded with both her and Helen living there—she had slept on a pullout sofa in the main living area—but in the aftermath of her parents' deaths, it had been eight hundred and thirty-six square feet of comfort and warmth that she would forever be grateful for.

There was a brief moment when she had been packing her things in Los Angeles that she had debated selling the cottage and buying a condo or something in town—taking over Atramentum would be reminder enough she was now alone in the world—but that moment had passed quickly. Reminder or not, there was no way she would ever be able to part with the quaint stone cottage tucked into the woods like something from a fairytale. This cottage and Atramentum had seen her through her darkest days before, and though she was older and more jaded and just looking for a chance to start over, she had faith that they would come through for her again.

Joss sighed and let her arms fall back to her sides with a smack as she started for the short cobblestone path that connected the driveway to the sweeping deck that wrapped around the front of the cottage and fanned out along the side of the house. A wood portico that had strings of fairy lights laced over and through its beams covered the seating area beside the kitchen that had an outdoor fireplace, and Joss smiled as she remembered sitting out there with Helen when she came home for the summer during college, sharing a beer or a glass of wine after a long day at Atramentum and talking about anything that crossed their minds. Helen had been more of an older, wiser sister than a surrogate parent, leading her with a gentle hand and a kind smile, allowing her to make mistakes and learn from them, ready to step-in if needed, but giving her the room she needed to grow into her own person. It was something Joss had appreciated more than she had ever been able to express and, as she pulled open the storm door to slide her key into the deadbolt on the front door, she wished she had found a way to tell Helen that.

The cottage smelled like dust and neglect even though it had been vacant for less than a month, and Joss was grateful for the warm spring weather outside as she threw open all the windows before she stood in the small foyer and surveyed what needed to be done.

She had arranged for Robert to have Helen's furniture donated to the local charity that benefited the women's shelter in town, so the cottage was empty except for a pile of boxes in front of the picture window on the far wall that held Helen's books, photographs, and other personal items, as well as the flat-screen television Helen had bought the year before. Joss had not even owned a television back in Los Angeles, choosing instead to watch the few shows she followed on her laptop, so the fifty-inch screen tucked into the corner, waiting for the stand she had ordered to hold it, seemed comically huge.

The layout of the cottage was such that only the sofa from her condo in LA would have fit in the space, but she had sold it with the rest of her furniture. Moving herself without help meant that lifting heavy items like couches was out of the question, and so she just tacked a comfortable-looking corner sofa to her cart when she was browsing Ikea's website. The warehouse down in Denver charged her an arm and a leg to deliver to Sky, but at least their guys would do all the heavy lifting and, in the end, even their outrageous fees were cheaper than hiring movers. She would still need to pick up the little odds and ends to make the cottage feel like home, but the new sofa and other items she ordered were a good first step to the fresh start she was hoping to make.

The main floor was a twenty-five by twenty-five foot square. To the immediate right of the front door was a closet that was just big enough to house the cottage's HVAC and water heater, as well as a small, separate closet that housed a stacked washer and dryer unit. Tucked on the other side of the laundry and mechanicals was the home's lone bathroom, which was surprisingly airy considering its small footprint.

Of course, "surprisingly airy" was the best way to describe the entire cottage. It was only two-thirds of the size of her condo back in Los Angeles, but it felt three times as big.

A large bookshelf that doubled as support for the sleeping loft served as a see-through divider of the open space. On the side near where she stood in the foyer, it created a small hallway that led to the bathroom and the black wrought-iron spiral staircase that led to the loft, and beyond it lay the main living area. A peninsula counter that did double-duty as both a work surface and eating area separated the kitchen from the rest of the space. Helen had loved to cook, and had spared no expense when she gutted the space a few years back to create the kitchen of her dreams, installing hand-milled maple cabinetry, gray granite countertops, and top-of-the-line stainless steel Wolf appliances.

It was easy to imagine the new furniture that she had ordered in the space, and Joss nodded to herself as she turned back to look at the stairs to the loft. She did not have to go up to know what she would find—a platform for a queen-sized bed tucked beneath the nearest gabled window and a small desk nestled in front of the other—but as she stared at the staircase, she had to wonder how in the hell the delivery guys were going to get her new mattress up to the bedroom.

After a moment of trying to figure it out, she shook her head and gave up. "You know what?" she declared to the empty cottage. "Not my circus, not my monkey."

Robert's guys had somehow managed to get the old one out, surely the delivery guys who would be arriving later that day would be able to get the new one in.

Joss checked her watch and sighed. There was just over an hour until the beginning of her scheduled delivery window. In an ideal world, she would be able to get as many of her things into the cottage for the truck arrived so she would have a better idea of where she wanted the delivery guys to set it all up, but to manage that, she was going to have to get moving. She left her sunglasses on the windowsill beside the front door and made her way back down the porch step to start unloading the trailer.

She worked quickly, shuttling boxes and clear plastic cartons with multi-colored lids from the trailer to the general area their contents belonged inside, building small towers to be deconstructed and sorted later. And she was glad she had been too busy working to acquire many tchotchkes as she hauled boxes up the narrow staircase to the bedroom, shoving them in the closet so that they were out of the way. For being as small as it was, the cottage had a ton of storage built into it, and the few things she brought with her would fit with more than enough room to spare.

With most of the boxes out of the way, she was able to lift a handful of hangers from the shower rod she had rigged to serve as a makeshift closet at the back of the trailer. She would not have much use for her old work clothes here in Sky, but they were too nice to just give away. And, she figured, if she ever found somebody to date, they might come in handy.

She smiled at the thought as she hopped back to the ground, and had just hooked the curve of the hangers over her fingers and draped the plastic-covered clothes over her shoulder when something crashed into her legs. She swore loudly in surprise as she went down, dropping the clothes she had been holding as her hands scraped over loose gravel in a painful attempt to cushion her fall. Her heart raced as she tried to see what had run into her, but she did not need to look far as a large tongue licked up the side of her face, leaving a slobbery trail from her chin to her temple.

"Fucking hell. Really?" Joss sat up and shook her head. A black Great Dane wiggled happily in front of her, the white blaze on its chest bobbing back and forth with every energetic hop as it stared at her with what she swore was a self-satisfied smile on its face. "Are you the one who took me out?" she asked the dog as she climbed to her feet.

The dog cocked its head, its tongue lolling to the side as it stared at her.

"You need to work on your approach, buddy. That is not how you pick up women," she lectured as she scratched the dog behind the ear, her olive-toned skin pale against the dog's dark coat. She spun the large red collar on the dog's neck to look for a tag, and pulled her phone out of her pocket as she read, "George Dylan. 2 North Star Drive." She gave the dog an appraising look. Her cottage was at 1 North Star Drive, which meant that George was one of her neighbors who lived in the house up the road by the lake. "Hello, neighbor."

George's tail wagged in an energetic circle that had his whole body shaking.

"Pleased to meet you, too," Joss chuckled as she began dialing the contact number on George's tag. She had just finished punching in the area code when a panicked, slightly breathless female voice rang out from just beyond the tree line, "Goddamn it, George! Where are you?"

Joss looked at the dog and grinned. "I think your mom's pissed."

George's tail dropped, and he looked warily over his shoulder at the woods.

"No, you can't run away." Joss gripped his collar tighter. "I've got him!" she hollered back, and she chuckled at the way George buried his head into the back of her knees to hide. "You are so busted," she teased the dog as she crouched down and scratched behind his ears.

George licked her face and rolled over, and Joss laughed as she began rubbing his belly. "Oh. George is a girl," she observed as she scratched up and down the dog's ribs. "My bad."

George, for her part, did not seem to mind being misgendered as she squirmed on her back, trying to force Joss' hands where she wanted them.

The sound of branches snapping beneath hurried footfalls drew Joss' eyes to the trees, and her jaw fell open when the woman who had been chasing George jogged out of the woods. The woman was of average height—though her height was the only thing that was "average" about her. On a scale from one to ten, she was easily a twelve, and Joss licked her lips as she watched her jog across the clearing, her thick blond hair bobbing around her shoulders with every step like something out of a shampoo commercial. She was dressed casually in a pair of dark wash jeans and a deep green fleece pullover that, Joss noticed as the woman stopped in front of her, highlighted the bright green eyes that stared at her from behind the woman's ridiculously sexy black-framed glasses. Her cheeks were pink with exertion and her lips were curled in a smile that was unabashedly relieved, though she did seem to be striving for annoyed as she stared George down.

It had been a long time since Joss had felt the heart-racing flutter of attraction that rippled in her chest now, and she cleared her throat as she pushed herself to her feet. She held out her hand and did her best to appear nonchalant as she said, "I take it you're George's mom?"

The woman ran a hand through her hair and nodded. "Yeah. That's my monster." She smiled up at Joss as she shook her hand. "Thank you for catching her."

Joss chuckled. If anything, George had caught her, but she was more than willing to let that be their little secret. "It wasn't a problem at all. I'm Joss Perrault."

"Maeve Dylan." Maeve looked at the open trailer behind Joss and the pile of clothes strewn over the ground. "George tackled you, didn't she?"

"No." Joss lied, feeling protective of her new four-legged friend. Not to mention her ego. "Not at all. I, uh…tripped over my shoelaces." They both looked down at her feet, and Joss groaned, clearly caught as the laces of her trail running shoes were still neatly double-knotted. She smiled sheepishly and amended, "It was really more of an energetic hug."

Maeve chuckled and shook her head. "That certainly sounds like George. I am so sorry about this. If you take your clothes to the cleaner's in town, I'll have them put it all on my account."

"That's not necessary." Joss crouched down and gathered her shirts. The plastic covering them all had done its job, and they were as pristine as they had been before George ran into her. "See." She held them up by the hangers and gave them a little shake. "They're as good as new."

"Still…"

The small crinkle between Maeve's eyebrows was positively adorable, and Joss smiled as she shook her head. "If they need it once I get them out of these bags, I'll take them in." She hooked the hangers around her left hand and draped them over her shoulder. "So, you and George live up the drive by the lake?"

"We do." Maeve nodded. A small, apologetic smile curled her lips as she ducked her head and added, "I'm sorry about Helen."

Joss nodded. "Thank you."

"Are you her daughter?" Maeve rolled her eyes at herself and shook her head. "Sorry. I don't mean to be rude, it's just that you look like her and I haven't seen you around before…"

Joss waved off the apology. "It's fine. Helen was my aunt. I was down in LA, didn't make it back much because of work. But with everything that happened..." Her voice trailed off and she shrugged, not wanting to burden Maeve with the gory details of it all. "I decided to move back here and give running Atramentum a try."

"It's a lovely bookstore," Maeve said. "I've been in there a few times and have always found something wonderful to read."

"I can't take any credit for that, but thanks. Maybe I'll see you in there sometime."

Maeve smiled, the simple expression making her entire face glow, and nodded. "Maybe you will."

Joss was trying to figure out how to respond when she was saved by the throaty rumble of a truck making its way along her driveway. She sighed as a bright yellow paneled truck rolled into view, both grateful for the save and sorry that her time with Maeve would be coming to an end.

Feeling like she needed to say something, however, Joss cleared her throat and explained lamely, "I ordered some new furniture for the place."

"Of course." Maeve nodded as she reached for George's collar. "Then we'll get out of your way so you can finish moving in. Again, I am so sorry about this. And, please, if you need to take your clothes in to be dry-cleaned, have them put it on my account."

"It's fine," Joss assured her with a smile. "Really." She reached out to give George's head a quick pat goodbye. "Later, bud."

George licked her hand and then looked up at Maeve as the delivery truck stopped behind Joss' jeep.

Still gripping George's collar, Maeve took a small step backward. "It was nice to meet you."

"Yeah." Trying to appear nonchalant, Joss went to run a hand through her hair, and she groaned when her fingers stuck. She had pulled it back into a ponytail for the day, and had just screwed it all up in her failed attempt to be suave. She sighed as the chestnut-colored strands she had dislodged fluttered around her face. *Smooth, Perrault*, she mocked herself even as she replied, "You too."

Maeve smiled and waved as she turned to lead George toward the small dirt path she had come down on.

"Ms. Perrault?" the delivery driver called out.

Joss nodded as she set her clothes back onto the ground. She pulled the rubber band from her hair, and combed her fingers through the wavy strands as she put it back up. "That's me."

He ran a finger down the manifest clipped to his clipboard. "You ordered a corner sofa, six bar stools, a television stand, coffee table, and a mattress?"

Joss nodded. "Yep. That's it."

"You wanna show me where you want all of this?"

"Yeah," Joss said, glancing at the path Maeve and George had come down as she led the delivery guy up to the porch, and she was sorry to see that her new neighbors had already disappeared back into the woods. She shook her head and refocused her attention on the burly deliveryman who was waiting for her to tell him where she wanted them to put everything. "It'll all go in here…"

Three

Even though there were still boxes and bins scattered around the cottage waiting to be unpacked, Joss was at Atramentum by eight the next morning. She had arranged with UPS for all the deliveries that had been held over the last few weeks to be delivered that morning, and while she would have liked one more day to settle into her new life, she had work to do. With the peak summer season beginning in eleven days, she needed to make sure that the shelves were stocked and the store was ready for the glut of tourists and weekend-warriors that would soon be descending upon the town.

Traffic on Summit Avenue behind her was light as she made her way up the sidewalk to the pale beige stone and glass façade of Atramentum. The wooden sign above the door—white circle with a bright fuchsia, typeset-style A in the middle of it that hung from a black metal bar—creaked as she slipped her key into the lock into the black front door, and she studied her reflection in the glass as she turned it over. Her normally vibrant, gold-flecked brown eyes were dulled, muted by the transparency of her makeshift mirror and the dim morning light, and her hair was a mass of flyaway strands tickling her face as it billowed with the breeze. The sleeves of her fitted flannel that she had rolled to her forearms were pulled closer to her elbows as she tucked her hair behind her ears, and the chunky steel Tag on her left wrist that Helen had given her when she graduated from UCLA slid as high up her arm as the loose band allowed. Her fingertips brushed against her dark wash jeans as she tried to shake her watch back into place, and she sighed as she pushed the door open.

Right, let's do this, she told herself as she walked into the store.

Willy Shakes was sitting on the register near the door waiting for her when she flipped on the lights, and Joss smiled as she tossed her keys onto the counter beside him. "What's shakin', Mr. Shakes?" she asked as she scratched his head.

Willy purred and turned his head into her touch, chasing her hand whenever she tried to pull away.

"Yeah, you won't be left alone like that anymore," she promised him. From the corner of her eye, she saw Dickens watching them from his usual spot atop the nearest bookcase, his back straight and his gaze perfectly reproachful, and she avoided making direct eye contact with him as she set her coffee cup beside Willy in case he saw it as a challenge and decided to attack her. "I'll be right back," she told them both, though only Willy seemed to care—Dickens just turned with a dramatic swish of his tail and curled himself into the small space at the end of the top shelf that was always kept empty for him to sleep in.

Joss wandered deeper into the store, the soles of her running shoes silent against the pale gray tiled floor, and dragged a finger along the spines of the books that packed the deep mahogany shelves. The store smelled of parchment and ink and dust and loss, and Joss swallowed around a lump in her throat as she gathered Helen's laptop from the office and took it back to the front counter.

This area beside the register had been her domain when she worked at Atramentum all those years ago, and she was much more comfortable by the till than in the office. Eventually, she would have no choice but to make the small room at the back of the shop her own, but for now she was more than content to avoid it.

She opened the laptop and powered it up, and sighed as it came to life with a beep and a hum. She sipped at her coffee as the computer booted, and then glanced at Willy as she double-clicked on the Excel icon. "Time to see where we're at."

Willy yawned and hopped into the window to nap in the sunshine pouring through the store's front windows.

"That's not very reassuring, you know," Joss told him as she turned her attention to her computer screen.

Willy snored contently on the counter beside her as she tried to decrypt Helen's shorthand notes in her inventory log. Author's names were easy enough pick out, along with the titles of their books and their publishers, but the letters and symbols that followed in the columns beyond did not make any sense at all.

"What in the world were you doing with all of this?" she muttered to herself as she leaned back on her stool, hoping that the distance she put between her eyes and the screen would be enough to make sense of what she was looking at. It did not, and she groaned as she ran a hand through her hair. "Fuck. I'm going to have to totally redo this."

The bell above the front door rang, and she looked up with relief, grateful for the distraction. She expected to see a brown uniform and a stack of boxes on a dolly, and she could not contain her grin when she instead saw a familiar face smiling at her. Scott Heitz had been her first friend when she moved to Sky fourteen years before, and she shook her head as she slid off her stool and walked around the edge of the counter into his warm embrace. "Hey, you."

"Hey, Joss," he murmured as he held her close.

Scott's arms tightened around her waist, and Joss sighed as she squeezed his neck one more time before pulling away. "You look good," she said, giving him a quick once-over. His warm brown eyes were no longer hidden behind the curtain of dirty-blond hair he had sported the last time she had seen him, but his shy smile and lanky build were exactly the same as she remembered.

"You do too." He sighed and shook his head. "I'm sorry I wasn't here for the funeral. Michelle and I were in France when we heard what happened, and we just couldn't make it back in time."

"It's okay," Joss assured him with a small shrug, touched that he seemed so genuinely upset about not being there. "It was unexpected."

"Still…"

"It's fine, man. But I appreciate the sentiment." Joss took a deep breath and flashed him a wry smile. "So, I guess I'm technically your boss now…"

He hooked his thumbs in the front pocket of his jeans and smiled. "Assuming you're not going to fire me."

"I'm not going to fire you," Joss chuckled. "It'll be nice to have a friend around."

"Yeah, it will. So, what do you need me to do, boss-lady?"

"I like the sound of that." Joss glanced around them. The cozy sitting area by the electric fireplace opposite the register at the front of the store was already nice and tidy thanks to the fact that the store had been closed for the last few weeks, so there was nothing immediately pressing to be taken care of. "It's business as usual, really. UPS should be bringing a shit-ton of inventory they couldn't deliver over the last couple weeks sometime this morning, and then it's just stocking shelves and getting ready for the summer season."

He nodded. "Okay. You want me to make sure the stacks are in order?"

"That'll work. I'll help, and you can catch me up on everything I've missed since I left."

Scott laughed. "Yeah. That's a lot, you know. You've been gone for a long time…"

"I know," Joss murmured. It was strange, being in Atramentum with Scott like nothing had changed, but she felt an undeniable comfort in the familiarity of his presence as well. "So I guess that means you better get started."

Even though Sky was one of the most popular tourist destinations in the Rockies above Denver, it was a small-town at heart, which meant that everybody pretty much knew everybody's business. Joss listened to the stories Scott was telling her about people they had gone to school with as they worked side by side, down one row and up the next, straightening books and rehoming those that were in the wrong place.

"And how did you meet your wife?" Joss asked after Scott finished telling her about the mayor's daughter's lavish wedding the summer before.

"She came in here one day looking for a book…" He shook his head as a positively awed smile lit his face. "She's so far out of my league, it's ridiculous. But, yeah, she was looking for a specific edition of *The Giver*, and when I was ringing her up, she handed me a business card with her phone number written on the back of it. It took me a few days to work up the guts to call her, but we met up for coffee one day after work, and the rest is history."

"That's sweet." Joss bumped him with her shoulder. "Good for you."

"Thanks. Anyway, what about you?"

"Honestly man, I was working so much I didn't even have time to meet anyone. It'd be nice," Joss admitted with a wistful sigh, "but I think that's something I've just kinda missed the boat on, ya know?"

"You're insane."

"No, I'm a realist."

Scott rolled his eyes. "Yeah, because thirty-three is definitely too old to find a good woman."

Joss laughed. After Helen, Scott had been the first person she had come out to the summer before her sophomore year of college, and they had spent their free time during her trips home playing wingman for the other on the weekends when Helen let them off work to go enjoy the town for the evening. Not that either of them ever did anything more than stare longingly at the pretty girls they desired from across the room, both of them far too chickenshit to make a move, but the intent to be a good friend had been there, and she knew by the way he was grinning at her now that it still was. "First of all, I doubt Sky is suddenly crawling with eligible lesbians, so whatever, and second of all, we just ran into each other again for the first time in years, and you're giving me shit about this?"

"Yeah, well…" He winked at her. "What can I say? I guess some friendships can just snap back on track like that like nothing happened."

"Yeah. I guess so—" The rest of Joss' reply was interrupted by the sound of the bell above the front door jingling, and she left Scott to sort through the rest of the science fiction section on his own as she headed toward the front of the shop. She smiled at the UPS guy that was waiting by the register, scratching under Willy Shake's chin as the cat purred contentedly. "Can I help you?"

He stopped petting the cat and looked up at her with a questioning smile. "Ms. Perrault?"

"That would be me."

"I'm Ben. Sorry to hear about Helen."

"Thanks," Joss murmured as he picked up the electronic clipboard that was on the top of the boxes on his dolly and held it out to her.

"Where do you want these?" he asked, motioning at the boxes.

"You can just leave them up here by the register," Joss said as she scribbled her name in the screen. "We'll get them taken care of."

"You got it." He wiggled the boxes off the dolly and left them at the edge of the counter. "Have a good day."

"You too." She used a pair of scissors to cut through the tape on the top box and scanned its contents. She picked it up with a soft grunt and carried it back to Scott. "More sci-fi," she announced as she dropped the box beside him.

"Yay," he cheered sarcastically as he reached out and pulled it closer. He looked up at her and frowned. "What happened to your hand?"

Joss looked down at her hands that were rubbed raw across the palms from when she had hit the dirt the day before. "Nothing. I was unloading my stuff yesterday and my neighbor's dog took me out." She rolled her eyes at Scott's amused smirk. "Don't ask. But, anyway, speaking of my new neighbor, what do you know about her?"

Scott sat back on his heels and shook his head. "Not a lot."

"Yeah right. If there's one thing people around here are good at, it's gossip. How long did it take everybody to find out I was gay after I came out? Like a week?"

"If that," he chuckled. "But I'm serious. Nobody really knows a lot about her. She moved in during shoulder season just after Thanksgiving, and pretty much keeps to herself. Helen always spoke kindly of her, which you know as well as I do says a lot because Helen wasn't a fool, and she seemed polite enough the few times she came into the shop when I was working. But, really, that's it. Why?"

Joss shrugged. "Just curious." She had thought about Maeve Dylan more than she cared to admit in the time that had passed since they said goodbye. She knew Maeve was beautiful and kind and funny and that her dog was a complete character, but she had hoped that he would have something deeper to share.

"You like her."

Joss scoffed and shook her head. "Don't be ridiculous. I only talked to her for like five minutes. I'm just curious about my new neighbor."

He laughed. "Yeah right. Sorry, Joss, but that's all I got for ya."

Joss rolled her eyes and flipped him off. "Whatever. You wanna handle these and I'll go grab another box?"

"Sounds good." Scott slid the book he had pulled from the box into its proper place on the shelf in front of him and picked up another one. "Hey, you wanna go get a drink at O'Malley's after work?"

The offer was tempting, but she still had too much to do to spend the night drinking with Scott. "That sounds fun, but I really need to finish unpacking. Rain check?"

"Of course." He smiled. "I know the situation kind of sucks, but it's nice to have you back, Joss."

Joss jammed her hands into the pockets of her jeans as she looked around the store. Willy was sleeping in one of the half-open boxes that would have to be emptied after he woke up and she spotted Dickens in the front window, soaking up the sun, and she smiled as she looked back at him and nodded. This was not the life she had been all but killing herself over the last few years, but she felt more at peace than she had in a very, very long time. "Thanks. It's good to be back."

Four

Joss shoved the sleeves of her compression shirt up her forearms as she jogged around Pine Lake, the small oblong-shaped lake that was just up the driveway from her cottage, and grinned at the feeling of the cool morning air tickling her legs as she hurdled the fallen log that marked the halfway point of her three-mile run. She had been a treadmill warrior back in Los Angeles, hitting the large gym on the first floor of her firm's building every morning before getting to her desk by five, and while she was still getting used to running at high altitude—after two weeks of running around the lake, the effects of the thinner air were less noticeable by the day.

So far, she had to admit that coming back to Sky had been a good move. She was working almost as much as she had been back in LA, but with none of the stress. There were no angry clients to manage or demanding bosses monopolizing her time and siphoning her sanity. Every day had a predictable routine to it that was refreshing. She woke up, went on a run, had breakfast, showered, and headed into town to open Atramentum by nine. There were two "high" or busy seasons for the resort town—summer and winter, which combined totaled approximately seven months out of the year—which meant that those months where the tourists were abundant meant long days for local shopkeepers looking to turn enough profit to keep themselves and their stores going. Because it was the beginning of the busy summer season, the store's hours were extended so they were open until ten every night to capitalize on the tourist dollars wandering the streets after dark, and she and Scott alternated nights closing up. Sunday was the only day the lights were turned off early, the "Closed" sign finding its place on the suction cup hook on the front door no later than six.

The sound of the birds singing overhead carried her around the northern side of the lake, and she corrected her form—straightening her back and tightening her elbows—when Maeve's house came into view. The sprawling two-story home was a classic mountain retreat with its split wood plank and stone façade, and it had a dozen oversized windows spanning the back of it that overlooked the lake and Sky mountain beyond. A large stone patio extended from the back of the house down to the lawn that spread all the way to the thin strip of sand that circled the lake, providing the perfect spot to enjoy those magical mountain nights where the temperatures were comfortable and the sky overhead was a breathtaking blanket of stars. It was a gorgeous property, and Joss studied the house as she ran by it each morning, both hopeful she might see Maeve again, and mildly anxious about what she would say to her if she did.

It had been a long time since anyone had caught her attention like Maeve had done in only a few minutes of awkward conversation and, during her more optimistic moments, she could not help but wonder if anything might ever come from the spark of attraction she had felt that day. Odds were, of course, that nothing ever would—it was one thing to be blessed with a beautiful neighbor, and yet another for that neighbor to be both single and queer—but it was still a nice to think about.

Joss had taken maybe a dozen steps beyond the edge of the trees when she spotted a familiar dark shape bounding off the house's back patio. George tore across the lawn, her lithe form looking almost greyhound-esque as she hit her stride, and Joss chuckled under her breath as she slowed to a walk, hoping that George would match her change of pace.

The last thing she needed was to get tackled again.

Thankfully, her plan seemed to work, and George's pace eased from an all-out sprint to a light jog, her tail wagging so hard that it was only a blur behind her. When George was close enough, she shoved her head under Joss' hand looking for loves, and Joss smiled as she scratched behind her ears.

"You're a vicious guard dog, aren't you?" Joss teased.

George whimpered and pushed into her harder, nearly knocking her over, and Joss laughed as she stumbled back a step before catching herself.

"It's nice to see you too," Joss assured her. She alternated scratching behind George's ears and under her chin for another minute or so, and then gave her a couple quick pats on the head. "Okay. That's enough."

George *aroo*-ed loudly in disagreement and shoved her head back under Joss' hand.

"You are too much, George Dylan," Joss muttered as she gave George's ears another quick scratch. George's eyes fluttered shut happily as she turned her head into the fingers digging into the hollow behind her ear, and Joss sighed as she pulled her hand away. "Sorry, bud, that's it. I have to go to work. Go find your mom," she added as she began walking away.

Instead of letting her go, George stood up and gave a mighty shake before hurrying to fall into step beside her.

"George," Joss half-groaned, half-laughed. "You need to go home so I can finish my run and get to work." George's big brown eyes twinkled merrily as she continued to match her pace, and Joss rolled her eyes. "You're going to follow me all the way home, aren't you?"

George shoved her head under Joss' hand again.

"Right." Joss gave George's head a disbelieving pat. She was going to have to take her back to Maeve before she could finish her run.

She eyed the house, weighing her options. The quickest thing to do would be to knock on the sliding glass doors that opened onto the back patio, but that seemed a little too forward when it was not quite eight o'clock on a Sunday morning. It would take longer to go around the house to the front door, but the doorbell would give Maeve time to throw on a robe or something if she was still in her pajamas and not ready for company.

Of course, Joss thought as she looked down at herself, after over two miles of running at high altitude, she was not exactly in the best shape to see Maeve, either. She was sweaty and gross, and though she really liked the idea of seeing the blonde again, she would have preferred it be after she had taken a shower.

She sighed as she looked down at George, who was smiling up at her. "Okay. You win. Let's take you back to your mom so I can get going."

Figuring that she may as well give George a little workout since the dog seemed to have quite a bit of energy, she patted her on the side and then took off at a quick jog. She normally followed the edge of the lake because it felt less like she was trespassing, but in deference to saving time, she cut across the lawn. She looked over at George, who was running easily beside her, and grinned. It was fun having somebody to run with, even if that somebody was the goofiest Great Dane she had ever met. "You're good company, you know that?"

George chuffed happily.

"Of course you do," Joss chuckled.

They slowed to a walk as they neared the deep front porch that was protected from the elements by an overhanging roof. Joss took a deep breath to try to get her breathing back under control as she and George climbed the stars between the large stone pillars that supported the high, peaked roof, and let it go slowly as they stopped in front of a pair of massive mahogany-framed glass front doors. She pressed the doorbell that was set into the frame, and grabbed George's collar as they waited.

"You're lucky you're cute," she told the dog when Maeve rounded a corner down the hall wearing a pair of black yoga pants that showed off her long legs, and a loose-fitting, pale blue Columbia University hoodie that fell to the top of her thighs. Her hair hung loose around her face in deliciously tousled waves that made Joss think of lazy mornings in bed, her feet were bare, and her eyes crinkled in adorable confusion behind the same black frames she had worn the last time they met when she spotted Joss and George on the porch.

"Joss?" Maeve asked when she opened the door.

The fact that Maeve remembered her name made Joss smile, and she nodded. "Um, good morning." She rolled her eyes at the raspiness that had crept into her voice and cleared her throat. "Sorry to bug you so early, but I was finishing my run around the lake and I ran into George. Not, you know, literally, this time," she added quickly when a horrified expression flashed across Maeve's face. "She just came out to say hi and then she seemed to want to follow me home, so I thought I'd better bring her back to you..."

"Did she?" Maeve asked, arching a brow at George, who dropped her head and tried to slink past her into the house. Maeve laughed and gave George an affectionate pat on the behind as she passed. "I'm sorry about that. She's usually very well-behaved."

"No. It was fine. I just didn't want to inadvertently kidnap her or something and have you be all worried."

"Well, thank you. I appreciate that." Maeve smiled and ran a hand through her hair as she gave Joss a quick once-over. "Would you like to come in for a cup of coffee?"

Having a cup of coffee with the woman who had captivated her thoughts over the last two weeks sounded like a dream come true, but Joss shook her head. For as much as she loved the idea of spending a little time getting to know her new neighbor, she had to get to the store. "I would love to, but I'm afraid I need to get ready to head into Atramentum for the day."

"Of course. Perhaps another time, then."

"Yeah," Joss agreed as her eyes dropped to the smile curling Maeve's lips, tracing what she was sure was not meant to be an incredibly seductive smirk before she forced her gaze higher. "That, uh, would be great."

Maeve curled her fingers around the edge of the door, letting it hold some of her weight, and nodded. "I look forward to it."

"Me too." Joss rocked back on her heels, trying her best to appear nonchalant as she tipped her head at the driveway behind her. "Right." She nearly missed the top step and had to grab the railing to keep from falling. *Fuck.* "Well. I'll, um, just…see you later, I guess."

Maeve's smile widened, though, to her credit, she did manage not to laugh. "Enjoy the rest of your run."

Joss backed slowly down the steps, feeling for the edge of each board with the toe of her shoe so she did not make an even bigger fool of herself. She flashed what she hoped looked like a confident grin, and waved a hand in the direction where George disappeared. "I'll do my best. Tell George thanks for running with me."

"Any time," Maeve chuckled, the rich sound of her laughter making Joss' stomach flutter. "Really."

"I'll keep that in mind," Joss said. She lifted her hand in a small wave goodbye that was immediately mirrored by Maeve, and she shook her head as she turned on her heel and started for home, a single thought running through her mind on an infinite loop with every step she took.

Was she just flirting with me?

Five

Sunday was typically Atramentum's slowest day of the week as tourists filtered in and out of town, more concerned with the logistics of their vacations than doing any kind of shopping. But this Sunday was not following true to form as Joss ran herself ragged, helping customers find the book they might not have known they were looking for and then ringing up their purchases. From the moment she flipped the sign on the door to "Open", she had been in constant motion, hurrying from one end of the store to the other and trying to keep a smile on her face as her first cup of coffee of the day went cold on the counter beside the register.

The unexpected business was great for her bank account, but it was even better for her sanity because it left her barely had any time to breathe, let alone continue to try to deconstruct her little run-in with Maeve from earlier that morning.

She was ninety-eight percent sure that Maeve's coffee invitation had been nothing more than a neighborly gesture, but there was a part of her that was not entirely convinced. Perhaps it was blind optimism on her part, but Maeve's smile had been so warm and easy that it was hard to ignore the little voice in the back of her head that whispered "*What if?*". She had replayed their brief conversation more times than she could count during her quick run home and even quicker shower— and the only definitive conclusion she had been able to reach was that she had been as bumbling and awkward as Maeve had been stunning and collected.

The constant flow of customers lasted until the early hours of the afternoon when Scott arrived to begin his shift, and Joss sighed with relief when he walked through the door.

"Oh, thank God," Joss said as the door closed behind him. She was half-tempted to lock it so he could not escape, but that would get in the way of them actually doing business. "It's been insane today."

His eyebrows lifted in surprise as he looked around the store. "Really?"

"Yeah. It's been beyond nuts." Joss rolled her eyes as her stomach growled. "I hate to bail right when you show up, but I'm starving. Can you handle things for half an hour so I can go grab a sandwich from the deli?"

He nodded and shooed her away from the register. "Of course. Oh, and before I forget—what are you doing tonight?"

"I dunno. Probably just hanging out at home. Why?"

"My softball team is down a woman for the next few months and we're looking for a replacement. Gotta field three to be legal, and we're down to two. You still play?"

Joss shook her head. She had grown up playing, and had been a decent player once upon a time, but the last time she had taken the field was for her sorority's Greek League. "I haven't played since college, honestly. Hell, I don't even know what happened to my glove. I guess I can run over to Dick's after work and pick one up if you guys are really that desperate."

"We are exactly that desperate." Scott grinned. "And I have a spare glove you can use if you want."

Joss appreciated the offer, but she had always hated using somebody else's equipment, preferring the feeling of a glove fit to her own hand. "Thanks." She stepped out of the way of a customer who was approaching the counter with a couple of books they wanted to buy. "Maybe I'll just use that until I can get one broken in?"

"You find everything you need?" Scott asked the man as he took the books from him and prepared to ring them up. The man nodded, and Scott looked over at Joss as he swiped the barcode of the first book in front of the scanner beside the register. "That can work too. I've got things here, go grab some food."

After the morning she had just survived, Joss did not need to be told twice, and she smiled her thanks as she ducked out the door before he could change his mind.

Traffic on Summit was bustling. The metered spaces along the curb were all taken—something that was unheard of for the last weekend in May because schools were not yet out for summer vacation—and Joss idly wondered if this was a sign of how the rest of the season would go. It would be great if it was, though the idea of having the next three months be as busy as her morning had been made her cringe a little inside.

Time-wise, it was a push between walking the block up Summit and then the two down Main to the deli and driving, and because the weather was nice, she decided to hoof it. She amused herself with watching the downhill mountain bikers that were streaking down the arcing dirt paths that were cut into grassy ski-slopes in front of her as she walked, and marveled at the fact that, to some people, barreling down the side of a mountain on a bicycle was a good time.

Although the lunch rush should have been over, the line inside the Italia Deli was still three deep, and she sighed as she took a number from the red dispenser just inside the door before retreating to the far wall to wait her turn. She took off the blue and green flannel she wore over a plain black tee and tied it around her waist as she waited, and rolled her eyes at a mid-twenty-something guy in a red fleece and cargo shorts who winked at her.

Fat chance, buddy, she thought to herself as she pulled her phone out of her pocket.

She studiously ignored the guy as she deleted a couple of junk emails from mailing lists she should just take the time to opt out of, grateful that he seemed to take the hint as he started talking to someone else. With her inbox cleared, she opened her twitter feed to catch up on the latest Hollywood gossip and the latest info from her friends scattered around the country. Twitter and Instagram were pretty much the only consistent form of communication she had with her friends from UCLA, and she was in the middle of typing out a reply to her senior-year roommate's tweet when a familiar voice interrupted her.

"Hello, again."

Joss's stomach flipped as she looked up to see Maeve standing beside her in a pair of faded jeans and a white T-shirt, with an amused smile quirking her lips. Her pink and gray Asics looked brand new, and she had a designer handbag draped over her left shoulder that probably cost more than a few of Joss' monthly car payments combined. She looked casual and elegant in a way that only celebrities ever seemed to be able to pull off, and Joss' heart fluttered into her throat when their eyes met. xx

It had been years since a woman affected her this acutely, and Joss smiled as she turned off her phone and jammed it into her pocket. "Hey. How's it going?"

"It's going." Maeve tucked her hair behind her ears and pushed her glasses back into place. "I'm just running some errands. George is almost out of food, and I needed to pick up some groceries for the week. What about you?"

Joss blew out a quiet breath and ran a hand through her hair. "I'm taking a well-deserved lunch break. It was an absolute zoo at the shop this morning."

"That's good though, right?"

"Oh yeah. Absolutely. It just makes for a really long day."

"I'll bet," Maeve commiserated with a kind smile. "What time are you done tonight?"

The guy behind the counter called out "Thirty-two!", and Joss double-checked her little slip to make sure it was not hers as she answered, "Six. We close early on Sundays."

"Well, at least your day's almost over with, then."

"If only." Joss shook her head ruefully. "I promised a friend I would play softball tonight because his team is down a player."

"Oh. Did you play in college?"

"Just for my sorority in intramurals. How about you?"

Maeve chuckled and leaned in closer as if confessing a deep, dark secret she wished to keep quiet. "I am completely hopeless when it comes to sports that require even the slightest amount of hand-eye coordination. It's pathetic, really. My brothers love to tease me about it even now."

The intoxicating scent of citrus and amber from Maeve's perfume lingered for a few heartbeats even after she pulled away, and Joss swallowed hard in an attempt to wet her suddenly dry throat. "How many brothers do you have?"

"Two. How about you?"

"It's just me." Joss sighed and changed the subject as the guy behind the counter called for the next number. "Is your family nearby?"

Maeve shook her head. "Nope. They're all back in Chicago."

Sky, Colorado was a world away from the bustling Midwest metropolis, and Joss arched a brow in surprise. "So, how'd you end up here?"

The smile that had tugged at Maeve's lips the entire time they had been talking dimmed, and her right shoulder lifted in what Joss was sure was supposed to look like a nonchalant shrug. "Long story."

"Sorry," Joss murmured, not knowing what else to say. Maeve had been so upbeat and affable in all of their run-ins so far, that she was completely thrown by the shadow of past hurt that clouded her expression.

Maeve rolled her eyes and sighed. "It's fine. Anyway—"

"Thirty-four!" the guy behind the counter called out, interrupting their conversation.

Even though she knew that was her number, Joss still double-checked her little paper before she looked up at Maeve with an apologetic smile. "That's me. Sorry."

"Don't be," Maeve assured her, a ghost of her earlier smile once again settling on her lips. "I should get going anyway. Lord knows what kind of trouble George is getting into at home right now. I just saw you in here when I was walking by and thought I'd pop in to say hello."

"Thirty-four!"

Joss rolled her eyes and held up her hand to signal she would be right there. "Somebody's anxious," she grumbled, and grinned at the throaty laugh the comment elicited from Maeve. "I'll see you around?"

"Definitely," Maeve agreed with a small nod. "Have a good rest of your day."

"You too." Even though the guy behind the counter was waiting on her, Joss did not move as she watched Maeve leave, too distracted by the way Maeve's jeans hugged her ass to care that she was holding up the line. She bit her lip and waved when Maeve glanced back at her just before stepping out the door, and shook her head when she disappeared from view. *Damn, she's gorgeous.* "Sorry," she apologized to the man behind the counter. "Can I get a turkey, Swiss, and mustard on a hard roll?"

"Dressing?"

Joss nodded. The house dressing the deli put on their sandwiches was what made them so much better than every other sandwich shop in town. "Yes, please."

She jammed her hands into the front pockets of her jeans as she watched him make her lunch, her eyes tracking the process as her thoughts drifted to Maeve. Seeing her had been a most welcome surprise, and Joss felt like an ass for ruining what had been an otherwise pleasant conversation. Not that she could have known that the reasons behind Maeve's move would evoke such a response, but still. It was clearly something big, and while Joss was curious about the story behind Maeve's reaction, she was more sorry that she had said something to upset her.

In the end, though, she mused as she paid for her lunch and started back to Atramentum, the fact that Maeve had interrupted her errands to come into the deli to say hello at least meant that her bumbling earlier had not completely scared the blonde off. Joss was still lost in her thoughts when the door to Atramentum closed behind her, the bell above the door announcing her return, and she shook her head as she dropped the plastic bag on the counter. No matter how much she wished otherwise, there was nothing about Maeve Dylan that pinged her gaydar, and she was being ridiculous trying to read something into what was just a friendly conversation.

"Stupid," she muttered to herself as she scanned the shop for Scott, who was nowhere to be seen. She pulled a bottled water from the small, dorm-style fridge tucked beneath the front counter—a much more convenient place than in the back because there was usually only one person working at a time—and rolled her eyes as she dropped onto the stool beside the register.

"What's stupid?" Scott asked, smirking as he popped out from between some nearby shelves while Dickens glared at him from his bed in the front window for disturbing his sleep.

"Nothing," Joss said. Willy Shakes jumped onto the counter and purred as she scratched the top of his head. "Everything go okay here while I was gone?"

"Of course." He leaned against the end of a nearby shelf and studied Joss carefully. "You seem off. Are you sure everything is okay?"

"I'm fine."

"You don't look fine. You look broody."

"I am not 'broody'." She sighed and shook her head. He was giving her that look that said he did not believe her, and she knew that he would keep pestering her until she gave him something. "I ran into Maeve at the deli," she admitted as she began unwrapping her lunch, hating the knowing look that flashed across his face.

"I see," he drawled, cocking his head interestedly. "And how is your beautiful, yet mysterious neighbor."

Joss snorted out a laugh. "Is that your best creepy screenwriter impersonation?"

"Not even close." He grinned. "To do it right, I need an ugly Hawaiian shirt, boxer shorts with a hole worn in the crotch from excessive, thoughtful scratching, three-day-old stubble, and an old, manual typewriter."

Joss chuckled as she took a bite out of her sandwich, and covered her mouth with her hand as she said, "That's quite the mental picture you just painted there."

"Yeah. I'm awesome." Scott buffed his fingernails on his shoulder. "Seriously though. You saw Maeve? What happened?"

"Nothing happened. She was out running errands, saw me waiting at the deli, and stopped in to say hi."

"Well, that sounds promising…"

Joss rolled her eyes. *I wish.* "She was just being nice."

"You don't know that for sure."

"No, I don't. I do, however, know that you have not told me the details about this softball game I've agreed to take part in."

"Ooh. Smooth segue." He laughed. "But, fine. I'll drop it. Game is at eight on field two over at the high school, so you'll have time to grab dinner beforehand. We usually start warming up like an hour before just so everybody has time to get a little batting practice in. You still play middle-infield?"

Joss shrugged. "I can play wherever as long as it's not pitcher," she told him as she took another bite from her sandwich.

He nodded. "So…Maeve…"

"Drop it, Heitz," Joss warned around a mouthful of food.

Her words may have been garbled, but her glare more than got her point across, and he laughed as he held his hands up in surrender. "Whatever you say, boss-lady." He tipped his head toward the back of the store and added, "I'm going to get started shelving some of that inventory we have piled up in the hallway."

Joss swallowed and nodded. "Yeah. You go do that." She lifted her sandwich. "I'm just gonna stay here, eat my lunch, and watch."

"Oh, well, in that case," Scott drawled, waggling his eyebrows and doing a perfectly cringe-worthy shimmy, "I'll make sure to try and give you a good show."

Joss laughed and threw a crumbled receipt at him. "You're such a dork."

Scott winked at her as he gave a small bow. "That's why you love me."

"If you say so," Joss retorted, shaking her head. "Go do something useful. I'll be back to help as soon as I finish eating."

Six

It was routine, plain and simple, that drove Joss from her bed when her alarm blared at half-past six the next morning. The game the night before had gone better than she could have hoped. Somehow, despite having not set foot on a field in ages, she managed to go three-for-four with two singles and an inexplicable triple thanks to a series of overthrows that had the other team swearing up a blue streak, but she was paying for it all now. Her back and shoulders ached from swinging a bat and throwing a ball around for the first time in years, and she groaned as she stepped onto the porch and closed the front door behind her.

"Christ, I'm old," she muttered as she walked down the steps, stretching her arms up over her head to try to ease the ache that had settled in her muscles overnight. The stretching helped, though not as much as she might have liked, and she shook her head as she dropped her arms to her sides and started jogging up the driveway toward the lake.

The game had ended around ten, but she had hung out in the parking lot afterwards to catch up with the handful of guys on the team she and Scott had gone to high school with, which meant that she did not get home until well after eleven. She could have used a few more hours' sleep, but she had had so much fun running around the field playing ball—something she had not realized she missed so badly until she was out there—that it was worth the exhaustion that was making her legs feel heavy and slow this morning.

The crisp air and the steady pounding of her feet against the dirt helped push the lingering fatigue from her system, and by the time she reached the lake, she was beginning to feel like her usual self. She picked up her pace as she followed the narrow trail through the woods along the edge of the water, and let her thoughts drift to the things she had to do that day.

There were boxes of books in the hall beside the office that needed to be shelved, and she had to go through the electronic record of sales from the week before so she knew what to order to restock their inventory. Both chores would have typically been completed the day before, but the insanity from the morning had picked up again not long after she finished eating lunch, and she and Scott had been too busy helping customers to get any of their usual housekeeping-type tasks done.

More immediately pressing than either of those tasks, however, were her bare pantry shelves and the dirty clothes overflowing from her hamper. Her Sunday nights were reserved for grocery shopping and laundry, but because she had gone to the sporting goods store after work for a glove, by the time she got home, changed, and scarfed down a frozen dinner that was barely palatable, it was time for her to head to the field. Thankfully however, Mondays were one of the two nights during the week that Scott stayed late to close up, so she would at least have time later that evening to begin chipping away at her personal to-do list.

She was in the middle of compiling a mental shopping list when she broke out of the woods at the edge of Maeve's lawn, and she smiled when she spotted George sprinting toward her, looking even more excited than she had the day before. George's lips flopped comically with every bounding leap, and Joss laughed as she danced out of the dog's way so she would not get run over.

"Hey, you," she greeted as she scratched behind George's ears. "Is this going to be a daily thing for us? Should I start bringing you treats?"

George perked up at the word "treats" and looked at Joss expectantly, her tail wagging a mile a minute.

"Should've known you'd know that word," Joss muttered as George began sniffing at her shorts. "These things don't have pockets, bud. I've got nothing for you."

George huffed what sounded like a completely disgruntled breath and glared at Joss.

"Right. Sorry. I will add Milk-Bones to my shopping list," Joss told her. That seemed to appease George, because her tongue lolled out of her mouth as she sat down and bumped her head under Joss' hand, content to just sit there and be loved on. "You are too much, George Dylan. You know that?"

George closed her eyes and sighed.

After a few more minutes of scratching behind George's ears and under her chin, Joss patted her on the head and pulled her hands away. "Okay, you. That's it. I'll see you tomorrow."

George stood up and shook, and then looked expectantly at her.

"You're going to follow me again, aren't you?"

She knew that she was projecting human traits onto the dog, but Joss could have sworn that George grinned.

"Fine. Let's take you back to your mom…"

Joss started across the lawn, not at all surprised the George followed her step-for-step. She was, however, surprised when she spotted Maeve watching them from a chair at the table on the wide stone patio that spanned the back of the house. Maeve was dressed similarly to the morning before—blue hoodie, black yoga pants, bare feet, hair that was so sexily tousled that it should have been illegal— and had a cup of coffee that was still sending thin tendrils of steam up into the cool morning air. There was an open spiral notebook on the table in front of her and a pen dangling from her fingers, and Joss smiled apologetically for interrupting as she neared the steps.

"I swear I'm not trying to steal your dog."

Maeve grinned and gave Joss a look that seemed to say, *Uh-huh. Sure.* "George Dylan, get up here."

George stared straight at Maeve and then sat on Joss' left foot.

"I swear to God that dog was perfectly well-behaved before she met you," Maeve grumbled, rolling her eyes in amusement. "George, come on."

George let out a loud yawn and laid down, her behind still anchoring Joss' foot in place.

Joss laughed and arched a disbelieving brow at Maeve. "Are you sure about that?"

Maeve chuckled and shook her head. "I don't even know anymore." She ran a hand through her hair, and Joss bit her lip as she watched the way the platinum strands fluttered back into place. "I'm sorry she ruined your run again."

"She didn't ruin anything." Joss wiggled her foot that was trapped beneath George's butt. "She was just saying hello."

"Yes, well, at least she didn't tackle you this time," Maeve noted wryly.

"Yeah. Once was enough for that." Joss smiled and rolled her shoulders. "I'm still sore from last night."

"That's right. How did your game go?" Maeve sat up straighter. "I'm sorry. Where are my manners? Let me get you a cup of coffee."

"Nah, that's okay. I'm good," Joss said. "I don't want to put you out."

"Yes, because sticking a fresh pod in the coffee machine is so much work." Maeve smiled. "If you have time, it really isn't any trouble."

Joss nodded, unable to resist the alluring smile curving Maeve's lips. She would have to rush through the rest of her morning to ensure that this impromptu coffee break did not make her too late, but that was a small price to pay to spend a little time with Maeve. "Okay then. Yeah. A cup of coffee sounds wonderful, thank you."

Maeve's smile widened as she pushed herself to her feet. "Great. I'll be right back."

George's tail thumped three times against the grass before she rolled onto her back and looked up at Joss, front legs folded in a way that clearly commanded, *Rub my belly*.

"You look way too pleased with yourself, missy," Joss said as she crouched beside the dog and began scratching her belly. "Was this all part of your evil plan?"

George yawned and turned her head just enough to look at Joss.

Joss rolled her eyes. "Of course it was. Does she ignore you? Is that why you keep hunting me down?"

"It is not possible to ignore that one," Maeve declared in an amused tone as she sauntered back onto the patio with a steaming mug identical to the one she had left on the table. "She won't allow it. Here you go."

George flipped over, jumped to her feet, and ran up the stairs and into the house.

Joss smiled as she took the coffee Maeve offered her. "Thanks." She pulled out the chair beside Maeve's and looked through the open slider at George, who was making herself comfortable on a sofa, as she sat down. "Your dog is a real kick in the ass—you know that, right?"

"She's definitely full of personality." Maeve picked up her coffee and tucked her feet up under herself. She looked over her shoulder at George and sighed. "She's a good dog, though. You know, when she's not running off and randomly assaulting people."

"It wasn't that bad." Joss sipped at her coffee as she leaned back in her chair and crossed her legs. Her eyes landed on the open notebook on the table that was filled with neatly printed lines of text that had sections scratched out and others circled. There were little drawings doodled in the margins, bumpy waves that traced the edge of the coiled wire that bound the notebook, and a rough timeline or something equally linear sketched in the white margin that spanned the top of the page.

Maeve must have noticed her interest in the notebook, because she said, "I was working when George bolted off the patio to greet you."

"I'm sorry."

"Don't be." Maeve arched her back and sighed as she settled back into her seat. "This final section is giving me fits, so I would much rather sit and talk to you than pull my hair out trying to figure out the stupid thing."

"Next section?"

Maeve flipped the notebook closed and shrugged. "The climax of my next novel. All the pieces are in place, I just can't figure out how I want it all to go down."

"Next novel?" Joss arched a brow as she sat up a little bit straighter. "So does that mean you've written others?"

"A few," Maeve demurred. She cleared her throat and shook her head. "None of that will matter, however, if I don't get this manuscript turned in on time. My agent has been riding my ass for the last two weeks, which is why I've all but turned into a hermit."

"I was wondering why I hadn't seen you around." Joss pursed her lips thoughtfully. "Do I sell your books?"

Maeve nodded, a light blush tinting her cheeks as she focused on the coffee in her hands. "You do, yes."

"How did I not know this?"

"I honestly don't know," Maeve replied. "I mean, I publish under my own name, and you do own and operate an incredibly well-stocked bookstore..."

Joss's forehead wrinkled with concentration as she wracked her brain, running through her mental catalogue of Atramentum's inventory. It was beyond frustrating that she could not picture one book with the name Maeve Dylan on its spine. "I really sell your books?"

"You do. I know, because I signed a stack of them for Helen not long after I moved here." Maeve sipped at her coffee, clearly uncomfortable talking about herself. "How did your game go last night?"

"Well, I didn't make a fool out of myself." Joss picked up her coffee again as she leaned back in her chair. "I actually went to high school with like half the team, so it was a fun little reunion."

"So you grew up here?"

"Not exactly." Joss shook her head. "I grew up down the mountain in Greenwood Village just outside Denver, but came to live with Helen in my junior year after my parents died in a car crash."

"Oh, Joss. I am so sorry."

It was a sentiment Joss had heard countless times over the years. Most of the time it was offered as an automatic platitude, but she could tell from the stricken look on Maeve's face that the blonde genuinely meant it. "Thanks." Joss shook her head and shrugged. The loss still stung, but enough time had passed between then and now that, for the most part, it was just a part of her past because life demanded she keep moving forward. Time really did heal all wounds, and after enough of it, even the scars that healing left behind were just marks on her soul, evidence to point at and say *I survived.* "But yeah. So I finished high school here, and then came back every summer during college to help Aunt Helen at the store. I lost touch with pretty much everybody after I graduated from UCLA because my work was so crazy, so last night was the first time I'd seen anyone in…" Her voice trailed off as she did the quick calculation. "Almost eight years." She grimaced. "Christ, I'm old."

Maeve smiled. "If it makes you feel any better, at least you graduated high school in this century."

"Just barely," Joss chuckled. Her eyes roamed Maeve's face as she wondered just how much older Maeve was than her. It could not be much, she figured, perhaps a year or two at most. "Though I doubt you were much before it."

"Three years," Maeve confessed as she took a sip of her coffee.

"And did you go to Columbia?" Joss asked, pointing at Maeve's sweatshirt with her mug.

"For my undergrad, yes." She sighed and pushed her glasses back up her nose. "I went to Iowa for my Master's."

Joss frowned. "Why Iowa?"

Maeve laughed. "They have the what's generally considered the best creative writing MFA program in the country."

"So it wasn't some weird love of cornfields."

"God, no." Maeve shook her head. "It was fun though. Lots of good memories. What made you choose UCLA?"

"Good math program. And my dad went there, so…"

Maeve's smile softened. "Westwood's a fun part of town. I enjoy going there for signings." She tilted her head and asked, "Math, huh?"

"Yeah. I was a public accountant before I came back here to take over Atramentum," Joss explained. Her phone that she carried with her on runs in an armband sleeve as a precaution began beeping, and she sighed as she tugged the phone from the pouch to silence off the alarm. "Sorry about that. That's my if-you're-still-in-bed-you-better-get-your-ass-up alarm."

"Oh. I'm sorry I've kept you so long."

"Don't be." Joss took one last sip of her coffee, selfishly allowing herself a few more seconds of Maeve's company, and then sighed as she set her mug onto the table. She smiled as she got to her feet, wishing she did not have to say goodbye just yet. "This was fun."

"It was." Maeve tucked her hair behind her ears and added, "Thank you."

"Thank you for the coffee."

"It was my pleasure."

The words *we should do this again soon* were on the tip of Joss' tongue, but she held them back. It seemed like it would be too much, too soon. "I'll see you around, then. Good luck with that climax."

Maeve smiled and tipped her head in a small nod. "Thank you. Have a good day."

"You too." Joss glanced toward the house. "Say goodbye to George for me?"

"After you've gone," Maeve promised. "That way I won't have to chase after her when she tries to leave with you."

Joss sighed and shook her head. "You're no fun. But sounds good. I'll see you later." She waved goodbye as she turned to jog down the stairs, more than a little bummed that she had to go.

Her left foot had just hit the grass at the edge of the patio steps when she could have sworn she heard Maeve whisper, "I look forward to it."

When she turned around to see if she had heard her correctly, however, Maeve was bent over her notebook, pen in hand, scribbling words on the page with a fervor that told Joss she must have been imagining things.

Seven

It was equal parts curiosity and embarrassment that she had not known that Maeve was an author that had Joss pulling up the store's inventory on her laptop as soon as she finished opening Atramentum for the day. Joss whistled softly as she typed Maeve's name into the search field and skimmed the list of titles and publication dates on her screen. Maeve had been playing coy when she claimed to have written "a few" books. She was prolific, having put out one book per year for the last thirteen years.

Snapping her laptop shut, Joss shoved her hands into the front pockets of her jeans and wandered toward the Crime/Mystery section of the store where her inventory list told her Maeve's books were shelved. She shook her head as she stopped in front of a full row of books with Maeve's name printed on the spine.

How in the hell had I never heard of Maeve Dylan before?

Because they always stocked books in the order they were released to make it easier for customers to find the beginning of a new series or the latest release from a favorite author, she pulled the top-left-most book titled *Smoke* and flipped it over to read the blurb on the back. It was a standard summary—clear, concise, with enough of a hook to grab her interest even though she preferred urban fantasy—and she rolled her eyes at herself as she took the book with her back to the front counter. She could have totally hated the genre and found the summary absolutely yawn-inducing, and she would have still read it just because Maeve wrote it.

She should have taken advantage of the otherwise empty store to begin working on the myriad of things that had not gotten done the day before, but she instead sat down on the stool by the register and opened the book to the first chapter. She crossed her legs as she laid the book on the counter and tucked her hair behind her ears as she leaned forward to read.

It only took her two chapters to realize that starting Maeve's book was a colossal mistake. Not because it was bad, but because she was already so completely sucked into the story that she had to remind herself not to snap at customers whenever they needed her help with something.

She knew that it was not their fault she was in full-on I'm-reading-leave-me-the-hell-alone mode, but that did absolutely nothing to temper her annoyance. She had begun reading the story thinking it would give her an interesting glimpse into Maeve's mind, but the more she read, the more she just wanted to know what happened next. Maeve's characters were engaging, her prose tight, her descriptions evocative, and Joss was begrudgingly forced to accept that she needed to put the book down when a young couple entered the store chatting happily, and then froze just inside the threshold when she glared at them for interrupting her.

"Chill, Perrault," she muttered under her breath as the couple scampered past her. She ripped a piece of receipt paper from the roll on the register and used it to mark her spot, and shook her head as she closed the book and set it off to the side.

You can read more later, she promised herself.

Of course, sitting down with the book later meant that she was most likely not going to catch up on the sleep she had missed the night before, but at this point that seemed like a perfectly acceptable sacrifice.

Even though she knew that she needed to avoid reopening the book, it taunted her from its spot on the counter, and she blew out an exasperated breath. "Do your work, Perrault," she lectured herself under her breath as she forced herself to go fetch one of the boxes of inventory from the back hall.

She glanced toward the row the couple had disappeared down as she used a pair of scissors to cut through the tape holding the box shut, and was pleased to see they each had a small stack of books piled near their feet even as they continued to peruse the shelves.

Restocking shelves was a task that kept her hands, if not her thoughts, occupied, and she was in the middle of delivering the contents her fifth box to their appropriate locations when Scott arrived to begin his shift.

He waved hello as he walked around the front counter to stash his brown-bag dinner in the fridge. "Hey, boss-lady."

Joss nodded. "Hey."

Scott arched a brow in surprise when he noticed the book on the counter beside the register, and glanced at Joss as he picked it up to scan the back cover. "Crime novel? When did you get into this stuff?"

Joss grinned, knowing that his reaction to this particular bombshell was going to be priceless. "You know my neighbor Maeve?"

"Yeah…" His eyes went wide as he put two-and-two together. "Wait." He tapped his finger on the cover of the book. "Your neighbor is this Maeve Dylan?"

"Yup."

"How did we not know this?" Scott muttered as he flipped through the novel. "I mean, I've heard the name before, she's probably the most influential author in the genre right now, but I didn't even think that your Maeve was this Maeve."

Joss rolled her eyes. "She's not 'my Maeve'."

"She kinda is." He smirked and set the book back down on the counter. "I mean, you're like the only one in town who's ever really talked to her."

"You're insane."

"Yep," he agreed easily. "Seriously though. This is awesome! We have a famous author living right here in Sky! Do you think you can get her to do a signing here or something? It would be great for business."

"I'm not bugging her about that." Joss shook her head. "Her agent is riding her ass about finishing her next novel; she has enough going on without us trying to exploit her like that."

"Next novel?" Scott perked up even more. "Same series? Or is she branching out into something new?"

"I don't know. I didn't ask." *Never mind the fact that I had no idea she was even some big-time author until I came into work and looked her up.* "She was working on it this morning when I stopped by to drop off George again."

"Again?"

Joss shrugged. "George likes to come out and say hello when I'm running around the lake in the morning, and since I don't want her to follow me home, I take her back up to Maeve."

"Hold up." Scott held up a hand. "Why haven't I heard about this before?"

"I don't know," Joss drawled, shaking her head. "Maybe because it's only happened twice, and it's not really all that important in the grand scheme of things?"

Scott rolled his eyes. "It's totally important."

"I'm afraid to ask why you feel that way," Joss muttered as she began pulling books from the open box on the floor and stacking them on the counter.

"Because," Scott said, drawing out the last syllable for a good four beats, "you like her."

"And you know that, how?" Joss challenged.

"Because I know you," he answered imperiously. "You keep bringing her up whenever we're just shooting the shit, and you were all broody yesterday after you saw her at the deli—"

"I was not broody," Joss interrupted. "And I do not 'keep bringing her up'."

"Fine. Introspective and wistful." He arched a brow and dared her to argue. When she just huffed in annoyance but did not correct him, he grinned. "And, you do. And *then,* come to find out, it was the second time you had seen her that day!"

"Why do I feel like a character in some story you're plotting right now?"

"Because you are," he retorted. "I'm calling it, *Joss Perrault Finally Finds Her Happily Ever After.*"

Joss chuckled and shook her head. "That is the worst title for a story ever. And, I hate to break it to you, man, but I'm pretty sure she's not even gay."

"How do you know?"

"I don't." Joss ran a hand through her hair and sighed as her thoughts drifted to the parting words she had thought she had heard earlier that morning. No matter where Maeve was on the spectrum, the last thing she needed was for Scott to try to play matchmaker should he accidentally cross paths with her. And, really, even if their spheres of attraction overlapped, there was still the fact that she was just a nobody who ran a bookstore, and Maeve was an internationally acclaimed author. "But, even if she were gay—which, for the record, I don't think she is—there's no way in hell a woman like her goes for someone like me."

"Now you're the one who's insane. You're a catch! If I weren't married and, you know, totally the missing the required assets to catch your attention…" He smirked and mimed grabbing a rather impressive set of boobs.

Joss feigned like she was going to throw one of the books she was holding at him. "That's so wrong…"

He laughed. "What? I thought we were in agreement about boobs being awesome."

Joss glanced toward the customers that had yet to emerge from the stacks, and rolled her eyes. "We are," she muttered. "But still… No, dude. Just no."

"Fine," he sighed dramatically, like dropping that entire line of conversation was the most difficult thing he had ever had to do. "Look, is she single?"

"I don't know. You're the one who went total fangirl when you found out who she was—you tell me."

He pulled out his phone. "I can Google it…"

"Oh my God, no." Joss took his phone and set it on the counter. "That's creepy."

"Wikipedia? It says here that she won an Edgar at the age of twenty-two for this one." He lifted the book he was still holding as evidence. "She's bound to have a Wikipedia page."

"No. I am not internet-stalking my neighbor."

"You won't be. I will." He smiled and reached for his phone.

Joss grabbed it before he could and put it in her back pocket. "No."

"You're no fun."

"I know." Joss picked up a stack of books off the counter and shoved them into his arms. "Go shelve these and then come back for more when you're done."

Scott blew a loud raspberry as he adjusted his grip on the books. "Fine."

"Fine."

The bell above the front door jingled as a mid-twenty-something brunette in a bright sundress walked in the store, and Joss smiled at her gratefully. "Hi, welcome to Atramentum. Can I help you find something?"

"Like the balls to make a move," Scott muttered just loud enough for Joss to hear.

She discreetly flipped him off as she kept her eyes on their customer, who was mumbling something and digging through her purse, thankfully too distracted to pay much attention to the playful spat happening in front of her.

Scott laughed. "We'll continue this later."

"Yeah, that's what I'm afraid of," Joss chuckled.

"Sorry," the woman apologized with a smile as she pulled a scrap of paper from her purse and handed it to Joss. "My friend recommended this author—do you carry her books?"

Joss read the name scribbled on the note and was grateful that Scott had already disappeared into the back as she nodded. There was no way he would be able to resist making some kind of comment designed to embarrass the hell out of her. "We certainly do. If you'll follow me, I'll show you where we have all of Ms. Dylan's books."

Eight

"Again, huh?" Joss arched a brow at the dog waiting for her at the edge of the lawn as she jogged out of the woods, back straight, ears alert, with the dopiest grin on her face.

George stood up and cocked her head, her muscles tensing as she waited for the command she knew was coming.

"Right then," Joss said, clapping once before waving a hand at the wide lawn that stretched in front of them. "Let's go."

This quick sprint with George had become a regular part of her morning routine over the last week, to the point that she had even begun to save a little energy during her run leading up to this point so she could try to outrace George to the patio. A familiar fluttery feeling settled in her chest as they neared the house and she saw that Maeve was sitting on the back patio, her laptop folded shut in front of her as she watched them over the rim of her coffee cup cradled in her hands. This was the best part of her new morning routine, and Joss returned Maeve's smile with an easy one of her own as she skipped up the steps to the patio.

She had learned a lot about Maeve over the past week of coffee and conversation, but she always said goodbye wishing she had just a little more time to spend with her. Maeve was funny and smart, with a quick wit and the most infectious laugh Joss had ever heard, and even the extra minutes she gained with Maeve by setting her alarm earlier and earlier each day were not enough to quench her need for more. None of their conversations revealed any hint where Maeve's proclivities lay, but the more time Joss spent with her, the more she was forced to admit that it did not matter. She was crushing, hard, but even if friendship was the end-all-be-all of their burgeoning relationship, it would be enough because she just genuinely enjoyed spending time with her.

But there was still that little part of her that could not keep from foolishly hoping…

"Good morning," Joss said as she stopped beside what she had come to think of as her chair at the table. She did not bother to glance at George, who was already making her way inside the house in search of a drink of water and a couch to sleep on.

Maeve relaxed in her seat and tilted her head in a way that was comically similar to the way George had done when Joss had happened upon her moments before. "Good run?"

"It was." Joss pulled out her chair and picked up the travel mug that was waiting for her as she sat down. She had been so surprised when the mug was waiting for her two days after they first had coffee together that she nearly tripped over the last step to the patio, but now the sight of it filled her with happiness because it meant Maeve enjoyed this time they spent together as much as she did.

"Good." Maeve smiled and sipped at her coffee, if one could even call it that. Joss had learned when she had offered to get Maeve a refill the day before last that Maeve liked her coffee to not taste anything like coffee. Three heaping scoops of Swiss Miss and a generous dash of milk more than covered up the bitterness of the brew, turning what was actually really good coffee into nothing more than a caffeinated hot chocolate.

Joss nodded and turned her head to the side as she yawned. "Sorry."

"Late night at the store?" Maeve asked sympathetically.

"Not really," Joss admitted, shaking her head. "Scott closes on Fridays. I was just up late reading this annoyingly brilliant novel…"

Her voice trailed off as she smirked at Maeve. She had been hesitant at first to admit to Maeve that she had started reading her books in case Maeve was uncomfortable about the idea of somebody she knew in real life reading her work, but she had been forced to fess up three days before when she could not stop yawning because she had stayed up into the murky pre-dawn hours finishing *Fire*—the second book in Maeve's series.

"Ah. Good. So my evil plan to turn the world's population into a horde of sleep-deprived zombies is working." Maeve's eyes twinkled with amusement as she pulled her right foot up to rest on the seat of her chair. "Are you still reading *Ash?*"

It was a surreal experience to be able to sit down and discuss a book with the woman who wrote it, and Joss sipped at her coffee as she shook her head. "I finished it at like two this morning," she shared as she barely stifled another yawn.

"And?" Maeve prompted.

Joss cradled her coffee mug in her hands and shook her head. "I can't believe you ended it like that. If I had to wait a year for the next one, I'd be beyond pissed about that cliffhanger."

Maeve laughed. "Quite a few people were. It was glorious."

"You are twisted," Joss muttered.

"Yes, well, I'm a writer," Maeve pointed out with a dismissive shrug. "It's all part of the deal, I'm afraid."

Joss chuckled. "I see."

"Seriously though." Maeve leaned forward in her seat and rested her arms on the table. "I'm interested to hear what you thought about it."

"It was amazing," Joss said, shaking her head as she tried to organize her thoughts on the story. She had fallen almost immediately in love with Maeve's main character, Faith Ricci, a decorated detective in the Chicago Police Department who had made a name for herself by capturing a serial killer that had been tormenting the city for years. Faith was one of the more well-rounded characters Joss had ever read, deeply nuanced and layered, with a dedication to her job that was both admirable and tragic in the way that it kept her almost painfully isolated from the world. Her only friend was the District Attorney—an equally dedicated woman named Greta Thrash—who took it upon herself to make sure that justice was served to the criminals Faith apprehended. "The case was riveting, which the bags under my eyes attest to, and I was half-tempted to drive up here and smack you when the book ended with Greta being abducted at gunpoint from the parking garage at her office."

Maeve grinned. "I'm sorry."

"No you're not," Joss retorted, waving off Maeve's wholly unrepentant smile with a frustrated hand. "Just promise me that Faith gets her back and I'll forgive you."

"Faith gets her back," Maeve promised. She bobbed her head from side to side for a few beats before adding, "Eventually."

Joss pointed an accusing finger at Maeve. "You do realize that is not at all encouraging, right?"

"I know." Maeve nodded. "But you can rest assured that I love them both too much to do any lasting damage to either."

"Good."

"Everyone else is fair game, however," Maeve added.

Joss shrugged and crossed her legs as she relaxed back in her seat. "I can handle that. So, how's the editing coming along?" Maeve had been positively adorable in her relief and excitement about having finished the first draft of her manuscript Tuesday morning when Joss stopped by to return George, and had seemed eager to begin what she called a "quick structural edit"—whatever the hell that was.

Maeve smiled a small, self-satisfied smile and nodded. "I finished them earlier this morning, and sent the manuscript off to my editor for her to do a more thorough job about thirty minutes ago."

"Congratulations." Joss smiled. "So what are you going to do to celebrate?"

"Laundry." Maeve sighed. "And grocery shopping. And cleaning. You know, all those things I put off for the last week while I was doing this."

"How exciting," Joss chuckled.

"Right?" Maeve shrugged and sipped at her coffee.

Joss shook her head. "No." Maeve's answering laugh was throaty and rich, and she grinned. "You need to do something to celebrate."

"I'm sure George will smother me with cuddles."

"I'm sure she will," Joss agreed. "If I weren't working late tonight, I'd take you out for a drink or something."

"That sounds like fun. Maybe some other time, then."

"Yeah." The small, lopsided smile quirking Maeve's lips caused hope to bloom in Joss' chest, and she cleared her throat softly as she shrugged and shook her head, like what she was about to say was not a big deal at all—despite the fact that she really, really hoped that Maeve accepted her offer. "Would you maybe... I mean, it wouldn't be much, but I'm having some of the softball team over tomorrow night around seven for a barbecue since we have a bye this week—why don't you come down join us?"

"I wouldn't want to impose..."

"You wouldn't be," Joss assured her. "It'll be a small thing, just some of the guys from the Brewers that I went to high school with and their better halves. I'll appeal to their inner caveman and put them in charge of the grill, and we can just hang out. It'll be fun, I promise."

"Well, if you promise..." Maeve murmured, a playful glint flashing in her eyes.

"I do," Joss said, trying to not look too eager. "Come on. Say yes."

Maeve bit her lip and nodded. "Okay. Yes."

Joss beamed as her heart swooped and her stomach dipped in excitement at the idea of spending the following evening with Maeve. "Excellent."

"What would you like me to bring?"

"Just you. I already divvied up the menu between the team. It's all taken care of."

"You're sure?"

"Positive," Joss assured her. Her phone strapped to her bicep began to beep with her time-to-get-moving alarm, and she groaned. "I'm sorry. I need to go."

"Don't be." Maeve smiled warmly as she stood with Joss. "What time should I come down tomorrow?"

"I'll be home by six thirty, so anytime after then is fine."

"Okay, then." Maeve ran a hand through her hair and nodded. "I'll see you then."

Joss grinned. "Perfect."

Nine

Joss checked her watch and sighed. She wanted nothing more than for her workday to be at an end so she could get home and get ready for the barbecue, so time was, of course, moving at a crawl. There were still over thirty minutes left before it was time to close up for the day.

"Okay. Seriously," Scott said, crossing his arms over his chest as he leaned against bookshelf she had been restocking in-between bursts of muscle-freezing anxiety. "That's like the two-thousandth time you've done that this afternoon. What's up?"

"Nothing," Joss muttered, shaking her head as she pulled the book she had just placed on the shelf and moved it to its correct location two shelves higher.

"Are you nervous about tonight?"

"No."

He chuckled. "Bullshit."

Joss blew out a loud breath and groaned. "It's nothing."

"That look of frustrated apprehension on your face is not 'nothing'," he pointed out. "You look like you're about to jump out of your skin and puke at the same time. It's kinda scary."

"Gee, thanks." Joss rolled her eyes. For as much as it killed her to admit it, he was really not all that far off. "I'm just..."

"Freaking out," Scott supplied with a knowing grin.

Joss swore to herself that she would fire his ass if he started singing "*Joss and Maeve sitting in a tree*" again like he had done his entire shift the day before after she had told him that Maeve would be coming to the barbecue. "I'm not freaking out. I'm just…" She groaned. "Seriously freaking out."

"I knew it. Okay." He clapped twice and nodded, then rubbed his hands together. "Why, exactly, are you freaking out?"

"You mean besides the fact that Maeve will be at my house in about an hour and that I promised her she would have a great time hanging out with me and a bunch of people she's never met before?"

Scott grinned. "Exactly. Besides that."

"What if she hates it?"

"Hates the cottage? Who can hate the cottage? That place is fucking awesome."

"No," Joss grumbled, smiling in spite of herself at Scott's playfully horrified expression. "I meant, what if she hates the entire evening?"

"How could she possibly do that? We're awesome!"

"If you say so, Heitz."

"Look. Joss, baby, darlin', it'll be fine," he drawled, his expression softening. "Everything will be great, I promise. Herold is in charge of bringing the hard stuff, Lennox is bringing the beer, and Green is bringing some of the wine they picked up on their winery tour thing last summer, so there'll be more than enough alcohol to keep things loose. I'll grill up some fucking amazing steaks, Michelle is bringing her salad that everybody loves, and Green's husband is making his famous cheesecake. What can go wrong?"

"Everything." Joss stared at him pleadingly. "Tell me this wasn't a mistake."

"Inviting Maeve to this little shindig was not a mistake," Scott assured her in a gentle tone. "You were so excited yesterday, what happened? Did she say something when you saw her this morning?"

Joss shook her head. For the first time in a week, she had not seen Maeve and George during her morning run—a fact that was undoubtedly contributing to her rising panic. She knew that Maeve had a busy, important life beyond their informal, impromptu coffee dates and that there was no reason for her to expect her to be there every single morning, but knowing that did not lessen the worry that had been twisting her stomach in knots from the moment she ran out of the woods to find Maeve's lawn and patio deserted.

"No." She sighed and shook her head again. "I didn't see her today. Which is why I'm worried that she's regretting accepting my invitation and is trying to find a way out of it."

Scott smiled and gave her shoulder a light, reassuring squeeze. "She was probably sleeping. Not everyone enjoys waking up at the ass-crack of dawn every day like you do. Never mind the fact that she was probably working herself to the bone to get her manuscript ready to send to her editor. Hell, I slept for almost eighteen hours straight after I submitted my last manuscript. It's *brutal*."

"I'm sure it is, it's just..."

"You like her."

Joss closed her eyes and nodded. "Yeah."

"You think she's gorgeous," he sang. "You wanna kiss her... You wanna..."

"Shut up, Gracie Lou," Joss laughed, smacking his arm. "And thanks for talking me down."

"No problem. Somebody's gotta do it." He checked his watch and then tilted his head at the door. "Look. It's almost six and we've been dead today—why don't you head home and make sure everything's ready for tonight. I'll lock up here."

"I can't—" Joss started to argue.

"Go, Perrault," Scott said, grabbing her by the shoulders and turning her toward the front door. "I got this."

"Scott..." Joss rolled her eyes as she began obediently marching with him.

"Joss." He arched a brow in playful challenge when she stopped beside the front counter to glare at him. "Don't make me throw you out."

"You can't throw me out. It's my store. I'm the one who signs your paycheck."

"Whatever. Just get the hell out of here." He gave her a light shove. "I'll lock up, swing by my place real fast to pick up Michelle, and then we'll be out to help with whatever you need."

Scott's expression was determined, and Joss sighed. She would continue to worry no matter where she was; at least at home there would be nobody around to witness it. "Fine. You win."

He gave a small fist-pump and nodded. "Good."

"Six thirty?" Joss asked as she hovered in the doorway, not quite ready to be alone with her thoughts just yet.

"At the latest," he promised.

Joss took a deep breath and nodded. "Okay." She paused with one hand on the handle and added, "Thanks."

Scott smiled. "You bet."

She sighed under her breath as she pushed the door open. An elderly couple in matching tan Bermuda shorts that was discussing where they wanted to go to dinner later that evening were just on the other side, and she flattened herself against the doorframe to let them enter. They smiled their thanks as they walked past her, and Joss swallowed hard as she turned to leave.

"Time to get this over with," Joss muttered under her breath as she glanced both ways before jogging across Summit to the lot where she always left her car.

If the lack of traffic on Main Street as she drove out of town was any indication, the next week was going to be a slow one for business, but Joss could not summon the energy to worry about what that meant for her profit margin as she turned off the main thoroughfare and onto her driveway. She stopped at the mailbox at the end of the lane to collect the mail she had forgotten the day before, and tossed it all onto the seat as she shifted the car back into gear and made her way home.

Evening shadows had already draped themselves over the cottage by the time Joss pulled to a stop in front of it, and she took a deep breath as she killed the engine and pulled her key from the ignition. She glanced around at the woods as she climbed out of the jeep, somewhat calmed by the familiar musical chatter of the birds hiding in the lush, verdant foliage surrounding her and the sound of the breeze rustling the leaves overhead. She took another slow, deep breath as she stood beside her car, letting the rich scent of dirt and pine and nature chase away some of the anxiousness that had plagued her all day, and let it go slowly.

You have no reason to be so nervous, she told herself as she made her way up to the porch. *It's just dinner with old friends and a new one. Maeve hasn't called or texted to say she won't be able to make it after all, so she'll be here.*

Joss left the front door open so that the breeze could filter through the open, screened half of the storm door as she made her way through the small foyer into the living room. She had cleaned from the moment she got home from work until she went to bed the night before, which meant that there was really nothing for her to do to get the place ready for her guests that would be arriving soon. She hesitated for only a moment before she set her keys on their usual shelf in the unit behind the couch and made her way up the spiral staircase to her bedroom. She flicked on the lights as she stepped into the loft, the recessed lights set in the beams overhead bathing the cozy space in gentle, golden light, and chewed her lip nervously as she opened her closet.

If it were just the team coming over, she would not have bothered changing from the jeans and heather gray UCLA tee she had worn to work that day, but she wanted to look good for Maeve, who only ever saw her in her running clothes. Joss scanned the clothes hanging up in front of her and laced her fingers on top of her head as she considered her options. She wanted something that was nice but still casual enough to not look like she was trying too hard, and eventually settled on a black silk, long-sleeved button-down shirt she had worn with her favorite charcoal suit back in LA. The shirt was anything but casual, but the worn, faded jeans she pulled from the built-in dresser below the hanging clothes more than balanced it out.

She was considering grabbing a quick shower when she glanced out the window behind her bed and saw Maeve pulling up the drive in a white Audi SUV, and she bit her lip as she realized she did not have time for that. Butterflies swooped and dove in her stomach as she hurried to change, and she was just buckling her belt when the doorbell rang.

"One minute!" The cottage was small enough that she knew her voice would carry well enough to be heard on the porch, and she combed her hands through her hair as she started for the stairs.

Joss rolled her sleeves as she padded down the winding staircase in her bare feet, and could not contain her grin when she stepped into the foyer and saw Maeve standing on the other side of the screen door, hands behind her back as she looked anywhere but inside the cottage. Joss' mouth went dry as she drank in Maeve's sinfully tight jeans and fitted red scoop-neck tee, and she swallowed hard when Maeve's piercing green eyes landed on her. A small, shy smile curled Maeve's lips as their eyes locked, and Joss had to remind herself to breathe as the flicker of hope she often tried her best to ignore roared to life, stealing the breath from her lungs.

"You made it," Joss said, as she opened the storm door and waved Maeve inside.

Maeve nodded. "Of course." She pulled her hands from behind her back, and Joss' heart leapt into her throat. Maeve had brought not only a bottle of wine, but also a small bouquet of wildflowers. "These are for you."

"I..." Joss cleared her throat and shook her head as she took the gifts, feeling more confused than ever about where, exactly, they stood. Wine might be a perfectly acceptable hostess' gift, but, in her mind, flowers carried an entirely different connotation. *Maybe...* the little voice inside her head murmured even as she told Maeve, "Thank you."

Maeve ducked her head as a light blush crept over her cheeks. "I know you said to not bring anything, but—"

"They're beautiful," Joss interrupted, her stomach fluttering at the pleased smile Maeve gave her response. "Would you like to come in?" She waggled the bottle of wine. "We can crack this while we wait for everyone else to arrive..."

"That sounds wonderful," Maeve murmured.

You got that right, Joss thought as Maeve brushed past, and she took a deep breath as she turned to follow.

Ten

Joss set the flowers Maeve had brought onto the counter that separated the kitchen from the great room and picked up the corkscrew she had set out the night before. She twisted the bottle of wine to study the label as she removed the foil cap. A rainbow-hued grasshopper was striking on the flat black label, and the vineyard's name was inscribed beneath it in an elegant silver script. "Spectrum?"

"It's a small vineyard in Washington state." Maeve tucked her hair behind her ears as she sat down on a barstool. "My brother still keeps in touch with a friend of his from law school who knows the owner."

"Wow," Joss murmured.

Maeve shrugged. "Yeah. Anyway, every once in a while Liam will just send me a case of their Merlot because he knows I love it. Although, they've recently released a Pinot Noir that's absolutely divine and has basically become my new favorite."

Joss nodded, feeling a little like an idiot because she knew pretty much nothing about wine beyond the fact she did not really care for whites. She tossed the foil cap aside and fit the levered corkscrew on top of the bottle, pushing the handle down to drive the metal screw into the cork. "Sounds amazing."

"It is," Maeve assured her with a smile as she crossed her legs. "Next time I get a bottle, I'll have you over and we can share it."

The offer, much like the smile curling Maeve's lips, was so unequivocally genuine that any lingering anxiety Joss felt about their missed coffee date that morning was immediately forgotten. Joss adjusted her grip on the corkscrew and shoved the handle up, away from the bottle, yanking the cork free. "That would be great."

Maeve rocked forward on her seat to grab the stems of two of the wine glasses on the counter and slide them closer to Joss. "Here you go."

"Thanks." Joss poured a generous amount into each glass, and clinked hers against Maeve's before she lifted it to her lips. "Cheers."

"*Salut,*" Maeve murmured as she watched Joss take a sip. "What do you think?"

The wine was smooth and crisp, fruity without being overpoweringly so, and Joss nodded as she swallowed. Though she was not a wine connoisseur, even she was able to tell that it was exceptional. "It's great."

A delighted look flashed across Maeve's face as she, too, took a sip. "I'm glad you like it."

"I do." Joss set her glass on the counter and turned to retrieve the crystal vase that had once belonged to her mother from the cupboard above the fridge. Her mother had loved fresh-cut flowers and her father had loved spoiling her, and Joss could not remember a time growing up when this vase had not been overflowing with flowers. She sighed softly at the memory, and shook her head as she took the vase to the sink to rinse it off.

"Do you need help with anything?" Maeve offered as Joss turned back toward her, drying the vase with a cornflower blue dishtowel that had been sitting beside the sink.

"There's nothing to do." Joss set the vase on the counter beside the wrapped flowers and smiled at Maeve. She had never been a flowers kind of girl, she always thought it was a waste to spend money on something that was already in the process of dying, but she had to admit that the wildflowers Maeve brought were beautiful. "These are gorgeous. Where did you find them?"

Maeve smiled. "I was down in Vail this morning checking out the farmer's market and art show because I've heard so much about it, and there was a vendor there selling these bouquets. I know you said I didn't need to bring anything, but I couldn't just show up empty-handed, so…" Her voice trailed off and she shrugged, as if it were no big deal.

Joss bit her lip as she forced herself to ignore the way her stomach sank at Maeve's explanation. She should have known that the flowers, like the wine, were nothing more than a "thanks for having me over" type of gift, but she had still hoped… She blinked hard and picked up a pair of scissors to trim the stems. "Well, they're beautiful."

"I'm glad you like them." Maeve's eyes lingered on Joss' face for a moment before she turned on her seat and looked around the cottage. "Your home is incredible. It's much so much bigger than it looks from the outside. I love it."

"Thanks," Joss murmured without looking up. She took a slow, deep breath to try to re-center herself as she placed the flowers into the vase. She spent more time and energy than was necessary on the arrangement, using the task as an opportunity to get her head back on straight. Maeve was her friend, and she would do her best to enjoy the evening. When she finally looked up, she saw that Maeve was standing in front of the bookcase in the living room. Maeve's expression was intrigued as she sipped at her wine and studied the titles lining the shelves, and Joss wondered what she thought about her choice in reading materials. Joss tried not to notice the way Maeve's hair curled enticingly around her shoulders or the way her jeans hugged her ass as she made her way out of the kitchen with the flowers. The kitchen counter would be too full later with food to allow room the bouquet, and the only other place the vase would fit was on the coffee table in the living room. She caught Maeve's eye through the open shelves as she set the vase onto the table and arched a playful brow, determined to keep things light and friendly. "No judging."

"I would never." Maeve waved her glass at the shelves. "So you're an urban fantasy girl, huh?"

"Yeah." Joss placed the vase in the center of the table, giving it a small turn so that the overhead lights caught the ridges in the crystal, and wiped her hands off on the seat of her pants as she straightened. "How about you? What's your favorite outside your particular genre?"

"I actually read very few crime novels. Or mysteries, for that matter," Maeve admitted with a small shrug.

Joss arched a brow in surprise. "Really?"

"Really." Maeve smiled around the rim of her wine glass. "I spend so much time lost in my own head thinking about that kind of stuff, that when I do have time to read, I just want an escape."

"Okay. That makes sense." Joss tilted her head as she looked at Maeve through the open shelves. "So, what's your fictional poison, Ms. Dylan?"

Maeve bit her lip and blushed as her gaze dropped to the books that separated them. "Which one is your favorite?" she asked, changing the subject.

"Depends on the week." Joss edged past the sofa and around the end of the bookcase. Joss grinned at Maeve's embarrassment as she leaned against the end of the bookshelf. "How about you?"

Maeve shrugged. "I read a little bit of everything," she answered evasively.

"Some day I will figure it out," Joss teased.

Maeve smirked and lifted her glass in a silent toast. "Good luck with that."

"I don't need luck." Joss winked at her. "I have receipts."

"That's assuming I've purchased books at your store," Maeve retorted.

Joss laughed and held a hand over her heart as if wounded. "You don't buy your books from me? That's very un-neighborly."

"I make you coffee every morning," Maeve pointed out. "Which is actually beyond neighborly, if you were to stop and think about it, so..."

"You're right," Joss conceded with a small bow. It was beyond neighborly, which is why she was so damned confused. Besides the flowers Maeve had brought her today—which seemed to be nothing more than a hostess gift—there was nothing in their interactions that gave her any indication where Maeve stood. Was everything between them just friendly gestures, or was it something more?

She ran a hand through her hair and sighed. *God, I really hate this second-guessing shit.*

"Knock, knock," a familiar voice called out as the storm door was yanked open, and Joss frowned as she looked at the door. How had she not heard Scott's car pull up?

"Gee, come on in." Joss shot Maeve an apologetic smile and shrugged. "Have you met Scott Heitz?"

"I believe so, yes," Maeve murmured as they watched Scott all but dump the ridiculously massive salad bowl he had been carrying onto the kitchen counter.

"Maeve, right?" Scott asked, smirking at Joss. "I've heard so much about you. It's nice to finally meet you properly."

If looks could kill, he would be dead after that comment, and Joss grit her teeth as she glared at him.

Maeve, however, smiled like he had just paid her the world's best compliment. "Really? And what have you heard?"

Scott looked at Joss, who was standing behind Maeve, vigorously shaking her head at him, and laughed. "Not much. Just that your dog is awesome and that you make good coffee."

"Well," Maeve drawled, sounding almost disappointed as she shot Joss a curious look, "that's all true."

Scott nodded. "I bet." He looked around the cottage. "Where is George the linebacker, anyway?"

"George," Maeve replied with a small laugh, "is at home, getting some good use out of the dog run that she pretty much never uses."

"You have a dog run?" Joss' brow furrowed. In all the times she had run past Maeve's house, she had seen nothing that even remotely resembled a dog run. "Where?"

Maeve pushed her glasses back up her nose as she turned toward Joss with a smile. "It's next to the garage. You can't see it from the back of the house."

"Oh," Joss breathed. She had not realized until this moment how close they were standing, and the intoxicating scent of Maeve's perfume sent her heart beating up into her throat.

Christ. I. Am. Fucked, Joss thought to herself as her gaze dropped of its own volition to Maeve's lips.

She was snapped back to reality by Scott, who was standing behind Maeve where only Joss could see him, waggling his eyebrows suggestively and miming running his hands down an especially curvy woman's body before smacking said imaginary woman on the ass.

"Joss?" Maeve asked, glancing over her shoulder at Scott, who gave her the most guilty-looking finger-wave as he leaned against the counter.

"Sorry." Joss cleared her throat. "Scott was just being a dork and distracting me. You were saying?"

"I wasn't," Maeve murmured, her head tilting just a little to the left as she looked at Joss.

It was clear that Maeve knew she was missing something, and Joss shook her head. The last thing she needed was for Maeve to push and for Scott to make little comments that would spill all her secrets. "Sorry," Joss apologized again. "It's nothing. I promise. Scott just thinks he's funny…"

"I'm hilarious," he declared.

"Yeah, you just keep thinking that," Scott's wife, Michelle, interjected as she ambled into the house. "Hey, Joss. Thanks for having us all over."

"My pleasure," Joss replied with a smile. She looked at Maeve and added, "Maeve, this is Michelle Heitz."

"It's lovely to meet you," Maeve said, holding out a hand.

"You too," Michelle replied breathlessly, looking absolutely starstruck as she shook Maeve's hand.

Joss groaned under her breath, remembering how Scott had reacted when he learned who Maeve was. *Please be more composed than your husband*, she pleaded silently.

Joss could tell by the way Maeve's easy smile turned just a little tight at the corners that she was uncomfortable with how things were progressing, and Joss did not stop to think before she slapped her imaginary white hat on her head and rode in to rescue her. She caught Scott's eye and tipped her head at the french doors in the kitchen that led to the deck. "Can you guys go make sure everything is set up outside while Maeve and I finish up in here?"

"Yeah. Sure." Scott nodded. "Babe?"

"Of course," Michelle agreed, looking more than a little disappointed that she was being called away as she turned to follow her husband outside.

"Sorry about that," Joss apologized once Scott and Michelle were out of earshot.

Maeve's smile softened as she reached out to run a light hand down Joss' forearm. Her touch was so gentle that it sent chills down Joss' spine, and Maeve sighed as she gave Joss' wrist a light squeeze. "Thank you."

"I..." Joss' voice trailed off at the feeling of Maeve's hand sliding from her wrist. A delicious shiver erupted at the top of her spine and tumbled slowly down her back, and she bit her lip to keep from visibly reacting to it. She wished she knew what had prompted Maeve to reach out like she had, but in that moment, all Joss really cared about was making sure she was comfortable. Having something beside her own tumultuous thoughts to focus on made Joss feel much more grounded and in-control, and she smiled at Maeve as she leaned in close and whispered, "Anytime."

Eleven

"You're drooling."

Joss pursed her lips as she turned to glare at Scott, and rolled her eyes at his shit-eating grin. "No, I'm not."

"No, you're not, what?" a deep, rumbling baritone asked.

Joss groaned as she turned to look at Brock Green. Brock was a beast of a man at over six and a half feet tall, with flawless ebony skin and a big, kind smile she could not help but return. "Nothing."

"Drooling over Maeve," Scott filled him in, tipping his head toward the dining table in front of the large stacked stone fireplace on the deck.

The novelty of Maeve's celebrity had waned well before the steaks had hit the grill, and she had seamlessly become part of the group, laughing and joking and trading barbs with the guys like she had known them for years. At the moment, Paul Lennox and Wesley Herold were at one end of the table, engrossed in their own little conversation, while Brock's husband Drew, Wesley's wife Kate, Michelle Heitz, and Maeve were having what looked like a light-hearted conversation amongst themselves.

Joss felt her pulse kick up as her gaze lingered on Maeve, drinking in the way she was relaxed in her chair, the fingers of her left hand playing along the side of her neck as she sipped at the glass of wine she held in her right. Her hair shone beneath the canopy of white fairy lights that were woven across the portico, and even from this distance Joss could see the light blush the wine had left on her cheeks. It was the first time she could freely appreciate how beautiful Maeve was without worrying about being caught staring, and the three glasses of wine buzzing through her veins made it impossible for her to pretend that she did not want to see if the smile tugging at Maeve's lips tasted as good as it looked.

"Yeah, well, I can't blame her there," Brock drawled, jolting Joss back to reality with a playful elbow in the side.

Scott nodded. "Right?"

"You are both married. Knock it off," Joss grumbled as she ran a hand through her hair, her eyes still glued to the slope of Maeve's jaw and the exquisite fall of her hair.

"We are." Brock smirked and added, "But we're not blind."

"Exactly," Scott chimed in. "You should just ask her out already."

Joss scoffed. "Yeah right."

As if sensing she was being watched, Maeve turned toward them, her smile widening by a fraction as she locked eyes with Joss.

"Fuck," Joss swore under her breath.

"You are so gone," Scott teased.

"Shut up," Joss muttered.

Maeve turned back to her companions and said something they could not hear, but it soon became obvious that she was excusing herself when she pushed her chair back and got to her feet.

"Here comes your girl," Scott whispered in Joss' ear.

Joss swallowed hard as Maeve ambled toward them.

"Breathe, Joss," Brock chuckled. "I'm gonna go take this beer to Drew," he announced more loudly.

"I'll go with you," Scott piped up, waggling his eyebrows at Joss before he followed Brock out onto the patio.

Joss shook her head at the way they turned around after passing Maeve to flash her matching excited grins and thumbs up. They were ridiculous, but the support—no matter how misguided—was nice. If anyone had told her she would ever find herself surrounded by this same group of guys so many years after they triumphantly said *sayonara* to Sky amid an auditorium full of flying mortarboard hats, she would have told them they were insane, but she was glad that Fate, for whatever reason, had seen fit to make sure they all found their way back together.

"Everything okay?" Maeve asked as she drew closer.

"Yeah." Joss nodded as she ran a hand through her hair and shrugged. "The guys were just being idiots. You doing okay?"

"I am." Maeve smiled and nodded. "Your friends are great."

"They have their moments." Joss waved at the glass in Maeve's hand. "Can I get you more wine?"

"I don't know," Maeve hedged, clearly torn between wanting to say yes and making the responsible decision. "I do need to drive home at some point tonight."

"I'm sure one of the guys would give you a ride home and you can come get your car tomorrow," Joss offered. "Or, you know, you could always crash here," she added before she could register what she was saying. She groaned inwardly at the comment, afraid that it gave away secret desires she would rather keep hidden, but there was no way she could not take it back. "I mean, if George would be okay with that."

"Oh, she could handle it. Whether or not she will be happy about being treated like a dog for a night, on the other hand..." Maeve huffed a small laugh as she glanced over her shoulder.

Joss' eyes followed, and she shook her head at the way everybody around the table suddenly became engrossed in anything that was not them. Before she could get annoyed with them for making an already awkward situation even more awkward, however, she was distracted by Maeve turning back to her, the right side of her lower lip caught between her teeth while a half-formed smile tugged at the left. She held her breath as she watched the way Maeve's lip slipped slowly free, pearl tugging at pink, and her pulse was beating so loudly in her ears she almost missed the words that tumbled from Maeve's mouth a split-second later.

"I guess one more glass won't hurt."

Joss smiled. "Really?"

Maeve nodded. "It's been a while since I crashed on somebody's couch. And, well, I deserve to celebrate a little. Right?"

"Of course you do." Joss took a deep breath and let it go slowly. "Though I couldn't possibly make you sleep on the couch if you ended up staying here."

Maeve arched a brow and looked around the open living area as she set her empty glass onto the counter. "I didn't realize you had a guest room."

"I don't." Joss shrugged. "But you can take my bed. I'll sleep on the couch. I end up doing that most nights, anyways."

"I can't kick you out of your own bed," Maeve argued.

Yeah, well, I couldn't possibly share it with you and not end up groping you, so we're kinda at an impasse here, aren't we? Joss shook her head. "We'll figure it all out later if we need to." She picked up the open bottle Pinot Noir that was sitting on the counter. "Pinot okay?"

"Of course." Maeve ran a hand through her hair and slid elegantly onto the end barstool at the counter.

Joss glanced at Maeve through her eyelashes as she refilled her glass. Maeve was staring off through the open door to the patio with a small, amused smile playing at her lips as she watched whatever antics Scott and the rest of the guys were up to. Raucous laughter filtered through the open door, and she shook her head as she slid Maeve's glass over to her. "Here you go. Do I want to know what's going on out there?"

"Probably not," Maeve said as she turned back to Joss.

It was tempting to turn and see for herself what had her friends laughing so hard, but the lure of Maeve's smile was too enchanting to resist. Joss returned Maeve's smile as she took a step back and leaned her forearms on the counter. Hostess duties had kept her from Maeve's side for too much of the night, and she selfishly wanted the opportunity to spend a few minutes alone with her. "Any word from your editor yet?"

Maeve shook her head. "Nothing yet. She's usually pretty quick with these initial notes, though, so I'm guessing I'll hear from her by the end of the week."

"And then what happens?"

"More revisions." Maeve rolled her eyes. "And then we'll start all over with copy edits. And then line edits…" She sighed. "It's a process."

"Sounds like it," Joss murmured. She cocked her head and toyed with the stem of her wine glass. No matter how much she liked the idea of spending more time with Maeve, she could not help but worry about her four-legged friend up the road. "Are you sure George will be okay?"

"Positive. She has plenty of food and water, and there's a dog door from her run into the garage, where I have my old futon from college for her to sleep on."

"Good."

Maeve smiled around the rim of her wine glass. "You really like her, don't you?"

"Sure." Joss shrugged. "I mean, that girl really knows how to make a first impression, you know?"

"That she does." Maeve chuckled and looked up at Joss through her lashes. "Truth be told, she's quite smitten with you, as well. She gave me the cold shoulder all afternoon in what I can only assume is retaliation for denying her your company this morning."

"Well, you can assure her that I missed seeing you guys too." Joss stared hard at her wine glass, trying to force back the blush she could feel tinting her cheeks. She had meant for her response to be playful, but there was an edge of longing that had crept into her voice she prayed Maeve did not notice. "I'll make it up to her next time I see her," she promised, plastering on a wry smile as she forced herself to look up at Maeve.

Maeve's expression was thoughtful, her keen gaze searching as her eyes roamed Joss' face. "Can I ask you a question?"

Joss nodded as her heart leapt into her throat. "Of course."

"What are you doing next weekend?"

Joss smiled. *Maybe Scott was right. Maybe I have been missing the obvious.* She cleared her throat and tried to look causal as she replied, "Just the usual. Why?"

Maeve shrugged, looking suddenly nervous, and spun her glass on the counter. "I was just wondering if…"

Joss leaned in closer. *Is this really happening? Is she asking me out?*

"…since you and George get along so well…"

Oh. Joss' heart sank. *George. Not a date.*

"I need to fly back to Chicago next weekend for my niece's birthday, and I was wondering if you'd be willing to keep an eye on George for me? It's just that she hates being kenneled, and…"

Joss took a deep breath, forcing herself to ignore the icy sting of disappointment that had settled heavily in her chest, and reached out to stop Maeve's spinning glass. "I'd love to spend some time with George. How long will you be gone?"

"Just a few days. I fly out Friday afternoon and fly back Sunday."

"That won't be a problem at all. Can I bring her down here?"

Maeve let out a relieved sigh and smiled. "If you'd like. I mean, she can always stay in the garage and her run if you don't want to deal with a hundred and twenty-five pound dog in your house. I just need somebody to make sure she has food and water, and I don't really know anyone else in town—"

"It's fine," Joss interrupted her with a smile. No matter how much she had hoped Maeve might have been gearing up to ask her something else, she was more than willing to look after George for a few days. "Honest," she insisted when Maeve's expression turned dubious. "It's been years since I've had a pretty girl spend the night, it'll be fun."

Maeve's smile turned thoughtful, and Joss realized that this was the first time she had ever hinted at her sexuality around her. "I… If you're sure," Maeve murmured, her eyes dancing over Joss' face.

Joss nodded. "Totally sure." Maeve's expression was indecipherable, and Joss sighed as she changed the subject. She was too close to drunk to even try to decipher what it meant. "So, when was the last time you crashed on somebody's couch?"

"I'm sorry?"

Joss waved a hand toward the open door where Maeve had made the quip earlier. "You said it'd been a while since you last crashed on somebody's couch."

"Oh." Maeve nodded. "I..." She lifted her eyes to the ceiling and sighed. "It was just about a year ago, after I'd caught my fiancé in bed with my best friend."

"Shit," Joss hissed, feeling like a total asshole. "Christ, Maeve. I'm sorry."

Maeve shook her head. "Don't be. It feels like it happened a lifetime ago, if I were to be honest."

"Still," Joss argued.

"It's fine. But I appreciate the sentiment," Maeve murmured.

Joss shook her head. How anyone in their right mind could ever treat Maeve like she was anything other than something to be cherished was beyond her. "Want me to go kick his ass?"

"Walker beat you to it," Maeve admitted with a wry chuckle.

That earned Maeve's baby brother a shit-ton of points in Joss' book. "Good."

"Anyway," Maeve said, her voice lifting on the first syllable in an obvious attempt to change the subject—not that Joss could blame her, "what about you? When was the last time you ended up crashing on somebody's couch?"

"God, I dunno...maybe in college? I wasn't kidding when I told you how much I worked back in LA," Joss added in response to Maeve's incredulous look. "Hell, my last girlfriend left me because I rescheduled our two-year anniversary dinner three different times and then blew off the fourth attempt so I could fly out to Vancouver for a last-minute meeting with a client. I was pretty much either working or sleeping for the last decade or so. I didn't have time for getting wasted and crashing on couches."

"Joss," Maeve murmured, shaking her head. "Seriously?"

Joss shrugged. "All I cared about was rising through the ranks at the firm. And then..."

"What?" Maeve asked after a moment.

"I didn't," Joss replied simply. "I was weird, really. I had poured everything into my career, and it should have been enough. But the hours at the office I used to thrive on became suffocating, for lack of a better word, and I began to realize exactly how much I'd missed out on." She shrugged. "That's why, when I inherited Atramentum, I came back to Sky. I was probably on the way out anyway, but having to decide what to do with the store kinda forced my hand, and yeah—here I am."

"I'm glad."

"Me too." Joss smiled. Even though she was still working all the time, it was different. She had a life. She had friends. She had Maeve. Not in the way she might have hoped, but that was life.

"Hey! Perrault! Get your ass out here!" Scott's voice echoed through the cool night air.

Joss rolled her eyes and glanced out the door to where the rest of her friends were gathered around her patio table. Andrew was shuffling a deck of cards, and a case of poker chips had magically appeared on the middle of the table. She sighed and shook her head. "I'm being paged."

Maeve laughed and nodded. "I noticed." She picked up the bottle of wine and distributed what was left of its contents it between each of their glasses. "Come on, Perrault. Let's go back outside."

"Ms. Dylan." Joss arched a brow at Maeve as she picked up her glass. "Are you trying to get me drunk?"

"Not at all," Maeve sassed with a playful wink.

"Bummer."

Maeve laughed as the guys outside began chanting Joss' name. "Maybe another night, then. For now, your public awaits."

"Assholes," Joss grumbled as she and Maeve made their way back out onto the deck. "Fine! We're coming! Happy?"

"Indubitably," Brock retorted, waggling his eyebrows. "Now, ante up. Daddy needs some new shoes."

Joss smirked and looked at Andrew. "You really make him call you Daddy?"

The table erupted, and Andrew blushed. "No."

"Shut up, Perrault," Brock said, grinning as he pecked Andrew on the cheek.

"Just keep it in your pants, big guy," Joss teased as she retook her seat. She smiled at Maeve, who angled her chair closer to hers as she sat down, and leaned back in her chair, thinking to herself that moving back to Sky was the best decision she had made in a long, long time.

Twelve

"What is that noise?" Maeve demanded in a rough, grumpy voice.

Joss blinked her eyes open and looked around, eventually finding the culprit behind the incessant beeping. She raked the top of her tongue against her front teeth three times, trying to dispel the rancid taste of too much wine from the night before, and leaned forward to grab her phone that was clattering around the coffee table as it chimed and vibrated with her wake-up alarm. "My alarm."

"Fuck," Maeve groaned. "What time is it?"

Joss laughed and flopped back onto the couch, not needing to look at the screen to know what time it was. It was early, perhaps only a few hours after they had fallen asleep—though when that had happened, she was not exactly sure. The rest of the group had filtered out sometime around eleven, but the two of them had polished off another bottle of wine as they lounged on the couch and talked about everything and nothing and all the things in-between.

It had been the most enjoyable evening Joss had had in a long time, which made the headache she was suffering now more than worth it.

"Quarter-to-six."

"Goddamn. You seriously get up this early every day?"

Joss nodded. "Yup."

"You're insane."

"Scott keeps telling me that," Joss agreed. She groaned and scrubbed her hands over her face, and could not contain her smile as she turned to look at Maeve, who looked as beautiful as ever. "Rude."

"What?" Maeve licked her lips as she turned her head toward Joss, her hair scrunching up behind her head as it rubbed against the back of the couch. Her eyes were clouded with sleep and her skin looked so soft and warm that Joss' lips tingled with the urge to kiss her.

Joss shook her head. She needed to stop thinking like that. "Nothing. Headache," she lied. "How are you feeling?"

"Like shit," Maeve grumbled. "But nothing a cup of coffee won't fix."

Joss smiled and shook her head. "I don't have any." Something dangerous sparked in Maeve's eyes, and Joss held her breath as her body reacted to it.

"How do you run out of coffee?" Maeve demand.

"Really?" Joss sniggered. "Coming from the woman who loads hers up with enough hot chocolate to send a three-year-old bouncing off the ceiling."

"The question is still valid."

Joss shrugged and leaned her head onto the back cushion of the couch so she was mirroring Maeve's posture. "I've been having my morning coffee with you. I guess I forgot to restock my stash because I never make any here."

Maeve huffed a disgruntled sigh and nodded. "Ugh. Okay. I'll give you that one. Good point."

"Thank you."

"We need to go to my house then."

"We do, huh?"

Maeve nodded. "Yeah. I need coffee." She frowned, her brow furrowing as she looked at Joss. "You're not actually going to go for your run today, are you?"

Joss laughed. "God, no."

"Good."

"Physical fitness is important," Joss intoned in a mock-horrified voice.

"Not as important as coffee," Maeve declared. She took a deep breath and pushed herself to a sitting position. "Fuck, I am too old to drink like that," she muttered as she cradled her head in her hands.

Joss giggled.

"What?"

"I've just never heard you swear before. I've been censoring myself because I didn't want to offend you."

Maeve waved her off. "Curse away, my friend. I have two brothers, I've heard it all." She sighed and leaned her elbows on her knees. A small, enigmatic smile curled her lips as she looked at Joss, and she shook her head. "Thank you."

"For getting you wasted?"

"Yeah. It's been a long time since I had fun like that."

"Good," Joss replied. "I'm glad."

"Let's wait a while before we do it again, though."

"I think that's a good idea," Joss agreed as her headache pulsed viciously behind her eyes.

"Come on, Perrault," Maeve groaned as she got to her feet. "Coffee."

"Just lemme shower real quick and then I'll meet you up there." Joss stood and stretched. "I've still got to open this morning."

"You need more employees."

Joss shook her head. "Nah. The summer season will be over in a couple months, and then I'll cut back the store's hours again until after Thanksgiving."

"You're a workaholic."

"I freely admitted that last night." Joss smiled. "Now, go home, Dylan, so I can shower and you can make us some coffee."

"Yes, ma'am," Maeve quipped, snapping off a quick salute for good measure. She rocked back and forth on her heels for a moment before she hummed softly and reached out to pull Joss into a light hug. "Seriously, Joss. Thank you."

"Oh." Joss wrapped her arms around Maeve's waist, just barely resisting the urge to bury her face in the crook of Maeve's neck. She smiled at the feeling of Maeve's head resting on her shoulder, and sighed as she squeezed her tight. Even after a night of drinking, Maeve smelled like heaven, and Joss pressed her cheek against the side of Maeve's head as she assured her, "It was my pleasure, Maeve. Anytime."

Maeve huffed a quiet breath that tickled Joss' neck and nodded. "Great." She smiled as she pulled away, raking a hand through her hair that was far too luscious for having spent the night on the couch. "So, I'll see you soon?"

"Of course." Joss nodded.

"Good."

Joss retrieved Maeve's car keys from the kitchen counter and then followed her to the front door. She stood at the threshold as she watched Maeve skip down the stairs to the driveway, her alabaster skin practically glowing in the dim, early-morning light. She waved once Maeve was behind the wheel, and only turned back inside once the SUV was out of sight.

She looked around her house in the absence of Maeve's company, and sighed. It felt emptier without her there, but that was a feeling she was just going to have to get used to. There were dirty glasses from the night before in the sink and empty bottles poking out of the recycle bin on the side of the fridge, but Joss ignored it all as she turned toward the spiral staircase to the loft. *I'll clean up later,* she mused as she climbed the stairs, her fingers trailing over the cool wrought iron with every step. She pulled her clothes for the day without too much thought— her wardrobe nowadays consisted of varying combinations of jeans and a T-shirt—and then headed back down to shower.

She undressed as the water warmed up, tossing her dirty clothes into the hamper in the bottom of the linen cupboard, and groaned once she stepped beneath the scalding spray. The heat and the steam helped clear away the remnants of the night before, causing the alcohol in her system to seep through her pores, leaving her feeling refreshed and ready to face the day as she dressed. Instead of taking the time to blow dry her hair, a task that would take a good twenty minutes to complete, she pulled it back into a french braid, her fingers dancing through her hair without thought as she worked. She opened the door to help the mirror un-fog as she brushed her teeth, and took a deep breath as she put her toothbrush back on its charger.

I caught my fiancé in bed with my best friend. Joss closed her eyes as the ghost of Maeve's words iced through her, snuffing out the ember of hope she had foolishly clung to.

She licked her lips as she opened her eyes, and shook her head at the disappointed woman that stared back at her from the mirror. "You're just going to have to get over this stupid crush of yours."

Maeve might not be a romantic possibility for her, but she was still a friend, and Joss would be damned if she did anything to risk spoiling that.

Despite the fact that there was a part of her that was brokenhearted over the loss of the possibility of someday with Maeve, Joss could not deny that she still wanted to spend as much time with her as she could before she had to head into town for the day. It did not take her long to gather her things and lock up, and minutes later she was making the familiar trek up the drive in her Jeep instead of on foot.

She pulled to a stop behind Maeve's SUV in the large driveway, and tossed her keys onto her seat as she jumped out of the car and slammed her door shut. She tugged at the hem of her shirt as she climbed the stairs to the front porch, and avoided looking at her reflection in the glass front doors as she pushed her thumb to the doorbell.

The melodic chime of the bell echoed loudly through the house, and Joss could not help the way her stomach flipped when she spotted Maeve sauntering down the hall to answer the door.

This crush is going to be hell to get over.

Even though she knew nothing would ever come of it, she still took a moment to just appreciate Maeve's beauty, awed as she ever was by the radiant smile that curled Maeve's lips. Her heart *ka-thumped* heavily in her chest as the door opened, and she returned Maeve's smile, feeling both disappointed that she would never know what it would be like to kiss those lips, and happy that her presence made Maeve smile like that.

"Hey," Maeve greeted, her smile brightening even further as she waved Joss inside. "You made it."

"Of course." Joss stepped into the foyer and looked around. "Where's George?" Before she had even finished her question, George's appearance was announced by the sound of nails clattering on the wood floor at a sprint, and Joss was just able to brace herself before the dog jumped at her.

Maeve laughed. "She's right there."

"I see that." Joss scratched her hands up and down George's sides as the dog spun happily in front of her. "Yes, George," she crooned as she continued to pet her, "I missed you too."

George made a sound that was a cross between a yip and a growl as she stared accusingly at Joss.

"I'm sorry," Joss apologized. "It won't happen again."

The promise seemed to appease the Dane, because she snorted and trotted down the hall toward the great room. Maeve and Joss followed, and Joss laughed at the loud *aroo* George let loose as she climbed up onto the couch that squeaked in protest beneath her paws before she flopped onto it.

"I guess she told me," Joss chuckled, shaking her head.

"That dog, I swear," Maeve muttered. "Are you sure you want to deal with her when I'm gone?"

George grunted and shimmied onto her back, the couch springs creaking with every wiggle, and hung her head upside down off the side of the couch as she made herself comfortable.

"Oh yeah," Joss said, laughing as she followed Maeve into the kitchen. "We're gonna have a blast."

Thirteen

"You're insane." Scott nodded at the hulking body behind the register with Joss. He grinned and picked up the last box of books to be shelved from their delivery that morning. "You know that, right?"

"I've worked with you for how many years and you're just figuring that out?" Joss quipped, smirking as she glanced over at George, who was standing beside her, paws placed squarely on the counter beside the register. George's tongue was hanging out, and she panted as she got her head scratched by the customer Joss was just finishing ringing up.

Maeve had left for Denver earlier that morning to fly home to the Midwest, and Joss had run out to pick up George as soon as Scott arrived for his shift. Friday was one of the few days where she got home early enough to have an actual dinner that was not from a bag or a microwave, but she felt bad leaving George alone until she got off work. Bringing a Great Dane that had a penchant for running into people to Atramentum was perhaps not the brightest idea Joss had ever had, but so far it was working out beautifully. George was loving all the attention she was getting from customers, Willy Shakes was purring happily from his spot in the window as he watched her, and Dickens was tolerating her presence better than he did most interlopers—even moving down a shelf on his usual bookcase to watch her.

"Have a good rest of the day," the man said, giving George a few solid pats on the top of the head before he smiled at Joss, picked up his books, and walked out the door.

George tilted her head to watch him leave, and Joss chuckled as pulled out her phone and snapped a picture of George standing at the counter. Maeve was probably still on her plane, but Joss still sent her the picture with a note, *George wants Scott's job. It's okay if I pay her in Milk-Bones, right?*

To her surprise, her phone buzzed with an incoming text not even twenty seconds later, and she smiled as she read Maeve's reply. *That's hilarious. Go for it.*

Joss looked over at George and winked. "Your mom says I can hire you."

George yawned and dropped back to the floor, giving a hearty shake before she turned in a small circle and curled herself up in a ball at Joss' feet.

"Don't look too excited," she told George as she typed out, *Wasn't expecting to hear from you so quickly. Are you already in Chicago?* Her phone rang a moment later, and Joss smiled as she answered it. "Hey, lady."

"Hey lady, yourself," Maeve replied with a laugh. *"Why is my dog at Atramentum?"*

"Because I felt bad leaving her home all alone while I worked," Joss answered matter-of-factly. "Besides, she's doing great. She sold three copies of your books already."

"Well done, Georgie-girl."

Joss laughed as she spotted the shop's more surly resident edge closer to the front counter. "Yeah. And she's even getting Dickens to loosen up."

"That's impressive."

"Tell me about it. So, are you in Chicago already?"

Maeve groaned. *"I wish. I'm still in Denver. Flight's been delayed twice already for mechanical issues."*

Joss hummed understandingly. "It's better than crashing though, right?"

"Well, when you put it that way…"

"You're welcome."

A tinny voice echoed through the phone and Maeve sighed. *"All right. They're saying we're going to board now. Here's to hoping we make it."*

"George and I will keep our fingers crossed. Hey, do me a favor and shoot me a text when you land. George is going to be worried sick until she knows you're safe and sound on terra firma once again."

Maeve chuckled. *"I will."*

"Good. Have fun this weekend."

"I will try my best. Give George a love for me."

"You bet. See you soon."

"Bye."

"Bye," Joss murmured.

"Bye," Scott repeated in a sickly sweet voice. "She's pathetic, isn't she, George?"

George huffed and covered her eye with her paw.

"Thanks for the support. Traitor," Joss teased, nudging the dog with her foot. She laughed when George just growled and tucked herself into a tighter ball.

Scott laughed. "Seriously, though. What's your plan for the weekend? Are you going to bring George in here with you every day?"

"Why not?" Joss shrugged. "She's used to being around Maeve all the time, so it'd be mean to leave her home alone all day while I'm here. Besides, it's not like she's causing any trouble."

As if to prove Joss' point, George let out a loud snore as Willy Shakes leapt from his perch to cuddle up against her, the normally affable cat giving Scott the stink-eye as he curled himself into a ball on her back.

Joss grinned. "See?"

"That is pretty cute," Scott admitted as he leaned against the edge of the counter. "So besides work, what do you have planned for your weekend with that one?"

"Haven't thought about it. I mean, it's not like George is an actual kid I have to keep entertained or anything. I'll take her on a walk at night, and on my run in the mornings, but she seems fine just hanging out."

The bell above the front door jingled to life with new customers, and George jolted back into action, dumping Willy onto the floor as she stood up to check out their arrivals. The women were pretty, one tall and blonde and the other a short brunette, and they both stopped just inside the door to gape at George, whose chin was resting on the counter beside the register as her tail smacked against the side of Joss' thigh.

"Wow. Big dog," the brunette said.

"You got that right," Scott agreed. "Welcome to Atramentum. Can I help you find anything today?"

George popped up into a textbook counter-surfing posture, back straight, forearms planted firmly on the countertop, and gave the woman a dopey grin. They both laughed and came over to pet her, and George chuffed happily as she soaked up the attention.

"You are adorable," the tall blonde told George.

"What's his name?" the brunette asked.

"Her name is George," Joss shared with a smile.

"As in, George Elliot?" the brunette guessed.

Joss shook her head. That had actually been her first guess too, and she had been surprised when Maeve revealed the true origin of George's name. "As in the character from the Nancy Drew novels."

"That's awesome," the brunette chuckled. "Great name."

"I didn't pick it, unfortunately, but I'll let her mom know." Joss winked. "I'm just babysitting her for the weekend."

The women nodded in understanding and looked at each other. "Well, should we pick up a few books? We're going to need to head out soon so we can get down to Denver to catch our flight home."

"Where are you two visiting from?" Joss asked conversationally.

"New Hampshire," the brunette answered, the blonde smiling shyly as she nodded and looked around the shop.

"And you came to Sky on vacation instead of somewhere with a beach?" Joss teased.

"Mackayla is doing research for her next novel," the brunette shared, smiling at her companion. "Besides, it's been a fun trip. We have trees back home, but the mountains are spectacular."

"Next novel? So you've written others?" Scott asked. When the woman the brunette called Mackayla blushed and nodded, he added, "Would we carry them?"

Mackayla shrugged. "Possibly."

"If we do, we would love it if you'd autograph our stock," Joss said. "It's not often we have authors through our door. We'll move them out to the front here, and set up a little display to draw attention to them."

"Oh, wow. That'd be great. Thank you," Mackayla murmured.

"Our pleasure," Joss assured her. "Well, yeah. We'll let you get to it, then. If you need any help finding something, just let us know."

"We will," Mackayla said with a smile as her companion gave George's head one last pat. "Thank you." She tilted her head toward the back of the store. "Charlotte?"

"You know you should totally ask Maeve to autograph her books too, right?" Scott asked once the women had disappeared into the stacks.

"I'm not taking advantage of my friend like that," Joss said, shaking her head. "Besides, George here"—she gave the dog's side a solid thump—"is moving enough of her mom's books on her own."

"I'm just saying…"

"I know what you're saying, Scott. And the answer is still no," Joss replied, perhaps a little more forcefully than she needed to. The edge in her tone had him instantly backing down and George regarding her curiously, and she sighed as she scrubbed her face with her hands. "Just drop it, okay?"

"Okay, fine," he said, holding his hands up in defeat. "Sorry."

Joss shook her head. She shrugged. She had been feeling especially protective of Maeve ever since she learned about what had happened with her ex-fiancé, and Scott's comments just pushed her buttons. "I'm sorry. I'm just…"

"Looking out for your lady. I get it."

"She's not 'my lady'."

"You want her to be."

"Doesn't matter what I want," Joss muttered. She had kept Maeve's revelation to herself, not wanting to betray her confidence, but she needed him to just back off. She knew that he was just teasing, but it hurt more, somehow, knowing for sure that friendship was the most she would ever have with Maeve. "She's straight."

Scott froze, his eyes widening in surprise at the definitiveness in Joss' tone. "You're positive?"

Joss ran a hand through her hair and sighed. "Yeah. So just back off, okay? She's my friend, and I'm not going to take advantage of that just to sell a few books."

"Okay." He studied her for a moment and then reached out to give her arm a gentle squeeze. "For what it's worth, she's missing out."

Joss shrugged. "Thanks."

"My pleasure. Now," he continued, his voice rising, "why don't you and George go hang out at your place for the rest of the day while I handle things here. You've earned a little break, and she looks like she could stand to stretch her legs."

Joss looked at George, who she swore was staring hopefully back at her, and laughed. "Okay." She glanced at Scott. "You're sure?"

"Positive," he assured her with a wink.

"All right, then." Joss reached beneath the counter for George's leash, and clipped it to the dog's collar. "You wanna go for a ride in the car, George?"

George licked her hand and dropped back to the ground.

"Looks like a yes to me." Scott moved out of the way so Joss and George could squeeze past him. "Have fun."

Joss gave George's head a light pet and nodded. "We will."

It took her almost twice as long as usual to get to her car because of people stopping her to ask about George, and Joss blew out a quiet breath of relief once she got George settled in the backseat of her car. "Let's go home."

She hurried around the back of the car, and laughed when she climbed inside to find George sitting on the passenger's seat. "Really?"

George grinned and licked her cheek.

"All right, but you better behave. No trying to climb onto my lap like you did on the way over."

George gave her a crestfallen look.

Joss shook her head. "No. It doesn't matter how cute you are. You're not driving."

George huffed and pointedly turned her head to look out the window.

Joss chuckled and lifted her phone to snap a quick picture. George looked too cute sitting there with the top of her head pressed against the roof of the jeep, and Joss knew that it would make Maeve smile. George looked over at her at the sound of the shutter clicking, and Joss nodded to herself as she got an idea. She dropped the phone into the cup holder and arched a brow at George. "Whattaya say we send your mom lots of pictures this weekend?"

George's tongue lolled out the side of her mouth and she made a happy chuffing sound.

"Good." Joss gave George's cheek an affectionate pat and just barely dodged another kiss. "You wanna go for a run when we get home?"

George barked and began practically vibrating on the seat, her entire body shaking with the movement of her tail that was trapped beneath her behind.

"Excellent." Joss cranked the ignition and shifted into reverse. She backed slowly out of the spot, and pulled to a gentle stop before putting the car in drive, mindful of her copilot who was not wearing a seat belt. George looked at her as they rolled forward, and Joss grinned. "This is gonna be fun."

Fourteen

Joss was sitting on the counter beside the register at Atramentum, swinging her legs back and forth as she watched George curled up beside a young girl on the rug in front of the electric fireplace that anchored the small reading area at the front of the store. The child's mother was sitting in a nearby chair, watching the scene playing out in front of her with a look of pure joy on her face. This was not the first time Joss had seen a child find strength in the unwavering, dutiful attention of an animal—Willy Shakes would often cuddle up to young readers while they tackled a new book—but there was something especially touching about such a small girl finding courage in such a big dog. George's eyes never left the girl's face as she read, and the slow, steady *thwump, thwump, thwump* of her tail against the floor was an organic metronome to the child's words.

"That is, without a doubt, the cutest thing I've ever seen," a husky voice murmured in Joss' ear.

"Right?" Joss smiled as she looked at Maeve, who leaned against the counter beside her. Maeve's left arm settled lightly on her thigh, and Joss sucked in a deep breath as she took a moment to just look at her.

The last few days of texting back-and-forth with Maeve had been fun—really fun, actually—but she had missed being able to see her. Missed the rumble of Maeve's smoky alto, and the laughter that always seemed to twinkle in her eyes. She had not been cognizant of feeling unsettled while Maeve had been out of town, and she had genuinely enjoyed her weekend with George, but there was no denying the feeling of serenity that settled inside her as she looked at her now. Joss knew that she needed to get control of herself, that it would do her no good to let her crush continue to grow, but that knowledge meant nothing when Maeve was so close she could smell the spicy scent of her perfume.

Maeve smiled and nodded, her eyes lingering on Joss' face for a few heartbeats before she murmured, "Indeed."

"How was your trip?"

"Good." Maeve ran a hand through her hair and sighed, looking perfectly relaxed as her gaze traveled back to George and the girl. "I loved all the pictures you sent."

Joss chuckled softly, not wanting to draw George's attention to them or disturb the young girl reading. She had taken dozens of pictures over the last forty-eight hours—some staged, some not, though all were amusing in their own way—and had sent them to Maeve in random bursts, hoping to make her smile. "Mission accomplished, then."

"Seriously, what made you think of that?"

"Well, you do have the most photogenic dog on the planet."

Maeve laughed. "She is. But, seriously, why?"

Joss shrugged. "I just wanted to make you smile."

"You did. I…" Maeve took a deep breath and let it go slowly, and then shook her head as she murmured, "You are too much, Joss Perrault."

The gentleness in Maeve's tone sent a pleasant flutter through Joss' chest, and had to focus on keeping her own voice steady as she quipped, "Yeah, I get that a lot."

Maeve smiled. "I'm sure you do."

Joss grinned and bumped Maeve's hip with her leg. "Honestly though, I'm glad you liked the pictures. George had lots of fun coming up with some of those."

"Did she, now?"

Joss nodded. "Oh yeah."

"Dare I ask which was her favorite?"

"Probably the one where she was sleeping on my bed."

Maeve laughed. "I don't doubt that at all. Please tell me you didn't actually let her sleep in your bed."

"I didn't actually let her sleep in my bed," Joss answered without missing a beat.

Maeve shook her head. "Why in the world would you let a hundred and twenty-five pound dog sleep in your bed?"

"Okay, first of all, I have a feeling that not even you 'let' George do anything—she does what she wants. And second of all, she was so cute with her sad eyes and shit that I couldn't tell her no even if I'd wanted to."

"Wow. Way to play hard to get, Joss," Maeve teased.

Joss rolled her eyes. "Whatever."

"Such an erudite response, Ms. Perrault."

"Such a snobby, elitist, quip, Ms. Dylan."

Maeve grinned, mischief sparking in her eyes. "You sound defensive. Please tell me you didn't take advantage of George while I was away."

Joss barked out a laugh that finally drew George's attention to the two of them at the counter, and she shot an apologetic look at the girl and her mother as George jumped to her feet and came bounding across the store. The mom smiled and knelt beside her daughter, who was pointing at the book in her lap and talking animatedly about whatever caught her interest. "You've been spotted."

"So I see," Maeve drawled. She stood up straighter and braced herself for George's greeting. George stopped in front of her and jumped up to place her front paws on Maeve's shoulders, and she laughed as she ducked away from the kiss George tried to give her. "Hey, beautiful."

George whined and wiggled closer, her tail wagging back and forth in an excited blur.

"Aww, I missed you too." Maeve rubbed her cheek against George's. She laughed as George's almost frantic cuddling pushed her back a step into the counter, and gave a few solid pats to George's sides before she said, "Down."

George immediately dropped to the floor and sat back on her haunches with a wide, goofy smile on her face as she looked up at Maeve.

"Damn. She didn't do that for me," Joss muttered, remembering back to the night before when she yelled the same thing after catching George counter surfing her way through the dinner ingredients she had spread out on the counter beside the stove.

"Dare I even ask?" Maeve asked.

Joss rubbed the back of her neck and shook her head. "Nope."

"Got it." Maeve looked at George. "Do you want to stay with Joss, or are you ready to go home?"

George stood up, gave a mighty shake, and hurried to the door, the breath from her nose fogging the glass despite the warm, summertime temperature.

"Gee, love you too, George," Joss drawled.

George looked over her shoulder at Joss, and wagged her tail.

"Do you have a game tonight?" Maeve asked as she took George's leash from Joss.

"Yeah, but I don't have to go. One of the paralegals from Brock's firm joined the team, so we're over the lady-limit."

"Oh. Well, in that case, would you like to come over for dinner tonight?"

"Dinner?" Joss parroted, her brow pinching in confusion.

A small, shy smile tugged at Maeve's lips as she nodded. "Yeah. I mean, It's the least I can do since you took care of George for me all weekend."

"Oh." Joss nodded. Yeah, she should have known that. "Sure. Sounds great."

"Wonderful." Maeve's smile widened as she clipped George's leash to her collar. "What time do you think you'll be done here?"

"We close at six, so…" Joss shrugged. "Six thirty? Six forty-five?"

"Perfect." Maeve took a deep breath as she stared at Joss for an extended moment, an unintelligible look clouding her eyes as they danced over Joss' face, before she shook her head as if to clear it as she tightened her hold on George's leash and pushed the door open. "We'll see you then."

"Yeah. See you then," Joss murmured, utterly confused by the way Maeve had just looked at her. Maeve had said the dinner was a way of thanking her for watching George, but there had been something in her eyes that made Joss wonder if she was still misreading the situation somehow.

"What's wrong with you?" Scott asked as he ambled into the store.

"Nothing." Joss ran a hand through her hair and checked her watch. "You're early."

"Yeah." He looked around the store. "I got a bone for George," he said, holding up a shrink-wrapped stuffed bone.

Joss arched a brow at him, wondering how in the world he had not seen Maeve and George out on the sidewalk. "You just missed her. Maeve's back from her trip and she just came by to pick her up."

Scott nodded. "Oh. Okay. Well, here." He handed Joss the bone. "You can give it to her next time you see her."

Joss bit her lip as she took the bone. "I'll see her tonight, actually. Maeve's invited me over for dinner as a thank-you-for-watching-George kind of thing." *Maybe if I say it enough times, I'll stop thinking about the way she looked at me just before they left.*

"So you're missing the game?"

"Yeah." Joss shrugged. "You've got Lila from Brock's firm now, I figured I could take a night off."

"Yeah. Totally." He pursed his lips and gave her a searching look. "You gonna be okay?"

"I'm pretty sure she's not going to poison me or something."

"That's not what I meant, and you know it."

"I know." Joss sighed. "I'll be fine. No matter how ill-advised this stupid crush of mine is, she's still a friend. I'll get over it," she added, more for her own benefit than his. Maybe if she kept telling herself that, it might actually happen. Someday.

"Okay."

She nodded. "Okay."

Fifteen

A veritable throng of customers spilled through Atramentum's door exactly four minutes before closing, and Joss bounced anxiously on the balls of her feet behind the front counter as she watched them meander through the stacks long after the store's posted closing time. Scott was flitting through the aisles, offering assistance, trying to get them to hurry, but it was still half-past six by the time the final customer left with their purchases. She knew that Maeve would not mind her tardiness, but that did nothing to quiet the panic that had her feeling distinctly unsettled. She hated being late—so much so, in fact, that she was habitually ten minutes early to everything.

Not that Maeve was expecting her at a specific time, she had just told her to come over when she was done with work, but still.

"Shit."

"Shit? What?" Scott asked as he pulled the cash drawer from the register and set it on the counter. He looked at her as he pulled the stack of twenties from their slot and thumbed through the bills, giving them a quick count.

"Nothing." Joss shook her head as she watched him write the amount he had just counted on a post-it before securing the bills together with a rubber band and setting them aside. She wanted to tell him to forget it, that she would take care of this in the morning, but he was already halfway through the drawer. Over ninety-six percent of

Atramentum's transactions were electronic, with only the rogue, random person choosing to pay with cash, which meant that the drawer never held more than a couple hundred dollars at a time.

"Can you get the bank bag from the safe for me?"

Joss nodded. "Yeah."

"What time are you supposed to be at Maeve's?" Scott asked as she started toward the office where the safe was hidden.

"She just said to come by after I was done here," Joss called over her shoulder. Dickens was watching her from the middle shelf on the bookcase nearest the office, and she gave his head a quick scratch as she walked by. He purred and closed his eyes at the touch, and Joss arched a brow in surprise as she lingered for a moment, tickling the soft fur between his ears. She hated to stop since he so rarely looked for attention, but Maeve was waiting, and so she gave him a small, apologetic smile as she pulled her hand away. "Sorry, buddy, but I gotta get going."

Dickens opened his eyes as he popped to his feet, and gave her one long, offended stare before he leapt from the bookcase and went in search of a new perch.

"I wasn't kicking you off your spot," Joss muttered as she watched him disappear.

She shook her head and ducked into the office to retrieve the square, blue canvas bank bag from the safe, and spun the combination lock to 5-2-9 as she made her way back toward the front of the store. Though she looked down each aisle she passed, Dickens was nowhere to be seen, but she spied Willy Shakes lounging on the same spot of rug George had occupied earlier that afternoon, rubbing his face on the carpet. He sat up to watch Joss as she passed and meowed as if asking where his friend went.

Joss chuckled under her breath and shook her head as she tossed the bag onto the counter beside Scott. She was definitely going to have to ask Maeve if George could come visit again soon. "Here you go."

"Thanks." Scott collected the banded bills he had finished counting while she had been gone and shoved them inside. "You want me to make the deposit tomorrow?"

"Nah. I'll do it." She picked up the pouch, zipped it shut, and spun the numbers on the lock out of position. "It's not a big deal."

"Works for me. So, is that it? We done?"

"We done." Joss stepped back and waved him toward the door with a small bow. "After you, sir."

Scott grinned and curtsied so low he almost fell over. "Thank you, ma'am."

"Good night, monsters!" Joss called into the store as she dimmed the lights and walked out the door.

Scott waited for her on the sidewalk as she locked up, his hands jammed in the pockets of his jeans, and then they could head across the street to their cars together. "Good luck tonight. Call me later if you need to vent?"

Joss smiled, grateful for his support. "I won't. But if I do, I'll definitely hit you up…"

"Good."

"Tell Michelle I say hello."

"Will do." He nodded. "See you tomorrow."

"Yep. Hit a few dingers for me tonight."

"I'll see what I can do," he promised as he climbed into his car.

Joss flattened herself against the side of her Jeep as he backed out, and took a deep breath as she returned his wave goodbye before opening her own door. She glanced at her watch as she slipped behind the wheel, and shook her head when she saw it was already ten till.

It would be after seven before she finally got to Maeve's house.

Despite the increased foot traffic Atramentum had just seen, there was very little traffic clogging the main road, and she somehow managed to hit every single green light on her way out of town.

Maybe the universe isn't totally stacked against me, she thought as she drove under the final signal separating her from her destination.

Evening shadows spilled in ragged diagonals across the drive, and even though Joss was running much later than she would have liked, she still took a few minutes to swing by her place on her way to Maeve's. She left her car door hanging open as she ran inside, pausing just long enough en route to the kitchen to toss the money bag from the store onto a half-empty shelf on the bookcase in the living room, and blew out a thoughtful breath as she surveyed the bottles filling her small wine rack. Her plan had been to stop and pick up a nice bottle of wine, but after getting out of Atramentum so late, that was time she was not willing to waste.

The glowing green numbers on the microwave to her right told her she was wasting even more time staring indecisively at perfectly ordinary bottles of wine, and she shook her head as she snatched a Merlot from the rack. Merlot was easy, everything went with a Merlot. She double-checked her hair and makeup in the mirrored coatrack that hung on the wall just inside the front door before locking up after herself and climbing back into her car. She laid the bottle of wine along the seam of the passenger's seat, trusting that the swell of padding and fabric would keep it from rolling onto the floor, and did not bother to buckle her seatbelt as she twisted the steering wheel to head toward Maeve's.

Warm, welcoming light spilled through the glass double doors at the front of Maeve's house as Joss drove up, and a familiar flutter of lightness settled in her chest as she picked up the bottle of wine she had brought with her and climbed out of her car. There would come a day where she would eventually manage to overcome her one-sided feelings, but it was going to take time; and Joss resigned herself to the fact that Maeve would remain the same beautiful, unattainable woman who sent her pulse racing and her stomach cartwheeling whenever they were close for a while longer.

She skipped up the stairs to the front porch, her eyes landing on a classic yellow post-it that was stuck at eye level on the front door, and she smiled as she plucked it from the glass. "Door's open. Come on in." She folded the note and slipped it into the back pocket of her jeans. Even though the note told her to let herself in, she still peered through the door as she reached for the sleek stainless steel doorknob, and she called out as she stepped over the threshold, "Hello!"

"In the kitchen!" Maeve hollered back.

Joss thought she heard Maeve start to say something else, but it was drowned out by a series of George's booming barks and the sound of nails clicking at a near frantic pace across golden oak planks. She set the bottle of wine in her hand on the console table in the foyer as she braced herself for impact, and burst out laughing when George rounded the corner too fast and slid right into the wall. It did not slow the Dane down for long, however, and the giant dog had Joss backed against the front door only seconds later as she whined and wiggled with excitement.

It was almost as exuberant a welcome as Maeve had gotten earlier that afternoon, and Joss smiled as she wrapped her left arm around George's neck and down onto her chest in a one-armed hug. "Hey, kiddo. Didya miss me?"

"Terribly, it would seem," Maeve's answered.

Joss's pulse tripped over itself as she looked up to see Maeve leaning against the corner of the wall, looking as breathtaking as ever in her bare feet, fitted white tank, and distressed skinny jeans. The laughter twinkling in her eyes was enchanting, and Joss swallowed hard as she tried to find her voice. "I…"

Maeve grinned and pushed off the wall as she nodded at George. "You have quite the way with the ladies," she teased. "George, come on. Let her in so we can have dinner."

George froze for a split-second as she processed what Maeve said before she whipped around and bounded down the hall toward the kitchen.

Maeve laughed, her smile softening and the laughter in her gaze became a little more muted as she turned toward Joss. She bit her lip as she hesitated for the briefest of moments, indecision tugging at the corners of her eyes, and then shook her head as she crossed the large foyer to pull Joss into a hug. "I'm glad you were able to make it."

Joss wrapped her arms around Maeve's waist in a loose hold and closed her eyes as she selfishly enjoyed the feeling of having Maeve in her arms. She knew that it was wrong to hold Maeve like this when the blonde was so completely unaware of the way she felt about her; knew that the memory of the way Maeve felt in her arms would linger, adding weeks and months to the time it would take her to move on— but she was too weak to do anything to resist. "Anytime."

"Is that a promise?" Maeve purred, her voice soft and rough and oh-so-goddamn-sexy that it should be illegal.

Joss cleared her throat as they broke apart. "Yeah."

There was an intensity to Maeve's gaze that held Joss frozen in place as green eyes searched for the answer to a question she wished she understood, and after a moment Maeve nodded. "Good to know. Are you hungry?"

"Starving." Joss offered Maeve the wine she was still holding. "This is for you."

"You didn't need to bring anything," Maeve protested as she took the bottle.

I would give you the world if I could, the least I can do is a bottle of twenty-dollar wine, Joss thought as she shrugged off Maeve's words. "I wanted to."

"Oh. Well…" Maeve ducked her head and smiled up at Joss through her lashes. "Thank you."

"My pleasure."

George barked at the back of the house, and Maeve rolled her eyes. "It would appear that her highness would like her dinner now."

Joss smiled and waved a hand down the hall. "After you."

George was waiting for them in the kitchen with her steel bowl dangling from her mouth, looking positively annoyed at having been kept waiting so long.

Joss laughed and looked at Maeve. "Does she do this every time?"

"Every damn time." Maeve's brow crinkled in confusion as she looked up at Joss. "She didn't do it for you?"

"No." Joss shook her head as she took the bowl from George. "Where do you keep her food?"

Maeve looked ready to refuse Joss' offer to help, but after a moment just waved a hand at the pantry on the far side of the kitchen as she made her way back to the large island where she had pushed a red plastic cutting board holding a couple of chicken breasts out of George's reach. "In there."

"Just sit tight, bud," Joss told George as she took the bowl over to the pantry. She spotted the clear plastic bin with an airtight lid pushed into the corner that held George's food as soon as she opened the door, and she groaned as she unlatched the lid and began scooping out the appropriate amount of food. "I'm sorry," she apologized as she closed the food bin and used the heel of her foot to pull the pantry door closed, "I meant to bring her extra food back to you but I was in such a hurry that I forgot."

"No biggie. Just bring it next time."

Joss smiled at the idea of 'next time', and held up George's bowl. "Where should I put this?"

Maeve pointed with the meat mallet in her hand at the elevated wooden stand near the sliding glass doors in the breakfast nook where George was waiting with a regal air to be served. "There."

"You are too much, Georgie-girl," Joss chuckled as she set the bowl into its cutout. She gave George's side a quick pat before turning back to Maeve, and was surprised to see that she was watching her. "What?"

Maeve shook her head and smiled. "Nothing. You're good with her."

"Thank you, though it's really not hard. George is pretty awesome." Joss glanced over her shoulder at the canine in question, who was watching them as she chewed her food with all the sophistication of a ravenous toddler. Joss rolled her eyes and leaned her hip against the edge of the counter where Maeve was working. "Except for when she's eating."

"Yeah, we're still working on that," Maeve murmured as she set the small metal hammer aside. "Do you like spinach artichoke dip?" she asked as she pulled a spoon from the drawer by her left hip.

"I love it," Joss admitted with a nod.

"Good." Maeve winked at Joss as she turned to pull a small, oblong container from the microwave in the island and set it beside the chicken. "Because that's what I'm going to use to stuff the chicken."

Joss nodded as she watched Maeve drop a generous spoonful of the dip onto one of the chicken breasts. Maeve used the back of the spoon to push it into a line down the center of the flattened meat, and then set the spoon aside so she could fold the edges over the filling and secure the flaps with a couple of toothpicks. Maeve's long, thin fingers deftly repeated the process with the second chicken breast, rolling and closing it up so the two breasts were identical, and she pushed the board back into the center of the island so she could wash her hands. With Maeve's back turned to her, Joss' gaze drifted to the tousled fall of hair cascading over her shoulders. She bit her lip as she was struck with an urge to sweep those luscious locks aside and pepper the side of Maeve's throat with kisses, and she quickly looked away. Not that averting her gaze helped her much, because now she was looking at the delectable swell of Maeve's ass in the jeans that seemed to be custom tailored to show it off, and her eyes zeroed in on a small hole above the right rear pocket that gave a peek-a-boo glimpse of crimson behind the denim.

Fucking hell, Joss thought as she yanked her eyes higher, trying to find something safe to focus on, and she groaned silently when her eyes landed on Maeve's. The skin on the back of her neck prickled at the way Maeve was looking at her, eyes dark with what she was sure had to be confusion because there was no way it could be anything else, and she swallowed hard as she asked as nonchalantly as possible, "Hmm?"

"Nothing." A small smile tugged at the corner of Maeve's lips as she picked up an emerald green dishtowel and began drying her hands.

Desperate for something to do that might keep her from making more of an ass of herself, Joss asked, "Can I help with anything?"

"There's really nothing to help with. You can go ahead and open the wine if you want." Maeve waved the towel in her hand at the bottle Joss had brought that was sitting on the counter next to her. "All this should be done in half an hour or so."

"I can do that. Corkscrew?"

"Center drawer in the island."

Joss opened the indicated drawer and, after scanning its contents, pulled out a corkscrew identical to the one she had at home. She used the tip of the metal screw to break the foil seal on the bottle, and tried to think of something they could talk about as she tore it free. "Did your niece like the books we picked out for her?"

"She did." Maeve nodded as she set a large skillet onto the stove. "She especially loved *The Paper Bag Princess.*"

"Ah, so I did good, then." Joss set the corkscrew over the mouth of the bottle and yanked the cork free. Maeve had chosen a handful of books to give as part of her niece's present, but *The Paper Bag Princess* had been her own addition to the pile.

"You did," Maeve confirmed as she drizzled a couple tablespoons of olive oil into the pan. "Everybody loved it, actually."

"What's not to love about a badass princess who saves the prince from a dragon?"

"Never mind the ending," Maeve agreed. "Between the book and all the pictures of George that you kept sending me, I think you made a bigger impact on the weekend than I did."

"I doubt that." Joss looked around the kitchen. "Glasses?"

"My family is pretty easy to win over," Maeve argued amiably. She pointed to a cabinet beside the pantry. "Glasses are over there."

"They must be," Joss teased as she retrieved two large goblets from the cabinet and set them on the island. She picked the bottle of wine and poured a generous amount into each glass. "Here you go," she said as she handed one to Maeve, who was standing at the stove. Their fingers brushed lightly together, and Joss bit the inside of her cheek to try to keep from physically reacting to the way her skin tingled from the brief contact.

Maeve took a small sip as Joss retreated to her previous spot at the edge of the counter a handful of feet away from the stove. "Very nice. Would you mind if I use some of this to cook with?"

"Go for it," Joss said, shrugging as she picked up her own glass, grateful to have something besides Maeve to focus on. "So, your family likes silly pictures of dogs, huh?"

"You have no idea," Maeve said, and though Joss could not be sure, she thought she detected a hint of embarrassment in Maeve's tone.

"What?"

"Nothing." Maeve pulled a pair of tongs from a spinning tool caddy and set them on the counter beside the stove as she turned back toward Joss. She sipped at her wine and arched a brow expectantly. "So, fill me in more on what happened here while I was gone."

"There really wasn't anything that exciting." Joss shook her head. "I mean, George and I sent you pictures of the highlights. It was just a lot of work and hanging out—no different than any other weekend, really."

"George behaved herself at the store?"

"Oh yeah. I actually wanted to ask you if she could come visit again on the weekend sometime. The girl who was reading to her when you came to pick her up wanted to know when George would be back."

Maeve's lips curled in a smile around the rim of her glass. "You may borrow her whenever you'd like. Just let me know, and if I can't bring her over, you are always welcome to pick her up."

"Great. We'll figure something out, then."

Maeve nodded, an indecipherable look flashing across her eyes as she set her glass back onto the counter and picked up her discarded tongs. Her hair fell in a curtain around her face as she flipped the chicken, and there was a slight husk in her voice when she agreed, "Yes. We'll figure something out."

Sixteen

"Your brothers seriously pushed you in the lake?" Joss arched a brow at Maeve as she spun the stem of her wine glass between her the pads of her thumb and middle finger. They were still at the table, their dirty plates sitting forgotten on the slate blue placemats in front of them as they talked. "I hope you got them back for that one."

"Oh, I did," Maeve replied, her eyes twinkling with laughter. "If there is one thing you learn early in my family, it's how to get revenge."

Joss lifted her glass to her lips. "I'm almost afraid to ask..."

Maeve lifted her right shoulder in a small shrug and finished off the last of her wine. "I waited until we were all out on the lake yesterday afternoon so the kids could go tubing, and my brothers—of course—had to have a turn. Then it was just a matter of unhooking the tow line and leaving them floating in the middle of the lake."

"Oh my God."

Maeve grinned. "Yeah, that was a long swim into shore for them. Especially because they had to tow the giant tube back in with them. That thing ain't light."

"Remind me not to piss you off," Joss chuckled as Maeve's phone rang.

"I think you're safe," Maeve assured her with a laugh as she got up to check it. Her smile faltered when she glanced at the screen, the joy that had been so evident in her features replaced with an unmistakable insecurity, and she licked her lips as she looked back up at Joss. "It's my editor. I'm so sorry, but I've got to take this."

Joss nodded. "I'm sure she loved it. Go talk to her, and I'll start cleaning up."

"You don't have to do that," Maeve protested as her phone continued to ring.

"Go talk to you editor, Maeve." Joss got to her feet, leaned across the table to gather Maeve's plate, and stacked it atop her own. "I've got this."

Maeve sighed and nodded. "Thank you."

"My pleasure. Go."

Maeve took a deep breath and swiped her thumb across the bottom of the screen as she turned toward the living room. "Amy. Hi."

Maeve's voice faded as she wandered further from the kitchen, and Joss smiled to herself as she saw George climb off of the couch to follow her. "Good girl, George. Go take care of your mom," she murmured as she carried the dishes to the sink.

Joss was just finishing up drying the baking sheet that had used to roast the vegetables that had been the perfect side dish to their main course when Maeve and George returned to the kitchen. "So, how'd it go?"

Maeve blew out a long breath and smiled as George yawned and flopped onto the ground at her feet. "Good. She loved it. I still have work to do, but she's sending me her notes."

"Do you need me to go?" Joss offered as she set the baking sheet on the stove. She had already cleaned the pan Maeve had used to cook the chicken, so she wiped her hands dry on the dishtowel she had been using and set it on the counter beside the sink.

"No." Maeve shook her head. "I'll start on it in the morning." She looked around the kitchen. "I appreciate you doing the dishes, but I really would have been fine doing them later."

"Yeah, but now you don't have to."

"You're too much," Maeve murmured. "Thank you."

"Thank you for a fantastic dinner," Joss replied just as softly.

Maeve glanced down at the counter for a moment before she looked back up at Joss through her eyelashes. "Would you like to go for a walk?"

"Sure."

George scrambled to her feet and gave a mighty shake before she all but raced to the back door, and they both smiled at her antics as they followed her. Though Joss could not put her finger on why, Maeve seemed conflicted—or maybe it was just the aftereffect of finally hearing back on the story she had poured her heart and soul into over the last year—but whatever the case, Joss was grateful for the way George's goofy excitement made her smile.

As soon as the door opened enough for her to squeeze through, George bolted through the gap and out into the night, leaping off the patio and soaring with surprising agility over the stairs before she landed with a small stumble on the grass. She turned and looked at them, her body vibrating with anticipation as she waited for them to follow.

Maeve shook her head at the dog as she waved a hand at the door. "After you..."

The moon was full, providing more than enough light to keep track of George as she sprinted toward the lake and they followed at a more leisurely pace. Their hands would brush against each other every so often, first every sixth step, then fourth, then second, and Joss had to force herself to keep from turning hers by a fraction to "accidentally" let their fingers hook together.

But damn, it was tempting.

Joss bit her lip as she glanced over at Maeve, wishing she could read the whatever was going on behind her placid expression. Their hands brushed together again, and she could have sworn she saw the smallest uptick at the corner of Maeve's lips.

Did she just smile?

Maeve's eyes remained locked on the shadow of George, who was running in a wild zigzag patter ahead of them, and Joss sighed under her breath.

Don't be ridiculous. It's just an accident.

The thought made her heart sink even though she knew that her feelings for Maeve would never be reciprocated, and she took a deep breath as she forced herself to look for George.

Get control of yourself, Perrault.

George stopped at the edge of the lawn to pick something up, and Joss was not at all surprised when the Dane came bounding up to them a moment later with the tattered tennis ball they had played with during their runs all weekend in her mouth. George dropped the ball at Joss' feet and then began inching away slowly, her head low, tail wagging in wide arcs as she waited for what she knew was coming next.

Joss stared at George as she picked up the ball and tapped it against her left hand once before she wound up to heave it as far as she could into the night. She chuckled at the way George barked excitedly as she turned to give chase, and turned to smile at Maeve. "How long do you think until she finds it?"

Maeve shrugged as she turned to look at Joss with a determined look in her eye. "Hopefully a while."

Joss could not look away from the way Maeve's tongue slid slowly over her lips as she took a step closer, the cool night air warming to an unnatural degree as Maeve moved closer still. Citrus and amber mixed with the sweet scent of wild summer grasses as the breeze kicked up, stirring the air around them, and Joss stared, utterly transfixed by the way Maeve kept coming closer, closer, closer.

She held her breath and tried to convince herself that this was not what it seemed, and yet—

Her eyes snapped down to her side in surprise at the feeling of Maeve's fingers ghosting down her forearm, goosebumps erupting across her skin in the wake of the hesitant touch. Her stomach clenched as Maeve's hand encircled her wrist, and she swallowed thickly as she forced her gaze higher. She wanted to ask Maeve what she was doing, but the question died on her tongue as she watched Maeve's head tilt ever-so-slightly to the right as she leaned in. The alluring scent of Maeve's perfume surrounded her as the blonde's breath fell in ragged waves against her lips, and she closed her eyes as the urge to capture Maeve's lips in a kiss that would ruin everything rocked through her.

She's so close...so close...

Maeve's thumb moved in short, hesitant strokes up and down the inside of Joss' wrist, and her voice was rough and broken when she whispered, "Can I kiss you?"

Joss snapped her eyes open to make sure she had really heard what she thought she had. Maeve's expression was almost pained as she stared back at her. The hand around her wrist trembled as Maeve waited for her response, and even though Joss did not understand where any of this was coming from, she did not have the power to continue to deny herself what she wanted.

Not when Maeve seemed to want it to.

The left side of her mouth quirked up in a small smile as she lifted her free hand to lightly drag the back of her nails along the line of Maeve's jaw.

Is this really happening?

She tilted her head to peer into Maeve's eyes, searching for some sign, some hint that this was all a dream as she tenderly cupped Maeve's face in her hand. Maeve's cheek was so warm soft beneath her thumb as she caressed the smooth skin, and Joss swallowed a gasp at the way Maeve's eyes fluttered shut as she turned her head into the touch, her lips parting with a quiet moan that was so raw and full of want that it nearly brought Joss to her knees.

Christ, she's beautiful.

Though Maeve's eyes were closed, Joss' remained wide open as she slowly closed the distance between them, letting the anticipation build to a ragged, needy crescendo before she let out a soft sigh and captured Maeve's lips in a sweet, chaste kiss.

"Oh God, yes," Maeve whispered into the kiss, letting go of Joss' wrist to loop both her arms around her waist.

That breathy plea destroyed the last vestiges of Joss' restraint. She whispered Maeve's name, the single syllable vibrating with all the tortured longing she had been repressing. She reached up with her left hand to frame Maeve's face as she pulled her closer, smoothing her thumbs over Maeve's cheeks as she kissed her again, letting herself become lost in the moment. Her stomach flipped at the feeling of Maeve's breasts pressing against her own as Maeve lifted herself onto her toes, fusing their bodies together as the arms around her neck tightened, pulling her closer, and she moaned at the first slow swipe of Maeve's tongue of against her own. Her right hand slid upward as the kiss deepened, tongues stroking together in languid exploration, and she groaned as she threaded her fingers through the thick, luscious strands of Maeve's hair like she had been wanting to do from the first time she laid eyes on her.

Maeve whimpered at the more possessive hold, and Joss tightened her grip as she took control of the kiss, plunging her tongue into Maeve's mouth with a tender recklessness that undoubtedly gave away every one of her most secret desires. And the way Maeve arched into her, head slanting further to the side as she opened her mouth wider, giving Joss everything she possibly could, said that she wanted it all too. The kiss was everything she had not allowed herself to dream it might be, and she squeezed her eyes shut even tighter as she broke the kiss and leaned her forehead against Maeve's, needing a moment to just breathe as the enormity of what was happening overcame her.

Joss combed her fingers through Maeve's hair as they clung to each other in the moonlit night beside the lake, their breaths tumbling together in ragged bursts between kiss-swollen lips. The taste of Maeve's tongue lingered on her own, and Joss groaned as she gave in to the want still spreading like fire through her veins and captured Maeve's lips in a passionate, awestruck kiss. She untangled her fingers from Maeve's hair and dragged them over the hinge of Maeve's jaw to the column of her throat, where the heavy beat of Maeve's pulse pounded an irregular rhythm against her fingertips that seemed to perfectly match her own racing heart.

Every time she tried to pull away, Maeve chased after her, claiming her lips with a smile that Joss could not help but return as she allowed herself to be swept away by the heady taste of Maeve's lips and the heavenly feeling of Maeve's body curled against her. She would have gladly stayed right there for the rest of the night, but a hard bump against their thighs reminded them they were not alone.

"Fuck, George," Maeve groaned as they broke apart, both looking down at George, who was grinning at them around the ball she held in her mouth, clearly proud of herself for succeeding in getting their attention.

"You have terrible timing, George," Joss muttered as she smiled down at the dog.

Maeve laughed as she brushed a quick, chaste kiss across Joss' lips. "I'm sorry about her."

"It's okay."

Maeve smile was beatific as she kissed Joss again, and she nuzzled Joss' cheek as she pulled back just far enough to whisper, "Should we go back inside?"

Joss nodded as she let her hand trail slowly from Maeve's neck, over the curve of her shoulder, and down the length of her arm until she was able to lace their fingers together. She gave Maeve's hand a gentle squeeze, and stole one last kiss before she agreed, "Sure."

"Good." Maeve squeezed Joss' hand back and looked down at George. "Home?"

George dropped the ball she had been holding in her mouth and took off for the house.

Joss chuckled as she and Maeve turned to follow. "That dog…"

"I know," Maeve agreed with a laugh as she leaned into Joss' side. "Believe me, I know."

Seventeen

As soon as they got back to the house, George let out a mighty yawn as she claimed her spot on the couch in the great room, and Maeve shook her head as she gave Joss' hand a light tug. "Whattaya say we leave her here and go somewhere she can't bother us?"

Joss' stomach fluttered at the idea, and she nodded. "Sure."

"Excellent." Maeve smiled. "Follow me."

Joss allowed herself to be led past George—who watched them go through half-lidded eyes, as if she were contemplating following—and down the hall toward a section of the house she had never been in before. The hallway was long, with large windows along the left side that overlooked the home's impressive property, and a few doors along the right that opened onto a couple of guest rooms and a laundry room. The only door that was not open was the one at the end of the hall, and Joss looked around interestedly when Maeve pushed it open and led her inside.

The room was not overly large, and the windows from the hallway continued all the way to the far wall, providing a breathtaking view of the woods and the lake. A low-pile blue and cream patterned rug covered the majority of the wood floor, giving the room a cozy feel. Pushed up against the glass was a six-foot long, table-style desk that had a mahogany work surface and white painted legs, which provided ample workspace without blocking the view. The edges of the desk were cluttered with stacks of books and papers, though the area surrounding Maeve's open laptop in the center was pristine, and the high-backed leather swivel chair pushed up to it looked like it was one of those ergonomically designed chairs that cost a fortune but were ridiculously comfortable. A navy blue upholstered loveseat anchored the far wall, which was filled with framed photographs Joss was eager to inspect, and the remaining two walls were taken up by built-in bookshelves overflowing with books.

"So this is where the magic happens, huh?" Joss murmured when she returned her attention to Maeve, who was watching her inspect the office with an interested smile.

Maeve lifted her right shoulder a small shrug as she closed the door behind them. "Something like that."

Joss smirked and turned toward the bookshelves, inspecting the titles on display much in the same way Maeve had done at her house. "I wonder what books a famous author has on her shelves. Maybe I'll finally figure out what your guilty reading pleasure is," she teased as her made her way to the nearest shelf. "Let's see...we have books about serial killers, police procedure, what looks like a few criminal law textbooks." She closed her eyes as Maeve moved came up behind her. "You're into the real page-turners, huh?"

Maeve chuckled and wrapped her left arm around Joss' waist as she lifted her right hand to sweep Joss' hair away from her neck. She leaned closer, so that her breasts pressed lightly into Joss' back, and kissed her ear. "Well, you know," she whispered huskily, "I do write crime-fiction."

"Oh, I know," Joss replied as she turned around and took Maeve into her arms. What she did not know was how in the hell they had ended up at this point. Happiness fluttered in her chest as Maeve sank into her, their lips fitting so easily together that it was hard to believe they had not kissed like this a thousand times before. And though she did not want to look a gift horse in the mouth, this dramatic shift in their relationship was almost too good to be true, and she could not help but wonder what had brought it on.

She wanted this—God, how she wanted this—but she also needed to know that, whatever this was, that it had a chance to become something lasting. Her feelings for Maeve were too strong for her to risk her heart on anything less.

Joss sighed as she pulled away, and bit her lip as she considered how to even begin broaching what she knew would be an awkward conversation

"That sigh sounds serious."

"Kinda…" Joss swallowed back the nerves that were making her throat feel impossibly tight, and tugged Maeve toward the sofa with her. "Can I ask you a question?"

Maeve perched herself on the edge of the cushion beside Joss and nodded as she folded her hands on her lap. "Of course."

Joss took a deep breath and looked down, hoping to find the words she needed. Her eyes landed on Maeve's hands, which were twisting subtly against each other in a show of nerves, and she shook her head as she reached out and covered them with her own. "It's not bad," she assured Maeve softly. "Or, I mean, I hope it isn't, I just…" She blew out a loud breath. "I thought you were straight," she blurted, and then groaned. *Smooth, Perrault. Surely there was a better way to lead into this whole thing…*

"Oh. I see." Maeve stopped fidgeting as a small, sad smile curled her lips. She straightened a little in her seat, like she was preparing herself to reveal something particularly damning, but did not pull her hands from under Joss'.

"I'm sorry," Joss apologized. "That was completely inelegant and far too blunt. Please don't get the wrong idea, I really, *really* want this…" She bit her lip as she cradled Maeve's face in her hand. "I just don't understand why…"

"I get it," Maeve murmured. She pulled her left hand free and laid it atop Joss' in a light hold that only served to make Joss' pulse race faster. "Yes, I have dated, and was even at one point engaged to a man, but I have not identified as straight since my junior year of undergrad. I'm bisexual, Joss."

"Oh." The tension in Joss' shoulders relaxed as she nodded.

Maeve gave Joss' hand a quick squeeze. "So, since we're being honest, I guess it's my turn to ask you a question: are you okay with that?"

Joss blinked, her brow furrowing in confusion. *Am I okay with it?* "Why wouldn't I be?"

"You'd be surprised." Maeve countered with a wry chuckle. "I've had a few women break up with me after they found out."

"Then they're idiots." Joss smoothed her thumb over Maeve's cheek and smiled at the way Maeve's eyelids fluttered at the gentle caress. "I'm sorry I was so tactless."

"Don't be," Maeve breathed. "It's good that we got all that out of the way."

Even though she knew that she should have handled things better, Joss nodded. "You are so beautiful." Her smile softened at the way Maeve's cheeks colored at the compliment. "I've wanted to kiss you from the moment I watched you come running out of the woods that first day when you were yelling at George," she confessed in a warm whisper.

Maeve's blush deepened, but playfulness sparked in her gaze as she looked up at Joss through her lashes. "So what's stopping you now?"

Joss laughed and nuzzled the tip of her nose along the side of Maeve's. "We're talking."

"Talking is overrated." Maeve grinned as she tilted her head and leaned in closer, her lips hovering just above Joss' as she purred, "Don't you think so?"

"Well, there's something to be said for flirty banter…"

Maeve ducked away from the kiss Joss tried to give her and arched a brow in playful challenge. "Speaking of flirty banter…"

"Hmm?" Joss smirked as she brushed a quick kiss over Maeve's lips.

"Did you honestly not notice me flirting with you every time I saw you over the last month?"

Joss rolled her eyes. "I just thought I was misreading the situation."

"Yes, because bringing a woman flowers in a completely platonic gesture."

"You know what?" Joss grumbled in mock exasperation.

Maeve grinned and flicked the tip of her tongue over Joss' lips. "What?"

"I honestly don't know," Joss admitted, unable to form a coherent thought with Maeve's lips so close to her own. There was nothing stopping her from taking the initiative and stopping this beautiful torture by capturing Maeve's lips with her own, but after what felt like years of wishing and hoping and wanting, she was enjoying the way her pulse raced and her stomach fluttered in anticipation. "God, Maeve…"

Maeve drew a shaky breath at the sound of her name falling so desperately from Joss' lips, and brushed the softest ghost of a kiss across her lips. "Joss?"

"Hmm?" Joss hummed, frozen in place as she waited for Maeve's lips to finally, finally claim her own.

"I've wanted to do this since that first day we met too," Maeve confessed in a husky whisper.

The kiss started slow and sweet—being with each other like this was too new for it to begin any other way—but it did not take long for it to become something more. Joss smiled against Maeve's lips as she obliged the hand on her shoulder and leaned back against the back of the sofa, and could not contain the soft moan that escaped her when Maeve moved with her, straddling her lap.

"Okay?" Maeve asked softly between kisses.

"Fuck, yes." Joss grabbed onto Maeve's hips and pulled her closer, loving the feeling of Maeve's body atop her own.

Any restraint either of them might have been exercising up to now disappeared as they came together with a desperation that made Joss' stomach clench. She had always loved being at the mercy of another woman's desire, and Maeve's was particularly intoxicating because she wanted her so desperately. Joss let her hands slide back to grab Maeve's ass as their kisses grew even deeper, encouraging the gentle rocking motion of Maeve's hips as she opened her mouth wider, meeting

Maeve's questing tongue thrust for thrust as a lustful fog clouded her brain. She tightened her grip and pulled Maeve's hips harder against her own, increasing the pressure with a deliberate grind, and the low, throaty moan that rumbled in Maeve's throat in response made Joss' eyes roll back in her head.

Oh, fuck me.

It was as if Maeve could read her mind as not a second later she began trailing hot, wet kisses along Joss' jaw before she ducked her head to nip at the sensitive hollow beneath her ear. Joss squeezed her eyes shut as the feeling of Maeve's teeth against her skin sent a rush of desire crashing between her thighs, and she groaned as she summoned the strength to gasp, "Wait."

Maeve pulled back to look at her with dark eyes and deliciously kiss-swollen lips that were pulled tight in a frown. "Did I do something wrong?"

"No. God no," Joss rasped, shaking her head. "I just..." She sighed and smiled sheepishly. "If you kept kissing me like that, there is very little I wouldn't have agreed to, and I don't want our first time to be some lust-fueled fuckfest on the couch in your office."

"Oh..."

"Exactly." Joss slid her hands back to Maeve's hips. Keeping them on her ass was just too much temptation to resist for long with the way her pulse was pounding against the seam of her jeans. "I mean, later on...I'm all for it, but not tonight."

A gentle smile curled Maeve's lips as she nodded. "Okay."

Joss blew out a loud breath, relieved that Maeve understood where she was coming from, and let her head drop back onto the couch so she was looking up at her. "You are an incredible woman, Maeve Dylan. Do you know that?"

"No I'm not," Maeve protested with a shake of her head.

The move sent a few random tendrils of hair tumbling over Maeve's cheek, and Joss felt her heart trip over itself as she stared at her. "You are." She reached up to tenderly tuck Maeve's hair back behind her ears, and then pressed a gentle finger to Maeve's lips to silence any further protest. "You are," she repeated as she pulled her hand away.

Maeve's gaze softened, and she leaned forward to capture Joss' lips in a sweet kiss. "You are."

Joss smiled into the kiss as George whined and scratched at the closed office door. "I think our chaperone has come to break this up."

"I'm sorry."

"Don't be." Joss nuzzled Maeve's cheek, just happy to hold her close. The force of their reactions to each other were so strong that she had no doubt they would end up in bed together sooner, rather than later, but she was perfectly content to spend the rest of the night cuddled up on the couch in the living room just like this. "What are you doing tomorrow night?"

"Nothing. Why?"

Joss smiled and kissed Maeve softly. "Scott's scheduled to close up the store, and I was thinking that I could maybe take you out to dinner?"

A small, shy smile lit Maeve's face as she nodded. "I would like that."

"Good. Then it's a date," Joss murmured, sealing her words with a slow, deep kiss that ended with them both laughing as George started barking her irritation as she clawed more insistently at the door that had not yet been opened for her.

Eighteen

The smile Joss had worn when she finally crawled into bed around midnight was still firmly in place when her alarm went off at six, and she rolled out of bed with far too much zeal for such an early hour of the day. She pulled on her running clothes and skipped down the stairs to the bathroom, where she hurried through her pre-run routine in her eagerness to hit the trail.

She took a deep breath as she closed her front door behind herself, and let it go in a *whoosh* as she jumped off the patio and took off at a pace that was much closer to a flat-out run than her usual jog. Her gaze drifted down the curve of blacktop that led to Maeve's front door as she passed, and her smile widened as she remembered the way they had lingered on the porch hours before, each of them taking turns extending their incredible evening by insisting upon "one last" goodbye kiss. They had stood out there for so long that even George had given up trying to break them apart, abandoning her post just on the other side of the doors with a distinctly disgruntled bark before she took off in search of her couch.

The entire night was so surreal that, were it not for the small hickey on her neck, she might have thought it had all been a dream. But that little mark was proof that all of it had happened, and her pace quickened further as she hurdled the log at the halfway mark around the lake. She had not asked Maeve if she would be waiting for her this morning, but she hoped that she would be.

Joss let out a small huff of a laugh when she spotted George waiting for her just beyond the trees, a four-legged sign that Maeve was indeed somewhere up ahead. She slowed just long enough to give George's head a quick scratch before she took off once again, calling out over her shoulder for George to join her.

George, sensing a challenge, bolted past her with an excited yelp, and Joss shook her head as she buckled down and forced herself to run even faster. She swore under her breath when George leapt up the stairs and sat haughtily at the top to watch Joss finish the sprint, her tongue hanging out of her wide, dopey grin as she panted in victory.

"Yeah, yeah," Joss grumbled, patting George's head as she gasped for air. After the pace she had set for the rest of her run in her rush to see Maeve, that little sprint thoroughly kicked her ass. "You win."

George chuffed at the validation, and licked Joss' hand as she got back to her feet. There was a jaunty little hop to her step as she trotted into the house, like she was proving that their race did not affect her at all.

Joss grinned and called after her, "Show off!"

"She doesn't usually beat you by that much."

Joss rolled her eyes and looked up at Maeve, who was curled up in her usual chair without any sign of work in front of her. Her smile softened as she made her way over to the table, and she sighed as she braced her hands on the arms of Maeve's chair and leaned in to capture her lips in a tender kiss. The feeling of Maeve's fingertips against her cheek, holding her in place, sent a pleasant shiver down her spine, and she hummed contentedly as one kiss became two, and then three.

"Good morning," Maeve murmured huskily when they finally broke apart.

"Good morning to you, too," Joss replied, nuzzling Maeve's cheek and then stealing one last kiss. She licked her lips as she stood up, and shot Maeve a curious look as she moved to take her usual seat. "Not writing today?"

"Not right now, anyway," Maeve confirmed with a small tip of her head. "How was your run?"

"Fast," Joss chuckled. "I think I did the whole thing at a sprint."

"Really?" Maeve purred, relaxing further into her seat, a small, pleased smile quirking her lips. "Any reason why?"

Joss shrugged and sipped at her coffee. "Eh. I might have been just a little excited to see this beautiful woman who always waits for me at the end of it."

"Well, I can assure you that George was quite excited to see you again, too," Maeve replied dryly.

"And what about her mom?" Joss sassed, arching a brow in playful challenge.

"Her mom," Maeve began with an embarrassed chuckle, "was up at five because she didn't want to miss seeing you."

Joss' heart soared at the confession, and she smiled as she leaned over and kiss Maeve softly. "I'm glad," she whispered, kissing Maeve again. "You know," she added as she lowered herself back to her chair, "part of me was afraid that you wouldn't be out here this morning."

"Why?"

"I dunno." Joss shrugged. "We were up late last night, and I just…"

Maeve's expression softened, and she shook her head. "I've been setting an alarm for the last month so that I would be out here when you came by. Which says a lot," she added with a smirk, "because I am not a morning person. At all."

Joss chuckled with Maeve at that, and bit her lip as she idly stroked her thumb back and forth across Maeve's knuckles. "Thank you," she said sincerely after a moment, looking up at Maeve through her lashes, her stomach flip-flopping at the affection shining in Maeve's eyes. "Seeing you every morning has been the highlight of my day."

"Mine too."

They stared at each other for a moment and then Joss blew out a soft breath as she took Maeve's hand and pressed a gentle kiss to her fingers. "Are we still on for dinner tonight?"

"Of course." Maeve nodded. "Just tell me what time to be ready."

Joss bobbed her head side-to-side thoughtfully. She had not actually decided where she was going to take Maeve, but she knew Scott would be fine with her skipping out earlier than usual. "Six?"

Maeve smiled. "You're leaving work early, huh?"

"Yeah. Scott can handle things." Joss kissed Maeve again. "Spending the night with you is much more important than working."

"Charmer," Maeve murmured, brushing their lips together.

"It's true," Joss assured her, shaking her head as the ghost of tear-filled accusations flung at her by her deservedly pissed-off ex floated across her mind. She did not want to be that person again, but she also knew that there would be times that Atramentum would demand most of her attention. She could only hope she remained aware enough to recognize when she was spending too much time at the store so she could take a step back from it all and make sure she did not screw this up.

The alarm on her phone began beeping, insisting it was time for her to get going, and she groaned and shook her head. Brilliant timing. She had just finished saying that Maeve was more important than Atramentum, and she was going to have to leave her now to get there on time to open.

"I'm sorry," Joss apologized.

"Don't be." Maeve got to her feet and used her grip on Joss' hand to pull her up as well. She smiled as she released her hold and looped her arms around Joss' neck. "Tonight isn't going to come if we don't get the day started."

"Well, that's one way to look at it," Joss said, wrapping her arms around Maeve's waist and pulling her into a light embrace. "Text me later?"

"Of course."

Joss smiled, already looking forward to the moment her phone would beep with a message from Maeve. "Can I get a kiss goodbye?"

Maeve pretended to consider the request for a few seconds before she laughed and leaned in closer. "Like I would let you go without one."

Joss moaned softly at the feeling of Maeve's tongue sliding lazily against her own. There was no urgency in the kiss, just a quiet affection and desire to enjoy the moment while it lasted, and she sighed when it reached its inevitable end. "I wish I could stay."

"I wish you could stay too," Maeve said with a smile. "But you have work to do, and so do I, I'm afraid."

"See you tonight?"

"Bet your ass you will."

Joss laughed. "Perfect."

"Anything special I should wear?"

"Wear whatever you want." Joss dropped a chaste kiss to the tip of Maeve's nose.

"So...yoga pants and a hoodie?"

"It'd save me the trouble of dressing up," Joss quipped as she took a small step back, keeping one arm hooked around Maeve's waist and pulling her along with her as she started for the stairs.

"Point taken," Maeve drawled with a small nod. "Then prepare to have your socks knocked off when I see you later, Ms. Perrault."

Joss laughed and turned her head to capture Maeve's lips in a tender kiss that was the antithesis of their playful conversation. Her stomach flipped at the feeling of Maeve melting into her, and she nuzzled her cheek as she whispered, "You take my breath away every time I see you, Maeve Dylan." She pecked her lips softly one last time. "I will see you tonight," she promised as she pulled away and started down the stairs.

Maeve's gaze was soft, her smile so achingly beautiful that it was all Joss could do to keep from reversing course and pulling her back into her arms, and she shook her head as she murmured, "Charmer."

Joss tipped her head in a small bow and blew her the kiss she would much rather have delivered herself. "See you at six."

"See you then," Maeve agreed softly.

Atramentum

Joss stared at her for a few more seconds, just committing to memory how Maeve looked in that moment, before she turned with one last wave and started for home.

Nineteen

"No, that won't work," Joss muttered to herself as she hit the back button on her browser and rubbed a hand over her face. She sighed and clicked the next result, not really expecting to find anything that would help, but hoping that it might spark an idea. She still had no idea where she was going to take Maeve for their date, and Google was failing to help her come up with any ideas.

The bell above the front door jingled, and she shook her head as she backed out of what seemed like the thousandth unhelpful page that promised prospective vacationers plenty of ideas about what to do in Sky at night. Willy Shakes, who had been stretched across the counter watching her work, sat up and swished his tail as he looked at the door.

"Oh God. Did your dinner not go well?" Scott asked, looking and sounding panicked as he stared at her.

Joss' shoulders relaxed, and she smiled in spite of her frustration. "No. Dinner last night was amazing. It's dinner tonight that I'm having trouble with."

Scott held up a hand. "Back that one up a bit, tiger. Amazing?"

"Incredible," Joss confirmed.

He grinned and pushed the lid of her laptop closed so he would have her full attention. "What happened?"

Joss took a deep breath as she leaned back in her chair and let it go slowly, knowing that the waiting was driving him insane and that his reaction was going to be priceless. She was half-tempted to pull out her phone to record it, but decided to take pity on him. Partly because he had been her biggest supporter over the last month, and mostly because she did not want to piss him off since he knew everything and everybody in Sky and could hopefully help her come up with an idea for her date that was in, she checked her watch, five hours.

Awesome, she thought to herself. *Five hours until I'm supposed to pick her up, I still have to figure out where we're going, and I haven't even begun to think about what I'm going to wear.*

"Joss..." Scott whined, pulling her out of her thoughts and back to the present.

"Maeve kissed me," Joss said, getting right to the point.

Scott's exuberant yell was so loud that a few people walking on the sidewalk outside Atramentum stopped to look through the front door, but he was too busy jumping up and down, pumping his fists in celebration to notice.

Joss did, however, and it only made her laugh harder as Willy Shakes looked at them both like they were insane before leaping gracefully from the counter and going in search of quieter digs. "Dude, calm down."

"I was right!" He pointed at her. "She is into you!"

"It would appear so, yes," Joss conceded with a smile.

He stopped hopping and stared at her expectantly. "And...?"

"And, what?"

"How was it?"

"It was..." Joss ran a hand through her hair and sighed. "Fantastic. Awesome. Incredible. Insert-your-favorite-superlative-here and it would still pale in comparison to the reality of what it is like to actually kiss Maeve Dylan."

He grinned and nodded happily. "Good."

"Yeah." Joss rolled her eyes. "But now I need your help."

"I always knew this day would come," Scott quipped with a mischievous twinkle in his eye. "See, Joss, when two people really like each other—"

Joss chuckled. "I know it's been a while for me, but I'm pretty sure I've still got all that down." *Hopefully*, she added silently. *It's like riding a bike, right?* "Though I am afraid to ask where your font of knowledge regarding lesbian sex comes from."

"Yeah, best we leave that one alone," he agreed quickly. "Seriously though, what do you need?"

"Date ideas," Joss groaned. "She promised to wear something that would, quote, 'knock my socks off'—and I don't know that many places in Sky that fall into the category of super-awesome-fancy-date locations."

Scott's expression turned thoughtful as he nodded. "O-kay. Right," he murmured. "Have you thought about taking her to Alpine?"

It had been one of the first places she thought of, to be honest. Alpine was the most exclusive restaurant in town, tucked on a small flat of land carved into the peak of Sky mountain and accessible only by gondola, and it certainly fit all the parameters of a "dream date". There was just one problem with the restaurant, and Joss shook her head as she pointed it out to him. "I called. Couldn't get a reservation. Seems they book two months out in advance for the high season."

"And that, my dear," Scott declared, "is why you need me." He pulled out his phone, tapped the screen a few times and did a couple swipes with his thumb, and then grinned as he lifted it to his ear.

"What are you doing?"

Scott held up a finger and winked. "Helping you get lucky. Now, shush."

Joss made a show of zipping her lips as she crossed her arms over her chest and leaned back in her chair.

After a beat, Scott's smile widened, and Joss assumed that whoever he was calling finally picked up. "Hey, man. Yeah, long time no talk. How's it going?"

Joss bit her lip and reached for her laptop. She didn't have time to listen to Scott shoot the shit with some buddy of his.

Before she could get it open, however, it was pulled from her grip. Scott shook his head and scowled at her as he listened to whoever was on the other end of the line. "I got this," he whispered. "Chill. No, not you man, sorry," he added, glaring reproachfully at Joss. "I'm here with a friend. Hey, do you remember Joss Perrault?"

Joss frowned. "Who is it?" she demanded quietly.

Scott blew out a frustrated breath and moved the phone to his shoulder. "Hunter Leblanc. Now, zip-it Miss Bossy Pants or I'm not helping you get any," Scott whispered back.

Joss' eyes widened. She had completely forgotten that the Leblanc family owned Alpine. Hunter had been a year behind them in school, but their paths would occasionally cross because he was on the football team with Brock and the basketball team with Herold.

Scott shot her a smug look as he lifted the phone back to his ear. "Yeah, that's her. Look, I hate to do this, but we were hoping you could help her out. She's got this big date tonight with this girl she's been drooling over *forever*, and…" His voice trailed off and his grin became absolutely shit-eating. "You can? That'd be awesome. Joss, what time would you want a reservation for?"

Joss' brow furrowed. Was this really happening? "Um…seven?"

"Would seven work?" he asked. "Awesome, man, thanks." Scott waggled his eyebrows at Joss even as he continued to talk to Hunter. "What? Oh, yeah, I can do pucks again this year. When does the season start? I'll need to get my insurance and shit lined up." He nodded along with whatever Hunter was saying. "Right. I'll get on that soon, then. Cool. Yeah. It'll be fun. Okay. I will. Thanks." He tapped his thumb to the bottom of the screen and slipped the phone back into his pocket. "And that, my dear, is how you network."

"You seriously just scored me a reservation?" Joss gaped at him. "At Alpine? For tonight?"

"Indeed I did." He blew on his nails and buffed them on his shoulder. "You're welcome."

"Thank you." Joss smiled. "Seriously. Thank you." She had a reservation at the fanciest, most romantic restaurant in town, now she just needed… "Fuck."

"What?" Scott asked, eyebrows rising in panic. "You said seven was okay!"

"It is," Joss said, shaking her head. "I don't know what to wear."

He rolled his eyes. "Do we need to close up the store for the afternoon so we can get your shit organized?"

It was a tempting offer, but a family of six walking through the door behind Scott nixed that idea before she could seriously consider it.

"Hey there. Can I help you find anything?" Scott asked.

The mother shook her head as the father said, "Nah. I think we've got it. Thanks."

"No problem. Lemme know if you need any help," Scott replied.

Once the family had moved out of earshot, Joss blew out a loud breath and picked up their conversation where they had left off. "No matter how much I would like to say yes, we can't. I am going to have to bail early tonight, though."

"No biggie." He shrugged. "I kinda figured as much with a seven o'clock reservation. You want me to have Michelle meet you at your place later to help you pick out something to wear?"

Joss shook her head. She liked Michelle, but she did not know her well enough to feel comfortable having her help with this. "Nah. I'll figure something out."

"You're sure?" Scott asked, looking unconvinced.

Not at all, Joss thought even as she nodded. "Yeah. I'm sure. Thanks, though."

"Of course." He tipped his head in a small bow. "I'm really happy for you, Joss. Really."

"Thank you."

"Excuse me," a quiet voice called out uncertainly from behind Scott, and Joss smiled as she looked at the smallest boy from the family that had just come in.

"What do you need, buddy?"

"Do you have any Minecraft books?"

"We do," Joss said, nodding as she got to her feet.

"Stay here and plan for your big date," Scott said, pushing her back onto the stool. "I've got this." He turned to the little boy. "You play Minecraft?" When the boy answered in the affirmative, he asked, "What's your favorite mod?"

Joss watched them go with a smile and shook her head. Scott was right. Their dinner reservation was taken care of, and she knew from Alpine's reputation that that portion of the evening would be fantastic, but there were still other things she needed to figure out if she was going to make their first date everything that a woman like Maeve deserved.

Twenty

Joss looked down at the items in her hands and frowned, concerned that what she had thought was a cute idea was just stupid. The voice of reason in the back of her mind told her she was being ridiculous, that this was just a manifestation of the nerves that had kept her pacing the aisles of Atramentum until Scott had enough of her silently freaking out and sent her home, but she desperately wanted this date to go well. Wanted to do all the right things and say the right words to make Maeve smile like she had earlier that morning, where the curl of her lips was so soft and shy and the crinkle at the corner of her eyes said how touched she was by the compliment.

She shook her head and looked up at her reflection that was staring back at her from Maeve's glass front doors. The fitted charcoal slacks she wore were nice enough, she figured, with their low-rise waist and the way they hugged her ass, but there was nothing particularly striking about the deep purple silk button-down shirt she had paired with them. Joss frowned at her hair, which she had left down so it hung loosely around her shoulders in her usual style, and sighed as she wondered if she should have done something else with it. She wanted to be smooth and suave and charming, and yet, here she stood, on the doorstep of the woman she had been crushing on from pretty much the moment she first laid eyes on her, in her old work clothes, holding a bouquet of lilies and a bone.

"Why in the name of fuck did I bring a bone?" she muttered. Bringing flowers for Maeve and a treat for George had seemed like a brilliant idea when she came up with it, since it was George who really first introduced them, but now that she was here, it just seemed...lame. "What kind of moron brings a treat for the dog on their first date?"

"The kind who knows that it would make said dog's mom smile," a soft, amused voice replied behind her.

Joss squeezed her eyes shut in horror. *No, no, no, no, no. Please tell me this is not happening!*

The soft hand on her elbow assured her it was, however, and she blew out a soft breath as she opened her eyes and allowed herself to be turned around. She desperately tried to come up with something witty to say in that half-second it took her to face Maeve, something that would make her seem like less of a dork for talking to herself like that, but her mind went blank the moment she saw her. She was pretty sure her mouth was hanging open as she stared at the blonde, but she could hardly find the wherewithal to care.

Maeve was positively stunning in a black, halter-style dress that highlighted the subtle line of her collarbones and the soft curve of her shoulders. The bodice was tight, hugging the amble swell of her breasts, and the loose skirt that billowed around her thighs before stopping just at the top of her knees added a touch of playful casualness to the dress. Joss' gaze continued its downward trek, over smooth calves to a pair of strappy black heels that were high enough to bring her and Maeve eye-to-eye. Maeve's makeup was impeccable, her hair was lusciously tousled in a way that Joss knew took quite a bit of effort to achieve while looking like she had just rolled out of bed after an afternoon of lovemaking, and her eyes sparkled with amusement and something Joss wished she understood.

A perfectly sculpted brow arching above Maeve's trademark black frames reminded Joss that she was still waiting for her response, and she bit her lip to try to stem the blush she could feel tinting her cheeks as she offered her the flowers, praying Maeve did not notice the way her hand trembled. "Um...hi. These are for you."

Maeve smiled as she took the wrapped bouquet. She twirled the flowers this way and that, her smile widening as she inspected the pink and white star-shaped flowers. Her voice was soft when she finally spoke, the look in her eyes even softer as she leaned in to press a light kiss to Joss' cheek. "Thank you. I love them."

The feeling of Maeve's lips against her skin was pure heaven, and Joss closed her eyes as she whispered, "I'm glad."

Maeve nodded and cleared her throat as she pulled away, and took a deep breath as she tilted her chin toward the bone Joss still held in her left hand. "George really likes bones, too."

"Yeah." Joss smiled sheepishly and handed Maeve the stuffed bone. "It seemed like a cute idea at the time…"

"It's perfect," Maeve assured her with a wink. "I just put her in her run, though, so you can give it to her when we come back."

With nothing left to occupy her hands, Joss shoved them in her pockets. "Okay."

"Do we have time for me to go put these in water?"

Joss did not need to check her watch to know that they had plenty of time before their reservation, and she rocked back on her heels as she nodded. "Of course."

A speculative look flitted across Maeve's face for a beat before she edged past Joss and opened the front door. Joss followed her down the hall to the kitchen, and leaned against the edge of the counter much like she had the night before as she watched Maeve set the flowers and bone on the counter beside the sink.

"I'll be right back." Maeve smiled and disappeared through the door to the butler's pantry that separated the kitchen and dining room.

Alone for a moment, Joss closed her eyes and took a deep breath to try to settle her nerves. *Okay, so Maeve heard me talking to myself. She seemed amused by it, so stop freaking out.* She blew out the breath she had been holding and shook her head. *Easier said than done.*

"You okay?" Maeve asked as she reentered the kitchen with a cut crystal vase.

Joss nodded, painfully aware of the way Maeve's eyes never left her face as she set the vase in the sink. "Yeah. I'm sorry."

"No reason to be sorry," Maeve murmured, her smile gentle as she abandoned her task and made her way over to Joss. Her touch was light as she stroked the line of Joss' jaw with the backs of her fingers, and she sighed as she leaned in, head tilting ever-so-slightly to the side as she closed the distance between them.

The kiss was slow and sweet, and Joss' eyes fluttered shut as she reached for Maeve's hips to pull her closer. The nerves that had been tormenting her all afternoon faded at the feeling of Maeve's body responding to her touch, allowing Joss to pull her in until they were hip-to-hip and breast-to-breast, and she let out a shuddering breath when they finally broke apart. "Wow."

Maeve hummed in agreement and pressed a chaste, lingering kiss to Joss' lips. "Indeed." Her expression was thoughtful when she pulled back and asked, "Feeling better?"

Joss blushed. "Yeah." She cleared her throat as she rubbed her thumbs over the soft fabric hugging Maeve's hips. "I don't think I've told you yet how incredible you look."

"Thank you." Maeve smiled and took a step back to give Joss a deliberate once-over. "You look pretty incredible yourself," she murmured, her eyes a shade darker than usual as she made her way back to the sink. "These really are beautiful," Maeve said as she cut the cellophane off the bouquet and began trimming the stems. "Where did you find them?"

Beautiful flowers for a beautiful woman, Joss thought to herself, though she did not dare utter such a clichéd phrase aloud. "Just the little florist shop in town."

Maeve grinned. "For Freesia's Sake?"

"That's the one."

"I haven't been in there yet, but I laugh every time I drive by. It's an absolutely genius name for a flower shop."

"Right?" Joss agreed with a small laugh. "Of course, the best is tourists' reactions when they ask for the name of a local florist and you tell them to go there."

"I'll bet," Maeve muttered as she finished trimming the final two stems before gathering the bunch to set into the vase. "There." She picked the bouquet up and let it drop one final time so that the flowers spread out and filled the entire vase. "Perfect."

Joss waited until Maeve had filled the vase with water and set it on the island before she asked, "Ready to go, then?"

"Absolutely. Where are we going?"

"That, my dear, is a surprise," Joss teased as she placed a light hand on the small of Maeve's back to guide her toward the front door.

"Oh, well, in that case..." Maeve gathered her black wrap and purse that were draped over the end of the banister. Her smile was blinding when she spun back toward Joss, and she chuckled softly as she took Joss' hand and threaded their fingers together. "I can't wait to be surprised."

Joss brushed a quick kiss across the backs of Maeve's knuckles as they walked out the door, and was pleasantly surprised when Maeve did not let go of her hand to lock up after them. She glanced toward the side of the garage as they walked hand-in-hand to her car, and had to laugh when she caught sight of George watching them from her run. "We've been spotted," she observed in a mock whisper.

Maeve rolled her eyes. "She has the garage and her run, she's fine."

George's sad eyes and droopy ears were utterly pathetic, and Joss shook her head as she opened the passenger's door for Maeve. "She's good at that."

"The guilt thing?" Maeve grinned and stole a quick kiss before sliding elegantly onto the passenger's seat. "You get used to it."

"If you say so," Joss muttered, making Maeve laugh. She winked at her and slammed the door shut, and looked over at George as she strolled around the hood to the driver's side. "We'll be back later, Georgie-girl."

George let out a loud, pathetic whine and then turned and disappeared into the doghouse that served as both shelter and camouflage for her super-sized dog door into the garage.

"She told you," Maeve said as Joss climbed behind the wheel.

Joss shrugged as she twisted the key in the ignition. The courtyard was wide enough that she could turn around without shifting into reverse, and she arched a brow at Maeve as she got them heading in the right direction. "Come on, like that's really surprising?"

"Well, no," Maeve teased, taking Joss' hand into her own once more as they started down the drive. "She's got you pretty whipped."

She's not the only one, Joss thought, shooting a glance at Maeve. "Shut up."

Maeve laughed. "Whatever. So, how was your day?"

Joss shrugged and filled Maeve in on the highlights of her day, omitting everything that had to do with her trying to plan their date and/or freaking out about said date, and once she was done, Maeve shared some of what she had accomplished with her editing. They chatted amiably on the drive into town, and Joss watched Maeve out of the corner of her eye as she pulled into the main lot at Buckskin Ski Resort, curious if Maeve had any idea where they were going. The small frown of confusion that wrinkled Maeve's forehead as she read the large billboard sign on the front of the ski shop advertising guided trail hikes told her she did not, and Joss grinned as she pulled into a space on the westernmost edge of the lot, nearest the gondola that would take them to the top of the mountain.

"Ready?" Joss pulled her keys from the ignition and turned to grab her blazer from the backseat just in case Maeve's wrap was not enough to keep her warm and she needed a coat later.

"Yes?"

Joss chuckled and leaned across the center console to kiss Maeve softly. "Excellent," she murmured as she pulled away and opened her door.

"We're not going hiking, right?" Maeve asked as she climbed out of the car.

"Maybe next time," Joss said. "George would like that, right?"

"I dunno, Ms. Perrault," Maeve teased with a smirk as she joined Joss at the front of the car. She slipped her hand in the crook of Joss' elbow and gave it a light squeeze. "Don't you think you should see how the first date goes before you start planning the second one?"

Joss laughed and led Maeve toward the small chalet at the base of the mountain where they would pick up the gondola. "Do you?" she retorted as she ushered Maeve inside. She caught the eye of the gondola attendant who was standing at a small podium just to the side of the loading area, and nodded. "Perrault."

The attendant checked the list on his podium and nodded. "The next car should be down in a minute or two."

"Great. Thanks." Joss walked over to where Maeve was looking out a window that overlooked a wide grassy area that, during the winter, served as the runout for the majority of the resort's runs. Aware of the fact that they were no longer alone and unsure of how much physical contact Maeve preferred while in public, Joss shoved her hands in the front pockets of her slacks as she stopped behind her, just close enough that they would be able to keep their voices from carrying to across the room to the attendant. "It won't be long."

Maeve nodded. "I heard." She leaned back into Joss and gestured at the runout. "Is that a deer?"

Joss looked across the meadow and nodded. "Yep. You know, a lot of the old-timers around here believe it's a good omen to see a deer on a first date."

"Really?"

Joss laughed and shook her head as she spotted the gondola approaching the bottom of the hill. "No." She laughed harder at the playful huff of exasperation her honesty earned her, and took a small step back as she gestured toward the loading area. "However, making one's reservation on time is. Your chariot awaits, m'lady."

"You're not as cute as you think you are," Maeve grumbled, bumping Joss with her shoulder as she passed.

Joss hurried to catch up to her, and hovered just off her elbow as they stood out of the way as an older couple climbed from the car. Joss smiled her thanks to the attendant as she followed Maeve inside, grateful to be free from prying eyes. Once the door was shut, and the gondola slid smoothly into motion, lifting them into the air, Joss wrapped her arms around Maeve's waist and pressed a light kiss to her ear. "You don't think I'm cute?"

Maeve shook her head as she spun in Joss' embrace and smiled as she kissed her softly. "You're so much more than 'cute', Joss. You're gorgeous."

Joss' stomach fluttered at the compliment, and she sighed as she captured Maeve's lips in a slow, sweet kiss. "You're gorgeous."

"I said it first," Maeve chuckled.

"Yeah, well, we can't all be wordsmiths around here, now can we?"

"And yet, you actually used the term 'wordsmith'," Maeve retorted.

Joss smiled and shrugged. "Whatever." She pressed a chaste, lingering kiss to Maeve's lips and then hummed under her breath as she pulled away. "You're still gorgeous."

Maeve tipped her head in a small bow. "Thank you." She kissed Joss softly and then sighed as she spun in her arms to look out the gondola's wraparound windows at the view spread before them.

Though the view beyond the glass was spectacular, Joss was more than content to watch Maeve take it all in. It had been years since she had last taken this ride, but majestic beauty of the mountain, with its thick strands of evergreens that filled the spaces between ski runs, and the wild grasses and flowers covering the open slopes that danced in the breeze, paled in comparison to the splendor of the woman in her arms. Her eyes danced over the gentle curve of Maeve's cheek and the regal slope of her nose as a warm, easy silence surrounded them, and a stab of disappointment shot through her when she felt the gondola begin to slow beneath her feet.

"This view is incredible," Maeve observed in an awed whisper.

Joss smiled and tightened her arms around Maeve's waist as she kissed her cheek. "Yes, you are." She closed her eyes and took a deep breath, letting the familiar scent of Maeve's perfume wash over her, and sighed as she pressed one last kiss to Maeve's cheek before releasing her.

Maeve's eyes were gentle and dark when she turned around, and she shook her head as she closed the slight distance Joss had put between them.

Joss' breath caught in her throat as Maeve's fingers skimmed over her cheek to lightly clasp the side of her neck. Maeve's breath was soft against Joss' lips as she leaned in closer, the kiss that followed so brief and tender that Joss swore her heart stopped beating altogether. The world came crashing back around them the moment the gondola door popped open, letting the indistinct hum of conversation from the restaurant beyond the small entryway pour into the car, and Joss licked her lips as she tipped her head at the door. "You ready?"

Maeve took a deep breath as her eyes flicked between Joss and the maître d' that was watching them from her spot just beyond the loading/unloading platform, and she let it go slowly as she nodded. "Yeah."

The feel of Maeve's hand slipping into her own made Joss smile, and she gave it a gentle squeezed as she led them from the car. The interior of the restaurant was mountain elegance at its finest with split-log walls and two massive deer antler chandeliers hanging from the elevated ceiling, the rustic elements blending seamlessly with the trappings one would expect to find at a Michelin star restaurant.

Joss watched Maeve take it all in as they approached the maître d', and sighed when she had to look away to give her name to the waistcoated woman at the podium. "Reservation for Perrault."

The woman nodded as she gathered the stack of menus she had already laid out in preparation of their arrival. Because the restaurant was reservation-only, Joss was not surprised that she had been expecting them. "Mr. Leblanc has recommended a table on the deck, if that's okay with you ladies?"

Joss looked at Maeve, who seemed to like the idea of dining alfresco, and nodded. "That sounds great, thank you."

They followed her across the restaurant and through a pair of french doors that opened onto a sweeping deck that seemed to hover off the edge of the mountainside. There was a large open area in the middle of the deck and small, square tables fanned out from it. The walkways between tables were wide, giving each table an air of intimacy that was generally lost when dining out, and Joss' eyebrows lifted in surprise when they were led to a table that was on the far end of the deck, tucked right up against the railing. Joss nodded her approval when the maître d' asked with a look if the table would be okay. She watched the way Maeve's gaze locked onto the view as she took her seat across from her, and they both murmured their thanks as they took the menus the maître d' offered.

"Your server Melanie will be with you shortly," she said as she handed them each a menu. She gave each of them a small bow as she stood the wine list folder on the edge of the table before retreating with a polite, "Enjoy your meal."

"I'm sure we will," Maeve replied.

Joss nodded her thanks, the maître d' already forgotten as she cocked an amused brow at Maeve. "Not bad, huh?"

Maeve shook her head as her eyes once again swept over the stunning vista spread before them. "Not at all."

At that moment, a tuxedoed man arrived at their table. "Good evening, ladies," he greeted as he took the wine list the maître d' had set out and laid it flat on the table. "My name is Jason, and I'm the sommelier here at Alpine." He smiled at them both as he held out a bottle of wine for inspection. "Courtesy of Mr. Leblanc."

Joss did not miss the surprised look Maeve gave her at that, and she smiled as she nodded her approval without examining the bottle. If Hunter sent it over, she knew it would be the best Alpine had to offer, and she made a mental note to give him a call the next day to thank him for everything. All she had hoped for was a table—and not even a good one, any table would have been fine—and she could not help but be touched that someone she had only the vaguest memories of from high school had gone so far out of his way to make sure they had an unforgettable evening. She sat up straighter as the sommelier uncorked the bottle and poured a small amount into her glass for her to sample the wine before filling their glasses. The red wine was light and smooth, with notes of raspberry, clove, and vanilla, and Joss nodded as she set her glass back onto the table. "Excellent."

He tipped his head in a small bow and poured them each a glass before setting the open bottle on the middle of the table. "Enjoy your evening."

"We will," Joss assured him, smiling at the flabbergasted look on Maeve's face. One they were alone, she laughed softly and explained, "Scott and I went to high school with the owner's son. And, as it turns out, reservations here are insanely difficult to come by, so Scott gave Hunter a call for me this afternoon and got him to pull a few strings."

Maeve's gaze softened, and she shook her head. "Thank you."

Joss picked up her glass of wine and held it between them in a toast. "To a lovely evening, with an even lovelier woman."

Maeve smiled as she lifted her glass and tapped it against Joss'. "Charmer."

Twenty-One

Though the temperature had dropped with the setting sun, the outdoor dining room was kept comfortable by the array of standing heaters scattered across the deck. Lights tucked high in the peaked eaves of the chalet-styled restaurant flickered on at dusk, draping a curtain of warm, golden light over the tables and patrons below. The candles on each of the tables added an intimate, romantic feel to the space, and the string quartet that that had begun playing not long after their entrees had been served only added to that idyllic ambiance. The quartet played classical covers of popular songs were at once both youthful and refined, loud enough to be heard but quiet enough to not drown out conversation.

It was the perfect evening that Joss had so badly wanted to give Maeve, and once their dessert plates were cleared away and the last drops of wine were drained from their glasses, Joss offered Maeve her hand with a smile. "Would you like to dance?"

Maeve smiled and nodded as she slipped her hand into Joss'. "I would love to."

They made their way through the surprising number of dinner guests on the open space in the center of the deck that had become a dance floor. The string quartet was playing a cover of *Love Story*, and Joss hummed along with the tune as she led Maeve past the crowd to the far side of the floor nearest the railing where the lights from the restaurant were dimmer and night cast a friendly shadow of anonymity over them.

Joss' heart stuttered in her chest as she pulled Maeve into her, her left hand sliding over smooth fabric covering Maeve's side, before ghosting down the warm skin revealed by the dress' enticing cut to press against the small of her back. She took Maeve's left hand into her right and cradled it between them as they swayed with the music, and touched their foreheads together as she inquired softly, "Are you having fun?"

Maeve nodded, the corners of her eyes crinkling with her smile as she wrapped her right hand around Joss' shoulder. She sighed and lifted her chin just enough to press a light, quick kiss to Joss' lips before pulling away to whisper, "Yes."

"I'm glad." Joss tightened her hold around Maeve's waist as she guided her into a slow, spinning box step. Maeve kept up with her easily, and she smiled as she began to add a little extra flair to their steps, picking up the speed, adding a little whip to each turn, grateful for the first time in years that Scott had talked her into taking ballroom dancing classes with him back in the day.

"Where did you learn to dance like this?" Maeve asked as their more involved pattern took them away from the shadows and toward the center of the floor.

"Scott and I took a few classes one summer when we were in college." Joss let her hand slip from Maeve's waist as she led her into an underarm turn, and laughed as she pulled her back into a more standard hold. "I honestly didn't think I remembered any of it, but apparently you bring out my inner Fred Astaire."

"Hmm," Maeve purred as she tightened her grip on Joss' shoulder. "So does that mean I'm Ginger Rogers?"

"Would you like to be?" Joss murmured, nuzzling Maeve's cheek as the more up-tempo music shifted to something slower, sexier, the cello player taking center stage as the violins shifted to a more supporting role. Joss did not recognize the song, but had no trouble picking up the beat and adjusting her timing accordingly.

Maeve laughed and looked around them for the first time, and when her eyes returned to Joss', they sparkled with mirth. "I believe all these people watching us already think I am."

"I don't care about them," Joss said, pressing her hand more firmly into the small of Maeve's back, pulling her so close she could feel the supple fullness of Maeve's breasts against her own. The loose skirt of Maeve dress wrapped around her right thigh as they began moving more deliberately together, step for step, closer, tighter, back, together, spin, together, their breaths falling in increasingly heated waves in the shrinking space between their lips.

The songs changed as they danced, some faster, some slower, but Joss paid just enough attention to keep them moving with the beat, too focused on the woman in her arms to care about putting a name to each tune. She had a vague memory of her dance instructor from so many years before telling them that dancing was akin to foreplay, but she had never truly understood that sentiment until now. Her every sense was attuned to Maeve—to the scent of her perfume, the warmth of her skin, and the intimate way Maeve's thighs held her own. Joss groaned softly at the feeling of Maeve's hips rocking against her leg. Forget foreplay. This was them having sex in the middle of a crowd with their clothes on.

Joss drew a deep, shuddering breath as the sound of Maeve whispering her name on a moan sent desire that had been flickering in her belly all night into a nearly uncontrollable blaze. She closed her eyes and just barely resisted the urge to capture Maeve's lips in a kiss that would have put on one hell of a show for everybody around them, and blinked them open as she asked in a rough whisper, "You ready to get out of here?"

Maeve nodded, her lips brushing against Joss' with the movement, both of them gasping at the electric contact. "God, yes."

The wait back at their table as they settled their tab was an excruciating experience as they kept their hands folded tightly on their laps and avoided prolonged eye contact in hopes that distance would mute the urge to touch that radiated between them. It worked, though only just, and Joss all but threw the small leather folder onto the table in her hurry to leave.

She did not dare reach for Maeve as they made their way back through the main dining room, and she blew out a loud sigh of relief when she saw a gondola already waiting at the front of the restaurant. "Thank God."

Maeve chuckled softly in agreement as she followed Joss inside. "Where's the fire?" she teased in a sultry whisper as she sidled up next to her, running the edge of her purse along Joss' inner thigh.

Joss swallowed thickly as Maeve's purse pressed against the seam of her slacks. "Right there," she muttered, unable to mute the whimper that escaped her as she fisted her hands at her sides, determined to control herself until they were alone. *My God, can somebody just close the goddamn door already!*

"Thank you for coming!" the maître d' called out as the gondola's door slid shut.

Maeve chuckled and smiled as she offered her a small wave. "Thank you. Everything was incredible."

The door sealed itself with a quiet pop and click seconds before the gondola slipped from its berth to begin its slow descent back down the mountain.

Joss licked her lips as she reached for Maeve's hips and pulled her closer. She groaned as Maeve obliged, the purse she had teased Joss with moments before falling to the floor with a thud as Maeve pinned her against the side of the gondola. Joss ran her hands slowly over the naked plane of Maeve's back, from the soft pile of fabric gathered at the small of her back and then up along the line of her spine to tickle the thin halter strap along the back of her neck that held the bodice of the dress in place, as Maeve's lips hovered just out of reach. "Maeve," Joss pleaded, tilting her head forward, her breath leaving her in a rush at the feeling of Maeve's hips pressing hard against her own and a possessive hand curving around her jaw.

Maeve's gaze was burning as she leaned in closer, letting the moment build for a few heartbeats more before she succumbed to the desire pulsing between them and crashed their lips together in a deep, probing kiss that ended in them both gasping for air. "I want you," Maeve whispered huskily.

Joss only time to moan in response before Maeve's lips sealed themselves to hers once more, but she managed to return the sentiment by grabbing Maeve's ass and pulling her closer as she ground their hips together. By the time the gondola stopped at the bottom of the hill they were both an absolute mess, and Joss avoided the attendant's lecherous gaze as they hurried out of the chalet and into the night.

She could not resist pinning Maeve against the side of her jeep once they stopped beside it, and she grinned as she wasted no time fusing their lips together once more. Her hands stroked boldly along Maeve's sides as they kissed, tracing the line of her ribs and caressing the swell of her breasts. A flood of arousal crashed between her legs at the desperate gasp that escaped Maeve when she dragged her thumbs over her nipples, and she sucked in a deep breath as she forced herself to pull away. "God."

Maeve licked her lips and nodded. "Take me home, Joss."

Joss nodded, offering up a silent prayer that they would actually make it there as she yanked Maeve's door open. "Okay."

Twenty-Two

The drive across town had been silent, the air filled with too much anticipation to allow for conversation, and Joss blew out a soft sigh of relief when she finally pulled to a stop in front of Maeve's house. They had made it.

"Oh thank God," Maeve muttered.

Joss huffed a small laugh and reached for Maeve, threading her fingers through silky blond locks and pulling her in for the deep, hungry kiss she had been denying herself for the last fifteen interminable minutes. She smiled at the sound of Maeve's seatbelt being unbuckled, but her amusement faded into a plaintive moan when Maeve pulled away from her. The light from the chandelier Maeve had left on in the foyer that spilled through the front doors and the large carriage-style lights flanking the entryway was more than enough for her to see the desire burning in Maeve's eyes, and she shook her head as she untangled her fingers from Maeve's hair. "Fuck, you're beautiful," she murmured as she traced the plump curve of Maeve's lips with her thumb.

Maeve smiled against Joss' thumb and puckered her lips against it in a chaste kiss before she reached for her door handle. "Come inside."

Though it was phrased as more of a direction than a request, Joss still nodded as she unbuckled her seat belt. The anticipatory tension from the drive returned tenfold as they made their way toward the front door, and Joss could not resist running her hands over Maeve's hips as she stood behind her, waiting for her to find her keys to unlock the door. She smiled at the breathy curse that tumbled from Maeve's lips as she pressed herself against her back, wrapping her left arm around Maeve's waist, drawing Maeve's ass firmly against her hips as she used her right hand to sweep the luscious fall of blond hair away from her neck. She closed her eyes as she pressed her lips to the Maeve's pulse point, wrapping her lips around sensitive skin in a wet kiss before flicking her tongue over it.

"If you don't stop, I'm never getting the door open," Maeve threatened breathily.

Joss smirked and nipped at the pulse beating heavily against her lips. It was a rush to know that she could make Maeve this flustered, and she dragged her mouth over the hinge of Maeve's jaw to brush a light kiss over her ear as she let her arm fall from Maeve's waist. "Hurry."

In a blink of an eye Maeve had the door open, a soft, triumphant cry escaping her as she pulled Joss inside. Her purse and keys hit the floor the moment she cleared the threshold, and she smiled seductively as she started for the stairs. "Close the door?"

Joss shoved the door shut hard enough to make the windows on either side rattle, and smiled sheepishly at the disbelieving look Maeve shot her from the second stair. "Sorry?"

Maeve laughed as turned her back to Joss and started to climb. "Come on."

Though Joss could have caught her without too much effort, she followed from a small distance, enjoying the way Maeve's calves flexed with each step and the subtle sway of her spine as she shifted from one foot to the other. Maeve did not look back at her when she cleared the last step, instead she just let her fingers trail over the top of the banister before she turned left and disappeared from Joss' sight.

Joss picked up her pace to follow, taking the final six steps two at a time. The second floor was wide open, a palatial master suite with a sitting room and floor-to-ceiling windows that overlooked the backyard, but Joss paid little attention to the architecture as she strode across the space, her attention focused on the woman pulling off her heels beside the fireplace that separated the sitting area from the massive four poster bed on the far side of the room.

Maeve heard her approach, and smiled as she turned around to look at her. "Hi."

"Hey." Joss cupped Maeve's face in her hands and captured her lips in a deep, wet kiss as she began walking her back toward the bed. Their tongues kept time with their feet, stroking needfully together with every step until they stopped beside the bed. Joss nuzzled Maeve's cheek as she let her hands fall to the sides of her throat before slipping beneath her hair to the back of her neck, tracing the line of fabric holding Maeve's dress in place, enjoying the way Maeve's breathing quickened as she pinched the clasp open. She guided the thin straps over Maeve's shoulders, lightly caressing the bump of her collarbones with the backs of her fingers as both her hands and the dress slid lower, across the plane of her chest. She let the dress continue its journey on its own as cradled two absolutely perfect breasts in her hands, squeezing and dragging her thumbs over hardened nipples as their mouths crashed desperately together.

"Yes," Joss whimpered when Maeve yanked her shirt free. She massaged Maeve's breasts as the cool air of the room spread across her stomach and ribs as Maeve slipped each successive button free with a quick flick of her wrist until it was hanging loosely from her shoulders.

She allowed her hands to be pulled from Maeve's breasts so her shirt could fall to the floor, and shivered at the feeling of Maeve's fingernails dragging up her sides to unhook her bra. The rest of their clothes were shed in a blur of motion as they came together once more, tongues stroking, hands pushing, guiding, touching, pulling. Joss gasped in surprise when Maeve spun them around and pushed her back over the foot of the bed, her body landing with a slight bounce atop the soft down comforter, but that gasp turned into a groan when Maeve followed after her, pushing her legs open wider as red lips blazed a ravenous trail along her inner thigh.

Joss watched, utterly entranced as Maeve took her glasses off and tossed them onto the nightstand, her lips never missing a beat as they continued to move higher and higher, her hands sliding beneath Joss' thighs, pushing her back farther onto the bed so she could kneel between her legs.

Joss' eyes snapped shut when Maeve's tongue stroked boldly through her before circling her clit. She tangled her right hand in Maeve's hair as she bucked against her mouth, her left finding purchase in the soft comforter beneath her. She cried out, her back bowing in pleasure as Maeve surged against her, tongue swirling, lips sucking, easily following every pitch and roll of her hips, strong arms wrapping around her thighs and holding her in place. Joss squeezed her eyes shut, trying to delay the orgasm she could feel building, but was unable to hold back when Maeve's lips wrapped around her clit, sucking lightly as that goddamn talented tongue flicked back and forth over her. She came with a long, low moan, her body twitching spastically against Maeve's mouth, which gentled against her as she trembled and gasped, lightly flicking, swirling, stroking her through her release.

She shakily untangled her hand from Maeve's hair and let it fall to bed beside her, but before she could bask in the afterglow of such a powerful orgasm, Maeve's fingers were inside her, stroking slowly, mindful of the fact she had just come, but allowing her no time to recover. Joss lifted her arms over her head and grabbed onto the bottom edge of the headboard as Maeve guided her closer and closer to the brink of ecstasy with every lick and suck and thrust. Her shoulders burned from the way she was pulling against the headboard, her back bowed so far forward it might surely snap, but she was too lost to the pleasure suffusing her body to care as she pulled harder, pushed further, forcing her hips down so that Maeve's tongue had no choice but to focus where she needed her most.

Stars exploded behind her eyes a split-second before she came again, and she collapsed against the bed as she floated on the waves of her climax, her mind too fogged with ecstasy to register the feeling of Maeve's body lying atop her own. The taste of herself on Maeve's lips guided her back to the present, and she moaned as she wrapped her arms around her neck and pulled her back down into another kiss.

"You're incredible," Joss murmured as she slipped her arms beneath Maeve's and let her fingers dance along her sides. She teased the outside curves of her breasts before traversing the length of her ribs, and licked her lips as she grabbed onto Maeve's hips and gave a small tug. "I want you," she whispered huskily, pulling against her again, hoping Maeve would understand what she wanted.

Joss' heart hammered in her chest as she watched Maeve push herself up onto her knees so she was straddling her waist. She rubbed her hands over Maeve's hips and tugged again, silently answering the question she could see in her eyes. She swallowed hard when Maeve nodded once, just the smallest tip of her chin as she allowed Joss to guide her where she wanted her.

Joss stroked the backs of Maeve's legs as she moved higher, her weight shifting from one side to the other as she maneuvered past her shoulders. Joss did not bother to try to contain the appreciative moan that escaped her as Maeve settled above her.

"So beautiful," she breathed as she ran her hands over Maeve's sides and up around her breasts. She smiled at the rumbling groan that rained down on her when she gave Maeve's nipples a firm pinch, rolling and tweaking the firm nubs as she peppered the soft skin of Maeve's inner thighs with kisses. She let her breath fall in teasing waves over sensitive folds as she slid her hands slowly lower, caressing Maeve's stomach and hips. She was utterly bewitched by the way Maeve was staring at her, mouth hanging slightly open so that each breath fell fast and ragged from her lips, her gaze scorching as she watched and waited, pleading for a more direct touch.

Demanding it.

Joss licked her lips as she ran the flats of her hands over the swell of Maeve's ass, and her mouth watered at how much wetter Maeve became after each slow circuit. She moaned as she trailed her lips from Maeve's inner thigh to full, outer lips, tasting, teasing. Maeve began to squirm above her, hips rocking from side to side, trying to force her mouth where it was so desperately needed, whimpering and moaning when each attempt failed to give the contact she so craved.

"Stop teasing," Maeve grunted, her right hand dropping from the headboard to tangle in Joss' hair, holding her still as she rocked against her mouth.

Joss groaned and grabbed Maeve's ass more firmly, pulling her down as she covered Maeve with her mouth. The hand in her hair tightened as Maeve's head fell back in pleasure, her hips rolling back, forcing her clit against Joss' tongue.

Maeve cried out ardently at the first slow swirl of Joss' tongue around her clit, her hips jerking away from the touch before pressing down harder in a desperate search for more.

Joss moaned against slick folds as she cradled Maeve to her mouth, licking and sucking at everything she could reach. She was in heaven, completely enveloped by the sight and sound and feel and taste of Maeve. She tightened her hold on Maeve's ass as she ravished her, matching every quick thrust and slow, heavy grind of the body writhing atop her.

Maeve's movement became more unpredictable the closer she spiraled to orgasm, desperation driving each pump of her hips as she tried to find the rhythm, the touch, the pressure, that would send her soaring.

Wanting nothing more than to experience Maeve's pleasure herself, Joss pulled her closer, smothering herself in soft skin and slick arousal, and she moaned as she sucked Maeve's clit between her lips and fluttered her tongue over it. Whether it was the focused attention or the rumbling moan or a combination of the two, she had no idea, but Maeve froze above her for a split-second before her hips pressed down hard and her pleasured cries shook the rafters.

Joss caressed Maeve's ass encouragingly as she lapped at the fruits of her labor, her eyes drinking in the exquisite beauty trembling above her. Maeve's gaze was smoldering as she looked down at her, and Joss smiled as she pressed a tender kiss to her still twitching clit.

"God, Joss..."

"You are so goddamn beautiful," Joss murmured.

Maeve blushed and shook her head, her sudden shyness so endearing that Joss wanted nothing more than to hold her and reassure her with an endless string of kisses that it was true. Before she could say anything to that effect, however, Maeve was already moving, hips rolling away from her mouth as she curled against her side.

Maeve propped her head on her hand and shook her head as she stared almost disbelievingly at Joss, her eyes dancing over Joss' face as she searched for the words that eluded her. "You..." She sighed and leaned forward, her hair creating a curtain around their faces as she kissed Joss' cheeks and chin before finally finding her lips in a deep, ardent kiss.

It was soft and awed and perfect, and Joss smiled as she cupped Maeve's face in her hand and guided her over onto her back so that she was hovering above her. She nuzzled Maeve's cheek and kissed her tenderly, again and again, bracing herself on her right arm and letting her left hand draw lazy swoops and swirls over Maeve's hip, stomach, breast, and shoulder. A warm shiver rolled down her spine as Maeve reciprocated the gentle touch, their tongues sliding languidly together as they basked in the moment.

Maeve groaning into her mouth when her fingers brushed over a straining nipple sent a current of desire rippling through her, and Joss groaned as she shifted her weight, edging her knees between Maeve's legs. The feeling of her nipples dragging over Maeve's as she moved was electric, and she slanted her head to the side to deepen their kiss as she settled between her thighs.

"Want you again," Joss grunted as Maeve's hips opened to cradle hers, smearing a hot, slick stripe of arousal down her stomach.

"Yes," Maeve moaned, lifting her hips.

Joss swallowed hard and used her chin to turn Maeve's head to the side as she laid a line of wet, heavy kisses from the corner of Maeve's mouth to the sensitive hollow beneath her jaw. She closed her teeth around Maeve's pounding pulse as she ground herself against Maeve, adjusting her position with each slow thrust until heat slid against heat, and they moaned in perfect harmony.

"God, Joss…"

Joss smiled and dragged the flat of her tongue up to Maeve's ear. "Yes?" she asked, punctuating the question with a thrust of her hips.

"Fuck," Maeve grunted as she pulled her legs higher, opening herself further to each delicious roll of Joss' hips.

Joss groaned at the feeling of Maeve's knees cradling her hips, and buried her face in the crook of Maeve's neck as she thrust again. "Maeve…"

"Don't stop," Maeve pleaded breathlessly.

"I won't," Joss confirmed huskily with a nod as she drove her hips forward again, grinding herself against Maeve and making them both whimper. "I won't."

Twenty-Three

Falling asleep after three that morning had little effect on Joss' internal clock, which still had her eyes fluttering open by ten to six.

Five whole extra minutes, she grumbled silently as she rubbed a sleepy hand over her face. *Gee, thanks.*

Of course, any annoyance she had about the staggering lack of sleep she was going to suffer from for the rest of the day was abated by the sight of a very naked Maeve Dylan laying next to her, tousled hair cascading wildly over the pillow she had captured in a stranglehold beneath her. The sheet she had pulled over them both after they made love one last time before collapsing in exhaustion lay bunched across the small of her back, and Joss smiled as she leaned onto her side to press a gentle kiss to Maeve's shoulder.

God, it would be so easy to fall for you, she thought to herself with a sigh as she pulled away.

Maeve hummed as she shifted in her sleep, turning her head so Joss could see the serene smile tugging at her lips as she snuggled closer to her pillow.

So easy.

The distant sound of barking crept into Joss' consciousness, and she shook her head as she slipped out of bed, careful to not disturb Maeve. She searched for her clothes from the night before in the dark, unwilling to turn on a light that would wake her sleeping lover, and she carried her clothes into the sitting area beyond the stone fireplace that divided the suite to get dressed.

One of them deserved to sleep, after all.

Once she was dressed, she made her way down the stairs and, after a quick stop in the powder room just off the living room, went in search of the four-legged monster whose barks were increasing in volume and hysterics.

"Fuck, lady, chill," she muttered as she hurried through the laundry room to open the door to the garage.

George launched through the door the moment it was opened, knocking Joss back against the washing machine as she smothered her with kisses, acting like she had been left alone for *ages* instead of just one night. Which, granted, she was used to sleeping on the couch and she had been forced to slum it on a futon instead, but still. It was not like they had made her sleep outside in some rinky-dink doghouse or something.

"Okay, okay," Joss laughed as she gave George's sides a vigorous rubdown. "I'm sorry, all right? We're terrible people for forgetting about you."

George *aroo*-ed and shoved the top of her head into Joss' hip.

Well, you told me, Joss thought to herself as she gave George's behind a light pat. "Okay, you. Ready to go outside?"

That was all the direction George needed as she took off down the hall, her nails skittering on the wood floor in the great room as she sprinted toward the back of the house. She was doing a doggy version of the potty dance when Joss finally caught up to her in the kitchen to open the sliding glass door to the backyard.

George bolted for the lawn as soon as the door opened wide enough for her to squeeze through, and Joss looked around for the ChuckIt that Maeve used to throw balls for her as she took care of business. She knew from the way George had pounced on her after being freed that if she did not do something to help her burn off her energy, the dog would be virtually impossible to contain.

Once George had circled the lawn and done what she needed to do, Joss held up the blue plastic handle that had a grimy tennis ball in its cup and waggled it back and forth, immediately grabbing George's attention. "Ball?"

George barked and spun in an excited circle before dropping her shoulders and staring at Joss, her entire body quivering with excitement as she waited for the ball to be thrown. Joss faked a few throws before letting the ball fly, and shook her head as she watched George run it down. Playing ball with George had not been on her shortlist of preferred activities for the morning, but seeing how much the Dane was enjoying herself made it impossible to not enjoy it just a little bit.

They had been at it for a good fifteen minutes when warm hands slipped beneath Joss' shirt, and she smiled as she leaned back against Maeve. "Hey."

"So you leave me in bed to come play with my dog, huh?" Maeve teased. She dragged her nails across Joss' stomach and laughed when Joss squirmed against her. "Should I be worried?"

Joss shook her head as she turned in Maeve's embrace, desire flaring low in her hips as she saw the loosely belted silk robe Maeve had thrown on that did little to hide the fact that she wore nothing underneath. "No." Her smile softened as she cupped Maeve's face in her hand, and she sighed as she guided their lips together. This was how she had wanted to spend her morning before she had to go to work. She nuzzled Maeve's cheek with her nose when she finally pulled away. "She was barking and I didn't want her to wake you up."

"That's very sweet of you," Maeve purred, rewarding Joss' thoughtfulness by pulling her closer and claiming her lips in a deep, lingering kiss. "But I'm awake now." She smiled against Joss' lips. "And I want you back in my bed."

Joss groaned. She wanted that too, but there was an insistent tail smacking against the back of her legs that told her that might not be happening any time soon.

Maeve chuckled and pecked Joss' lips. "Come on." She slipped away with a sultry smile and then looked at George. "Bone?"

George froze, eyes wide and her mouth half-open as she looked at Maeve hopefully.

"Come on, George." Maeve smacked the side of her thigh as she turned toward the house, a sixth sense guiding her to her left just as George bull-rushed the door, a move that saved her from being knocked over.

Joss laughed under her breath as she followed them inside. Maeve was flipping open a pair of scissors to slice the plastic off the bone, and she grinned as she caught her eye. "So that was a good idea then."

Maeve nodded. "Pure genius." She unwrapped the bone at set it in George's waiting mouth. "Take that to the rug," she said, tipping her head at the great room.

George bumped Maeve's hand with her head one time and then obediently padded into the other room.

"Now"—Maeve winked at Joss—"let's go see about that bed."

Joss took the hand Maeve offered her and allowed herself to be led toward the stairs. "What about George?" She lifted Maeve's hand to her lips and kissed the back of it. "With the exception of the bathroom, there really aren't any doors we can close up there to keep her out."

"George," Maeve declared as she stopped at the hall closet and pulled the door open, "is terrified of the vacuum." She pulled said vacuum from the closet and used her foot to kick the door closed. "So all we have to do is this," she continued as she rolled it to the foot of the stairs.

Joss climbed ahead of Maeve, stopping on the second step, and turned to see her carefully standing the vacuum in the center of the first tread.

The stairs were wide and George could squeeze by the vacuum if she really wanted, though she would probably knock it over in the process, and Joss eyed the purple Dyson skeptically. "I know she doesn't like it, but you think that will seriously stop her from coming upstairs?"

Maeve shrugged. "Only one way to find out." She smirked as she pushed Joss' back against the wall and joined her on the second stair.

There was no mistaking the mischievous twinkle in Maeve's eyes as she leaned closer, and Joss whimpered as she felt her shirt being unbuttoned. "Bed?"

"We'll get there." Maeve kissed Joss as she continued to work at the buttons on her shirt, and pulled away with a smile as the last one slipped free. "Much better," she observed as she reached for Joss' breasts.

Joss arched a brow in playful challenge and reached for the sash of Maeve's robe. She held Maeve's gaze as she gave it a tug, and licked her lips when Maeve was revealed to her. "God, I was an idiot for leaving you in bed this morning," she muttered as she slipped her hands around Maeve's waist and pulled her in for a bruising kiss.

"Yes, you were," Maeve agreed as gave Joss' breasts a playful squeeze before turning her attention lower. She flicked her tongue over Joss' lips as she reached for the clasp holding her pants closed, and a low, appreciative moan rumbled in her throat as she caressed the bare skin that was revealed to her. "Commando is a very good look on you."

Joss groaned and closed her eyes as a rush of arousal crash between her legs. They needed to get this off the stairs before they gave George one hell of a show.

"Very, very good." Maeve rubbed against Joss as she slipped two fingers between Joss' legs, and she moaned when she felt how ready Joss was for her. She pressed their lips together as she swirled her fingers around Joss' clit, and then sighed as she forced herself to pull away. "Bed."

"Absolutely." Joss smirked and shrugged out of her shirt before she pushed Maeve's robe from her shoulders. They left their clothes where they fell and hurried up the stairs with identical, wide smiles curling their lips, and Joss laughed as she caught Maeve beside the bed and pulled her into her arms. "Gotcha."

Maeve sank willingly into Joss' embrace and wrapped her arms around her neck. "You do."

The playful rejoinder was belied by the quiet earnestness in Maeve's voice, and Joss swallowed thickly as an unmistakable affection bloomed in her chest as she kissed Maeve softly. *It really would be so easy to fall,* she thought as she brushed their lips together. "Let me," she whispered as she guided Maeve back toward the bed.

Joss' breath caught in her throat at the sound of Maeve's breathy moan of consent, and she used her lips and body to push Maeve back onto the bed. She cradled Maeve's right breast in her hand as they maneuvered into the center of the mattress, and sighed as she stretched out over her. Maeve's nipple strained against her palm as she squeezed and massaged her breast in time with their deep, languid kisses, and she pulled back to look at Maeve as she adjusted her hold enough to give the hard bud a firm pinch.

Maeve gasped and arched into the touch, and Joss echoed the sentiment as her clit twitched in sympathy.

"Joss..."

"I know," Joss breathed, tweaking Maeve's nipple one last time before letting her hand wander down her stomach and between her parted thighs. A low moan tumbled from her lips as she ran her fingers through the copious wetness that welcomed her touch, and she kissed Maeve softly as she rubbed slow circles over her clit. "What do you want, sweetie?"

Maeve rolled her hips against Joss' hand. "An orgasm."

Joss froze, and then fell on top of Maeve laughing. "Oh my God."

"Do it right and I'll be saying that, too," Maeve quipped, laughing with her.

Joss licked her lips and cleared her throat as she pushed herself back up onto her elbow to look at Maeve, and was struck speechless by the amused affection that was staring so plainly back at her. She shook her head as she pressed a hard kiss to Maeve's lips, and sighed as she rested their foreheads together once the kiss finally broke.

It really would be so easy...

Her hand was still nestled intimately between Maeve's legs, and she took a deep breath as she slid two fingers lower and gently eased into soft, clinging warmth. "How's this?"

"Perfect," Maeve sighed.

Atramentum

Joss' eyes fluttered shut as she dipped her head to capture Maeve's lips in a slow, sweet kiss. *Yes, you are.*

Twenty-Four

Guess who just finished revisions on her eighth chapter of the day?

Joss smiled as she typed out a quick reply. *George?*

How'd you guess? She's feeling quite proud of herself and is looking to get out of the house for a while to celebrate. What are you doing for dinner?

Joss yawned and looked around the bookstore. Perhaps it was because it was a Tuesday and three different New York Time's bestselling authors released new books that day, but Atramentum had been crawling with customers, and the stream of people flowing through the door did not look to be easing any time soon. *Probably order a pizza. And a two-liter of Mountain Dew to help me stay awake. Somebody kept me up all night. ;) How about you?*

Maeve's reply came a few seconds later. *I'll figure something out. Hold off on ordering that pizza for a few?*

From the corner of her eye, Joss saw the elderly woman Scott that had been helping shake her head and motion toward the register. *Even if I wanted to do it now, I couldn't. We're swamped.*

"Hey, hickey," Scott teased for the thousandth time of the day as he set the stack of books he had carried up for the woman on the front counter.

Joss rolled her eyes and self-consciously tugged at the collar of her shirt. She had noticed the faint pink mark low on her neck earlier that morning, and by the time Scott arrived after noon to begin his shift, it had blossomed into a full-blown bruise. The memory of how she acquired it—Maeve's fingers digging into her back, the strangled cry of pleasure that trumpeted her orgasm muffled as she bit roughly at her neck—made her smile, but she knew that a giant hickey was not the most professional accessory to wear at work. She had noticed a few customers staring at it over the course of the afternoon, and, of course, Scott commented on it every chance he could get.

Because, apparently, they were back in high school when shit like this was fucking hilarious.

"Hello, soon-to-be-former-employee," Joss retorted. She smiled and looked at the customer Scott had been helping. "I'm sorry. Did you find everything you were looking for?"

"That's fine, dear," the woman replied with a grin. "That is quite the impressive hickey though."

"Yes, thank you." Joss sighed as she pulled the books toward her and started ringing them up.

"I'm sorry," a new voice called out. Joss, Scott, and the older woman all turned to look at a thirty-something father with two tow-headed boys at his side that looked just like him. "Can you tell me where I might find the *Spirit Animals* books?"

Scott nodded. "I'll show you. Follow me."

Joss smiled at the man and then redirected her focus on finishing the transaction she had been working on.

"You guys are really busy," the woman commented.

Joss nodded. "It's been a good day for business." She looked at the register screen. "That'll be sixty-two forty-eight."

"Here you are," the woman said, handing Joss her credit card.

Joss took the card and swiped it through the point-of-sale terminal beside the register. She glanced at the back of the card before handing it back to the woman, and then drummed her fingers on the counter as she waited for the charge to go through. She ripped the slip from the machine and turned it toward the woman. "If you could just sign here, please," she said as she pulled a plastic bag from beneath the counter. "Receipt with you, or in the bag?"

"The bag is fine."

Joss nodded and tucked the woman's books and her copy of the receipt into the bag and traded it for the signed receipt. "Here you go. Have a good night."

The woman smirked and winked as she collected her purchases and turned toward the door. "You too, dear."

"Everybody's a comedian," she grumbled under her breath, forcing a tight smile as three people wandered into the store before the door could close after the old woman.

The next hour passed in a blur, and Joss groaned when the grumbling protests of her stomach became too loud to ignore any longer. She reached for her phone. She needed food.

The bell above the door jingled as she pulled up the number for the closest pizza joint, and she froze with her thumb hovering millimeters from her screen as she saw two familiar faces walk in.

"That dog is as big as a horse!" a little kid screeched from across the room.

Joss shook her head in disbelief and smiled as her pulse tripped over itself at the sight of Maeve standing only a few feet away in a pair of jeans and the Columbia hoodie Joss knew she liked to wear when she wrote. She had a large bag from DiAmico's—the best Italian place in town—in her left hand and George's leash in her right, and she arched a playful brow over the rim of her glasses as she announced, "I come bearing gifts."

"I see that," Joss replied as she turned off her phone and slipped it into her back pocket.

"Have you eaten yet?" Maeve asked as she set the bag of food onto the counter.

Joss shook her head. "I was just getting ready to order a pizza. That looks a lot better, though."

"Hey, Carmilla!" Scott greeted with a grin as Willy Shakes jumped up onto the counter and bumped noses with George. "And Georgeasaurus Rex."

Carmilla? Maeve mouthed to Joss.

"I'm a little disappointed in you right now, Maeve Dylan," Scott chuckled. "Nineteenth century, ridiculously Sapphic vampire novella..."

Maeve was adorably confused even with his explanation, and Joss rolled her eyes as she turned her head and motioned at her neck.

"Oh." Maeve cringed and flashed an embarrassed smile. "I didn't realize... I'm sorry."

Joss just smiled and shook her head. While she could have done without Scott's sophomoric teasing all day, there was not one thing from the night before that she was sorry about.

"Anyways..." Scott dramatically began as he leaned against the edge of the counter. "How'd the big date go?"

Recovering quickly from her embarrassment, Maeve gave him a disbelieving look. "If you need to ask after seeing that"—she pointed at Joss' neck—"then I'm afraid you don't deserve an answer."

Joss flushed bright red and reached for the bag of food. "You're as bad as he is."

Maeve laughed. "Sorry. It was just too easy to pass up. Can I take George off her leash, or is it too busy for her to do that?"

"Go for it." Joss waved a hand in the air. "Her and Willy can go entertain everybody and hopefully buy us a few minutes to eat. What'd you bring?" she asked as she rifled through the bag. There was a crimped bag of what was most likely breadsticks on top of two cardboard cartons, which were balanced on top of something else.

"Lasagna, salad, bread sticks." Maeve unhooked George's leash and set it on the counter. She gave George's head a quick pat, and then smiled as she watched the Dane—with Willy on her heels—amble over to the little kid who had trumpeted her arrival. "I brought enough food to feed a small army," she said, looking back at Scott, "if you'd like some too."

"I would love some," Scott moaned, staring longingly at the takeout bag. "But," he continued with a disgruntled sigh, "Michelle is making some new ginger chicken something she saw online, and she'll kill me if I eat before I get home."

"Such a good hubby," Joss teased. It was a bit of a low blow since she knew exactly how much Scott loved DiAmico's lasagna, but after putting up with his shit all day, she would take any shot at him that she could get.

"Shut up." Scott laughed and discreetly flipped her off. "Look, why don't you guys take that back into the office so you can enjoy your mouthwateringly delicious dinner that I really wish I could share, and I'll hold down the fort up here."

"You sure?" Joss asked as she glanced around the bustling store.

"Yeah. Go for it," Scott said. "Just, you know, don't take forever." He glanced at his watch. "I need to be home by eight."

Joss checked her watch. It was ten till seven, which meant he still had another forty minutes on his shift. Plenty of time for her and Maeve to have dinner before she had to get back to work. "You're awesome."

"Save me some leftovers?" he asked.

Maeve gathered the bag of food in her hand and nodded. "Any leftovers are yours. I'll leave them in the fridge here for you to have tomorrow. Joss, can you grab a couple of the waters you keep in there?"

Joss nodded and pulled two bottles of water from the fridge as she and Scott switched places. "Thanks, man."

"Yeah, yeah. Go, eat your delicious dinner with your girl," Scott grumbled as he dropped onto the stool.

"Your sacrifice is much appreciated, Scott," Maeve assured him with a small laugh as she hefted the large bag of food in the general direction of the office.

Joss nodded and motioned for her to go on ahead. "Call me if you need help up here."

"I will. But I won't need you. Me and the monsters have this shit covered." He tipped his head at George and Willy, who were both belly-up on the rug, soaking up the attention they were getting from their adoring public. "Just make sure you save me some food."

"I'll try," Joss said, saluting him with the water bottle in her right hand. She laughed at the loud raspberry he blew at her in response, and turned on her heel to hurry after Maeve, grateful for the few minutes Scott was giving them together.

Maeve had pulled the top two cartons from the bag and set them out on the desk by the time Joss stepped into the office, and she smiled as Joss closed the door behind herself. "Hey, you."

"Hey, you, yourself." Joss returned Maeve's smile with a gentle one of her own as she made her way over to the desk. She licked her lips as she ran a tender hand over Maeve's jaw, and sighed as she leaned in to kiss her. The taste of Maeve's lips made her stomach flip, and Joss hummed as she wrapped her arms around Maeve's waist and pulled her closer. *Heaven. Pure heaven.* "I'm so glad you came by."

"Good." Maeve nuzzled Joss' cheek, and laughed at the sound of Joss' stomach loudly making its presence know. "Hungry?"

Joss smiled against Maeve's lips and shook her head. "Not at all." She gave her a quick peck and then reached past the cardboard cartons on the desk to retrieve one of the aluminum ones with a steamed-over plastic lid that was inside the bag. Salad could wait. Right now, she wanted real food. "You're an angel for doing this," she enthused as she wheeled her chair around the edge of the desk so she could sit next to Maeve.

Maeve laughed as she lowered herself gracefully into the lone visitor's chair and picked up one of the salads. "So the way to your heart is through your stomach, huh?"

"Tonight it is," Joss admitted as she pried the lid from her entrée. Steam wafted from the container, carrying the heavenly scent of cheese and sauce and spices, and she licked her lips as she reached for the package of utensils that Maeve nudged her way. "God, I am so hungry."

"Did you eat lunch?"

Joss shook her head. "Was too busy. Had a protein bar, but that didn't help for long," she said as she shoved a piece of lasagna that was so big, it just barely fit past her lips into her mouth. She moaned happily at the taste and smiled at Maeve. "Thank you for doing this."

Maeve set her salad back onto the desk and reached for her entrée, clearly swayed by Joss' reaction to the lasagna. "It was my pleasure." She grinned as she tossed her lid into Joss' discarded one on the desk and added, "Maybe, if you're lucky, I'll do it again Thursday night."

Joss smiled at the idea of being able to spend time with Maeve on the nights she had to work late—something she had not even considered a possibility until this moment. They could have peanut butter sandwiches for all she cared, she just liked the idea of this becoming a thing. She licked her lips and tipped her head in a small nod as she admitted, "I'd like that."

"Me too." Maeve's gaze softened as she stared at Joss, and after a few heartbeats, she took a deep breath and shook her head. "Stop looking at me like that."

Joss arched a brow in mock confusion. She knew what she was doing, and she rather liked the way Maeve was responding to it. "Like what?"

"Like you want to kiss me."

"I do want to kiss you. Do you not want me to want to kiss you?"

"Oh, Joss." Maeve's eyes sparkled mischievously. "I want you to do so much more than that."

Joss' breath left her in a whoosh as Maeve's words landed wetly between her thighs. "God…"

Maeve laughed and used the side of her fork to cut into her lasagna. "But, since that's not an option, how about we just eat dinner instead?"

"You're mean."

"You are more than welcome to come by the house tonight after you close up," Maeve pointed out with a smile.

It was clear that she meant it, but Joss still asked, "Really?"

"Yes." Maeve nodded. "Though if you're too tired or need to do something at home, I understand."

"What? No. I'd love to. I just…" Joss rolled her eyes. "I don't want to be too clingy. Or whatever." She shook her head. "I was actually going to ask if you wanted to come down to the cottage tomorrow night for dinner. It's the only other night this week Scott'll close, and—"

Maeve leaned forward in her chair and silenced her with a kiss. "That sounds great."

Joss nodded. "Okay, then." She took a deep breath and let it go slowly. "So, you said your edits went well?"

"They did." Maeve used the side of her fork to cut into her lasagna. "Do you really want to talk about that, though?"

"Sure. Why not?"

"Most people find it boring."

"I'm not most people," Joss pointed out with a smile.

"Yes, I'm staring to see that," Maeve murmured. "Okay, then…"

The shift in their relationship did not affect the ease with which conversation flowed between them as they shared the details of their generally unremarkable days, which led to tangential discussions about books, grammar, and dog bones, of all things. Long before either of them were ready to call their makeshift evening to an end, the real world descended upon them as Joss' phone buzzed with a text from Scott asking how much longer they were going to be because he did "kinda sorta have to get home for dinner at some point this evening."

"I'm sorry, but I have to get back out there," Joss apologized. She shook her head as she looked at the emptied cartons littering the desk, genuinely baffled at how they had all become that way. It seemed like only a couple minutes ago they sat down together, and yet it was already fifteen minutes past the time Scott's shift should have ended.

"It's fine. I didn't realize it had gotten so late." Maeve began stuffing the empty cartons back into the bag.

"Me neither," Joss chuckled. Once the desk was cleaned, Joss took the bag from Maeve and pressed a quick kiss to her lips. "Wait a second, okay?"

Maeve nodded. "Of course."

"Thank you." Joss winked and ducked out of the office and down the hall to the rear entrance they pretty much never used. She tossed the bag of trash into the dumpster and wiped her hands off on her jeans as she hurried back inside to find Maeve waiting right where she had left her.

"I wasn't sure if you meant here, or..."

"Here is perfect," Joss interrupted with a smile. They did not have much time, but that did not stop her from closing the distance between them and capturing Maeve's lips in a slow, deep kiss. She cupped Maeve's face in her hands as they kissed, and took a deep breath when she forced herself to pull away. She stroked her thumbs over Maeve's cheeks as she took a moment to just look at her, and she sighed as she leaned in and kissed her again. "I am really glad you came by tonight."

Maeve smiled, pure happiness lighting her eyes as she nodded. "Me too."

Joss' phone buzzed again, and she chuckled as she reached for it, knowing who the message would be from.

"Scott?" Maeve asked.

Joss nodded and turned the phone around so Maeve could see his text.

"Don't make me send George in there after you two..." Maeve laughed. "No. We certainly don't want that."

Joss dropped a quick kiss to the tip of Maeve's nose and nodded as she forced herself to take a step back toward the door. "I'll call you later."

"I'd like that," Maeve admitted as she followed Joss from the office.

"So you are alive!" Scott crowed when they made their way back to the front of the store.

"Yes, Scott," Maeve chuckled. "I'm sorry we lost track of the time."

"Eh, it's fine. Michelle says congratulations, and she wanted to know if you're coming to the game Sunday."

Maeve blinked in confusion and looked at Joss. "I...don't know. Am I?"

"Only if you want to," Joss said, not wanting Maeve to feel pressured. She liked the idea of Maeve being at the game, if only because she could duck out of the dugout to say hi to her between innings and stuff, but she had no idea how comfortable Maeve was with being out with their relationship, either.

She need not have worried, though, because Maeve immediately smiled and said, "That sounds like fun, then. Sure. Will you pick me up?"

"Sure." Joss nodded, unable to keep from grinning. "If you want me to."

"God, you two are just disgustingly cute," Scott muttered as he edged past them. "I guess I should go home to my wife. Here's to hoping my dinner is as good as yours was since I see no leftovers coming my way."

Joss shrugged. "Sorry. I was starving."

"You can make it up to me later." He fished his keys out of his pocket. "Have a good night. Maeve, it was nice to see you again."

"You too."

Scott winked and snapped off a quick salute as he spun on his heel. "See you tomorrow, boss-lady."

Joss rolled her eyes. "I can't wait," she grumbled as the front door swung shut behind him.

Maeve laughed and whistled for George, who appeared a moment later from the kids' section. She snapped George's leash into place and bit her lip as she reached out to give Joss' hand a quick squeeze. "I'll see you later?"

Joss nodded and gave George's head a quick pet when Maeve's hand slipped from her own. "Yeah. I'll call when I'm leaving."

"Okay." Maeve glanced around the store. There were murmurs of conversation floating toward them from the stacks, but the immediate area around them was empty, and she smiled as she leaned in to steal a quick, goodbye kiss. "I can't wait."

Twenty-Five

Joss smiled and closed her eyes as she relaxed back into Maeve on the blonde's couch, letting herself be lulled by the feeling of Maeve's fingers stroking up and down her arms. It had been a long week of trying to find time to spend together, and she was grateful that the crowds that had filled Atramentum all week had disappeared so that she and Scott could close up an hour earlier than usual. "That feels nice."

"Good." Maeve brushed a gentle kiss over her temple. "What time do we need to leave for your game?"

Joss shrugged as she failed to stifle a yawn. She had not gotten nearly the amount of sleep she needed over the last week. Though, really, the exhaustion she had been suffering from the last few days was a more than fair tradeoff for being able to spend time with Maeve every night after work. Given the choice, she would much rather stay and enjoy her first early night off since Wednesday with Maeve, but she knew that if she did, the team would have to forfeit since Brock's paralegal could not play that night, and she could not do that to the guys.

Not with only two weeks left to go in the season.

Knowing that, however, did not stop her from wishing for a sudden rainstorm to show up so the game would be cancelled.

A glance out the windows showed a cloudless indigo sky, and she sighed as and checked her watch. It was already a quarter after eight, which meant that she should have been at the field fifteen minutes ago. But, she figured, this was much more important than warming up for a stupid game. "I figure we've got maybe another ten minutes or so."

"Really?"

Joss chuckled. "Are you trying to kick me out?"

"No." Maeve wrapped both her arms around Joss' waist and squeezed her tight. "I'm just surprised. Don't you need to get there early to warm up or something?"

"Eh." Joss leaned her head back on Maeve's shoulder and looked up at her. "Probably, but I'd rather spend as much time with you as I can. The guys'll understand, as long as I'm there before the ump checks us all in."

"You are too sweet." Maeve kissed her softly.

"Says the woman who brings me dinner when I have to work late." Joss reached back with her left hand and pulled Maeve's lips back to hers. The position was not ideal, however, and she smiled into the kiss as she rolled over, her hips fitting into the familiar cradle of Maeve's open legs. "Much better," she whispered as she braced her forearms on the arm of the couch behind Maeve's head.

"Mmm, yes." Maeve grabbed onto the backs of Joss' shoulders and pulled her down on top of her. "Much, much better." She smiled against Joss' lips. "Kiss me."

Joss flicked her tongue over Maeve's lips, and moaned when an agile tongue swooped lightly around her own. Her nipples hardened instantly at the feeling of Maeve's tongue stroking against her own, slowly, deliberately, pressing forward before retreating and forcing her to chase, and the taste of Maeve's soft sigh of pleasure sent a rush of arousal crashing between her legs.

It would be so easy to forget her responsibilities and lose herself in the softness of Maeve's body and the slick heat she knew she would find waiting for her, and Joss groaned when the urge to strip Maeve bare and bury her mouth in the sweet crux of her thighs became almost too much to resist. Maeve's whimper of protest nearly shattered Joss' reserve to do the right thing, and she just barely managed to swallow the *Fuck it*, that was poised on the tip of her tongue.

It was incredibly, impossibly unfair that she had to leave this beautiful creature staring at her with such open desire to go play a fucking game.

"I know," Joss whispered as she brushed a chaste kiss over Maeve's lips. "I'm sorry."

Maeve shook her head. "Don't be. I love the way you kiss me."

Joss blushed. She wanted to bury her face in the crook of Maeve's neck to try to hide it, but she could not look away from the enchanting emerald eyes that held her captive. "How's that?" she murmured, her heart beating a mile a minute.

Maeve smiled and slipped an arm under Joss' to cup her cheek tenderly. "Like you can't get enough."

"I can't." Joss sighed and shook her head. "It's…"

"Amazing. And incredibly flattering. And exactly how I feel when I kiss you," Maeve whispered. She smirked and shifted her hips under Joss. "And it's also, you know, really, really arousing."

Joss dropped her head to Maeve's shoulder. Yeah, she did know. "Fuck."

Maeve laughed. "Exactly." She nuzzled Joss' cheek. "Would it help if I reminded you that I was going to go to the field with you?"

"Yes." Joss kissed Maeve's neck. "It definitely would."

"Good." Maeve turned her head to the side so Joss could savor as much skin as she wanted.

"Very good," Joss agreed as she nipped at Maeve's pulse point. She took a deep breath and forced herself to pull away. *Later*, she promised herself.

George yawned loudly from her spot on the other sofa, and Joss laughed as she looked up at a pair of sleepy eyes that were watching them.

"I forgot she was there," Joss admitted as she regretfully disentangled herself from Maeve.

"Because she wasn't snoring for a change." Maeve she sat up beside her. "Can we bring her along?" She waggled her eyebrows. "It'd wear her out so she sleeps better later."

"Oh, well, in that case…absolutely." Joss pushed herself to her feet and offered Maeve her hands. A light tug had Maeve standing in front of her, and she shook her head as she just resisted the urge to kiss her again. She did not need to look at a clock to know that they would be pushing it to get to the field in time, and if she kissed Maeve again, odds were very good that they would never get there at all.

"My car's set up for her already, so I'll drive." Maeve pecked Joss' lips and then turned to George. "You wanna go for a ride?"

George shot upright with a bark and leapt from the couch to bolt down the hall toward the garage.

"I guess that's a 'yes'," Maeve laughed. "I just gotta run upstairs to grab a sweatshirt."

"Sounds good. I'll go get her highness into the car, and then I can grab my stuff after I open the garage."

George's excited barking echoed down the hall, telling them to hurry things along so she could go for her ride.

"Pushy little thing, isn't she?" Joss muttered.

Maeve nodded as she started for the foyer. "Yep."

George barked again.

"Yeah, yeah," Joss hollered as she stared for the hall. "We're coming."

"God, I wish," Maeve grumbled from the other side of the living room.

Joss laughed and shook her head. *Not going there*, she thought to herself as she watched George bound back down the hall in search of them, clearly worried they had somehow gotten lost on the way to the garage. "Okay, you monster." She gave George's side a solid pat. "Let's go."

Twenty-Six

The sight of Maeve chatting with Brock and Scott's better halves made Joss smile as she jogged out onto the field to take her spot at second base for the bottom of the third inning. Maeve was sitting on the lowest row of the small, aluminum bleachers behind home plate, and George was lying in the dirt at her feet, happily ripping the stitching from an old softball Herold had given her when she showed too much interest in the game ball.

"Stop drooling over your wife and focus on the game," Scott teased, bumping her with his elbow as he jogged past her to his position in center field.

Joss smirked as she whirled in place and just managed to smack him with her glove, leaving a dusty print on the shoulder of his navy blue jersey. The guys had been giving her shit ever since she and Maeve showed up ten minutes before the game started and, while she knew it was their way of saying they were happy for her, it was still annoying. "I'm not drooling."

Scott laughed and turned around, continuing to jog backward into the outfield with outstretched arms. "You're not exactly focusing on the game, either. What was with that K? You never strike out."

"I was distracted."

"By what?" Brock asked with a laugh as he took his spot at short.

"Yeah!" Wesley Herold chimed in from the pitcher's circle.

Joss set her hands on her hips and shook her head. There was no way in hell she was going to tell them that she had been completely flustered by the sound of Maeve cheering for her when she stepped up to the plate. "I was distracted by your ugly ass."

"Ooh," Brock laughed, pointing at Herold. "She got you!"

"How do you know she was talking to me?" Herold challenged.

"Because I'm too pretty." Brock winked at Herold and emphasized his point with a dramatic hip thrust to the side as he snapped his fingers in an especially sassy Z in front of him.

"Dude, that was so gay," Joss chuckled.

Brock grinned. "Thanks! You too, Miss-my-pretty-lady-friend-cheers-for-me-and-I-go-down-on-three-straight-pitches."

"Betcha that's not the only thing she's going down on tonight, though," Paul Lennox chimed in with a laugh.

Joss' cheeks burned with embarrassment as everybody who had heard the jibe erupted in boisterous laughter, and she shook her head as she turned on their normally quiet first baseman. Part of her was proud that he managed the quip at all, but that pride had to take a backseat to her protecting her own. She arched a brow at him as her lips curled into a slow, dangerous smirk. He visibly gulped beneath her stare, and she chuckled under her breath as he took a small step away from her and almost fell onto his ass when his heel hit the base. "You jealous, Lennox?"

He blushed and nodded and, just like that, he was that dorky guy who had sat behind her in AP Calc their senior year.

Joss sighed, feeling bad about the way the guys were turning their attention onto him. She could handle the teasing, but she doubted he could, and she shook her head as she threw him a bone. "Herold is too, don't worry about it."

"Hey!" Herold smiled and threw his hands in the air in playful protest.

The guys could be brutal, but they all knew that Paul was to be handled with kid gloves, and Joss winked as she blew him a kiss. "Problem, Herold?"

"ARE WE PLAYING BALL HERE, OR WHAT?" The batter for the other team hollered from the batter's box.

"OR WHAT!" The entire Brewer's infield retorted in perfect unison, sending them all into another fit of laughter as they took their positions.

They were still chuckling under their breath as Herold stepped up to the rubber and smacked the neon yellow game ball into the pocket of his glove. The batter was a big guy, and Joss took a step behind the base path as the ball arced high in the air to give herself more time to react. The familiar *ping* of bat on ball rang across the field, chasing away any lingering amusement, and Joss swore when she saw a streak of neon flying at her head.

She ducked her head out of the way as she stuck her glove in the air, and blew out a loud sigh of relief as she felt it smack into her glove. *That was close.*

"FOCUS, PERRAULT!" Scott sing-songed from the outfield.

Joss tossed the ball to Herold and then turned and flipped him off. "SUCK IT, HEITZ!"

"THAT'S WHAT SHE SAID!" somebody from the opposing team's dugout yelled.

That timely rebuttal ensured a solid two-minute game delay as everybody within earshot burst into raucous laughter—including the umpire, who laughed so hard that he had to take his mask off to wipe at the tears streaming down his face. Even Michelle was laughing in the stands, and Joss arched a cocky brow at Scott as she shrugged and held up her hands in a *See what you started?* gesture.

Scott laughed and waved her off with his glove as he shook his head.

"ALL RIGHT, ALL RIGHT, ALL RIGHT!" the umpire hollered as he pulled his mask down over his face and stepped back behind the plate. He motioned the next batter up to bat as he settled into position behind the catcher and pointed at Herold to get the game going again.

Joss bit her lip as she locked eyes with Maeve through the backstop. Even from this distance, she could see the amusement etched across Maeve's face, and Joss smiled as she offered her a small shrug. Maeve's answering shake of the head made her laugh, and Joss was so focused on her lover that she completely missed Herold winding up to deliver the next pitch.

Ping!

Joss' eyes snapped back to the field as she tried to find the ball. "Shit," she swore as she spotted it a flying right at her. She instinctively tried duck out of the way, but the ball still ended up smacking her where her collarbone and shoulder met. Tears immediately erupted in her eyes from the pain, and she groaned as she reached down with her good arm to grab the ball and lob it weakly toward first before she crumpled to the dirt, not really caring if they got the out or not. She cradled her injured shoulder as she rocked back and forth, her eyes squeezed shut to try to block out the pain that was radiating across the top of her chest and down her left arm.

A gentle touch pulling her glove from her now useless arm told her she was not alone, and she shook her head. "I'm okay."

"Sure you are," Brock said as he tried to pull her hand away from her shoulder so he could look at the injury. "Lemme see, Jay."

"I'm fine," Joss choked out. "It's just a stinger. Gimme a sec and I'll be good."

"Bull-fucking-shit," Brock chuckled. "And, while I appreciate the bravado, I'm going to warn you now that Maeve is like five yards away, looking like she wants to either kiss you or kill you."

"Awesome." Joss groaned and forced a tight smile as she opened her eyes right as Maeve dropped to her knees in front of her. "I'm fine," she assured her.

Maeve rolled her eyes. "Bullshit."

Brock guffawed. "I like this one," he told Joss in a mock whisper.

"Me too." Joss nodded.

"Yes, well, this one," Maeve declared as she reached for Joss' hand, "wants to see the shoulder."

"Let her look," Scott chimed in from somewhere behind her.

"It's not that bad," Joss protested weakly as she allowed Maeve to pull her hand away. She grit her teeth as the loss of pressure sent a fresh rush of pain surging through her, making her head spin, and she focused on her breathing as Maeve gingerly pulled the collar of her jersey aside to inspect the damage.

"Fuck, Joss," Maeve breathed as her fingers hovered millimeters above Joss' skin. "You're gonna need x-rays on this."

Joss shook her head. The last thing she wanted to do was spend the night in the ER. "I just need an ice pack."

Maeve huffed and shook her head. "It's already purple and swollen, and I can count the stitches from the ball on your skin. It looks like it hit right on the acromioclavicular joint, and while your deltoid might have softened the blow a little, there's still a good chance you broke something."

Brock whistled. "How you know all that?"

"She kills people for a living," Joss quipped through gritted teeth.

Maeve ignored Joss' quip and looked at Brock. "Can you guys finish without her?"

"Yeah," Scott said. "Michelle's here. She's not the most athletically inclined—please don't tell her I said that—but we can hide her behind the dish and basically play down a man for the rest of the game."

"Scott..." Joss started to argue.

"What, Joss?" Scott scoffed. "You can't move your arm. How are you going to play?" He shook his head and added in a softer tone, "Let Maeve take you to go get checked out, and call me later. I can cover the store all day tomorrow, and if it gets busy, Michelle's on break for another few weeks before summer school starts and she can come in and help."

Joss shook her head. "I can't ask you to do that."

"You're not asking. I'm offering. This is what having friends is like, remember?"

Joss took a deep breath. She had been on her own for so long that she honestly had forgotten what it was like to have people looking out for her. Helen had tried, but she had also respected Joss' need to do things her own way and had never pushed. "Fine." She looked at Maeve. "We'll need to take George home first."

Maeve nodded as she pushed herself back to her feet and bent down to place a light hand under Joss' uninjured arm. "I know."

Joss pressed her good hand into her shoulder as she allowed Maeve to help her to her feet. The blue wall of concerned teammates surrounding them broke apart as she stood, and she nodded her thanks to the other team that was politely applauding her efforts.

"We can watch George tonight if you want," Brock offered.

"She'll do better at home," Joss told him as she squeezed her eyes shut against a stab of pain that radiated through her. Hooking her thumb in the waistband of her warm-up pants helped take some pressure off the joint, and she sighed as she opened her eyes again.

"Joss?" Maeve asked, her tone and expression worried.

"I'm fine," she assured her. "I promise."

"That has yet to be proven," Maeve said, shaking her head as she placed a gentle hand at the small of Joss' back to lead her from the field.

"Keep us posted," Scott said.

"We will," Maeve promised.

"I'll need my bag," Joss said as they got to the dugout. "My wallet with my insurance card and everything is in there."

"I'll get it," Herold said as he hurried past them to grab the black duffle that Joss had left on the end of the bench. He handed it to Maeve. "Here ya go."

"And this is for you," Brock said as he popped an instant ice pack and handed it to Joss.

Joss smiled her thanks as she took the ice and pressed it against her shoulder. *Come on, baby, start working your magic,* she thought as the ice pack began chilling the fabric of her shirt covering the injury.

"Thanks." Maeve shouldered the bag and tipped her head toward the parking lot. "You ready?" she asked Joss in a low tone.

"Yeah." Joss looked at Michelle, who was watching from the bleachers with a hand on George's collar. "Can you fill in for me?"

"Badly," Michelle replied with a smile as she let go of George's collar. "But yes."

"Thanks."

"Thanks for keeping an eye on George," Maeve said. She whistled sharply, and George was at her side in an instant.

The usually goofy dog was surprisingly subdued, somehow understanding that something bad had happened. She walked slowly beside them as they made their way to the car, stealing worried glances at Joss the whole way.

"Let me help," Maeve whispered as she opened the car door for Joss.

Joss let out a soft hiss as she angled herself onto the passenger's seat, and shook her head when Maeve started to buckle her in. "I can do that."

"I'm sure you can," Maeve said as she pulled the seatbelt all the way out and carefully leaned across Joss' lap to snap it into place. She guided it into place as it retracted, and kissed Joss tenderly. "Let me take care of you."

Joss sighed and nodded. "Okay."

Maeve kissed her again. "Good."

Even though Maeve closed the car door as softly as she could, the vibration of steel meeting steel still sent a shock wave of pain shooting down Joss' chest, and she grit her teeth to muffle the pained "*Fuck!*" that escaped her. She focused on keeping her breaths long and even as Maeve helped George into the car, and forced a tight smile when Maeve climbed behind the wheel.

"I don't know where the hospital is," Maeve admitted as she started the car.

Joss smiled. "Let's worry about taking George home first, and then I can tell you how to get there."

"You sure you don't want me to drop you off and then deal with George?"

"Nah, it's okay." Joss shook her head as Maeve shifted the car into drive and pulled out of the lot. The absolute last thing she wanted was to be in a hospital by herself. She hated hospitals. The last time she had been in one was the night her parents had died, and she had gone out of her way to avoid them ever since. She knew from the amount of pain she was feeling that Maeve was right and that she needed x-rays, but she also knew that the only way she would make it through the ordeal was with Maeve by her side. "I'll be fine."

Maeve looked like she wanted to argue, but some of the panic Joss was feeling about going to the ER must have shown on her face despite her best efforts to hide it, and she just nodded instead. "Okay."

Joss blew out a soft breath and closed her eyes as she leaned her head back against the headrest. "Okay."

Twenty-Seven

By the time Joss climbed back into Maeve's car after spending three long hours in the emergency room, waiting to get x-rays taken so that a doctor could confirm what Maeve had suspected back at the field, she was beyond exhausted. "I can't believe I actually broke my goddamn collarbone." She tugged at the strap of the sling cutting into the side of her neck. She had only been wearing it for half an hour and it was already driving her insane—there was no way she was going to wear this stupid thing for the next week until her follow-up visit. "Scott's going to have too much fun teasing me about this one."

"No, he won't."

Joss shot her a disbelieving look.

Maeve laughed and tipped her head in defeat. "You're right. It's going to be open season on your pathetic ass."

"Hey!" Joss protested with a laugh. Pain shot through her from the small lift of her shoulders that accompanied the laugh, and she hissed under her breath as she shook her head at the look of concern Maeve gave her. This really was going to suck. "You're supposed to be on my side, you know."

"I am at your side, as I've been all night." Maeve smiled sweetly.

Joss rolled her eyes, only marginally annoyed at how well it worked. "You're lucky you're cute."

"I know, right? It's come in quite handy over the years." Maeve winked as she twisted her key in the ignition. "So, Ms. Grumpy Butt, can I interest you in a lazy late-night-slash-holy-shit-it's-already-morning cuddle in my ridiculously comfy bed where we fall asleep to the melodious sounds of whatever the hell is on Food Network?"

Joss smiled. "Well, gee, how can I say no to an offer like that?"

"Pro tip, Perrault," Maeve teased as she shifted into drive. "When the woman you've just started dating asks you to come to bed with her, you should at least pretend to be excited about the opportunity."

"Ah, okay. Got it," Joss sassed with what she hoped passed for a playful smirk. She shook her head and wished that her left arm was not rendered completely useless so that she could reach out and take Maeve's hand into her own. "In that case, I would love to go to bed with you, Maeve Dylan."

"Good." Maeve rolled her eyes as she pulled her phone from her pocket and quickly glanced at the screen. "You need to call Scott and let him know that you're okay so he stops blowing up my phone."

Joss laughed. "Has he really been that bad?"

"He's worried about you," Maeve said with a small shrug. "It's cute."

"I'll make sure to tell him that," Joss chuckled as she pulled her phone out of her pocket. Even though Maeve had said that he had been texting her all night checking-in, she was still surprised when he answered before the end of the first ring.

"You're alive."

"And kicking," Joss confirmed. "Maeve was right, I broke my damn collarbone. Doc is delusional and told me to keep a stupid-ass sling on for a couple weeks, but he said there should be no lasting damage. Oh, and Maeve says you're cute."

Maeve laughed and shook her head.

"While my ego appreciates the compliment, do I want to know why?"

"I dunno, Sir Textsalot. Do you?"

Scott laughed. *"I was worried."*

"I appreciate it." Joss smiled. "But I'm fine. I'll see you tomorrow."

"Nah. Take a day to rest. I got the store for tomorrow."

"Scott..."

"Joss," he countered. *"I'm serious. Atramentum will still be there on Tuesday—just take a day off. You've been working yourself to the bone since you got back, it won't kill you to just relax for twenty-four hours and let your body begin to heal."*

It was clear by his tone that he meant it, and Joss sighed as she scrubbed her good hand over her face. He was right, of course, even Helen took the occasional "mental health day" during the high seasons, but she hated the idea of abandoning Scott when the store would most likely be bursting with customers. "You're sure?"

"Yeah. You need a break. Just hang out with that pretty girlfriend of yours for a day and watch some Netflix or something."

"I like the sound of that," Maeve spoke up before Joss could argue with him further.

Joss looked at her and arched a brow in surprise.

"Sorry. But you've got the volume turned up really high on that thing." Maeve waved a hand at Joss' phone. "And, since I can see that you don't want to do it, I figured I'd add my two cents."

"You're in the middle of edits. You don't have time to waste an entire day watching TV," Joss reminded her.

Maeve shrugged. "So? I'll add a chapter or two to my schedule for the next few days to make up the difference. It's one of the perks of being self-employed."

Joss sighed. "Two against one isn't fair."

"Deal with it," Scott chuckled. *"Nicely done, Maeve."*

"Thanks!" Maeve replied loudly. "I'll keep her home tomorrow, but come Tuesday, she's your headache again."

"I wish I could say that I look forward to it, but..."

"You guys do know that I'm the one holding the phone you're conversing through, right?" Joss grumbled.

"Whatever, Perrault," Scott said through a yawn. *"Right, well, I'm gonna go to bed now. Call me if you need me."*

"I won't," Joss promised.

"I will," Maeve assured him.

Joss shook her head. Part of her wanted to be annoyed by their meddling, but there was a part of her that found it sweet. It had been a long time since anyone had cared enough to insist she put herself first. "Yeah, yeah. You're best buddies," she muttered. "Call me if anything happens tomorrow, Heitz."

"You got it, boss. See you Tuesday," Scott signed off with another yawn.

"You need to rest so your body has time to heal," Maeve said when Joss flicked off her phone and dropped it onto her lap. She reached across the center console and gave Joss' leg a gentle squeeze.

"I know." Joss looked down at Maeve's hand on her thigh and covered it with her good hand. "I don't do sitting still well," she confessed, stroking her thumb over the back of Maeve's knuckles as they turned off the main road and onto their driveway. "I honestly couldn't tell you the last time I spent an entire day doing nothing. I'll probably drive you nuts by noon," she added only half-jokingly.

"Nah, maybe by dinnertime, though," Maeve sassed. She chuckled and gave Joss' thigh a light squeeze. "I'm sure we'll be able to come up with something to do to keep you from going stir-crazy. Hell, worst-case scenario, I'll just make you take George on a walk or something."

Joss sighed and shook her head. "You're sure you want me to bug you all day tomorrow?"

"Today," Maeve corrected with a grin as she nodded. "And, absolutely," she added as she pulled to a stop in front of her garage and killed the engine. "In case you haven't noticed, I kinda like spending time with you."

Joss smiled. "I kinda like spending time with you, too."

"I'm glad," Maeve murmured. She leaned across the center console and kissed Joss softly. "Do you want to shower before we get in bed?"

Joss grimaced as she imagined how much it was going to hurt to take off the sports bra she had managed to talk the doctors into letting her keep on during her exam, and nodded. "I probably should."

"What's that face for?" Maeve asked.

"Getting this sports bra off is gonna suck."

Maeve waggled her eyebrows. "Oh, well, lucky for you, I'm pretty good at getting you naked."

Of all the responses Joss might have expected, that one was nowhere on the list, and she huffed a small laugh that had her wincing in pain as she nodded. "Yes, you are."

Maeve smiled, clearly pleased that her quip was well-received, though her brow wrinkled with concern at the grimace on Joss' face. "In all seriousness, though, would you like me to help you?"

Joss nodded, her amused smile softening to one of gentle affection as she whispered, "I would."

Twenty-Eight

Joss sighed as she caught sight of her reflection in the windows beyond the large, cast-iron clawfoot tub at the far end of Maeve's expansive en suite master bath. She looked even more exhausted than she felt. Her hair was falling out of the ponytail she had pulled it back into for the game, the usually wavy strands falling imply around her ears and over her jaw, and there was an anguished slant to her mouth that belied the pain she was doing her best to pretend she did not feel.

The sound of water beating against travertine-tiled walls drew Joss' eyes to the shower on the other side of the bathroom that was more than large enough for two and had enough shower heads for six. It was the kind of shower that graced the pages of design magazines, and even though she was practically dead on her feet, a small smile tugged at her lips as she imagined how nice it was going to feel to step into the hot water.

"You ready?" Maeve asked.

"As I'll ever be," Joss muttered. She grit her teeth to keep from wincing as she gingerly removed her sling, and blew out a soft breath as she tossed it onto the vanity behind her. She averted her eyes as she hooked the thumb of her good hand into the waistband of her pants to push them down over her hips, and looked up in surprise when Maeve's hands took over the task.

"Let me help," Maeve whispered, her gaze cautious and concerned as she watched Joss' face for any sign of discomfort as she began undressing her.

Part of Joss wanted to insist that she could handle her pants and stuff herself, but it was late and she was exhausted, and the light brush of Maeve's fingers against her skin felt so nice that any words of protest died before they could form on her tongue. She braced her right hand on the edge of the vanity to steady herself as Maeve knelt before her, tossing her warm-ups and underwear aside before starting on her socks, and smiled shyly when Maeve stood back up in front of her.

"Hi."

"Hey, beautiful," Maeve murmured, a small, lopsided smile quirking her lips as she reached for the hem of Joss' tee. "Ready?"

Joss nodded and held her breath, knowing that this part of the process was going to hurt. They worked her good arm around of the shirt first, and she angled her head through the neck opening that Maeve lifted carefully higher. Sliding it off without putting too much stress on her affected shoulder was easy at that point, and Joss let the breath she had been holding go in a long, slow stream as she prepared herself for the next part. There were tears in her eyes when Maeve finally finished removing the sports bra, and she swallowed hard against the pain as Maeve tossed it aside. "I'm okay," she insisted, trying to soften the worry that was written on Maeve's face as she cradled her left arm in her right hand, taking the weight off her shoulder.

The hold granted her immediate relief from the intense, stinging pain that had burst through her shoulder and upper chest moments before, and she sighed as she realized she would be wearing the stupid thing for the next couple weeks like the doctor had suggested.

Damn it.

Maeve did not look at all convinced by Joss' assurance, but she nodded. "Okay, then." She bit her lip as she looked at Joss' injured shoulder, and shook her head as she leaned in to press a soft breath of a kiss to the very edge of the bruise that marred her upper chest, avoiding the raised bump beneath the angry, purple-black center of the bruise that marked the spot of the fracture.

The feeling of Maeve's lips against her skin was heavenly, and Joss sighed as she leaned her cheek against the side of Maeve's head. "That feels good."

"Good." Maeve lifted her head and dusted a similar kiss across Joss' lips as she pulled the rubber band from her hair. She smiled and took a small step back, her fingers trailing over Joss' sides and hips as she glanced over her shoulder at the shower, whose glass door was already beginning to steam over. "Looks like the water's ready. Do you think you'll need help washing your hair?"

Pride demanded Joss say no, that she would find a way to manage the task on her own somehow, but exhaustion forced the truth from her lips instead. "Probably."

"Okay." Maeve nodded. "Why don't you get in before you get too chilled, and I'll be there in a sec."

Joss nodded and slipped past Maeve to pull open the shower door, and she adjusted the water temperature as she stepped inside. The feeling of hot water shooting against her back was glorious, and she groaned as she tilted her head back beneath the spray, turning her body enough that the falling water did not hit her injured shoulder. Maeve had already anticipated how the various showerheads would hit her, and she had only turned on the two on either end that were more traditional fittings. There really were few things in life that were better than a hot shower with incredible water pressure.

One of those things that was better, however, was the feeling of soft hands sliding lightly over her waist as Maeve joined her.

"Keep making noises like that and I'm going to get jealous of my shower," Maeve teased as she ducked her head under the spray shooting from the shower head opposite the one Joss was under.

Joss chuckled as she blinked her eyes open, and smiled when she saw Maeve standing across from her. "I don't think you have anything to worry about," she murmured as she let her eyes sweep over Maeve's body.

"Sweet talk like that will get you exactly nowhere tonight." Maeve winked and picked up the bottle of Dove body wash and a loofa from the array of shower products that lined the built-in shelf that spanned the back wall of the shower.

"That's good," Joss admitted. "Because I'm tired. And sore."

"I'll bet," Maeve murmured as she knelt down and started spreading the soap over Joss' legs. She worked quickly and efficiently, moving up over shins and thighs and hips, and she waggled her eyebrows as she swirled the loofa in a languid figure-eight around Joss' breasts.

"Having fun?" Joss teased as Maeve continued to trace the same looping path over and over again.

"I am." Maeve stepped closer and reached behind Joss to give her back a quick scrub. "Are you?"

Joss wiggled her fingers against Maeve's stomach and nodded. "There are certainly worse ways to shower."

"I'm afraid to ask what those are, but okay." Maeve pecked Joss' lips as she gave the loofa a quick rinse. She set it back on the shelf, picked up her shampoo, and poured a generous amount into her left hand. She put the bottle back in its place and tilted her left hand over her right to redistribute the suds as she turned back to Joss. "Come here."

The slight push and pull of Maeve's fingers working through her hair had Joss swaying on her feet, and she bit her lip as she reached for Maeve's hips to steady herself. Not actively supporting her injured side made her shoulder throb, but the pain lessened somewhat when she wrapped her fingers around Maeve's hip, letting that hold take some of the pressure off her shoulder.

Maeve's touch gentled. "You okay?"

"Yeah. Moving just hurts."

"I know, sweetie," Maeve soothed as she tilted Joss' head back and began pushing the shampoo from her hair.

Joss closed her eyes to keep the soap out of them and smiled at the way Maeve's fingers tickled her back for a moment after she finished combing them through her hair. She stroked her thumbs over Maeve's hipbones as she gave herself over to her touch, and was pleased that the small movement sent only a tolerable amount of pain through her shoulder and chest.

A comfortable silence surrounded them as Maeve gave Joss' hair the same treatment with her vanilla-scented conditioner, their hips and breasts rubbing against each other every so often as Maeve worked. In any other context, Joss mused, this entire scene would have been an exquisite form of foreplay—wet skin, gentle touches, bodies moving together beneath the steaming spray of the shower certainly made for a fun lead-in to a night of lovemaking—but instead of aroused, she just felt safe.

Cared for.

"All done," Maeve declared, letting her hands slip from Joss' hair to cradle her face. She kissed her sweetly, and sighed as she nuzzled her cheek. "How you doing?"

"I have a beautiful, naked woman in the shower with me." Joss blinked her eyes open. "I'd say I'm doing pretty good."

Maeve chuckled and shook her head. "Charmer."

"I try." Joss took a deep breath and let it go slowly as she pulled her hands from Maeve's hips and once again cradled her injured arm in her good hand. "Do you want to wash up real fast?"

"I'll do it in the morning," Maeve said, shaking her head. "Let's get dried off and into bed."

Joss nodded as she leaned in to capture Maeve's lips in a quick, chaste kiss. "I like the sound of that."

"Me too." Maeve turned off the water and pushed the shower door open just far enough to grab a towel off the heated rack on the wall. Joss tried to take it from her, but she shook her head. "Let me."

In what seemed like no time at all, Maeve had them both dried off, and Joss stole a quick kiss before she stepped out of the shower. "Thank you."

"You're welcome." Maeve hung up the towel they had used and turned back to Joss. "Do you want something to sleep in?"

Joss nodded. She had packed a just-in-case bag with clothes for the next day so she had clean underwear and stuff, but had not bothered with anything resembling pajamas because, so far, on those nights she stayed over, they ended up collapsing in a spent, naked heap beneath Maeve's fluffy down comforter. But, thanks to that stupid line-drive, that was not an option for now. "Do you have a shirt I can borrow?"

"Of course."

Joss picked up her sling and followed Maeve back into the bedroom. Unzipping the backpack she had brought with extra clothes took far more effort than it should have, and she let out a relieved sigh when it opened far enough for her to rustle around inside it for her underwear. Once she was dressed, she could put the sling back on, and then maybe the arcs of fire shooting through her left shoulder and down her chest would go away.

"Here," Maeve said as she tossed two T-shirts and a pair of pink bikini briefs she had pulled from her dresser onto the bed beside Joss' bag. She eyed the pair of black boy shorts in Joss' hand and asked, "You want help with those?"

"I got it," Joss said, shaking her head as she leaned against the foot of Maeve's bed. The entire process of putting her underwear on would have been a lot less painful had she been able to sit down, but the height of Maeve's mattress made that impossible. She tucked her injured arm against her stomach and grabbed onto her hip to try to hold it there as she leaned down and slid her left foot, and then her right through the appropriate holes.

"I could have done that for you," Maeve pointed out when Joss finally stood up straight, her jaw clenched tight against the pain radiating through her injured side. She picked up the shirt she had tossed onto the bed. "Will you let me help with this?"

Joss nodded.

"Good." Maeve looked at Joss' bag and pursed her lips. "Um, okay. What about a bra? You're going to be more sore tomorrow, so if you want to wear one it'd probably be easier to get it on now, but the strap will put some pressure on your shoulder…"

"Fuck," Joss swore under her breath. She had not thought of that. She hated the feeling of not being supported, to the point that she usually slept in the sports bra she would wear for her morning run— though that habit had fallen by the wayside over the last week as she instead spent her mornings naked in bed with Maeve. Joss sighed as she looked through the open bathroom door and spotted the sports bra she had worn to the game on the floor by Maeve's hamper. "I'll put the one I wore to the game back on," she said. "The strap hits higher than the break, so it'd probably be more comfortable."

"Okay. That makes sense. You want to do that now, or in the morning?"

Joss shook her head. It was going to suck either way, but she had a feeling that it would probably suck just a little less now. "Let's just get it over with now."

"I'll go grab it, then." Maeve brushed a quick kiss across Joss' lips and then hurried into the bathroom, oblivious to the fact that she was still completely naked.

It spoke volumes to the level of discomfort Joss was suffering that she just leaned back against the foot of the bed and closed her eyes against the pain in her shoulder instead of ogling Maeve's naked body. She opened her eyes when she felt the air stir in front of her, and forced a tight smile to try to alleviate the wrinkle of concern that was creasing Maeve's forehead. "I'm good."

"If you say so," Maeve muttered as she twisted Joss' sports bra to slide it over her injured arm. "Reverse of before, okay?"

"Sounds good," Joss agreed.

Maeve worked quickly, her eyes never leaving Joss' face as she stretched and tugged at the fabric to try to make the process easier on Joss, and she blew out a soft breath of relief when she pulled it down over Joss' breasts. "How was that?"

Joss nodded. She had some adjusting to do, but she could do that once she had her sling back on. "Incredible." Joss kissed her softly. "Thank you."

"Shirt?"

"Sure." The heather gray Columbia shirt Maeve had pulled for her was easier to get on than the sports bra, and Joss shook her head when Maeve offered to help with her sling. "I got this. You worry about you, now."

Maeve nodded, but kept a wary eye on Joss in case she needed help as she began to dress. Once Joss had her sling fitted snugly into place, she smiled and said, "Go ahead and get comfortable. I'm just going to run down and take George out one last time, and then we'll be up."

Joss frowned at the plural pronoun. So far, they had gone with the vacuum at the bottom of the stairs thing every night, and she remembered all too well how George had pushed her out of her own bed back at the cottage when she wanted to snuggle.

Her concern must have been easy to read, because Maeve laughed. "George usually sleeps on the couch in the sitting room out there." She tipped her head at the sofas on the other side of the fireplace as she unfurled a faded blue Cubs tee in front of her before pulling it on.

"Right," Joss murmured as she moved toward what she was beginning to consider "her" side of the bed.

By the time she had gingerly slid onto the bed, Maeve had disappeared down the stairs, and she clenched her jaw as she laid down on her back. Relief flooded instantly through her the moment she was flat on the mattress, and she sighed as she arranged the comforter along her left side to support her elbow. Arm supported, she reached through the neck of her shirt to finish getting comfortable, and then closed her eyes.

The energetic pounding of George's paws up the stairs announced Maeve's return, and Joss smiled at the way Maeve was talking to her, warning her that she needed to be good or else she would have to go back downstairs.

Joss had suspected on several different occasions that George could actually understand her, and the uncharacteristically reserved way the Dane laid her head on the edge of the mattress by Joss just further confirmed that suspicion. "Hey, George," Joss said as she carefully reached across her body with her good arm to pet the dog's head.

George licked her hand as she stared sadly at her for a moment, and then sighed as she turned and padded toward the sitting room.

"Sorry about that," Maeve apologized as she hovered beside the bed, waiting to make sure that George really was going to lay down. "I just figured she'd behave better if she was up here with us, too."

"It's fine," Joss assured her through a yawn. "Come to bed."

Maeve nodded and slipped beneath the covers. She curled up on her side at the far edge of the bed, clearly worried about doing anything that might cause Joss pain. "Is this okay?"

"No." Joss shook her head and smiled. "You're too far away. Come here."

"I don't want to hurt you."

"You won't." Joss wiggled her fingers atop the comforter. "If I can't hold you like I usually do, the least you can let me do is hold your hand."

"Oh, it is, huh?" Maeve smiled and inched across the mattress, settling herself close enough that she was able to press a tender kiss to Joss' uninjured shoulder as she took her hand. "How's this?"

Joss smiled and closed her eyes as she gave Maeve's hand a light squeeze. "Much better." She yawned and added sleepily, "Thank you for all your help tonight."

"It was my pleasure," Maeve murmured, sounding as tired as Joss felt. She squeezed Joss' hand and sighed. "Sweet dreams."

"Sweet dreams," Joss whispered as the events of the day caught up to her in an instant, dragging her into unconsciousness.

Twenty-Nine

Quiet bursts of sporadic typing coaxed Joss back to consciousness the next morning, and as she blinked her eyes open, she was surprised to see that the bedroom was flush with sunlight. The entire left side of her torso felt stiff, but the stabbing pain from the night before was replaced for the moment by a dull ache that thankfully did not morph into something more when she turned her head toward her bedmate.

Maeve was sitting up against the headboard, legs stretched out in front of her to support the laptop she was busy plucking away at, so engrossed in her work that she was oblivious to the fact she was being watched. Which was just fine with Joss, as she loved these moments where she could just freely look at Maeve and marvel at how truly beautiful she was, even when hair was the very definition of bedhead and her Cubs tee was wrinkled from sleep. Joss smiled as she watched Maeve push her glasses back into place with the middle finger of her right hand as her eyes roamed back and forth across the screen, silently mouthing the words as she read as if she were tasting their cadence on her tongue.

"It's not nice to stare." Maeve grinned and double-clicked her touchpad to mark her spot as she looked at Joss.

"I didn't think you'd notice," Joss said, taking a deep breath as she stretched her legs beneath the covers. The ache in her shoulder remained constant, and she offered up a silent prayer that it would remain that way as she rolled onto her side to sit up. It did not, of course, but the pain was also not as sharp as it had been the night before, and she let out a small hiss of discomfort as she carefully levered herself into a sitting position.

Maeve closed the lid of her laptop and reached for Joss in case she needed help. "How you feeling?"

Joss shook her head. "Not as bad as I thought I would, honestly. Stiff and sore, but it's manageable."

"Here." Maeve turned toward her bedside table and then turned back to Joss, offering her a small, open bottle of Advil and a glass of water. "I brought these up for you."

"You are an angel," Joss murmured as she held out her hand. She quickly tossed the pills Maeve shook into her hand into her mouth, and smiled her thanks as she took the glass of water to wash them down. She placed the glass back in Maeve's waiting hand when she was finished with it, and sighed. "What time is it?"

"Almost ten. You slept much later than I thought you would," Maeve reported as she set the glass back onto her nightstand. She smiled and tucked her hair behind her ears. "I actually had to take George downstairs and put the vacuum back on the stairs to keep her away because she kept sneaking over to your side of the bed to try to wake you up."

"It's because she has a thing for morning breath." She grinned at the way Maeve laughed and nodded in agreement. "Anyway, you can get back to work if you want, I'm just going to go use the bathroom."

Maeve set her laptop on the bed between them. "I'll do it later. Do you need help getting up?"

Joss shook her head and flipped the covers aside with her good hand. She tightened her core to try to keep her shoulder from moving too much as she twisted her hips and swung her legs toward the edge of the bed, and was pleased to note that it seemed to help. No surge of pain, just the same teeth-gritting ache.

I can live with that.

She inched her butt toward the edge of the mattress and then slid forward until her feet touched the floor. Discomfort flashed through her as she straightened, but it disappeared quickly, and she smiled as she turned back toward Maeve. "See? I got it."

"Yes, you do," Maeve confirmed with a soft smile. "Would you like some coffee? What about food? I can grab whatever you'd want from the kitchen."

"You don't have to wait on me."

"I know I don't have to," Maeve said, rolling her eyes as she climbed out of bed. "But I want to. So, tell me what you want."

Joss bit her lip as her eyes trailed slowly up Maeve's bare legs, past the hem of her wrinkled blue tee, to the tantalizing swell of her breasts, noting the way Maeve's nipples pressed against the soft fabric, and she smirked when her gaze finally landed on green eyes that were regarding her with obvious surprise. "Well..."

"Down, girl," Maeve chuckled, shaking her head. "I think your eyes are bigger than your abilities at this point."

Joss smiled and nodded as she rounded the foot of the bed and shook her head. She knew that Maeve was right, but she was feeling good enough that she could not resist pointing out, "I have many abilities."

"Oh, I know you do." Maeve sashayed up to Joss and hiked a brow in playful challenge as she toyed with the strap of her sling. "But do you honestly think you could exercise any of those abilities right now?"

Joss made a show of pretending to think about it. "I dunno. Maybe." She smiled against Maeve's lips as she kissed her. "Is your strap on still in the middle drawer of your nightstand?"

Maeve threw her head back and laughed. "You're insane." She shook her head and pressed a sweet, chaste kiss to Joss' lips. "I am going to go get you some coffee. And you should probably eat something, too. I've got bagels, English muffins, or I can scramble up some eggs real fast. What sounds good?"

"I dunno... Seriously, Maeve, you don't need to make me anything."

Maeve tilted her head as she thoughtfully appraised Joss. "How about a bagel with peanut butter?"

"Sure." Joss nodded, not wanting to argue about it any more. If it made Maeve feel better to bring her breakfast, then she would eat it—even if she was not feeling all that hungry at the moment. "That sounds great."

"Good. And, do you care if I let George back up?"

Joss frowned. "Why would I?"

"I dunno. She can just be a lot to deal with."

"Let my girl back upstairs."

"Oh, your girl, huh?"

Joss grinned. "Yep."

"Right, then," Maeve chuckled, shaking her head. "Next time she's being a monster, she's all yours."

"I look forward to it," Joss sassed. She grinned at the way Maeve rolled her eyes at her before she turned toward the stairs, and let herself enjoy the hint of cheek that flashed beneath the hem of Maeve's shirt as she walked.

Joss turned toward the bathroom when Maeve finally disappeared from view, and winced at the flash of pain that streaked through her shoulder at the sudden movement.

"Yeah, my eyes are definitely bigger than my abilities at the moment," she muttered under her breath. "Goddamn it."

Having only one functional arm doubled the time her morning routine usually took, and by the time she made her way back into the bedroom, Maeve was stretched out on the bed and George was lying on the floor beside her.

Joss smiled at the way George's tail thumped heavily against the floor when she saw her, and braced herself to receive the dog as she scrambled to her feet. "Good morning, beautiful," she greeted George as she scratched behind her ears. George smiled her dopey smile as she turned and pushed against Joss' leg to try to force her hand where she wanted it. Joss should have expected the move—it was trademark George, after all—but it caught her by surprise and she could not stifle the whimper that escaped her as pain shot through her shoulder when she stumbled back a step. She sucked in a deep breath to try to put a lid on the discomfort before it could get out of hand, and gave George's head a few quick pats. "Okay. All done."

"George, come," Maeve said.

Joss shook her head at the concerned look Maeve was giving her as George padded back to the side of the bed and laid down on the floor. Between being up and about for the last however long she had been in the bathroom and George, her shoulder was throbbing and she hoped that bracing her injured arm with some extra pillows would help. "Sorry. I didn't think it'd take me so long to brush my teeth and stuff."

"That's not at all what I'm worried about right now," Maeve said, frowning as she watched Joss slowly round the foot of the bed. "Are you okay? Did she hurt you?"

"Of course she didn't," Joss said, groaning as she angled herself onto the bed. "I'm fine," she muttered through clenched teeth as she scooted toward the head of the bed so she could sit up against the headboard.

"Let me get a pillow behind you," Maeve said as she shoved a large, square pillow behind Joss' back. "How's that?"

Joss nodded and carefully wedged the pillow she had slept on the night before between her bad arm and her side. "Good." She took a deep breath and nodded again. "I'm good."

Maeve did not look at all convinced, but she just set a small plate with the bagel she had promised on Joss' lap. "Okay. Here you go, then."

Joss' stomach growled at the sight of the food, and she smiled a more genuine smile as she picked up one of the halves. "You are an angel, Maeve Dylan. Thank you."

"Of course I am." Maeve winked and picked up the television remote that had made its way from her nightstand to the comforter between them. "Any requests?"

"I honestly don't have any idea what's on TV this time of day," Joss said. "Whatever you want is fine."

As it turned out, there was pretty much nothing worth watching—even the movie channels Maeve subscribed to were useless—and Joss smiled as Maeve made a small noise of annoyance as she turned the set to Food Network and tossed the remote back onto the bed.

"Bobby Flay, it is, I guess," Maeve said.

Joss laughed. "You love Bobby Flay."

Maeve grinned. "Do not."

"You know his ex-wife is like, ten thousand times hotter, right?"

"Says you."

Joss chuckled and lifted her peanut butter bagel at the screen. "I'm sure I'm not the only one with that opinion. But this is fine, Anne Burrell is on this one." She had never heard of the spunky chef before she had started hanging out with Maeve, but if she was going to have to watch cooking shows, at least the female chef with the wild bleached-blond hair made it entertaining.

"Should I be worried?" Maeve teased, nudging Joss' leg beneath the covers.

"No." Joss smiled and turned her head to look at Maeve. "I'm perfectly happy with the way my life is right now, just as it is. I've got you and George, and—" Her phone buzzed on the nightstand beside her. She dropped her bagel onto her plate and set it on the bed between her and Maeve before as she carefully turned to grab it. The only people who ever called her were Scott and Maeve, and she immediately became worried that something was wrong at the store. "Heitz?"

"I'm just checking in," Scott said quickly. *"How are you feeling?"*

"Everything's okay?"

"Everything's fine, Joss. I was just worried because I totally expected you to call and check in by now. Are you okay?"

"Fine," Joss said, blowing out a soft breath as she leaned back against her pillow. "I just woke up a few minutes ago. I'd figured I'd call you when I finished eating breakfast."

"Well, now I've saved you the trouble. What's your plan for the day?"

"Right now we're watching Food Network," Joss reported. She smirked at Maeve and added, "Maeve has a thing for Bobby Flay."

"Hey!" Maeve protested with a laugh.

"I guess he's kinda cute, if you're into dorky-looking Irish dudes," Scott agreed without missing a beat.

Joss laughed. "Exactly. You're sure everything's okay there? I can come down…"

"Everything's fine. Enjoy your cooking shows, relax, and I'll see you tomorrow. And if you're not up to it, just lemme know and I'll do the whole day again. It's not a big deal."

"I'll be fine," Joss assured her. "But thanks."

"My pleasure. Now, gimme to your girl, Perrault."

Joss rolled her eyes and handed the phone to Maeve. "Sir Textsalot wants to talk to you."

"Lucky me." Maeve smiled as she took the phone. "Yes?"

Joss rolled her eyes and picked up her bagel as she listened to Maeve's half of the conversation, which was mostly a lot of *uh-huh*s and *I will*s.

Maeve laughed and nudged Joss' leg with her foot again. "I will make sure she rests. Thanks for taking care of things there. … She's lucky to have us both."

Joss nodded. "I absolutely am," she agreed loudly.

Maeve winked at Joss. "Will do," she told Scott. "Talk to you later." She disconnected the call and tossed Joss' phone onto the bed next to the remote. "He's a good guy."

"Has been ever since I met him back in high school," Joss said. "And I know I'm lucky to have you."

"Yes, you are." Maeve smiled and leaned over just far enough to drop a sweet kiss to Joss' lips. "As am I. My life here has been much more enjoyable ever since I met you."

Joss grinned and pecked Maeve's lips again. "George is the best matchmaker ever."

"Yes, she is," Maeve agreed, as she pulled back to lean against her own pillow. She glanced over the side of the bed at George, who was doing her best chainsaw impersonation, and shook her head. Her left hand found its way onto Joss' thigh, and she hummed under her breath as she stretched her legs out in front of her.

It was not her typical Monday at all, Joss thought as she looked down at Maeve's hand on her leg, but there were certainly worse ways to waste a day. "So, the plan for the day is to stay here and watch TV?"

Maeve nodded. "Yup. Unless you have something you need to do."

"All I have is a pile of laundry sitting at home waiting for me." Joss sighed as she envisioned how much that particular chore was going to suck.

"We'll go down to your place after lunch and I'll help you get that done," Maeve said.

"You don't have to do my laundry," Joss protested, shaking her head. "I'll figure it out."

"Jocelyn why-don't-I-know-your-middle-name Perrault," Maeve grumbled, "knock it off and accept the fact that I'm going to help you."

"It's Marie," Joss supplied. "And okay. Thank you."

"Good." Maeve grinned and nodded. "Now shut up and eat your bagel. You're distracting me from Mr. Flay."

Joss laughed. "Yes, ma'am."

Thirty

"You know," Scott said as he slid the last box of new stock on the register counter closer to himself, "it's kinda nuts how fast your shoulder healed."

"Right?" Joss lifted her left arm to ninety degrees and moved it in a small circle. In the last two weeks, she had gone from not being able to use her arm at all, to being completely sling-free and able to do stupid, everyday things like wash her hair without suffering crippling levels of pain. The doctor said at her recheck the day before that she had about another week to go before the fracture was completely healed, but he had signed off on her chart, telling her that he did not need to see her back again unless she felt something was wrong.

"Can't wait until you can help with this stuff again, though," Scott grunted as he picked up the box of books.

Joss made a show of making herself comfortable on her stool at the register. "Yeah, me neither. Sitting here watching you do all the heavy lifting has been brutal."

Scott stuck his tongue out at her as the bell above the shop's door jingled. "Maybe I'll break my shoulder or something and make you do all this on your own."

"I swear, you two are worse than me and my brothers," Maeve declared. "Are you sure you aren't related?"

"Nah, I'm much better looking," Scott quipped, winking at Maeve as he turned toward the stacks with his box. "I'm just gonna go shelves these."

"Yeah, you do that!" Joss called after him. She chuckled under her breath and turned to Maeve, who, by this time, had rounded the end of the counter and was standing right beside her. She smirked as she dragged her eyes over Maeve's long, tanned legs, enjoying the high cut of her olive green hiking shorts and the body-hugging fit of her white tank, and hiked a playful brow when their eyes met. "So, dare I ask, what brings a beautiful woman like yourself into our fine establishment this afternoon?"

Maeve shook her head and smiled as she leaned down to press a quick, chaste kiss to Joss' lips. "You're ridiculous. I was thinking that since it's Scott's night to close, that you might let me take you out to dinner?"

"I'd like that."

"Good." Maeve's smile softened, and she ran a gentle hand along the side of Joss' face. "Me too."

Joss turned her head to press a lingering kiss to Maeve's palm, and sighed when the bell above the door jingled and Maeve pulled away. She turned to the young family entering the shop and smiled. "Welcome to Atramentum. Is there anything I can help you find?"

"Kids section?"

Joss pointed. "Right back there."

"Great. Thanks."

The family moved en masse toward the indicated area of the store, and Joss ran a hand through her hair as she looked back up at Maeve. "So, Ms. Dylan, is there anything special you'd like me to wear to dinner tonight?"

"You don't need to dress up." Maeve shook her head. "I was just thinking we'd go to DiAmico's."

Joss' mouth watered at the thought of steaming bread sticks and rich tomato sauce. "Works for me. We should probably make a reservation though. Town's been busy this week."

"Already done," Maeve confirmed. "They only had one opening at seven forty-five, though, so call me if you end up getting out of here late and I'll just meet you there."

Joss shook her head. "I should be okay. You want me to come up to your place after I've changed?"

"I can pick you up."

"Yeah, except it's easier on George if we stay at your place," Joss pointed out.

Maeve laughed. "Oh really? I believe I only offered to take you to dinner. What kind of girl do you think I am?"

"The kind who likes cuddling in bed and making out during the commercials of her favorite cooking shows." Joss grinned and tickled the back of Maeve's knee. It had taken a few days to get back to that point, but she had several fond memories from the past two weeks of laying flat on Maeve's bed, surrounded by a curtain of silk as Maeve's tongue did toe-curling things to her own. "Doc says I can do anything that doesn't hurt," she repeated her orthopedist's instructions with a suggestive wink. "But if you're not interested…"

Maeve rolled her eyes and took a step back, out of Joss' reach. "Fine. Meet me at my place and we'll go from there."

"It was the cooking show thing that won you over, huh?"

"Bet your cute ass it was," Maeve sassed as she sidled back around the edge of the counter. "We'll need to leave no later than seven thirty to make the reservation."

"Got it."

"Got what?" Scott asked.

Joss grinned. "A date. She's taking me to DiAmico's."

"Ugh. Lucky," Scott whined. "Bring me some lasagna?"

Maeve smiled and arched a playful brow at Scott. "Will a slice of lasagna guarantee Joss an early exit from work this evening?"

Scott nodded. "Absolutely."

Joss laughed. "Wow, way to play it cool, man."

"Whatever. I've got dried out chicken and rice to reheat for dinner. Promise me a fat slice of oozy-gooey-delicious lasagna and you can leave now for all I care."

The bell above the door jingled again, spilling a handful of customers into the store, and Joss shook her head.

"That's very tempting…" Joss checked her watch. It was still only a quarter to five. "But I'll hang around for a bit longer to help with the pre-dinner rush."

"Hey guys. Let us know if you need any help finding something," Joss greeted the group.

"You don't want her now?" Scott asked Maeve as the small crowd filtered past. "You could grab an early-bird dinner and get me my lasagna sooner?"

Maeve shook her head. "Unfortunately, I have a call with my agent at five thirty so he can try and talk me into going to some convention in Cincinnati in October. So I'm just going to ignore your implied insinuation that I'm old and need to have dinner before the sun goes down and leave you to deal with her on your own for a bit longer."

"Gee, thanks," Scott grumbled. "I mean, damn, woman. What'd I ever do to you?"

Joss crossed her arms over her chest and pretended to be offended by the slant their conversation had taken. In truth, however, she thought it was great that Scott and Maeve were getting along so well. Even if their budding friendship meant that she was on the receiving end of their tag-team teasing. "You two sure know how to make a girl feel good."

"Well, I don't want to brag, but…." Maeve smiled sweetly and blew her a kiss. "You did tell me that very same thing several times last night."

Scott barked a laugh and held up a hand for a high five. "Nice."

"Thank you," Maeve chuckled as she slapped her hand against his.

Joss shook her head and did her best to try to hide her smile. "Yeah, well, see if I ever tell you that again."

"Ooh." Scott elbowed Maeve in the ribs. "I do believe she just threw down a challenge."

"You wish," Joss retorted.

"I believe you're right," Maeve said to Scott, though her gaze was locked squarely on Joss.

Joss swallowed hard and had to force herself to not look away as she watched a perfectly sculpted brow lift behind black frames in playful challenge or silent confirmation or...fuck if she knew. Judging by the way her heart was fluttering in her throat, though, she definitely liked it. "I..."

Maeve laughed—the sound low and rough, with more than a hint of a promise woven through those husky waves—and winked. "I'll see you soon."

"Yeah." Joss nodded.

"And I'll be sending you some lasagna soon," Maeve promised Scott.

"And you are the my new favorite person in the whole wide world," Scott told her with a grin.

Joss rolled her eyes. "Yeah, yeah. Don't you have books to stock or customers to help or something?"

"I do," Scott agreed. "Later, Maeve."

Maeve waved goodbye as Scott sauntered down a nearby aisle, and shook her head as she looked back at Joss. "I'll see you soon?"

"Of course," Joss promised. "I'll try and get out of here around a quarter till, which'll give me plenty of time to change and get to your house before we have to go."

Maeve looked around them and smiled as she leaned across the counter to steal one last, quick kiss. "I can't wait."

Thirty-One

DiAmico's was even busier than Joss had thought it would be, but even the loud din of chinking silverware and competing conversations did nothing to distract her from the woman sitting across from her. Maeve's hair was radiant in the dimly lit restaurant, a golden halo of waves that cascaded regally around her bare shoulders. She had changed from her shorts and tank into a cute summery dress that billowed enticingly around her legs when she walked. Joss felt a little underdressed next to her since she was just wearing the same jeans she had worn to work and a long sleeve, pale blue linen shirt, but thankfully—judging from the way Maeve's hand had stroked up and down her thigh throughout dinner—she did not seem to mind.

"Here you go," their waitress said as she dropped a leather billfold with their check on their table en route to tending to another of her tables.

Joss reached for the bill, but Maeve snatched it out of her grasp before she could even register what was happening.

"Nice try," Maeve said, shaking her head at Joss. "But this was my idea. I'm paying."

Joss laughed and held up her hands in defeat. "Sorry. But, really though, you can't blame me for trying. I mean, you went above and beyond the expected girlfriend responsibilities over the last few weeks. I kinda owe you a night out, ya know?"

Maeve's playfully stern expression shifted, her eyes positively melting as her smile softened into that gentle, awed look that sent Joss' stomach fluttering. "Girlfriend?" she asked as she slipped her credit card into the billfold and laid it over the edge of their table.

It might have taken her an unforgivably long time to learn how to read Maeve, but Joss knew exactly what that tone and that look meant. "Well, yeah." She smiled. "I mean, unless you don't—"

"I do."

"Okay, then," Joss said, unable to keep her smile in check. "Good."

Maeve huffed a small laugh and shook her head. "Why do I feel like I'm back in high school right now?"

"God, I wish I was this aware of myself in high school," Joss said. "It would have made my life so much less confusing."

"Right?"

Joss nodded and glanced at their server, who had just grabbed the check as she passed their booth with a tray of dirty dishes. "Anyway, you never said how the call with your agent went."

"It was fine." Maeve shrugged and picked up her nearly empty glass of wine. "I get to go spend the first weekend of October in Cincinnati. There's a panel they want me to sit on, and it'll be a good way to hype *Storm*." She eyed Joss over the rim of her glass. "You want to come with?"

Joss sighed and shook her head. "I would love to, but that's still shoulder season here. It won't be as busy as now, and it could be completely dead, but we typically see a fair number of hikers and bikers coming through town during that time of year because of the shift in foliage. Two weeks later and I'd totally do it, but I just can't then."

Maeve nodded. "It's not a big deal. I just thought I'd ask."

"I'm sorry," Joss apologized again, feeling like she had let Maeve down.

"It's fine," Maeve assured her. "Really."

"Would you want me to watch George while you're gone?"

"If it's not too much trouble, that would be great."

"George is never too much trouble."

Their server returned with Maeve's card and the credit slip for the charge, and Maeve smiled as she opened the folder and picked up the pen. "Okay, then." She filled in the tip and total lines on the bill for their meal—she had taken care of sending Scott his lasagna when they first arrived—and scribbled her name across the bottom. "You ready to go?"

"Sure. You want to walk around town for a bit before we head back?"

Maeve nodded as she slipped her card back into wallet and dropped it into her purse. "That would be fun."

"Good." Joss pushed her chair back and got to her feet. She waited for Maeve to do the same, and then smiled as she motioned for her to go first. Maeve's fingers slid over her right wrist as they stepped onto the sidewalk outside the restaurant, and Joss smiled at her as she took Maeve's hand into her own and gave it a light squeeze. "Anywhere in particular you'd like to go?"

Maeve shook her head. "Let's just wander."

"Works for me." Joss tipped her head and turned to the left, figuring that any direction would do since they had no real goal in mind.

The boutiques lining the boulevard were flush with tourists looking to spend their hard-earned money, and Joss waved to the few familiar faces she spotted as they strolled past. Night had fallen on the mountain while they had been inside the restaurant, and Joss sighed as her gaze drifted over the brightly lit, multi-colored awnings and shop signs on either side of them.

"It's been ages since I've done this." Joss smiled as her eyes landed on a weathered statue of a man in full winter gear balancing a pair of skis over his shoulder. She nudged Maeve with her elbow and pointed. "See that statue?"

"Yeah."

"Wesley Herold nearly got us all arrested on the corner right there senior year."

Maeve pulled up short. "Herold? Seriously? How?"

Joss laughed and tugged Maeve onward. "We were all on our way home from prom, and he thought it'd be a good idea to stand up through the sunroof of the limo. He was holding his hands up in the air and yelling that he's the king of the world and shit like that—it was actually pretty hilarious until blue and red lights started flashing behind us."

"Heh, I bet."

"Right? So, cops pull us over, and we all freak because a couple of the football players had brought flasks to the dance that we'd been passing around like a bunch of delinquents. Herold decides he's sober enough to try and talk us out of trouble—which was crazy because he was the drunkest out of all of us. So he, of course, failed spectacularly, and we all ended up sitting on the sidewalk in front of the statue."

"Oh my God," Maeve chuckled, shaking her head. "What happened next?"

"Well, thankfully for us, Brock's dad was the Deputy Chief for Sky P.D. at the time—he's Chief, now—and he heard about it on the radio. Now, you know how big Brock is..."

Maeve nodded.

"Well, his dad has a good six inches and probably sixty pounds on him. He's built like a tank with this deep, gravelly voice that just screams 'don't fuck with me'. Anyway, Deputy Chief Green hears about it on the radio, gets in his car, and comes out to scare the shit out of us for a few minutes. Once we were all convinced we were going to jail, he had the patrol guys who pulled us over call all our parents to have them come pick us up."

"What happened? Did they charge you?"

Joss smiled and shook her head. "Nah. Green's dad kept it to our families, so even the school didn't find out so we weren't punished there. Though, really, even if the school had found out, it would have come back on them because we had all been drinking right under the noses of the chaperones."

Maeve bobbed her head as if to say, *Maybe, maybe not.* "What'd Helen say when she found out?"

"She was surprisingly cool with it. I mean, my mom would have flipped her shit, but Helen was just like, 'At least you were being responsible about it and not driving', and let it go."

"Lucky," Maeve said.

"Yep." Joss arched a brow at Maeve. "What about you?"

"What about me?" Maeve asked.

"You ever almost get arrested?"

Maeve laughed. "No. I was a good, sheltered, innocent child who was terrified to put one toe out of line."

"Aww, that's no fun."

"I had fun. It was just, you know, legal," Maeve sassed as she pulled Joss to a stop in front of Sky Fudge Shoppe.

The confectioner on the other side of the glass had just knocked a gigantic brick of fudge from its mold onto a large slab of marble, and Joss smiled as she watched Maeve's tongue slide slowly over her lips as she eyeballed the treat.

"Come on," Joss said, nudging Maeve with her elbow as she tipped her head at the door.

Victor, the owner and head confectioner for the store, looked up from his work as they walked into the small shop that smelled like heaven, and grinned. "Joss!"

"Hey, Vic." Joss smiled and waved as she eyed the slab of chocolate on the marble worktable behind the glass display case. Victor came into Atramentum every Saturday morning with his kids Marco and Emilio to get them each a new book, so she knew him better than most since they chatted while the boys looked through the shelves for something new to read. "Whatcha making?"

Victor grinned. "Just my famous turtle fudge."

"Victor makes the best fudge in the entire world," Joss told Maeve with a smile.

"Of course I do," Victor boasted with a wink. He wiped his hands off on his apron and extended his right to Maeve over the counter. "Victor Gonzales."

Maeve shook his hand. "Maeve Dylan."

Victor's eyes went wide. "Like the author?"

Maeve smiled and nodded. "That's me."

"Oh, wow! Really?" He turned and picked up a slice of fudge from the brick he had been cutting when they walked in. "Here, let me know what you think."

"Thank you." Maeve smiled as she took the offered chocolate.

"What about me?" Joss asked, batting her lashes at Vic.

"Yeah, fine, whatever," Victor teased as he handed her a piece. "Here."

"Thanks. My favorite." Joss popped the chunk of fudge into her mouth.

"Oh my God, this stuff is deadly," Maeve moaned.

Victor grinned. "One pound?"

Joss laughed. "Sure. Gimme a variety, and split it into two boxes. We'll drop half off with Scott before we head home."

Victor nodded and wiped his hands off on his apron. He pulled a couple of small, white boxes stamped with the store's logo from beneath the counter, and set them on top of the glass. "Any preferences?"

"The turtle fudge," Maeve said immediately.

Victor beamed and nodded. "Of course. Anything else?"

"Surprise us," Joss said, shaking her head. "How are the boys doing?"

"They're driving their mother insane," Victor shared with a laugh. "She's already counting the days until they go back to school."

"I remember my mother doing the same thing," Maeve said.

"Mine too," Joss agreed. "They still playing soccer?"

"Of course. Mary will be down in Parker with them this weekend for a tournament."

"Sounds like fun," Joss said. Once Victor had finished boxing up all their treats, she paid for them all and tipped her head at the door. "You ready to keep wandering?"

Maeve nodded. "Sure."

"Tell Scott I say hi," Victor said as the door to the shop opened and more customers came inside.

"Will do. Say hi to Mary and the kids for me. See you guys Saturday?"

"Of course." Victor nodded. He looked at Maeve. "It was a pleasure to meet you."

"You, as well," Maeve replied with a smile as she followed Joss out the door. "You have to keep that stuff at your place or the store," she told Joss when the door closed behind them. "If we bring it home, I'll eat it all."

"There are worse problems to have than half a pound of gourmet fudge in your fridge," Joss pointed out with a chuckle.

Maeve groaned. "So many calories."

Joss smirked and waggled her eyebrows. "I'm sure we can come up with a way to burn them all off."

"Yeah." Maeve sighed dramatically. "But I really hate running."

Joss laughed. "Lucky for you, there will be no running involved."

"I like that idea."

Joss nodded. "Me too."

"So, what do you have in mind?" Maeve asked, waggling her eyebrows.

Joss pecked her lips. "After we drop this stuff off at Atramentum, I'll take you home and show you."

Thirty-Two

Joss licked her lips as she sank to her knees, her fingers lightly caressing the curve of Maeve's breasts. She pressed a wet kiss to soft satin and breathed deep, her eyes fluttering shut for the briefest of moments as the sweet scent of Maeve's arousal enveloped her.

Heaven. Pure heaven.

"Joss…"

Joss smiled up at Maeve as she dragged her fingers down her sides, bumping over her ribs to grab hold of the final article of clothing that separated them. She nuzzled the smooth fabric as she tugged the panties down slowly, revealing Maeve to her in millimeters. She kissed soft skin and even softer curls as they appeared, and dipped her tongue into the shadowed fold between Maeve's legs, reveling in the muted sighs and strangled moans that rained softly down on her from above.

Her lips followed the path of her hands, searing a path down toned thighs and over the knob of a knee, and they both moaned softly when she finally slipped the panties from Maeve's legs and dropped them to the floor.

"You are so beautiful," Joss murmured, stroking her hands over the back of Maeve's legs as she drank in the vision above her. Her lips tingled with the need to taste every inch of skin, to tease and kiss and worship, and she sighed as she leaned in to press a lingering, open-mouthed kiss to Maeve's right thigh.

Maeve groaned and adjusted her stance, opening herself wider to Joss' slow, adoring kisses. "Please…"

Joss smiled and grabbed the backs of Maeve's thighs as she pushed herself up onto her knees, enjoying way Maeve's eyes darkened with every kiss. She felt herself clench at the low, rumbling moan that escaped Maeve when she nipped at her inner thigh, and the sight of Maeve sucking in a deep breath as she bit her lip was almost enough to make her speed things along.

Almost.

The tips of Maeve's fingers played with her hair as she kissed her way higher, alternating from one leg to the other, delighting in the naked desire that played across Maeve's face. Legs opened wider before her, beckoning her forward, begging for her touch, and Joss sighed as she slid her hands higher, over the taut swell of Maeve's ass, kneading and massaging as she gave in to their shared need and finally kissed the slick, warm skin nestled between the apex of Maeve's thighs.

"Oh God." Maeve leaned back against the edge of her bed, her right hand strangling the duvet as she combed the fingers of her left hand through Joss' hair.

Joss moaned, wordlessly echoing the sentiment as pushed herself up onto her knees and lightly flicked the tip of her tongue over half-hooded nerves.

"You are so good at that," Maeve encouraged breathily, her eyelids falling to half-mast as Joss continued to lap lightly between her legs.

"I'm glad you think so," Joss murmured, the words muffled by soft folds.

She used the very tip of her tongue to coax Maeve's clit from hiding, and smiled as she felt it swell and harden against her tongue. She nuzzled closer, teasing the sensitive bud with broad licks, slow swirls, and light, fluttering flicks, breathing deep the sweet, heady scent of Maeve's arousal. She stroked her hands along the back of Maeve's thighs as she made love to her with lips and teeth and tongue, touching, tasting, teasing, loving the way Maeve's hips rolled against her mouth, searching for more, seeking the touch she so desperately needed.

"Joss," Maeve groaned, her voice rough with need. "Please…"

Joss rubbed her cheek against a silky thigh as she looked up at Maeve through the valley between her breasts. "What do you want, sweetie?"

"You."

"Like this?" Joss teased Maeve's clit with the tip of her tongue.

Maeve licked her lips and shook her head. "Drawer."

The single word was all the instruction Joss needed, and she sucked Maeve's clit between her lips as she reached for the middle drawer of the nightstand that was to her left. It took her a moment to find the knob that would help her open the drawer, and a shuddering whimper of relief bubbled in her throat when she finally felt smooth, cold metal against her fingertips. She continued to kiss and lick between Maeve's legs as she began blindly rifling through the drawer's contents, pushing aside soft tees that served as both cushion and camouflage as she searched for her desired prize. The entire process would have gone so much faster had she pulled away to look, but she was too focused on savoring the sweetness that coated her tongue to do that.

She huffed in victory when her fingers found what she was looking for, and she smiled at the low, ragged moan that tumbled from Maeve's lips when she pulled the L-shaped length of purple silicone from the drawer.

She continued to tease Maeve's clit with light licks and heavy swirls as she ran the shorter end of the toy between her own legs a couple of times before slowly easing it into place. The feeling of fullness and the sound of Maeve's pleasure made her clench, and she groaned as she buried her face between Maeve's legs with renewed vigor. She grabbed onto Maeve's hips to try to control their rocking as she guided her higher and higher with her lips and teeth and tongue, following the unspoken direction given by the moans raining down on her from above and the firm hand tangled in her hair.

Joss smiled when Maeve's hips stilled and she cried out in pleasure, and once the hand in her hair loosened, she began kissing her way up the blonde's body. Maeve's nipples, so tight, pink, and delicious were too exquisite to pass up, and she took her time bathing each with hard licks and forceful sucks before eventually sweeping higher to claim Maeve's lips in a deep, searing kiss. She tangled her right hand in thick blond hair as she pressed their bodies together, pinning the dildo between them, and began rolling her hips in a slow grind, hips and tongues settling into a complementary rhythm that drove their shared anticipation higher with every thrust.

Had Joss' shoulder been fully healed, she would have grabbed Maeve by the ass and lifted her up onto the bed, but the same goal was accomplished with a hand on her hip and a huskily whispered, "Up."

Maeve bit her lip as she slid up onto the edge of the mattress, her feet gliding up Joss' legs as she hooked her knees around Joss' hips to pull her up to the side of the bed. She wrapped her left hand around the back of Joss' neck as she reached between them with her right, nimble fingers tickling soft curls before dipping lower, teasing Joss' inner thigh and then sliding higher, curling around the firm length that was going to bring them both so much pleasure.

"Fuck," Joss rasped when Maeve gave the cock a firm tug.

Maeve grinned wolfishly and nodded as she tugged again.

Joss shuffled closer, allowing Maeve to lead her where she wanted her, but resisted that final pull that would have guided her inside. "I want you just like this," she whispered, rocking her hips lightly forward. Her injured shoulder made it impossible for her to have Maeve in a more traditional missionary position, but here, with Maeve sitting in front of her, she could at least look her in the eyes and kiss her lips while she brought her to the heights of pleasure.

Maeve nodded and looped her arms around Joss' neck, holding herself up as she rubbed herself against the head of Joss' cock. "Please…"

The unabashed need in that single syllable made Joss' stomach clench. She swallowed back a moan as she dropped her hands to

Maeve's waist, holding her still as she canted her hips forward, thrusting shallowly at first, coating the tip with the copious amounts of arousal pooled between soft folds before pushing further, inch by inch until she was buried inside her.

"Mmm, yes," Maeve groaned, her eyelids fluttering as Joss ground their hips together.

Joss smiled and flicked her tongue over Maeve's parted lips. "Good?"

"So good." Maeve kissed her firmly. "God, I want you."

"You have me." Joss rolled her hips back before driving herself forward again, her grip on Maeve's hips tightening as she finished the thrust with another slow grind, the press of warm, slick silicone against her clit sending delicious sparks shooting through her body. She kissed Maeve as she rolled her hips back, and smiled at soft gasp that tumbled from Maeve's lips when she pushed inside again.

She began pumping into Maeve in a deliberate rhythm, gradually increasing the tempo of her thrusts as she basked in the feeling of Maeve's body around and against her own. Soft gasps punctuated quick thrusts, while long, drawn out moans marked slow, heavy grinds, fingers digging into sweat-slicked skin as chests arched and bodies rolled as one, back and forth in a toe-curling dance of pleasure.

Joss grit her teeth as she felt herself begin to peak, and pressed her forehead against Maeve's. "God…"

Maeve groaned and arched into Joss, her arms tightening around the brunette's neck as Joss' long thrusts became shorter, faster. She stared unblinkingly into Joss' eyes as she rocked against her, mouth open, breath coming hard and fast and ragged as she rode the wave of ecstasy building inside her. "Come with me," she demanded in a husky whisper.

Joss moaned and squeezed her eyes shut, trying to hold her climax at bay so she could do just that.

"Look at me, Joss."

Fuck. Joss blew out a rough breath as she forced herself to comply, and she gasped as she watched ecstasy explode in Maeve's eyes, dark and fathomless, flashing with the brightness of a thousand stars, begging for her to give in, to feel, to fall. Maeve squeezed her tight, pulling her deeper, strong muscles clenching and unclenching to the heavy beat of Joss' pounding heart. It was all too powerful to resist any longer, and Joss captured Maeve's lips in a desperate kiss as she drove herself forward one last time, burying herself to the hilt as the universe tilted and she fell, tumbling into ecstasy, her broken cries of pleasure muffled by the supple softness of Maeve's lips.

They stayed pressed tightly together until long after the last aftershock of pleasure faded, trading soft kisses, basking in the feeling of closeness that surrounded them. Joss expected the warmth of happiness flooding her body to ease like it eventually always did, but it remained as strong as ever, tethering her to the beautiful woman she held in her arms, and she smiled against her lips as she closed her eyes and breathed Maeve in, hoping that if she did it enough that she would never lose this feeling.

Maeve shifted in front of her, and Joss complied with the unspoken request, canting her hips back as Maeve's hands cradled her face, holding her close as she kissed her with such aching tenderness that Joss' hand shook with the emotion swelling inside her as she tugged slick silicone from between her legs and let it fall to the floor.

She followed Maeve up onto the bed, mindful of not putting too much weight on her injured shoulder as she moved. The fluffy down duvet was as soft as a cloud when Maeve urged her with a kiss onto her back. She sighed as she settled into it, her legs falling open to welcome the toned thigh that slipped between them as Maeve hovered over her, the look in her eyes as tender as the lips that pressed against her own. Joss held Maeve to her as they came together once more, hips rolling, rubbing sensitive skin against firm muscle, breaths crashing lightly together between parted lips, lust-blown eyes full of affection locked in awestruck wonder as their separated universes aligned, seamlessly merging into one. It was as irrevocable as it was absolute, and Joss smoothed her fingers through Maeve's hair as she debated putting everything she was feeling into words—worried that it was too soon to give voice to such powerful emotions.

"I love you," Maeve whispered.

Joss smiled, her heart fluttering with joy that she was not in this alone, and kissed Maeve softly. "I love you, too."

Thirty-Three

Scott handed Joss a bottle of beer. "Here's to surviving another season."

"I'll drink to that." Joss nodded and tapped the neck of her bottle against Scott's.

Somehow, without her really noticing, July had turned to August, and next thing she knew, it was the Tuesday after Labor Day weekend—the official end of the summer high season, and the beginning of the fall shoulder season. It had ended up to be quite a good summer for her and Atramentum, with the store making more than enough to clear overhead costs for the next few months until the winter high season hit while still leaving a nice chunk in the bank, but her body and mind very much appreciated being able to roll into town around eleven each morning and being home by six each night.

Especially since "home" had become Maeve's sprawling mountain retreat. It had been a gradual, organic change where Joss just slowly stopped taking clothes to-and-from the cottage after spending the night—instead just adding to her collection that was spreading along the left side of Maeve's spacious walk-in closet. There had been no discussion about the change in her residence, no formal "will you move in with me" proposal, just a shirt hanging in the closet that was gradually joined by the rest of Joss' clothes until the wardrobes at the cottage were bare.

"Oh, and Maeve wanted me to tell you that dinner would be done in five," Scott said.

"Okay." Joss nodded and slapped the cup of the ChuckIt over the ball George had just dropped at her feet and winged it toward the lake. George was dragging as she chased the ball, and Joss was pretty sure that the Dane would most likely trot right past her and into the house with it so she could not take it from her and throw it again.

Mission accomplished. Joss gave herself a mental pat on the back. "Okay. Pretty sure George is ready to crash, anyway."

"Is this your job every night when you come home?" Scott chuckled.

"Yep. Every morning, too." Maeve had started working on her next book not long after final edits had been finished and approved on her last, and as soon as Joss' shoulder healed enough for her to run comfortably, she had started taking George with her on her morning excursion around the lake so that the energetic dog would sleep during the day and let Maeve work in peace. Making sure George was good and tired at night provided a completely different set of benefits, and Joss smiled as memories from the night before—a soft silk scarf wrapped around her wrists, holding her in place as even softer hair trailed over her stomach, following the path blazed by Maeve's lips and teeth and tongue—flashed across her mind. She cleared her throat and bit her lip, grateful for the shadows that surrounded them and hid the blush she could feel burning her cheeks.

"You sure you don't want me to work tomorrow night?" Scott asked, thankfully not picking up on her discomfort.

"Nah. I got it." Saturday was the only day of the week during the shoulder season when the store was open late—though the eight o'clock closing was still far earlier than during the high season. "Maeve has something she needs to go to in Vail tomorrow evening anyway, so you may as well enjoy the extra time with your wife. I'm sure Michelle is happy you'll be around more."

"Fuck. That's one way to put it. You should see the size of my Honey-Do list," Scott groaned.

"Ah, so that's why you want to work." Joss smirked as she watched George trot right past them without making eye contact.

"Exactly." Scott nodded. "Come on, help a guy out."

Joss shook her head. "I would love to, man, but Michelle knows that we're alternating weekends at the store. Never mind the fact Maeve and I are planning on taking George out to the Bells to go hiking next Saturday and I'm not going to screw that up."

"Sounds like fun, but I swear I saw you grimacing when you picked up that box this afternoon. I don't want you hurting your shoulder again."

Joss laughed. "Nice try. But no." She smiled around the mouth of her beer as she took a long swig. "You need to take care of your shit at home so your wife doesn't come after me about it. Now, come on." She tilted her head at the house. "Let's go back. I'm starving."

"Yeah. Whatcha making for dinner?"

Joss shrugged. "Chicken, steak, the usual. Did Michelle bring her salad?"

"Of course."

"Cool. Is everybody here?"

"Pretty sure. It's just us, the Greens, the Herolds, and Lennox—right?"

"Yeah. Did Paul bring anyone? I know Maeve went out of her way to make sure he knew that he could…"

Scott shook his head. "Nope. Michelle is trying to set him up with a science teacher from her school, but he's so damn shy that it's slow-going."

"Yeah," Joss murmured. "What if we all met up at O'Malley's one night for beer and pool and she just invited her to meet us there? Then it's not a date-date, but they can at least meet up."

Scott nodded. "That could work. Lemme talk to Michelle, and we'll figure out a day. Can we count you two in?"

"Of course."

"Sweet."

"PERRAULT!"

Joss laughed and waved at the Herolds and Greens, who were relaxing in around the large patio table. "Hey, guys," she greeted as she skipped up the stairs. She waggled her eyebrows at Wesley as she leaned down to kiss Kate's cheek. "How you feelin', momma?"

Kate laughed and rubbed her stomach, which was still relatively flat considering she had just entered her second trimester. "Tired."

"Can I get you another glass of water?" Joss offered.

Kate nodded. "That would be wonderful, thank you."

"I aim to please," Joss quipped with a grin.

"What about us?" Wesley whined.

"What about you?" Joss sassed. She laughed at their looks of mock disbelief and tipped her head in a small bow. "Fine. Is there anything I can get you gentlemen?"

"Nah, we're good," Brock answered for the group. He kicked a chair out and added, "Sit. Hang out. We haven't seen you in forever."

"I will in a minute," Joss promised. "I just need to go get Kate's drink and check-in with the boss real quick."

"Lemme know if you need help with anything," Scott said as he pulled the chair out a bit further and made himself comfortable.

Joss nodded her thanks and started for the house. She could just make out George's head propped on the arm of her favorite couch in the great room as she made her way through the open sliding glass door to the kitchen, and she chuckled at the sound of the dog's loud, rumbling snore.

"You did good," Maeve declared when Joss caught her eye.

"Thank you." Joss grinned and made her way over to where Maeve was standing at the island. The long, rectangular counter was covered with the different side dishes everybody had brought to go along with the main course she and Maeve were providing—spinach and artichoke stuffed chicken breasts and steaks that were sitting on a cookie sheet beside the sink, waiting to be grilled. "Hey, guys," she greeted Michelle and Paul as she squeezed past them to refill Kate's glass.

Paul just waved, while Michelle smiled and said, "Hey." She looked at Maeve and added, "If you're sure you don't need help with anything, I'm going to go outside."

"I'm sure." Maeve waved her along. "Go enjoy yourself. We'll be out in a minute to start cooking. I just want to give the barbecue a bit longer to warm up."

"Can you take this back to Kate?" Joss asked, holding the glass of water out to Paul.

"Of course," he agreed affably, smiling as he followed Michelle out the door.

"Thanks." Joss turned to Maeve with a frown. "I turned the barbecue on when I took George out like half an hour ago. Is something wrong with it?"

"Nothing's wrong with it," Maeve said, smiling as she wrapped her arms around Joss' neck. "I just wanted a minute alone with you."

"Oh." Joss reached for Maeve's hips and pulled her closer so she could claim her in lips in a sweet kiss. "Well…I definitely won't argue with that."

"I had a feeling you wouldn't." Maeve kissed Joss again. "George barely made it onto the couch, she was so beat."

"Good." Joss took a deep breath as she nuzzled Maeve's cheek. "Because I have plans for you later that I don't want her interrupting."

Maeve hummed and turned her head to the side as Joss kissed her ear. "What kind of plans?"

"The kind of plans that make me happy I don't have to go into work until noon," Joss whispered huskily against her ear. She chuckled at the shudder she felt ripple through Maeve and nipped at her earlobe. "Mmm, exactly."

"You two are so cute it's gross," Brock declared, his booming baritone tinged with laughter. "Christ, knock it off already. You're setting a bad precedent for us old married folks."

Joss rolled her eyes. "Yeah right. I saw your hand on Andrew's thigh out there."

Brock bowed his head in defeat. "Touché, Perrault. Maeve, the natives out there are getting restless—would you like me to start grilling up all this food?"

"Sure. That would be great." Maeve nodded.

Brock picked up the sheet pan and gave them a small bow. "I shall take care of this, feel free to carry on, ladies."

Joss grinned. "Thanks, man. Appreciate it."

"I'm not doing it for you," Brock sassed, winking at Maeve. "I'm doing it for your girl there. But yeah. You're welcome, too, I guess."

Maeve laughed. "Thanks."

"Anytime," Brock promised, chuckling to himself as he turned and headed back out onto the patio.

"He's a good man," Maeve said as she watched him go.

"Yep," Joss agreed.

"Joss…"

Joss looked back at her and a warm, wet shiver rolled down her spine at the mischievous smile tugging at Maeve's lips. "Hmm?"

"Kiss me."

Joss arched a brow and pinned Maeve against the countertop with her hips. "Like this?" she asked as she lifted her hands, lightly dragging the backs of her fingers along the line of Maeve's jaw.

"Yes…"

"Okay," Joss breathed. A familiar flutter settled in her chest as she captured Maeve's lips in a slow, deep kiss that had them both breathing hard by the time it reached its inevitable end. She hummed softly as she dropped a tender kiss to the tip of Maeve's nose. "I love you."

Maeve licked her lips before stealing one last lingering kiss that left Joss completely weak in the knees. "I love you." A shrill wolf-whistle split the air, and she laughed. "I believe our time alone is up for now."

Joss flipped their audience off over her shoulder and kissed Maeve again, sucking on her bottom lip before coaxing her mouth open to deepen the kiss, swirling her tongue around Maeve's as she began rocking against her. She groaned when Maeve's legs parted just enough for her to slip a thigh between them, and rolled her hips in a slow, teasing grind a couple times before she forced herself to pull away, silently cursing the fact that they were not alone. "Okay. Fine. Now I'm done," she declared roughly.

Maeve laughed and shook her head. "I'm going to get you back later for that one."

"I'm counting on it." Joss grinned and slapped Maeve's ass as she took a step back, putting some much-needed space between them so she did not succumb to her desire to strip Maeve down and have her way with her right there in the kitchen. Although, once they were alone... She cleared her throat softly and shook her head. "Oh, and I told Scott that we'd be in for setting Paul up with a teacher from Michelle's school. We were thinking an 'accidental'"—she framed the word in air quotes—"meeting at O'Malley's one night."

"That could work. Michelle brought her up, but Paul just blushed and made up some excuse about being busy at school." Maeve paused and looked out the back door to make sure she could not be overheard before she asked in a low whisper, "He is into women, right?"

"My gaydar is for shit," Joss said, rolling her eyes at the way Maeve chuckled and nodded in a *yeah tell me about it* kind of way, "but I'm pretty sure. Scott said Lennox had a pretty serious girlfriend for a few years a while back, but she ended up taking a job in Orlando or something."

"Well, if it's just everybody hanging out, I guess there's no real pressure for anything to happen," Maeve said. "Besides, it'd be fun to actually go out and do stuff together now that you're not working yourself to death."

Fuck. Joss' stomach clenched. She thought she had been managing her time between Maeve and the store well, but maybe she was wrong. "I'm sorry. I didn't..."

Maeve cut her off with a kiss. "I was just kidding, babe. I know that your hours at the store will be insane during the busy seasons, and I'm fine with that."

"I don't want you to feel like I'm ignoring you. If you do..."

"I don't." Maeve smiled and shook her head. "And if I ever do, I will tell you. Okay? I promise."

Even though everything about Maeve's tone and expression told her that she was serious, Joss still asked hesitantly, "You're sure?"

"Positive." Maeve kissed her softly. "Besides, after these next few months, I'll probably be chomping at the bit for you to go back to work," she teased.

"Oh really?" Joss arched a brow and dug her fingers into Maeve's sides.

"Hey!" Maeve laughed and danced away from Joss's wiggling fingers. "No tickling."

Joss grinned. "But I like when you writhe against me."

Maeve stopped and pointed a warning finger at her. "You're insane. We have company."

"They have food and drinks, they won't miss us."

"STOP PLAYING TONSIL HOCKEY WITH MAEVE AND GET YO ASS OUT HERE, PERRAULT!" Brock bellowed.

Joss laughed and shook her head. "YEAH, YEAH, WHATEVER!" she yelled over her shoulder at the patio.

Maeve chuckled and picked up her glass of wine. "Come on, Joss. Your public awaits."

"My public," Joss scoffed. "They all like you better."

"Well, come on," Maeve teased, "can you blame them?"

Joss smiled and dropped a quick kiss to Maeve's lips. "No. Not at all."

Thirty-Four

"Goddamn it," Scott swore, shaking his head as he dropped his phone in disgust onto the front counter at Atramentum. Business was slow because it was nearing the end of the shoulder season, and they were both taking advantage of the lull in activity to do nothing of actual importance. "People who trap their town hall are assholes."

Joss chuckled at his outburst but did not look up from the Sunday New York Times crossword puzzle she was in the middle of trying to complete. Maeve usually stole the puzzle before she could get her hands on it, but because Maeve was in Cincinnati for the convention she had booked the month before, Joss figured she would give the puzzle a shot.

She had half the puzzle filled in and a total of four holes torn through the flimsy paper from repeatedly erasing incorrect answers, but it was the perfect thing to distract her from the fact that she had no work to do at the store and there were still several hours left for her to kill until she would be able to talk to Maeve again. Maeve's agent had put her on every panel he possibly could and filled the time between panels with book signings on the convention floor, which meant that the only time she had to herself was before the doors opened or after her final appearance of the day.

"Seriously," Scott continued his rant as he picked his phone back up and began searching for a new base to attack. "Such a dick move."

"You take that game way too seriously." Joss tossed the puzzle onto the counter and sighed. She was never going to finish the stupid thing. How Maeve did it every week without fail—and in pen, no less—was beyond her.

"Whatever," Scott grumbled as he squinted at his screen, assessing the base the game had pulled up for him to attack.

Joss rolled her eyes, and was about to respond with a crack about his being a total geek, when her phone started dancing across the counter, the vibration matching the beat of Maeve's ringtone. She frowned as she looked at the phone—it was the middle of the afternoon, Maeve should not be calling her right now—and reached for it with a growing feeling of trepidation. "Hey, you. Everything okay?"

"Fine. I'm just taking a break from signing for a few minutes and thought I'd call to say hi. How's my girl?"

Joss blew out a soft sigh of relief and nodded to herself, her pulse slowing to a more regular tempo now that she knew everything was okay. "I'd be doing better if you were here, but, you know..."

Maeve laughed. *"I was talking about George."*

"Oh." Joss made a small sound of playful disappointment as she got to her feet and wandered into the stacks for privacy. "Well, she's perfect, as usual. She's sleeping on the rug in front of the fire with Willy Shakes and Dickens at the moment."

"Wow. Dickens?"

"I know. It's weird, but he's actually been following her and Willy around a lot the last few days. Maybe he's mellowing in his old age or something."

"Maybe," Maeve agreed with a soft laugh. She sighed and added, *"Is it bad that I wish I were there right now instead of here working?"*

"Not at all. I'd rather have you here with me, too. George is good company, but she's not you."

"Charmer."

Joss smiled. "Just for you, beautiful."

"Good."

Joss laughed. "How's the con going today?"

"It's the last day, so things here are beyond crazy. It's fun though. There's something that's just really great about seeing people so genuinely excited about stuff."

"I'll bet. Any good cosplayers?"

"There's a Deadpool going around who's pretty awesome. He was chasing a Superman around with a bouquet of fake roses earlier. Oh, and I actually had two women dressed as Faith and Greta come by my table earlier with some fan art and books for me to sign."

"You had people dressed as your characters come see you?" Joss repeated in surprise. "That's awesome!"

Maeve chuckled, sounding both pleased and a little embarrassed, and Joss could just picture the faint blush that was no doubt creeping over her cheeks at that very moment. *"It was very cool. They gave me a picture one of them drew—I think it was the one dressed as Greta—you'll really like it."*

"I will, huh? Why?"

"Because you have a thing for pretty ladies kissing each other," Maeve replied in a playful whisper.

Joss laughed. "That's true. But I mostly have a thing for me kissing you…"

"And I very much appreciate that."

Joss nodded and sighed. "I can't wait for you to get home."

"Me neither. Anything exciting happening there?"

"Not really," Joss answered. She laughed when she realized where she was in the store, and shook her head as she remembered what had happened in this very spot not even two hours earlier. "But, you'll never guess what happened here"—she kicked the bookshelf in front of her—"this afternoon…"

"It snowed?"

"No, but that would be cool. I got to play disapproving adult and break up a couple of kids who were getting all hot-and-heavy in the stacks."

"Please tell me you didn't embarrass the hell out of them."

"Oh, I totally did. I even sicced George on them. It was awesome."

"You're awful," Maeve chuckled.

"What? If I can't make out with my girlfriend, then why should some preppy teenager get to get his mack on in my store?"

"Because all book geeks have a secret fantasy about doing it in a library?"

"This isn't a library," Joss pointed out. She smiled as Maeve's words sunk in and added, "And, really? All book geeks?"

"All book geeks," Maeve confirmed in a low, suggestive purr.

Joss' mouth went dry. "And, um, have you ever"—she cleared her throat—"fulfilled that fantasy?"

Maeve laughed. *"Not yet."*

"Fuck…"

Maeve laughed harder. *"Well, that's the idea…"*

"You are so mean." Joss ran a hand through her hair and groaned.

"I'm sorry," Maeve apologized, though the apology carried no weight because she was still laughing softly. *"It was just too easy, though."*

"Evil."

"But in a good way, right?"

"That depends. When are you coming home?"

"Soon," Maeve promised.

"Good."

"I know," Maeve sighed. *"I'll be right there,"* she said, her voice somewhat muffled. *"Just let me finish this up."*

"You need to go?"

"Yeah. The panel for Kick-Ass Female Leads is up next."

"Well, you go kick some ass then, beautiful, and I'll talk to you later."

"Okay." Maeve sighed. *"I love you."*

"Love you too," Joss murmured. "I'll see you soon."

"Give George a kiss for me."

"I will."

"And save a few for me."

"I'll save you all the really good ones."

"I can't wait." Maeve sighed again. *"I'll call later."*

"I'll be here," Joss promised. When the line went dead, she pocketed the phone and meandered back toward the front of the store. She had missed Maeve the last time the author had gone on a business trip, but that sense of longing was magnified now, leaving her feeling like a piece of herself was missing. A five-foot-six inch, beautiful blonde piece of her heart was too far away for her liking, and she blew out a frustrated breath as she cleared the end of the stacks and wandered back into the main front area of the store. Scott was where she had left him at the counter, hunched over his phone, thumbs tapping quickly against the screen as he mumbled incoherently to himself, and George, Willy Shakes, and Dickens were still snuggled together on the rug in front of the fire. It was all so much more than she had hoped to find when she moved back to Sky, but with Maeve missing from the picture, no matter how happy all this made her, it was still not enough.

"What's wrong?" Scott asked without looking up from his phone.

"Nothing." Joss shook her head.

"You sound sad."

Joss rolled her eyes. "I didn't even say anything."

"Your breathing was depressed. Don't argue with me, I'm a writer. I know these things."

"And how's that writing thing going for you, Mr. Author?" Joss teased.

"Good." Scott looked up and grinned. "My agent sold my latest collection of short stories to Macmillan."

"Wait. What?" Joss said, her eyes widening in surprise. "When? Why didn't you tell me?"

"Book. Sold," Scott enunciated slowly. He laughed and ducked out of the way of the punch Joss threw at his shoulder. "Friday. And I didn't work yesterday, remember?"

"Technically, you're not working now?"

"True, but I'm hiding from my responsibilities at home while simultaneously keeping you from going stir crazy because Maevey-wavey is out of town."

"Shut up."

Scott laughed. "Whatever. But yeah." He nodded, his smile absolutely untamable. "Macmillan. Can you believe it?"

"That's so cool, man," Joss said, shaking her head. His other collections had gone through small publishers and done well for the market, but selling a manuscript to a powerhouse publisher like Macmillan was huge. "You've hit the big time."

"Or it's gonna hit me," he said, a sliver of insecurity creeping into his tone.

"What? You're gonna do great. Maeve is going to flip her shit when I tell her." Joss grinned. "We need to celebrate. Call your wife," she told him as she pulled out her own phone, "and tell her we're going out for beer and billiards later. Have her call that friend of hers for Lennox, and we'll kill two birds with one stone. I'll round up the rest of the crew. You, sir, are going to get totally shitfaced tonight."

"You're crazy."

Joss laughed and nodded as she unlocked her phone. "You say that like it's a bad thing."

Thirty-Five

Joss smiled as she stepped out of the coffee shop and into the blustery fall afternoon. After years of having only fire, flood, earthquake, and drought as seasons, being surrounded by colorful leaves and a nip in the air was an absolutely decadent experience, and she took her time walking back to Atramentum to just soak it all in.

"God, I've missed this," she said to herself as she pulled the door to the bookstore open and stepped inside.

"Missed what?" Scott asked, looking up from his phone. "Not being hungover?"

"You were the only one hungover yesterday." Joss smirked as she set the cardboard tray she was carrying down onto the counter and handed him his drink. "I meant that it's nice to have actual seasons."

He nodded and sipped at his mocha "Yeah. I don't know how you managed in LA. I couldn't give this up."

"It's one of those things you notice at first, but by the second year of wearing shorts and flip-flops on Christmas Day, you just kinda stop paying attention to it all," Joss said with a shrug. "Anybody come in while I was gone?"

He nodded again. "Just one. She's in the stacks." He took another sip of his coffee and sighed. "Look, would you mind if I bailed? We've been dead, and I just—"

"Scott," Joss interrupted. "Go. It's fine. Get out of here." She ran a hand through her hair and checked her watch. They had not had a single customer all day, and she was planning on calling it an early night too so that she could make sure she was at the house when Maeve got back from her trip.

"You're sure?" Scott asked as he got to his feet, right hand reaching into the front pocket of his jeans for his car keys.

"Yeah. There's no reason for us both to suffer. Hell, I'm half-thinking I won't even bother to open tomorrow."

Scott laughed and waggled his eyebrows. "Big plans?"

"None that I'm telling you about," Joss shot back with a smirk. She sipped at her coffee and sighed. "I'll figure it out."

"You want me to cover the store?"

Joss shook her head. "Nah. It's fine. If I get in, I get in. Otherwise, whatever. It's not like we've been doing much anyway."

"I dunno, that game of gin we played this morning got pretty cutthroat."

Joss chuckled and nodded. "Exactly." She took a deep breath and let it go slowly. "Get out of here. Go surprise your wife with dinner or something nice. I'll see you Friday."

"Thanks." He shouldered his backpack and grinned. "Have a good night."

"I plan on it," Joss assured him. They both laughed, and Joss sipped at her drink as she watched him leave.

The store was silent in his absence, and she shook her head as she locked the front door after him and flipped the sign. There was no reason to stay open after the customer in the back left, and this way nobody else would come wandering in to draw her afternoon here out any longer.

Her thoughts drifted to Maeve as she stood by the front counter, sipping at her coffee, and she idly wondered where she was at that moment. It had been a long week of evening phone calls and bursts of text-messages, and while George had been her usual charming self, Joss was really looking forward to having her girlfriend back. She lingered near the register, replaying their various conversations from the last few nights in her head until her drink was gone, and then tossed the cup on the trash before heading into the stacks. She still had a couple hours until Maeve was supposed to get home, but she was going stir-crazy sitting in the store waiting, and if she could speed this customer along, she could get out of here for the day. Every aisle she passed was empty except for the very last one near the office, where she found a woman in a short black skirt and an ivory silk blouse that had an enticing third button open at the neck. A black pea coat was draped over the purse she had set on the floor by her feet, leaving her hands free to browse, and Joss' heart did an ecstatic flip-flop as what she was seeing truly sank in.

Maeve was home early.

It was dramatic and entirely unnecessary, but that did not stop Joss from giddily tiptoeing down the row toward her. She grinned, just resisting the urge to laugh as she stopped behind Maeve, and she held her breath as she reached out to wrap her arms around Maeve's waist. Joss chuckled when Maeve jumped in surprise, and pressed a gentle kiss to her cheek. "Can I help you find something?"

"You know, I think I just found what I was looking for," Maeve replied with a smile as she turned her head to press their lips together. "I missed you."

Joss hummed as she cradled Maeve against her. She knew she had missed her, but she had not realized exactly how much until this very moment. "Me too." She kissed Maeve again, slowly, sweetly, lingering in the caress before doing it again and again and again until her head spun and her heart felt like it was about to burst with happiness. She closed her eyes and took a deep breath as she buried her face in the crook of Maeve's neck, savoring the warmth of Maeve's skin against her lips and the scent of her perfume. "So, so much."

Maeve moaned as she leaned her head to the side, giving Joss more skin to worship. "Joss…"

"Maeve," Joss murmured, tightening her arms around Maeve's waist as she laid a string of slow, wet kisses down Maeve's throat. The feeling of Maeve's hips rolling back against her as she nipped at her pulse point brought one particular conversation of theirs from the past week to mind, and Joss' pulse spiked as she slowly, purposefully let her hands slide from Maeve's waist down to the top of her thighs.

The door was locked, and they were alone, she figured, so why not?

Joss stroked her fingers back and forth along the edge of Maeve's skirt, keeping her touch light as she tested the waters. This was not how she had planned for their reunion to happen, her plans had ran more along the line of a romantic dinner before retiring to the luxurious confines of their bedroom, but the idea of having Maeve here and now was too much to resist. "How serious were you the other day?" she asked, flattening her palms against Maeve's thighs and holding her close as she thrust her hips forward.

Maeve let out a shaky breath as her head fell back onto Joss' shoulder. She braced her right hand on the shelf in front of her as her hips rocked back to meet Joss' next thrust. The way her body was responding was proof enough she knew precisely what Joss was talking about, but she smiled as she whispered coyly, "About what?"

"About word nerds all having a fantasy about doing it in a bookstore."

"I believe I said a library."

Joss ran the flats of her hands heavily over Maeve's thighs, letting her thumbs dip between her legs as much as the tight skirt allowed. She smiled at the sound of Maeve's breath catching, and lingered there for a moment before moving higher. "Is that really so much different than a bookstore?"

"Not really," Maeve conceded when Joss' fingers began tracing back and forth along the curve of her breasts.

"The door is locked, and it's just us in here," Joss murmured against Maeve's ear, understanding where Maeve's hesitation was coming from. It was one thing to fantasize about something like this, but neither of them could afford the backlash that would come from being caught. "We can stay or we can go home, sweetie. No pressure. I just thought…"

Maeve groaned, her body melting back into Joss as she nodded. "Yes."

"You're sure?" Joss cupped Maeve's breasts and stroked her thumbs over her straining nipples. When Maeve turned her head to kiss her hungrily in response, Joss could not help but let out a soft groan of her own. She massaged Maeve's breasts, rolling and pinching her nipples as they kissed, teasing them to hard, tight points. She nipped at Maeve's lower lip as the need for more drove her hands lower, and she traced the plump, captured flesh with her tongue as her thumb uncovered the small zipper at Maeve's hip.

The quiet whimper that tumbled from Maeve's lips as she gave it a tug made Joss' knees weak, and she swallowed hard as she began pulling it slowly downward. Their breaths tumbled together in ragged waves in the small space between their lips as Joss worked the zipper lower and lower, the air around them rippling with anticipation as the skirt hugging Maeve's hips became looser and looser.

"You are so beautiful," Joss whispered as she gave the skirt a push and sent it cascading to the floor. Her stomach clenched with desire as she drank in the view afforded her once the garment was kicked aside, and she licked her lips as she traced the black satin garter straps that stretched along the backs of Maeve's thighs. She lifted the tail of Maeve's shirt to get the full view, and her mouth went dry as she drank in the vision before her. Toned thighs, lace-topped stockings, garters drawing dark lines across unobstructed alabaster skin that was left on tantalizing display thanks to the black lace thong Maeve was wearing. "Fuck."

Maeve chuckled throatily, clearly pleased with Joss' reaction. "You like?"

Joss stroked her palms over the swell of Maeve's ass. "That's one way to put it," she whispered huskily, squeezing the firm cheeks under her hands hard enough to lift Maeve up onto her toes.

"Good. I was hoping you would."

"I do." Joss pressed a wet kiss to Maeve's ear and nipped at the lobe as she relaxed her grip. "Very, very much," she elaborated as she began unclipping the garters from Maeve's stockings. She let her breath fall in hot, heavy waves against Maeve's ear as she moved from clip to clip, and hummed softly when the final one released. "So beautiful," she murmured as she hooked her thumbs under the waistband of Maeve's thong. She lowered herself to her knees as she worked the scrap of lingerie lower, covering the delicate skin of Maeve's behind with kisses as helped her out of the panties.

"Fuck," Maeve groaned, her head falling back in pleasure as her free hand reached out to join her other on the shelf in front of her for support.

Joss stroked the front of Maeve's thighs as she nipped at a cheek and then soothed the pink mark with the flat of her tongue.

Maeve rocked her hips back needfully. "God, Joss."

Joss licked her lips as the scent of Maeve's arousal hit her, and she took a deep, steadying breath as she reached up and gave the small of Maeve's back a gentle push. "Bend over." It was a plea more than a command, but she was not above begging when she really wanted something—and in that moment, there was nothing she wanted more than to take Maeve into her mouth and make her cry out with pleasure.

A low, breathy whimper escaped her when Maeve obeyed, her grip on the shelves tightening as her head dropped between her shoulders. Joss moved with her, walking backward on her knees as Maeve settled into a comfortable position, her hips lifting beseechingly, showing Joss exactly how aroused she already was.

"So beautiful," Joss murmured as she leaned forward, teasing swollen lips apart with the tip of her tongue before flicking lightly over Maeve's clit. Maeve cried out softly at the gentle touch, her back bending further, opening herself up even more to Joss' touch, and Joss moaned as she grabbed onto Maeve's thighs and dove in.

Maeve's quads trembled beneath her hands as she licked and sucked everywhere she could reach, more concerned with bringing Maeve to release as quickly as possible than teasing. The task was made more difficult by the incessant way Maeve's hips were rolling against her mouth, but Joss would not have wanted it any other way. She loved it when Maeve lost control like this, loved the soft cries and rumbling moans that escaped her as she closed her eyes and rode the wave of pleasure building inside her. Maeve was art personified, beautiful in every line and curve of her body, the composition of the sounds of her pleasure the most captivating opus ever created, and Joss would gladly worship her for the rest of her life if allowed.

She pressed a hard kiss to Maeve's clit at the thought, and moaned in surprise when the firmer touch sent Maeve tumbling into orgasm. She dug her fingers into Maeve's thighs as she lapped at the sweetness of her release, drawing out her pleasure for as long as possible. When Maeve's trembling eventually eased, Joss pressed a reverent kiss to each of her cheeks and climbed slowly back to her feet, just barely containing the groan of protest her aching knees wanted her to let out.

Joss wrapped her arms around Maeve's waist in a tender embrace as she molded herself against her back, the fly of her jeans pressing against sensitive skin and making Maeve gasp. She smiled and gave a small thrust. "Okay?"

Maeve moaned and nodded, her head lifting as her back straightened, and she sighed contentedly when Joss began lightly stroking the inside of her thighs. "That feels good."

"You feel good." Joss kissed the side of Maeve's throat as she stroked higher, and smiled when Maeve shifted in front of her, widening her stance in a silent plea for more. She dipped a fingertip between soft folds, gathering some of the arousal lingering there before sliding higher to rub small circles over Maeve's clit. She lifted the hem of Maeve's shirt up and out of the way with her free hand, and began thrusting her hips against Maeve's ass in time with each slow circuit.

It did not take long for Maeve to begin rocking against her, and Joss wrapped her left arm around Maeve's waist as she flexed her right wrist and slipped two fingers into slick, clinging heat. They both moaned when her first thrust bottomed out, and Joss raked her teeth over the line of Maeve's jaw as she began thrusting in earnest, long and hard and deep, her hips following suit as if they were responsible for every plunge and retreat. Maeve's knuckles whitened as the sounds of her pleasure increased in volume, and Joss squeezed her eyes shut as she tried to ignore the way each thrust of her hips against Maeve's ass pushed her that much closer to her own climax.

Maeve first, she told herself. *Maeve first*.

Joss' thrusts became frenzied as Maeve's cries became louder and more plaintive as she sought her release, hips rolling, body rocking, back arching as she tried to press as much of herself against Joss as possible. It was raw and rough and primal, the need to take and the need to give driving them together, pushing them harder and faster as ecstasy continued to hover just out of reach until it was finally within their grasp.

Joss buried her face in the hollow between Maeve's shoulder blades as Maeve came undone with a deep, rumbling moan. She thrust deep one last time before stopping, leaving her fingers sheathed in spasming velvet as she held Maeve to her, too spent to offer any other comfort. Her jeans clung uncomfortably to her crotch, soaked through from her arousal that she had so far ignored. However, with Maeve spent and lax in her arms, she could no longer ignore the way her clit was pulsing with every beat of her heart, and she groaned as she ground herself weakly against Maeve's ass.

It won't take much. Just a little...

Maeve seemed to understand because she reached down and pulled Joss' fingers from her and spun in her arms. Her gaze was smoldering as she took the fingers into her mouth and sucked them clean, the look and the touch so erotic that Joss felt herself begin to peak.

"Please," Joss whispered, wanting it to be Maeve's touch that sent her over the edge.

Maeve smiled and nodded, her hands dropping to the button on Joss' jeans as she leaned in and kissed her.

Maeve's tongue tasted like her arousal, and Joss moaned as her jeans loosened and a slim hand slipped beneath her underwear. She leaned her forehead against Maeve's and grabbed onto her ass for balance as talented fingers brushed over her clit, rubbing and circling twice before easing deep inside her. She bit her lip as she stared into

Maeve's lust-blown eyes, silently pleading for her own release. It only took three thrusts for her to come undone, and she whimpered with relief as she trembled and shook in Maeve's arms.

She fell forward, capturing Maeve's lips in a deep, wet kiss that was equal parts satisfaction and exhaustion, and sighed contentedly when they finally broke apart. "Wow."

"Indeed," Maeve agreed with a chuckle as she pulled her hand from Joss' pants. She nuzzled Joss' cheek affectionately as she looped her arms around her neck, and smiled as she dropped a sweet, chaste kiss to her lips. "That was quite the welcome home."

Joss laughed and nodded, releasing her hold on Maeve's backside and wrapping her arms around her waist in a firm embrace. She took a deep breath and let it go slowly, unbridled contentment warming her soul as Maeve's smiling lips pressed against her neck.

Welcome home, indeed. After years of feeling like she was adrift in the world, she had finally found her home—and it was right here, wrapped in Maeve's arms.

Thirty-Six

Scott grinned and dramatically laid his cards out on the front counter. "Gin, baby. That's three games in a row."

"Fucking cheater," Joss grumbled as she threw her cards down beside the discard pile next to the register.

It was the Friday before Thanksgiving, which meant that the last of the leaf peepers had disappeared weeks ago, ushering in the off-season and leaving Sky and the trails around it to the various two- and four-legged creatures that called the mountains home. The street beyond Atramentum's front windows was as empty as the hotels clustered around the ski resorts, and if Joss had not received a delivery notification email earlier that morning, she would have been at home enjoying the afternoon with Maeve and George instead of sitting in the store.

Willy Shakes did not seem to mind getting two visits from her in a day, however—she spent a couple hours at the store every morning taking care of basic housekeeping tasks and spending time with the cats—and she had to admit that, despite the fact that she would rather be home with Maeve, it was also nice to hang out and shoot the shit with Scott. He had shown up around two to visit with the cats while his wife was at work, and because there was no real work to be done around the store, they had immediately picked up with their usual time-wasting activities—cards and gossip. "Add 'em up, Heitz."

"How do you cheat at gin?" Scott chuckled as he tallied their scores for the hand.

Joss rolled her eyes. "You tell me, Mister Three-in-a-row."

Scott smirked. "Jealousy doesn't become you, Perrault."

"Fuck you."

Scott laughed. "So, how're the big Turkey Day preparations coming along at Casa de Dylan?"

Joss sighed and ran a hand through her hair. Maeve had offered to host Thanksgiving dinner since the Dylans always stayed in Chicago for Christmas so Santa could make his rounds, so Maeve's parents, brothers, and their families were all coming to Colorado for the big feast. She was looking forward to meeting Maeve's family, but she was also feeling completely overwhelmed by the idea of being surrounded by Maeve's family for a week. "They're coming along as well as can be expected, I guess. Maeve's cleaning like a madwoman and freaking out about making sure everything's perfect, and me and George are just trying our best to stay out of her way."

"Sounds familiar," Scott commiserated with a wry smile. He and Michelle were going to be hosting both of their families at their place for a joint holiday celebration, which she figured was probably why he was hiding out at Atramentum with her rather than doing stuff at home. "Why didn't you bring George in with you?"

"She was sleeping and Maeve said she was going to try to get some work done while I was here, so I didn't see a reason to wake her up and bring her along."

"Is everybody from Maeve's family staying at the house with you guys?"

Joss nodded. "Well, her older brother Liam and his family are going to use the cottage since his kids are older and are okay to camp out on the couch for a few days, but her parents, Walker, and his family will be at the house with us."

"You guys have any plans for when they're all here?"

"Honestly, man, at this point I'm just doing what I'm told and not asking too many questions," Joss confessed. "I know they're all big hikers, so we'll probably hit the trails around here if the weather holds. If it doesn't..." She shrugged. "Who knows? Maybe we'll swing over to Target and pick up a Wii U or something to keep the kids occupied."

"Get that new Mario game if you do!" Scott said excitedly. "The one where you can make Super Mario levels. It looks so awesome!"

Joss laughed. "I'll see what I can do."

Scott grinned, clearly excited by the prospect of reliving his childhood in bigger, better graphics. "So, when do they all get in?"

"Her parents get in Monday, Walker and his family will fly in Tuesday, and because Liam's kids are in school, they'll be flying in Wednesday night so that they don't miss class."

"You're gonna have a full house."

Joss nodded. "Yeah. It's going to be weird. George is going to love all the attention, though."

"And you?" Scott asked, his expression growing more serious as he studied her knowingly. "How are you going to do with all the attention?"

Joss blew out a soft breath and shrugged. "I don't know."

Scott sighed and started to say something, but stopped when the bell above the front door rang as it was pushed open by a familiar face in a brown uniform.

"Hey, guys. Busy at work, I see" Ben teased, eying the cards on the counter as he spun his dolly with three small boxes of books toward them.

"You know it," Joss replied, grateful for the distraction his arrival provided.

"You ready for the holidays?" Ben asked as he handed Joss his electronic clipboard.

"As we'll ever be," Scott answered for them both as Joss scribbled her name in the little window. "How about you?"

"Pretty much the same," Ben admitted with a smile. "Where do you want me to put these?"

Joss handed him back his clipboard. "Just leave 'em there. We'll move them later."

"You sure?" Ben double-checked even as he began sliding the boxes from his dolly.

"Yeah," Joss said. "Have a good weekend."

"You too," Ben said, snapping off a small salute as he headed back to his truck that was idling at the curb.

"Are you okay with Maeve's family descending on you guys for the holiday?" Scott repeated as soon as they were alone again.

Joss blew out a soft breath and nodded. "Yeah."

"You need to work a little harder to sell that one, tiger."

"Shut up," Joss chuckled. "It's just a lot, you know? It's been a long-ass time since I've done the big holiday get-together thing."

"Yeah, I know. But you're happy?"

"Yeah." Joss smiled. "I'm happy. Very, very happy."

"Good." He picked up the cards on the counter and began tapping them into a neat stack. "So…should I kick your ass again at cards, or should we shelve those books Ben just dropped off and call it a day?"

Joss checked the time on her phone, and was surprised to see that Maeve had texted her a little over half an hour ago. *Muse is AWOL. Am going to take George on a walk around the lake and see if I can't find the sneaky little bitch. Call when you're on your way home. XO* She smiled and shook her head. If Maeve was not going to be working, there was no reason for her to continue killing time at the store. "The books can wait until this weekend." She set her phone facedown on the counter as she stood and began pulling on her coat. "Let's get out of here."

"What'd Maeve say to make you so eager to get home?" Scott teased, reaching for Joss' phone.

Joss snatched her phone from his grasp and waggled her eyebrows as she slipped it into the chest pocket of her coat. "What makes you think Maeve texted me?"

"Please," Scott scoffed. "You smiled your I'm-so-in-love-with-Maeve-smile and you've got the biggest heart-eyes right now."

Joss chuckled and shook her head. She was busted, but there was no way she was going to cop to it.

He laughed, knowing he was right. "Come on, what'd she say?"

"Wouldn't you like to know."

"I would!"

Joss grinned. "Sucks to be you, then." She spun her keys around her finger. "You coming? I mean, I'm not going to stop you if you want to stay here and shelve those books…"

"Nah, I'm good," Scott said as he jumped to his feet.

"That's what I thought." Joss held the door open for him. "You got tomorrow afternoon?"

Scott nodded. "Yeah. You got Sunday?"

"Yep," Joss confirmed as she locked the door after them. "Though I don't know why we bother," she continued, pocketing her keys as they walked across the street to the lot where their cars were parked. "We at least see a few people while they're out running errands on Saturday. On Sunday everybody's watching football."

"So don't come in Sunday," Scott said, shrugging. "Me and Michelle can come by and check on the cats since we're closer and make sure their food and water is all topped off. She got some new toys for them the other day at the market anyway that I keep forgetting to bring in with me, so she can give them to Willy and Dickens then."

Joss pursed her lips thoughtfully. "Thanks for the offer. If Maeve isn't working, maybe I will just hang out at home instead."

"Good. Lord knows we're going to be back at our insane schedule soon enough, may as well enjoy this time while we have it, you know?" Scott held out his right fist for a bump. "Call me if you need me."

"Ditto, man," Joss confirmed, tapping their knuckles together. "Tell your wife I say hi."

"Will do. Say hi to Maeve and George."

"Of course." Joss nodded and climbed into her car as Scott did the same beside her. She started her car and let it idle to warm up as she pulled her phone from her pocket to call Maeve. She was surprised when the call went to voicemail after a handful of rings, and frowned as she disconnected the call without leaving a message, knowing that Maeve would see the missed call and call her back.

Atramentum

The only time Maeve ever turned off her ringer was when she was working, and Joss sighed as she spotted Willy Shakes watching her from one of Atramentum's front windows. If Maeve had found her Muse, there was no telling when she might emerge from her office, but the idea of shelving books held very little appeal to her at the moment.

"Sorry, bud," Joss apologized to Willy. "Scott will come play with you tomorrow," she continued as if the cat could hear her. And maybe he could, because Willy swished his tail once and jumped down from the window, out of sight.

Joss dropped her phone into the cup holder beside her seat and shifted her Jeep into gear, hoping that the fling Maeve was having with her Muse would be a short one and that she would get her girlfriend back at a halfway decent hour that night.

Thirty-Seven

George had a keen ear for the sound of garage door opening, so when Joss made her way into an otherwise empty mudroom after returning home, she figured Maeve was still out on the walk she had texted about. She checked the time on her phone as she toed off her shoes and kicked them into her cubby, and arched a brow in surprise when she realized that a full hour had passed since Maeve texted her.

Maeve's walks around the lake never took more than forty minutes.

"Maybe her Muse is harder to find than usual," she muttered to herself as she shrugged out of her coat and hung it on a hook above the shoe cubbies. She slipped her phone into her back pocket as she padded through the attached laundry room and made her way to the kitchen for a snack.

The slow cooker Maeve was so fond of was plugged in on the counter beside the stove, filling the house with the delicious scent of simmering tomatoes and spices. Joss lifted the lid on the earthenware pot to see what Maeve was cooking, and her stomach growled when she saw Maeve's homemade chili bubbling away.

"Lucky me," Joss said, smiling as she gave the pot's contents a quick stir. She rinsed the spoon off and left it in the sink, and grabbed an apple from the bowl on the middle of the island to stave off the rumble of hunger in her belly while not spoiling her appetite for later.

She stared out the back windows as she ate, watching the way the fat, gray clouds spread at a snail's pace across the slowly darkening sky. The weatherman had predicted flurries later that evening—the first of the season that might stick—and she hoped he was right. She had always loved watching it snow, there was something so relaxing about the way the flakes of varying heft tumbled gracefully through the air, and she could think of no better place to do so now than on the sofa in front of the fire with Maeve snuggled in her arms.

She pushed off the counter she had been leaning against and wandered closer to the windows, hoping to see something that would hint at them getting not just flurries, but some measurable snow. A small smile tugged at her lips as she imagined building forts and getting into snowball fights with Maeve's nieces and nephews, and she laughed softly to herself as she pictured George rampaging through it all, knocking kids down and snatching snowballs out of the air.

It was almost hard to believe that only a year ago she was living alone in a sparse one-bedroom condo, with no real friends actively involved in her life, working herself to death eighteen hours a day, six days a week. Of course, during the busy seasons her hours at Atramentum were not much better, but the rest of her life was the complete opposite of what she had left behind in Los Angeles.

Her gaze drifted over the naked trees that framed the perimeter of the lake as she chewed, and she had just finished swallowing when her eyes landed on something unusual in the yard. From this distance it was hard to discern what, exactly, she was looking at, and she squinted as she tried to make sense of the small, still shadow on the back lawn.

Did something blow off the patio?

The wind stirred, and the clouds parted just enough to let the sun shine through, and Joss felt like she had been punched soundly in the chest when she realized what she was looking at.

It was not random debris.

God, how she wished it was.

"No."

She dropped the apple she had been eating and ripped the sliding glass door open. She took off through the door at a sprint, leaping from the back patio to the grass beyond. Her socks were instantly soaked by the grass that was still damp from the rain showers that had passed through the night before, but the wet and the cold did not register with her as she ran, heart hammering in her throat, stomach twisting like she was going to be sick at any moment.

What?

How?

She ran faster, unaware of the tears that were streaming down her face as she got close enough to make out the details distance had hidden from her before. Soft hair usually the color of sun-kissed straw was now matted and muddy. A black coat smeared with mud and dirt, jeans dark with what she prayed was just damp and not blood. And beyond that, black fur and a blaze of white stained pink with blood that was just as motionless, just as sickening.

"No. God, no."

Joss dropped to her knees and slid those final few yards across the grass to Maeve's side, her hands hovering above the still form of her lover, wanting to comfort, needing to feel that she was alive, but afraid to touch, terrified to do anything that might make things worse. Her eyes darted over Maeve's body, analyzing, assessing, noting the way her left eye was black and swollen and the way her right arm was bent at an unnatural angle beneath her. Her glasses were laying on the grass beside her, and Joss' hands shook as she picked them up, telling herself Maeve would need them to see when she woke up.

Oh, God, baby, what happened to you?

She slid the glasses into place and carefully brushed Maeve's hair from her forehead. Maeve's skin was cool but with an underlying warmth that told Joss she had not been out here for too long, and Joss shook her head as she trailed her trembling fingers along Maeve's cheek to the hollow beneath her jaw to check for a pulse.

Please let me find it.

"Oh, baby…" Joss murmured as she surveyed Maeve's body as she pressed her fingers against Maeve's carotid artery, trying to figure out what had happened. Her heart skipped a beat when she finally found Maeve's pulse—it was weaker than she would have liked for it to be, but it was there—and she blew out the breath she was unaware she had been holding as her eyes raked over the unusual array of thick, dark hairs that were stuck to the fabric of Maeve's coat.

George shouldn't shedding this time of year…

Joss looked up at George, finally giving the dog her full attention. Whatever happened to the two of them, George seemed to have taken the brunt of it. George was bleeding freely from her side, and Joss had to turn away to keep from being sick when she saw the ragged gash torn across her ribs. It was then that she saw the prints pressed into the wet earth between Maeve and George, and she was unable to keep the apple she had just eaten down as she spun and emptied her stomach on the ground behind her.

Bear.

The tracks came from the lake and disappeared toward the driveway, and it was not hard at all for her to put two-and-two together.

"Oh George," she breathed, wiping her hand across her mouth as she turned back to her brave, loyal friend, who she just knew had done her best to protect Maeve.

George whimpered, and Joss shook her head as she knelt at her side. She took off the sweatshirt she was wearing and pressed it against the dog's side as she pulled her phone from the back pocket of her jeans. She leaned down to press a kiss to George's cheek as she dialed 9-1-1, and despite knowing that she needed to be strong and take care of her girls, it was impossible for her to stem the tears that spilled down her cheeks as the call rang through.

"It'll be okay," she promised George. It had to be okay. They had to be okay. The call was answered on the second ring, and she did not let the woman finish her standard greeting as she shouted, "There's been a bear attack. I need an ambulance at 2 North Star Drive right now."

The energetic clattering of keyboard keys accompanied a terse, *"Can you describe what happened, please?"*

"I just found my girlfriend and our dog in the yard. She's unconscious, the dog is bleeding heavily, and there's a bear print in the grass between them, which I'm assuming means it was a bear that got them. They need help!"

"Ma'am, I am sending an ambulance to you now. However, I am afraid we cannot transport animals."

"You WHAT?" Joss shouted, her voice cracking. "George is bleeding! She needs help!"

"I understand that but, unfortunately it's against regulations for EMTs to transport animals. I can put in a call to animal control, or—"

"My hundred and twenty-five pound Great Dane was attacked by a fucking bear and you won't help her?"

"Like I said, ma'am," the operator said in an annoyingly composed tone, *"I can call animal control and they can transport the animal to the closest emergency clinic, or you can provide your own transportation."*

Joss blew out a frustrated breath and shook her head. She did not have a choice. She could not transport George herself, even if she wanted to. The dog was too big for her to pick up. "Fine. Send them too."

More clattering keys. *"I'm afraid there may be a bit of a delay with animal control, they are on a call dealing with a trapped raccoon at the moment."*

"You have got to be fucking kidding me! They can't leave the damn raccoon and come help?" Joss repeated indignantly. "Fuck it. I'll get her to the stupid clinic."

How she was going to pull that off, however, was the real question.

"I apologize ma'am, but—"

"Your apologies mean shit right now when my dog is bleeding to death on my back lawn," Joss interrupted. "The ambulance is on the way?"

"Yes, ma'am."

"Great. Tell them to drive around the side of the house. They won't be able to miss us. I need to help my dog now." She hung up on the woman and immediately dialed Brock. He was the strongest man she knew, and if anyone could help, it would be him. And he drove a SUV, which would be needed to get George to the vet. He picked up on the third ring, laughter ringing out behind him, and Joss choked out a broken, "Brock."

"Joss. What's wrong?"

"Maeve and George were attacked by a bear and the ambulance won't take George. I need help getting her to a vet."

"Where are you?" She heard frantic snapping, and a hushed, *"Get your shit. We're leaving NOW. Fuck the cheesecake, Joss needs help!"*

"We're in the backyard." Joss glanced over at Maeve, who was still unconscious. She had never felt so torn. Her heart ached for her to hold Maeve, to stroke her hair and watch over her, but she felt compelled to stay by George, who was conscious and staring at her with the saddest eyes, whimpering in pain as blood continued to spread across the sweatshirt Joss had pressed against her side.

"We're on our way. Five minutes, tops. I will run every red light on the way if I have to."

Joss closed her eyes and pressed another kiss to George's cheek. "Thank you. Please hurry."

"Like the devil's riding my ass with a pitchfork," Brock promised before hanging up.

"It'll be okay," Joss promised George, petting her head softly as she watched Maeve, wanting nothing more than for her to wake up and tell her what the hell she was supposed to do because she had no idea what she was doing.

The next five minutes were the longest of Joss' life. The sweatshirt she was holding against George's side had become soaked with blood, and the dog's normally vibrant eyes became dulled as pain and exhaustion threatened to pull her under. Joss continued to soothe her as best she could, murmuring soft words of reassurance, stroking her head, kissing her cheek, trying to keep her awake because she was terrified that if George fell asleep, she would never wake up.

Maeve began to stir just as the sound of sirens finally, finally shattered the otherwise silent mountain air, and Joss sucked in a sharp breath as she watched Maeve's legs shift in discomfort, a low moan spilling from her lips as consciousness brought with it the unfortunate awareness of pain.

"Maeve, sweetie, don't move," Joss called, wanting to rush to her side but afraid to leave George. She forced a tight, strained smiled as the one eye Maeve was able to open found her. "The ambulance is on the way. Just try and stay still, okay?"

"George?" Maeve asked, her voice rough and panicked. She tried to move her broken arm and cried out in pain.

"You've got to stay still, baby, okay? I've got her," Joss promised, her voice so tight she could barely get the words out, and she hoped to God it was true because if they lost her... She shook her head. "Brock and Andrew are on their way to take her to the vet."

"We need to take care of..."

"We can't," Joss said, her voice cracking as the weight of the situation squeezed her chest. God, she was so fucking scared. What was taking everyone so long? "We can't, sweetie. You need to get to the hospital, and the ambulance won't take her. Can you tell me what happened?"

Maeve squeezed her eyes shut and gave a small nod. "We were coming out of the woods, and there was a black bear at the bird feeder. We startled it, I think. I grabbed George's collar and started to lead her slowly toward the house. We didn't turn our backs on it because I read somewhere that that was bad, and just when I thought we were safe, that it was going to let us go and escape into the woods, a cub came out of the woods just there." She pointed over her feet. "Pretty sure it was a momma bear, because it roared and started chasing us away from the cub."

Shit. Joss swallowed hard and glanced warily toward the woods. With the exception of the rare mountain lion that wandered into town, there was nothing in the woods around Sky that was more dangerous as a mother bear intent on protecting her cub.

"George jumped in front of me and started growling at it," Maeve continued, her voice choked with tears. "It took this big swipe at her." She made a small swiping motion with her uninjured arm. "And she just...flew. It charged at me next and just crashed into me like a linebacker or something, and I don't remember what happened next."

The sirens grew closer, and Joss looked up to see the ambulance driving around the side of the house with Brock's black Explorer hot on its heels. Reinforcements had arrived.

George whimpered and made like she was going to crawl to Maeve's side.

"No no no, sweet girl," Joss murmured, holding George still. "You gotta stay still." She looked back and Maeve. "She'll be okay." *Please let her be okay.*

"Joss!"

Joss looked up at Brock, who was running toward her with a large blanket under his arm. Andrew had stopped to pop open the hatch of the SUV, but even with that delay, he only was four or five steps behind him, looking as freaked out as Joss felt. "Help."

"Bet your ass," Brock said as he knelt beside Joss and George. He looked up at Maeve and smiled. "Hey, beautiful."

"Don't let her die," Maeve replied, her tone flat and serious.

"I will do my best." Brock spread the blanket on the ground behind George and looked up at Andrew. "Ready?"

Andrew nodded. They had clearly worked out a plan on the way over, because they wasted no time getting down to business, sliding the blanket under George as carefully as they could, both offering continuous soft words of encouragement and apology as they worked. Joss continued to hold her sweatshirt to George's side as she watched the paramedics tended to Maeve. One was securing a C-collar, while the other had begun splinting her arm, and all the while Maeve stared past them, her jaw set against the pain of having her injured arm manipulated, her one good eye boring into Joss, pleading for her to not let George die.

Joss had never felt so useless in her life as she watched the four men in their backyard take care of the two most important women in her life.

"Joss," Brock called, snapping her back to the present. "We're going to lift her now. We'll try and keep her as still as possible, but I'm going to need you to climb into the back of my car and help us slide her in. Can you do that?"

Joss looked at Maeve, who was watching them with watery eyes full of fear, and nodded. "Yeah."

The cry that George let out when they grabbed the ends of the blanket and lifted her into the air broke what was left of Joss' heart into a million pieces, and she sprinted, vision blurred by tears to Brock's car. She clambered through the open hatch, and by the time she turned around, Brock and Andrew were at the tailgate.

"We're going to lay her down as gently as we can, and I'm going to need you to pull the end of that blanket toward you," Brock instructed, his tone calm and confident, like he had done this very thing a million times before.

Joss stifled a hysterical laugh—because when the fuck would he have ever done anything like this before?—and nodded. "Yeah." She forced a small smile when George's panicked eyes sought her out as her head and shoulders were laid onto the floor of the hatch. "You're okay, baby girl," she cooed as she grabbed the end of the blanket and began to pull.

Andrew braced George's hind end as Brock scampered around the side of the car and climbed in beside Joss.

"Here we go," Brock said, grabbing the blanket with Joss and helping her guide George into place. Once the dog was completely in the car, Andrew slammed the hatch shut and sprinted to the driver's door. Brock touched Joss' hand and smiled reassuringly. "We've got her, Jay. Go take care of Maeve. I'll call you as soon as we know anything."

Joss nodded, grateful that he was there to take charge. She leaned down and pressed one last kiss to George's cheek. "I love you," she whispered against George's soft fur.

"I won't let anything happen to her," Brock promised as he placed one large hands on the sweatshirt on George's side and the other on her head to calm her. "Now go. Maeve needs you, and we need to get George to the vet. I called them on our way over, they're expecting us. It'll be okay."

Joss swallowed hard and reached for the door handle, her eyes never leaving George as she slipped out of the car. Andrew cranked the ignition as her feet hit the dirt, and as soon as the door was closed, the car was in motion, driving slowly toward the driveway where they would hopefully pick up speed en route and the only vet in town.

Joss scrubbed the tears from her face and took a deep breath to keep them from returning as she turned to Maeve. Maeve's arm was splinted, and the paramedics were easing a yellow backboard beneath her in preparation for transit. Joss hated the fact that she had, for all intents and purposes, just handed her injured child off to friends to take care of, but she was simultaneously grateful for their friends rushing to help and leaving her free to focus on Maeve.

She hurried back to Maeve, her wet socks flopping uselessly in front of her toes as she ran. She wormed her way to Maeve's side as the paramedics began strapping her to the board and took her uninjured hand.

"George?"

"They've got her. Vet's expecting them. She'll be okay."

"Ma'am, we need to get her on the stretcher now. Do you want to ride with us, or follow in your own car?"

Joss shook her head as she looked at Maeve. What did people do in cases like this? She knew that they would need a car eventually, but the idea of watching another person she loved drive away from her was enough to make her sick to her stomach. "I don't..." She shivered violently, the shock of what had happened fading enough to allow her body to register exactly how cold she really was. "Maeve?"

Maeve squeezed her hand. "You need shoes and a coat, and my insurance card is in my purse on the hook in the mudroom. I'm okay to ride on my own, there's not a lot of extra room in the back of the ambulance anyway. Just follow us in the car so we have one at the hospital. George is going to need you, too."

Joss drew a slow, ragged breath and nodded. "Okay."

"Okay." Maeve squeezed her hand again. "I love you."

Completely ignoring the two men surrounding them, Joss leaned down and kissed Maeve softly. "I love you, too. I'll see you in a few minutes." She swallowed hard as she pulled away, and shoved her hands in the front pockets of her jeans as she watched the paramedics lift Maeve onto the rolling stretcher.

She was glad Maeve could not see her crying as she watched the paramedics load her into the ambulance, and as soon as the doors were slammed shut, she took off for the house. She yanked her ruined socks off on the patio and tossed them aside as she leapt through the door, the cool hardwood floors feeling positively hot against her freezing feet as she sprinted upstairs for a new pair. Not thirty seconds later, she flew back down the stairs, her new socks sliding dangerously on the wood floor as she ran toward the mudroom. She shoved her feet into her shoes as she gathered her coat, Maeve's purse, and the car keys, her heart beating wildly as she raced through the garage door to her car, her every thought focused on only one thing—getting to the hospital as fast as she could.

Thirty-Eight

Joss stood at the large, floor-to-ceiling windows flanking the eastern wall of the surgical waiting area at Sky Memorial Hospital watching the snow she had been eagerly anticipating fall. The sky was dark, the flakes invisible except for where they tumbled through the pale, golden glow of the lights in the parking lot outside. The lights inside the waiting room were dimmed in deference to the fact that it was now the middle of the night and not everyone's circadian rhythm was accustomed to being awake at such a time, and the otherwise empty room silent except for the quiet hum of the air conditioner that was pumping more cool air into the already too-cold space. Somewhere behind several sets of swinging doors behind her, Maeve was undergoing surgery to set her broken elbow, and Joss closed her eyes as she resisted the urge to begin pacing again. The constant back-and-forth across the long, rectangular room had been making her even feel more sick with nerves than just standing still, but at least if she was moving she felt like she was actually doing something.

She took a deep breath and held it. *Maeve is in good hands. The doctor assured us it was safe for her to go under general anesthesia. She'll be fine. She'll be fine... Keep it together. Don't break now. She needs you.*

"Coffee."

Joss opened her eyes and smiled her thanks at Scott's reflection in the window as she took the white paper cup he held out to her, noting the black duffle he carried in his left hand. She hoped Michelle had thought to grab a coat for Maeve since the rangers had taken the one she had been wearing during the attack for their dogs to scent while they tracked it. "Thanks."

He hefted the bag and nodded. "Michelle dropped this off while I was getting the coffee."

"Thanks." Joss took the bag from him. She sipped at her coffee and sighed. The drink warmed her hands and throat, but she doubted she would feel properly warm again until she was able to see Maeve and know for certain she was okay. "You wanna sit?"

Scott shrugged. "Only if you do."

He had arrived at the hospital earlier that evening after she had called to tell him what had happened, asking him to handle things at Atramentum until further notice, and had stubbornly insisted that he had nowhere else he needed to be when Joss tried to convince him that he would be much more comfortable at home than sitting in the main lobby of the hospital. She was grateful for his stubbornness now, however. The waiting room was eerie—cold and shadowed, the only sign of life their ghostly reflections in the windows—and his presence was doing wonders to help keep her rampaging pessimistic thoughts at bay. He knew when to talk and when to keep silent, and she knew that without him to keep her company, she would have surely lost it by now.

The orthopedist handling Maeve's case had said the surgery would take about an hour—but she had already been gone for close to two—and Joss was beginning to fear that all of the surgeon's assurances about Maeve being perfectly fine to go under general anesthesia despite her concussion were false.

"Have they come out to talk to you yet??"

Joss shook her head and checked her phone for the thousandth time that evening. Her throat was tight, and if she had eaten anything since that apple seven hours earlier, it surely would have come back up by now.

"Any word from Brock?" Scott asked, nodding at Joss' phone.

The local vet had done everything she could to stabilize George, but the Dane's injuries were too critical for the small clinic to manage, and they had referred her case on to the veterinary hospital at the Boulder campus of the University of Colorado. With her handful of broken ribs and punctured lung, the large veterinary hospital was better equipped to perform the required lifesaving measures, as well as monitoring her twenty-four hours a day afterwards. They had called to update her on George's status as they drove the Dane down the mountain, and the hospital had called once they arrived there to get a credit card number to cover George's expenses, but news on that front was as sparse as it was here with Maeve.

Joss shook her head. "Nothing since he texted to say they had just taken her back for surgery."

"Fuck."

"Yeah." Joss blew out a loud breath and dropped into a nearby chair. She slumped in the seat and took a sip of her coffee. "I dunno… I mean, he sounded optimistic when he called on their way down the mountain, like the vet in town felt this was something she could recover from, but I hate that she's all the way down there and we're up here."

Scott dropped the bag he was holding at her feet as he sat in the chair to her right, giving her leg a reassuring bump with his knee. After a few minutes of sitting in silence, he asked, "How much longer is Maeve supposed to be in surgery?"

"I dunno." Joss ran a hand through her hair and sighed, her stomach twisting as she looked at the clock on the wall. *What was taking so long?* "She's already been in there longer than they were saying she would be."

"Joss?"

Joss bolted upright and looked at Dr. Lewis. The blonde orthopedist was young, probably not much older than she was, but the nurses had all raved about her skill in the operating room. "Yes?"

"Maeve is in recovery and starting to come around if you'd like to come back and join her."

Joss nodded and grabbed the bag of clean clothes from the floor as she jumped to her feet, only vaguely aware of Scott doing the same thing beside her. "How is she?"

Dr. Lewis smiled. "It all went perfectly," she said, her voice soft and reassuring. "It was a little more difficult to realign than I'd anticipated, which is why the surgery took longer than we thought it would. I used three pins to set the elbow"—she bent her left arm in front of herself and pointed to where she had placed the pins—"but that's not at all uncommon, and Maeve should recover beautifully from this. Provided she continues to do as well as she has been, she could possibly be discharged tomorrow." She frowned and checked her watch. The day had changed over while she had been in surgery, and she shook her head. "Sorry. Later today."

Oh thank God. Joss looked over at Scott. "Do you want to come back too, or…"

"Nah." He yawned and made a show of stretching his arms over his head. "It's late. I'm going to head home." He wrapped an arm around Joss' neck and pulled her into a light hug. "Go take care of your woman. Lemme know if you need anything. I'll text Brock and let him know he can hit me up if he needs help while you're with Maeve."

Joss sighed and leaned her head on his shoulder. "Thanks."

He kissed her forehead. "Of course. We got your back, Perrault. I'll call after the sun comes up to check in. Try and get some sleep."

Joss nodded, even though she was certain that sleep was nowhere in her future, and turned toward Dr. Lewis. She forced a tight smile as she took a deep breath, and nodded that she was ready. "Thank you."

"Of course." A nurse in navy blue scrubs was waiting on the other side of the swinging doors, and Dr. Lewis smiled as she waved a hand at her. "This is Carrie, and she'll be taking care of you guys from here on out. I begin my rounds at six, so I'll see you again bright and early."

Joss shook the doctor's hand. "Great. Thank you so much."

Dr. Lewis nodded and disappeared down a small corridor just behind them.

"Ms. Perrault?" Carrie spoke up. "Shall we?"

"Absolutely." Joss swallowed hard as she followed Carrie through a second set of doors to the recovery area. There were three other nurses at the central desk station in the middle of the ward, and Joss bit her lip as she gave them a small nod in greeting. Her throat was too tight with worry despite the nurse's assurances that Maeve was okay to do anything else.

Joss sucked in a deep breath when her eyes landed on Maeve—the lone surgical patient in the ward at the moment, laying on a slightly elevated hospital bed with her casted arm draped over her stomach. Her blackened eye had completely swollen shut in the time that had passed since the attack, but the eyelashes on her other eye were fluttering as her body shook off the anesthesia that remained in her system.

She was waking up.

She was alive.

Joss closed her eyes and blew out the breath she had been holding as the fear that had been twisting her stomach from the moment she watched them take Maeve back for surgery disappeared, leaving her feeling weak-kneed and slightly dizzy.

Maeve was okay.

She swallowed back her tears as she opened her eyes and hurried into the draped-off area where Maeve was waking up, the duffle bag she had been carrying landing with a quiet thump on the floor beside the bed. Her eyes darted over Maeve's arm that had just been operated on, and she frowned when she saw the elastic bandage that covered the cast she had been expecting to see. "Why the Ace bandage?" She glanced at the nurse as she picked up Maeve's glasses that were sitting on the small, rolling table beside the bed and gently set them in place.

"Because of the trauma to the arm, Dr. Lewis bivalved the cast in case of extreme swelling. When she comes back for her recheck in a couple weeks, it'll be taken off and replaced with a regular, uncut cast."

"Oh." Joss took Maeve's un-casted hand in her own as she stood by the side of the bed as Maeve continued to shake off the drugs that had kept her asleep, and her heart clenched at how cold it was. She looked at the nurse. "She's cold."

The nurse smiled and draped another blanket over Maeve's legs. "She'll warm up soon. It's just a lingering effect from the anesthesia."

Joss nodded, taking the woman at her word as she turned her attention back to Maeve, watching the way her non-blackened eyelid fluttered, waiting for the moment it opened for good. *There you go, baby. Come back to me.*

One long blink later, Maeve smiled as her gaze became more focused, her normally vibrant emerald-colored eye dulled by the medication that was still working its way from her system. "Hey, you."

Thank God. Joss clenched her jaw as she forced a small smile and gave Maeve's hand a light squeeze. "Hi," she rasped.

The automatic blood pressure cuff came to life with a low hum, and the nurse gave Joss' shoulder a light pat as she turned her attention to the machine, giving them as much privacy as the unit allowed.

Joss took advantage of the woman's kindness and leaned in to press a tender kiss to Maeve's forehead. "How are you feeling?"

"Sleepy," Maeve murmured. "How'd it go?"

"Three pins, but the doctor assures me you'll be good as new in no time," Joss reported.

"George?"

Joss shook her head. "Brock texted not long after you went into surgery that they had taken her back. But I haven't heard anything since."

"We need to get to her," Maeve said.

"I know." Joss squeezed her hand reassuringly. "But first, we need to get you taken care of here."

"Blood pressure is good," the nurse reported. "Maeve, I need to listen to your heart," she said as she reached for the collar of Maeve's hospital gown.

"I'm fine," Maeve insisted even as she had a stethoscope pressed to her chest. "You should go to her."

Joss shook her head as tears stung at the backs of her eyes. Oh, how she wished it were that easy. "Sweetie, I love George as much as you do, but Brock is taking care of her there. He will light a fire under their asses to make sure she gets everything she needs, but right now we need to get you everything that you need so we can take care of her once she's out of the hospital."

"When can I go home?" Maeve asked, changing tactics. She looked at the nurse expectantly.

The nurse smiled as she draped her stethoscope around her neck and patted Maeve's leg. "It usually depends on how well you're managing your pain," she said in a calming tone as she made a note on Maeve's file. "The doctor will check on you during her morning rounds in a few hours and she'll make the decision then. I'm not making any promises, mind you, but in most cases like this, the patient is able to go home within twenty-four hours."

Maeve's eyes were like lasers, determination focusing her gaze as she looked back at Joss. "I'll need clean clothes so we can get down there after I'm discharged."

Not at all surprised by Maeve's insistence that she get to George as quickly as possible, Joss nodded and waved a hand at the bag that was on the floor by her feet, hidden from Maeve's view. "I figured that was what you'd want to do, so I had Scott send Michelle to the house to grab us some clothes. Thought you'd be more comfortable with her rifling through your drawers than him."

Appeased, Maeve yawned and nodded. "Good."

"Everything looks good here," the nurse piped up as she set Maeve's chart on the foot of the bed. She made a waving motion to the other nurses in the unit and then kicked the brakes off the wheels of the bed. "We can move you back to your room now."

"Great," Maeve said.

Joss could tell by the determined set of Maeve's jaw that she was eager to get things moving along so she could prove to the doctor she was ready to go home, and she just hoped that Maeve would be honest about the pain she was feeling. It would do none of them any good for her to be discharged before she was really ready. She gave Maeve's hand one last squeeze before letting it go, and picked up the duffle from the floor. "Do you need me to do anything to help?" she asked the nurse, who had already unplugged Maeve's I.V. machine and looped the cord over an unused hook on the unit, and hooked the thin metal pole between the webbing between her thumb and forefinger and the back of the bed.

The nurse smiled and shook her head. "Nope. I've got her, but I recommend following behind us so I don't accidentally run you over."

Joss nodded and stepped out of the way to give the large bed room to move. The trip from the recovery unit to Maeve's room on the eleventh floor took no time at all since the majority of the hospital was sleeping, and she set the bag of clothes on the small chair beside the bed as the nurse rolled it into place and locked its wheels.

Once Maeve was properly situated—I.V. plugged back in, pulse ox in place, blankets adjusted—the nurse smiled and asked, "Is there anything else you think you'll need right now?"

"No, thank you," Maeve said in a flat, weary tone.

Joss added, "I think we've got it."

"Okay then." The nurse nodded. "I hope everything goes smoothly for you from here on out."

"Me too," Joss agreed. She looked at Maeve, whose lips were pulled tight in pain, and sighed. "Me too." Once the nurse had left the room and closed the door after herself, Joss used the remote attached to Maeve's bed to dim the lights as she leaned in and pressed a lingering kiss to her temple. It was late, and they had more long days ahead of them. "Get some sleep, baby."

Maeve nodded, the dimmed lights and the drugs lingering in her system effectively trouncing any desire she might have had to resist. "Okay."

Joss' throat tightened with emotion as she watched Maeve slip back under, and she swallowed thickly as she kissed her forehead. "I love you. Oh God, do I love you..."

She knew that she should sleep while she could as well, but once she was sure that Maeve would not be waking up anytime soon, she retrieved the clean clothes Michelle had picked for her and disappeared into the small en suite bathroom. She closed the door quietly and then turned on the lights, and blinked at the harsh glow the florescent bulbs above the sink cast against the gleaming white tiled floor and walls. She turned on the shower and undressed quickly as it warmed up, and closed her eyes as she stepped beneath the hot, beating stream.

Alone and utterly, completely exhausted, she sank to the floor, barely registering the cool tile against her skin as she pulled her knees to her chest. She bit her lip nearly hard enough to draw blood as she tried to fight back the chest-rattling sob that she could feel building inside her, but it was no use. She pressed her forehead against her knees as she let it go, tears of fear and relief pouring hotly down her face as she rocked in place, comforting herself as best she could.

She had almost lost Maeve.

They still might lose George.

She squeezed her eyes shut as she fought back against the mental image of her trying to comfort Maeve as they received that final, irreversible news.

What would they do if George didn't pull through? What would they do if she couldn't be saved?

Joss could not stop the small cry of anguish that escaped her as she rocked back and forth on the tile floor of the shower, terrified that the small family she had managed to find might be irrevocably torn apart forever.

The sound of a phone ringing on the other side of the bathroom door forced her from the stall, and she hurriedly wrapped a towel around herself as she stumbled into Maeve's room. Her phone was on the small couch where she had left it, and the brightly lit screen called her forward like a beacon. She watched Maeve as she picked it up to answer the call, and offered up a quick prayer that she stayed asleep.

"Hello?" she answered, her voice rough from crying.

"Ms. Perrault? This is Henry Dyson from Boulder Veterinary Hospital. I am the one overseeing George's case."

Joss swallowed hard and clenched the towel to her chest as sat on the edge of the vinyl covered sofa. "Yes. How is she?"

"She's resting peacefully at the moment. There was not a lot we could do for her broken ribs, but we did end up having to remove half of her left lung. The trauma was just too extensive to save it."

"Will she be okay?" Joss whispered hoarsely.

"It'll be touch and go for the next twenty-four hours. She's still in critical condition and she lost a lot of blood, but seeing as she took on a bear, I'd say she's got enough fight in her to hopefully pull through. We'll keep her sedated through the day to allow her body time to begin to recover, and will start weaning her from the drugs probably later this afternoon. She's going to be in a lot of pain though, so we will keep her on a steady regimen of morphine to try to manage it all."

Joss sucked in a deep breath. "Okay. So…what are we looking at, here?"

"Best-case scenario," Dr. Dyson hedged, *"and, really, this is dependent on how well she responds to the lobectomy and how affected she is by her broken ribs— she might be able to go home by Thanksgiving. But, again, it really depends on her. I won't release her until I'm sure she's one-hundred percent ready to go home."*

Joss blew out the breath she was holding and nodded. "Okay. Thank you so much. My girlfriend and I will be down to check on her as soon as she's released from the hospital up here. Do we need to call ahead, or…?"

"No need. Mr. Green, has filled us in on the situation there, and I will put a note in George's file that our staff is to allow you to see her whatever time you arrive."

"Great. Thank you."

"My pleasure. If I don't see you by the afternoon, I will call again then and let you know how things are going here."

"Thank you," Joss repeated, knowing that she sounded like a broken record but not knowing what else she could say.

"Of course," Dr. Dyson said warmly before he hung up.

Joss pulled her towel tighter around herself as she got back to her feet. She sighed as she looked at Maeve, who was sleeping far more peacefully than she knew she would personally be able to manage. Maeve's bruised face and casted arm were stark reminders of how close she had come to losing her, and Joss bit her lip as she turned and padded back into the bathroom where she had left her clothes.

It was going to be a long few days, she needed to get dressed so she could try to steal a few hours sleep before she had to hit the ground running again.

Thirty-Nine

"We just need to stop by the house real quick to get clothes and stuff for the next few days before we head down the mountain," Joss said as she helped Maeve into the passenger's seat just before ten the next morning.

Maeve had woken up before dawn determined to get out of the hospital as quickly as she possibly could, and by the time Dr. Lewis came by her room at half-past six that morning, she was already dressed and sitting beside Joss on the uncomfortable, too-small sofa Joss had used as a bed the night before. To the orthopedist's credit, she just smiled pleasantly as if she had expected to walk in and find Maeve already dressed and demanding to be discharged.

Joss had been half-afraid that Dr. Lewis would insist on keeping Maeve a few hours longer. Not because she felt Maeve did not need to be hospitalized any longer, but because the storm clouds in Maeve's eyes threatened World War Three if anyone dared suggest she stay longer. Thankfully, however, after perusing Maeve's vitals from the night before and performing a quick exam, asking multiple times about Maeve's pain levels—which Joss was pretty sure Maeve downplayed in her rush to get to George—she scribbled out a prescription for some Tylenol3 in case over-the-counter pain meds were not enough and signed off on her release.

"We don't need to go home. We can get whatever we need in Boulder."

"The house in on our way out of town, and the vet said that they're not going to begin waking George up until later this afternoon." Joss shook her head and pressed a gentle finger to Maeve's lips to silence the argument she could see sitting there. "Look, it'll take me five minutes to run inside and throw some clothes and toiletries into a bag for us, and then we'll be on the road, okay?"

Maeve pulled the finger from her lips and shook her head. "I need to see her."

"I know. I do too. But this quick stop will save us time in the end. I promise." Maeve's phone rang, and Joss sighed, grateful for the distraction as she closed the door and jogged around to the driver's seat. When she climbed inside, Maeve's phone was still ringing, and Maeve was staring at the screen. "What's up?"

"It's my mom," Maeve groaned. Her parents still had no idea what had happened.

Joss nodded as she started the car. "You gonna answer?"

"Yeah." Maeve sighed and swiped her thumb over the screen a split-second before the call was kicked to voicemail. "Hey, Mom," she said, closing her eyes and leaning her head back against the headrest. Her mother must have asked what she was doing, because she said, "We're just leaving the hospital."

Joss bit her lip and shifted the car into drive.

"I'm fine," Maeve continued. "I just broke my arm."

Nothing about the situation was funny, but Joss still smiled at the sound of Elizabeth Dylan screeching, *"YOU WHAT? HOW?"* Of course, listening to Maeve recount the events from the day before for her mother completely wiped any look of amusement from her face.

Maeve was just finishing up her retelling of everything that had happened when Joss turned off the main road onto their driveway, and Joss reached across the console to give Maeve's leg an affectionate squeeze as she drove past the turnoff to the cottage. While she did not envy Maeve's situation—from the way Maeve was trying to talk her mother down, it was clear that parents really never stopped acting like, well, parents, no matter how old you were—she was glad that Elizabeth's call gave her the opportunity to swing by the house like she wanted without having to fight with Maeve about it.

Joss scanned the woods as she drove, looking for any sign of the bear that the rangers had been unable to track down. There was no sign of life to be found, however, causing a conflicting mix of relief and guilt to settle heavily in her stomach. Relief because she had no desire to go head-to-head with a mamma bear, and guilt because she hoped the bear and her cub would continue to evade the rangers looking for them. She knew that she should want the bear that attacked Maeve and George to be killed, but she held no malice toward the animal, whose habitat was shrinking by the hectare every year due to human encroachment. She just hoped they would all be able to stay out of each other's way from now on.

She turned around in the courtyard so that the front of the car was pointed toward the road and glanced at Maeve as she killed the ignition. "Two minutes," she whispered, grabbing the duffle with their dirty clothes from the backseat as she reached for her door.

Maeve nodded and continued her conversation. "I don't know when George will be released or when we'll be home."

Joss shook her head as she hopped out of the car and slammed her door shut. Even though she knew that she was there to grab clothes and toiletries for the next few days so they could be near George at the veterinary hospital in Boulder, she still keenly felt the dog's absence when she entered the house. There was no happy bark to greet her, no sound of nails clicking on the hardwood floors. Just cold, unforgiving silence.

Joss swallowed hard and offered up a silent prayer to whoever was listening to help George make it through this. She hurried up the stairs to their bedroom and dumped their dirty clothes onto the bed to be dealt with later. She shoved a few days' worth of clothes into the duffle before ducking into the bathroom to grab their toiletries. She zipped the bag closed as she hefted the strap over her head so that the strap cut diagonally across her chest, and then jogged back down the stairs. A quick glance through the front doors assured her that Maeve was okay as she used the end of the bannister as a fulcrum to propel her away from the door toward the mudroom. Maeve's arm needed to stay in the sling that looked identical to the one Joss had worn a few months before, and she would need a coat that was big enough to zip over her cast.

Once she had everything she needed, Joss headed back to the car. She turned on the front porch lights and the chandelier in the foyer before she locked up—just in case they, or Maeve's family, arrived back at the house when it was dark—and took a deep breath as she twisted her key in the deadbolt.

Maeve was pinching the bridge of her nose as if to ward off a headache when Joss opened the door to the backseat and tossed the bag inside, and she frowned as she slammed the door shut and climbed back behind the wheel. "Everything okay?"

"Yeah," Maeve said, shaking her head. "Just…Thanksgiving stuff."

Joss made a small sound of understanding as she started the car. She had been so worried about Maeve and George that she had forgotten about the Dylans' impending visit. "So, what's the plan for next week?"

Maeve blew out a loud breath and shrugged. "I dunno. My parents are still coming for sure—my mom is beyond pissed that I didn't call her right away to let her know what happened—and she's going to talk to my brothers to see what they want to do because their plane tickets are non-refundable. I told her they are more than welcome to use the house and whatever even if we're not here, I just…"

The uncertainty in Maeve's tone broke Joss' heart, and she wished there was some way she could just magically make everything okay. "She'll be okay," she promised.

"Will she?" Maeve whispered, her voice cracking.

Joss nodded, hoping that by force of will alone she could make it happen. "Yeah."

Maeve sighed and looked out her window as Joss turned back onto the main road. "I hope you're right."

Me too, Joss thought as she reached across the center console to give Maeve's thigh a reassuring squeeze.

The drive down the mountain felt like it took forever when, in reality, Joss managed the four-hour trip in just under three-and-a-half hours. Even though the lunch hour had come and gone while they had been on the road, Joss knew better than to suggest they stop for food. There was no way Maeve would go for it and, truth-be-told, there was no way her stomach would be able to handle her putting anything in it until she saw George and was assured that she was okay anyway.

Joss looked over at Maeve as she pulled to a stop in a space near the main doors to the veterinary hospital. For as sick with worry as she felt, Maeve looked like she was ready to pass out or throw up— or both—and Joss worried about her being able to make it inside on her own. "Wait for me get your door, please." She turned off the ignition but did not otherwise move until Maeve nodded. "Thank you."

It was warmer in Boulder than it had been in Sky, a fact that Joss was grateful for as she hurried around the rear of the car to the passenger's side because she knew Maeve would not want to waste time being helped into a coat. She offered Maeve her hand as she opened her door and did her best to smile reassuringly as she laced their fingers together once Maeve was standing beside her. There was an unmistakable tremble in Maeve's hold that Joss wished she could soothe, but she knew that there was nothing she could do to help Maeve than what she was already doing. "You ready?"

Maeve shook her head. "No."

Joss sighed. *Me neither.* "It'll be okay. Let's go see our girl."

The lobby was eerily quiet when they walked through the front door, the small room occupied by only a handful of chairs and a mid-twenty-something woman behind the front counter who looked up at them with a kind smile. She had long brown hair pulled back in a ponytail, warm chocolate-colored eyes, and bright red lipstick that was more befitting a night on the town than work at a veterinary hospital, but there was something about the way she carried herself—even just sitting behind a desk—that said she knew what she was doing. "May I help you?"

"We're here to see George Dylan," Maeve said, every ounce of strain she was feeling creeping into her tone.

Joss gave her hand a squeeze as the woman typed George's name into their system. The nametag clipped to her lightweight fleece hoodie embroidered with the veterinary hospital's logo identified her as Ruby French, and below her name was the title Veterinary Technician.

"I was here when she was brought in last night. I have a special fondness for big dogs, but she really is a super-sweet girl," Ruby said as she clicked through whatever she was looking at on her screen. She nodded at whatever she saw. "Can I just see your I.D.s real fast?"

Joss and Maeve produced their driver's licenses and held them out for Ruby to see.

"Thank you," Ruby said as she got to her feet. "If you'll follow me, she's just back here."

Maeve nodded, her grip on Joss' hand tightening as she started after Ruby. The waiting area of the hospital might have been silent, but as soon as the swinging doors to the treatment room were pushed open they ran right into a wall of sound made up of people talking, dogs whimpering, barking, and crying, and a mix of other, unidentifiable sounds of animals in distress.

"Wow," Joss muttered.

Ruby turned and smiled. "George is this way," she said, waving a hand at a narrow corridor. She caught another tech's eye and said, "Can you tell Dyson that George has visitors?"

"Will do," the woman replied with a nod.

The noise from the main treatment area faded as they made their way down the hall, making Joss suddenly aware of how loud her pulse was pounding in her ears. She felt like she might be sick at any moment, and she held her breath as she and Maeve were led through an open door.

"These are our kennels for larger animals," Ruby explained as she walked further into the room.

The room was long, with a half-dozen cinderblock kennels along the right-hand side with chain link doors that looked more like miniature jail cells than actual kennels. George would not be happy about her accommodations once she woke up, but they were far better than an actual kennel would have been. George was the room's lone occupant for the moment, and Joss blew out the breath she had been holding as she looked at the sleeping dog. George's torso was wrapped in gauze and there was a three-inch band of yellow tape around her right front leg. She was laid out on a cot made of what looked like vinyl stretched over a PVC frame—snoring lightly and whimpering as the expansion of her chest with each breath stressed her injured ribs and lung. A plastic cone of shame hung from a hook above the bed, an accessory Joss knew for certain that George would not appreciate, and beside it hung a thin slip-leash.

"Can we?" Maeve asked, pulling her hand from Joss' to gesture at the door to George's kennel.

"Of course." Ruby opened the door and waved them inside.

Joss hung back as Maeve made her way to George's side on unsteady legs, feeling like it was not her place to join her just yet, and bit her lip as she watched the blonde drop to her knees beside George's cot. Tears rolled freely down Maeve's cheeks as she whispered something and leaned in to press her lips to George's cheek, her uninjured hand lovingly stroking George's head. Joss was beckoned forward by an open, watery gaze, and a distinct feeling of lightheadedness settled over her as she knelt at Maeve's side.

They pet George's head together, their fingers brushing against each other atop soft fur, unified in their feeling of utter helplessness. This was their child, and they could do nothing to take away the pain she was feeling. No matter how badly they might have wanted to, there was nothing they could do to make everything better.

Joss swallowed around a lump in her throat as she glanced up at Ruby. "Will she be okay?" she asked, pleading with her eyes for good news.

"She should be," a vaguely familiar, masculine voice answered.

Joss looked at the new arrival—a man with curly blond hair in navy scrubs and a white lab coat—but did not stand to greet him.

He smiled and leaned against the open door to the kennel. "I'm Henry Dyson. I spoke to…" His voice trailed off as his eyes flickered between her and Maeve. "You," he continued, his brow wrinkling as he looked back at Joss, "last night?"

"Yes," Joss confirmed, nodding.

"Okay. So you must be Maeve?" Dyson said, looking at Maeve.

Maeve nodded. "Yes. Sorry," she apologized as she tried to wipe the tears from her face.

"Nothing to apologize for," Dyson assured her with a kind smile. "Your girl there"—he nodded at George—"is doing beautifully, all things considered."

"Thank God," Maeve breathed, sinking into Joss' side.

Joss steadied herself with a hand on George's cot and wrapped her free arm around Maeve's waist. "When will she wake up?" she asked the doctor.

"Well, we've been slowly backing down her meds since, oh, about eleven this morning, and as you can see—or hear, rather—she is becoming more aware. I'm going to keep her on some pretty strong meds that will keep her feeling sleepy so she won't be tempted to move around too much just yet, but her numbers are looking really strong. We need to keep an eye out for any sign of infection, but at this point I'm cautiously optimistic that she should pull through just fine."

Maeve's breath was warm and ragged against Joss' neck and she could feel Maeve shaking with the fresh tears that were damp against her skin, and she sighed as she pressed her lips to Maeve's forehead. "She'll be okay," she whispered.

Maeve buried her face in the crook of Joss' neck and nodded as her tears fell faster, wetting the collar of Joss' shirt. "Yeah…"

Joss looked back up at Dr. Dyson, who had turned to talk to Ruby to give them a moment of privacy, and took a deep breath. She knew Maeve was going to want to be by George's side as much as possible, but Maeve was still recovering herself, and it would be up to her to make sure that both her girls were taken care of. Which meant she needed to find them a place to stay until they could take George home. "Is there a hotel nearby that you'd recommend?"

Ruby grinned. "My grandmother runs a bed-and-breakfast not five minutes from here. You'd have your own room and bathroom, and she'll take care of your meals for you so you're not eating out all the time. How's that sound?"

"That sounds perfect," Joss said, flashing the brunette a grateful smile.

"Thought it might." Ruby tipped her head at the door and added, "I'll go get you her information."

Joss nodded. "Thanks."

"We'll let you guys visit with George," Dr. Dyson spoke up. "Please let us know if you or she need anything."

"We will," Joss promised, stroking her fingers up and down Maeve's back comfortingly. "Thank you," she added as Dr. Dyson and Ruby both disappeared through the large open doorway, leaving their little family to begin to heal together. Maeve shivered against her side, and Joss licked her lips as she gave her waist a light squeeze. "How you doing, sweetie?"

"Fine." Maeve's voice was flat.

Joss shook her head. "How's your arm?"

"Fine."

"Maeve," Joss cajoled. "Look at me." The sight of Maeve's black eye was still shocking, but it was the tears that were still spilling down her cheeks—because even though her one eye was swollen shut, its tear ducts still worked perfectly—that really rocked Joss to her core, and she blinked back her own tears as she tenderly kissed Maeve's away. "It will be okay."

"I know."

Joss tucked Maeve's hair behind her ears and sighed. George whimpered beside them, the pained sound drawing their immediate attention, and Joss grit her teeth as she looked down at the fitfully slumbering Dane. George's cheek quivered as her front legs twitched, the canine version of sleepwalking.

"What do you think she's dreaming about?" Maeve murmured.

George growled low and soft in the back of her throat, a muted bark scraping its way free, her feet twitching faster.

Joss wanted to lie, to say she was sure George was dreaming of their runs around the lake where she would chase bunnies through the underbrush before returning triumphantly at her side, but she knew that there was no point. There was no mistaking the anguish in the sounds George was making. "Probably that fucking bear."

George cried out louder in her sleep, all four of her legs moving at a gallop as if confirming Joss' statement.

"Oh, sweetie," Maeve cried, wincing in pain as her injured elbow was trapped between her legs and stomach as she leaned down to press her lips to George's ear. "I'm okay, George. I'm okay."

The choked promises seemed to do the trick, because George let out a trembling, breathy-bark and then started snoring again as her body relaxed and her limbs became still.

"Joss," Maeve cried, shaking her head as she watched George.

"I know, baby," Joss closed her eyes and pressed a reassuring kiss to Maeve's hair. "I know."

They remained in silent vigil at George's side until the last of the anesthesia keeping her under faded, and the pained whine that greeted them when George's big brown eyes blinked open was softened by the small wag of her tail.

"Hey, kiddo," Joss greeted the dog with a watery smile.

"George," Maeve whispered as she stroked the dog's head.

George's tail thumped softly against the cot.

"Ah, I see somebody woke up," Ruby announced as she sauntered into the kennel. She knelt at the head of the cot and peered into George's eyes. "How you doing, beautiful?"

George whined softly and licked her hand.

Ruby smiled. "Yeah, I know." She held out a folded piece of paper. "This is the address for my Gran's bed-and-breakfast. I called and filled her in on everything, and she said she will have dinner waiting for you whenever you arrive."

"That's too kind, thank you," Joss told her.

Maeve shook her head. "We can't leave her," she protested weakly, her voice strained.

Joss checked her watch and did some quick mental math. It was pushing five o'clock, which meant that Maeve's pain meds had worn off about half an hour ago. "We can't sleep here," she pointed out as gently as she could. "And you need food so you can take your meds again."

"I'll stay with her tonight," Ruby spoke up. "It's my night to work overnight anyway, and since she's our only 24-hour guest at the moment, I'll set up one of the spare cots in here and we'll have a sleepover."

"You don't have to do that," Joss murmured, risking Maeve's wrath.

"I do it all the time," Ruby said, brushing her off with a grin. "Like I said earlier, I have a soft spot for big dogs and I just know that George here is going to be my new best friend. Aren't you, George?"

George chuffed softly and turned her head to lick Maeve's hand as if promising that she would be okay for the night.

Joss smiled, grateful as ever that George seemed to be more human than canine. "You'll call us if anything happens?" she asked Ruby, mostly for Maeve's benefit. She had no doubt that the tech would keep them in the loop.

"Absolutely," Ruby promised.

"Maeve, sweetie." Joss leaned in to catch Maeve's good eye. "You aren't going to be any good to George if you're in too much pain to do anything," she reasoned. "Let's go get some food so you can take your meds, and then we'll see how you're feeling," she reasoned, knowing that as soon as the pain medication hit her system that Maeve would be too tired to come back to the veterinary hospital. She trusted Ruby to watch over George, and it was up to her to watch over Maeve. Come hell or high water, she was going to do whatever it took to get her little family back home together where they belonged.

"You'll call us?" Maeve demanded.

Ruby held her hand up as if swearing an oath. "I will call you if anything happens."

Maeve yawned and nodded, the events of the last twenty-four hours that she had been fighting to ignore finally catching up to her. "Okay." She kissed George's cheek. "I'll see you soon."

Joss petted George's head and added, "Be good for Ruby."

She could have sworn George grinned in response.

"Okay," Joss said as she got to her feet so she could help Maeve up. "Thanks again for everything," she said to Ruby.

"My pleasure." Ruby smiled. "I wrote down some directions on how to get to Gran's from here—shouldn't take you more than five minutes."

Joss flipped the paper over and scanned what Ruby had written. It seemed straightforward enough, and she nodded as she looked back up at her. "Thanks." She took Maeve's hand into her own and gave it a light squeeze. "You ready?"

Maeve shook her head. "Yeah."

Knowing that was as good as she was going to get, Joss gave George one last lingering look before she led Maeve out the door. "All right. Let's get going, then."

Forty

Joss took a slow, deep breath as she watched Maeve and George make their way back through the clinic to where she waited by George's kennel, the Dane's cone bumping into Maeve's knee every so often, her eyes tracking their progress. George's first few trips to the yard at the back of the clinic where she took care of business had been pure agony to witness, the dog's normally exuberant gait slow and pained, her steps halted, her breathing labored as she adjusted to her decreased lung capacity. By Monday evening, however, George began to look more like herself. She still walked slowly, but the happy swish of her tail and her refusal to come back inside after taking care of her business were both welcome signs that she was adjusting.

That she was healing.

And with every day that passed with George showing more and more of her personality, Maeve's condition improved as well. She still winced whenever she moved too quickly, and could not keep from crying out in pain whenever she accidentally bumped her elbow on something, but Joss knew that seeing George make such progress in the four days since they had arrived in Boulder sped along her own.

Joss smiled as she watched Ruby fall into step with Maeve and George, her wide, red smile as contagious as the happy swish of George's tail. She said something that made Maeve grin, and Joss crossed her fingers that they might get to go home soon.

Though Maeve had avoided talking about it, Joss knew the fact that her parents were up at the house without them weighed heavily on her mind. Her brothers had decided to stay back in Chicago—mindful of the fact that their kids running around would not be good for George and that having all of them around would just be more stress for Maeve—but the guilt of staying with George and basically ignoring her parents who had flown in to spend the holiday with them was wearing on her.

They understood, of course, but it was still an unusual situation—one that Joss fervently hoped they would never have to live through ever again.

"What are you guys smiling about?" Joss asked when Maeve, Ruby, and George were within earshot. George barked happily, though not as boisterously as usual, as if she were sharing the secret, and Joss laughed. "Okay, how about somebody else fill me in?"

Maeve smiled down at George and shook her head affectionately as she scratched behind the dog's ears. "How does spending Thanksgiving at home sound?"

"Like a dream come true." Joss got to her feet and checked her watch. It was pushing four o'clock, which meant that Thanksgiving Day technically kicked-off in eight hours, and she arched a brow at Ruby. "Are we getting sprung from this joint?"

Ruby laughed and looked over her shoulder at Dr. Dyson, who was making his way over to them. "I'll let him share the good news," she said, winking at Joss.

Dr. Dyson, bless his soul, did not waste any time as he joined their small group. "Who wants to go home?"

"Me!" Ruby exclaimed.

"Too bad," Dyson chuckled. "You're on until eight tonight."

"Ah, hell." Ruby shrugged. "Oh well, it was worth a shot."

"You really think George is okay to go home?" Joss asked.

Dyson nodded. "I do. She'll need to be kept as calm as possible over the next week or so, but I see no reason to keep her here. Just make an appointment with your regular vet for her to be seen sometime next week, and they'll be able to oversee her care from here on out. George is healing beautifully, so"—he rapped his knuckles on the side of his head—"knock on wood, she should be back to her old self before you know it."

Joss looked at Maeve, who was positively beaming back at her. "I can't wait."

"Me neither," Maeve echoed.

"I have our pharmacy preparing the medications George will need now," Dyson continued with a smile. "So as soon as those are ready, you ladies are free to go."

Joss nodded. They would need to stop by the bed-and-breakfast to check out and pick up their things, but with any luck they should be home before nine that night. "Thank you."

"Our pleasure," Dyson assured her with a grin. He patted Ruby on the shoulder and added, "I'll leave it to Ruby to walk you through the discharge paperwork. If you need anything or have any questions, please don't hesitate to give us a call."

"We will. Thanks," Maeve said.

"What kind of car do you have?" Dr. Dyson asked.

"An Audi SUV," Maeve answered.

"Okay." He nodded. "So you'll need a ramp to help George into it. I don't want her jumping."

"Right," Joss spoke up. "Makes sense." She looked at Maeve and frowned. They could use the veterinary hospital's ramp to get George into the car, but that still left the issue of getting her out of it back at the house.

Maeve nodded, understanding what Joss was thinking. "I'll call the vet in Sky and see if they have one we can borrow. I'm sure my dad'll go pick it up for us."

"Honestly, a length of three-quarter ply works just as well," Dr. Dyson spoke up. "It doesn't need to be anything fancy, and it'll just have to support her weight for a few seconds."

"Good to know." Maeve ran her good hand through her hair and shrugged. "So, worst-case scenario, he goes to the hardware store and picks something up."

"I'm sure Brock or Scott would do it too, if we asked," Joss pointed out as she wrapped a light arm around Maeve's waist. "I mean, do you know what kind of car they rented?"

Maeve shook her head. "I'll run it all by him and see what he says."

"Well, since that's settled"—Dyson lifted George's file in the air and gave it a flick—"good luck on the drive home." He nodded at Ruby, who grinned and flashed him two thumbs up, and then turned on his heel and left.

"You excited to go home, George?" Ruby asked as she checked the bandages wrapped around the Dane's torso. George speared her with the edge of the cone tied to her neck, and Ruby laughed. "Sorry, girlie, but that needs to stay on for a bit longer." Ruby adjusted the cone and glanced up at Maeve and Joss. "Your vet back in Sky will let you know when she can stop wearing it. I can tell you they'll want her in it until the bandages come off and her stitches are out, though."

George whined and stared unhappily at Maeve.

Maeve chuckled and shook her head. "Sorry, George. But we gotta do what she says."

George growled in disagreement and looked at Joss.

Joss laughed and held up her hands. "You gotta listen to your mom on this one, bud."

Ruby giggled. "George, my girl, you have the most personality of any dog I've ever met." She scratched behind George's ears and kissed the tip of her nose. "You need to get your moms to bring you back to visit one day when you're all better so we can have some fun."

George laid a long, fat lick up the middle of Ruby's face and chuffed.

"Excellent," Ruby declared.

"She has quite the way with the ladies," Joss murmured playfully against Maeve's ear.

Maeve grinned and arched a brow at Joss as she retorted, "Why do you think I let her out in the yard that morning when you were running by the house after you moved into the cottage?"

Joss gaped. "You're lying."

"I don't think she is," Ruby piped up with a laugh as she pushed herself back to her feet. "I'm going to go check on George's discharge paperwork."

Joss waved a distracted hand at Ruby as she continued to stare at Maeve. "You really set George on me?"

Maeve shrugged. "I'd been watching you run by the house every morning from my office, and I figured that since George was the whole reason I got to meet you in the first place, that she could help me out again." She grinned unapologetically. "It worked, didn't it?"

"Yeah, it did." Joss bit her lip as she looked at Maeve, and shook her head as she leaned in to kiss her. George speared them both with the edge of her cone, unhappy with being ignored, and Joss laughed as she looked down at George and scratched her head. "Thanks for doing me a solid, George."

George barked and wagged her tail.

"You're welcome," Maeve translated. She sighed and leaned her head on Joss' shoulder. "I love you."

Warmth bloomed in Joss' chest as she held Maeve close and pressed a lingering kiss to the top of her head, her eyes drifting from Maeve to George, who was watching them with her typical goofy smile. "Love you too," she whispered.

"So! Who's ready to get out of here?" Ruby asked as she strode back into the kennels waving a stapled packet of papers.

"We are," Maeve spoke for the group as she disentangled herself from Joss' embrace.

George barked her agreement, and Joss shook her head as she asked, "What do we need to do?"

"Sign here," Ruby said, holding out the papers to Maeve. "And here." She smiled apologetically as she tapped the small credit card receipt stapled to the front of the papers.

"Gladly," Maeve said as she scribbled her name on the receipt, not bothering to see what the final total for George's care the last six days actually was. She took the discharge papers Ruby handed her when she gave her back the receipt, folded them in half length-wise, and slipped them into the back pocket of her jeans.

"Check her stitches every day. Keep the cone on. Change the bandages as necessary. Call your vet and get an appointment sometime early next week," Ruby instructed as if reading down a mental bullet-point list.

"Will do," Maeve promised.

"Then you are good to go," Ruby declared. "Gran knows you're coming by to check out, so she'll have everything waiting for you there so that way you can get back up the mountain as quickly as possible. I'm sure you're all more than ready to go home."

"We are," Joss confirmed, looking from Maeve to George and then back to Ruby. "Thanks for everything, Ruby."

"It was my pleasure," Ruby said. She glanced at Maeve's casted arm and then offered Joss a black and gold slip-leash. "Since she didn't come in with a leash, you guys can take this one."

"Perfect. Thanks." Joss took the leash and carefully looped it around George's neck. "You ready to go home, George?"

George did her best jousting impersonation in response, pushing Ruby out of the way without a second glance as she headed for the door.

"Gee, thanks," Ruby laughed. "Love you too, George."

The best Joss could do was laugh and offer Ruby an apologetic smile as she hurried after George, not wanting her to pull too much on the leash. She heard Ruby tell Maeve to follow them and that she would meet them out front with the ramp to help George into the SUV, and was glad that George slowed down as they neared the exit.

After spending so much of the last few days indoors, the sight of wispy white clouds streaking across a strikingly blue sky was especially beautiful, and Joss followed George to the small strip of grass in front of the veterinary hospital so she could sniff to her heart's content while Ruby got the ramp.

Less than five minutes later, George was safely loaded into the back of the SUV and had already made herself comfortable on the blankets Maeve always kept in the car for her. Joss waved one last thank you to Ruby as she slammed Maeve's door shut, and took a deep breath as she jogged around the front of the car to get behind the wheel.

Time was going to be of the essence as they rushed to get back to Sky as quickly as possible since they did not have a ramp to help George in and out of the car if she needed a bathroom break mid-trip, and she glanced at Maeve as she slipped behind the wheel. "You can just stay here with George while I run into the bed-and-breakfast to check out and grab our things."

Maeve nodded. "Okay. And while you're doing that, I'll call our vet in Sky to see if they have a ramp we can borrow, and then I'll call my mom to let them know we're on our way home and what we need them to do."

It felt good to actually be doing something after days of sitting around, twiddling her thumbs, waiting for this moment, and Joss smiled as she started the car. "Sounds good." She glanced over her shoulder. "You ready to roll, Georgie-girl?"

George yawned and closed her eyes.

Joss chuckled and winked at Maeve. "I think we're good."

Maeve smiled. "Good. Take us home, Joss."

Forty-One

The sight of warm, golden light spilling through the glass front doors overlooking the driveway had never been more beautiful and welcoming than it was when Joss pulled into their garage after what felt like forever on the road. The combination of holiday traffic and her overprotective need to take every turn at five miles per hour below the suggested speed added an extra hour to the trip, and she blew out a loud sigh of relief as she killed the engine.

They were home.

Joss looked over at Maeve, who was sleeping peacefully in the passenger's seat. She was curled into the seat, her left shoulder pressed into the supple leather, her feet tucked up beneath her. Maeve had been watching George when she had fallen asleep, and though Joss hated to wake her up, she knew that she needed to. "Sweetie." Joss gently swept Maeve's hair from her cheek and tucked it behind her ear. "We're home."

The garage brightened as the door to the house was opened, and Joss flashed a quick smile as she waved at Maeve's parents. Elizabeth Dylan smiled and waved as she leaned against the open doorway, looking very much like her daughter with her dark-framed glasses, blond hair, and lean build. She was dressed casually in a pair of dark jeans and a rose-colored sweater, while Maeve's dad sported a pair of faded 501s and a classic red and black lumberjack flannel. He was tall and built like a power forward, his red hair muted with streaks of gray, and Joss saw when he smiled at them as he walked toward the mouth of the garage that he had the same bright green eyes as Maeve.

Joss shook her head as she turned back to Maeve. "Maeve," she tried again, this time brushing her thumb over the blonde's lips. She smiled when they puckered to kiss her thumb.

"Love you," Maeve murmured.

"I love you, too. So very, very much." The urge to lean in and kiss Maeve awake was strong, but not nearly as strong as the knowledge that Maeve's parents were watching. Joss figured she should at least meet them before she started kissing their daughter in front of them. "But I need you to wake up. We're home, and your parents are waiting for us."

Maeve blinked her eyes open and mewled softly as she stretched, arching her back and gingerly straightening her legs. "I'm sorry. I didn't mean to fall asleep."

"You needed it." Joss lifted her arms over her head in a small stretch. She caught sight of Ben Dylan in the side mirror, hovering just to the side of the rear bumper with a long plastic ramp that was identical to the one they had used to help George into the car in Boulder, and reached for the door handle. "I'll help your dad get George out of the car."

"I can—" Maeve started to argue.

Joss shook her head. "Sweetie, we got it. I don't want to risk you bumping your arm on anything. Can you get me her leash? I'd rather not use the slip one Ruby gave us."

"I can do that."

"Thank you." Joss smiled and gave Maeve's leg a light squeeze. "Once we get George on solid ground again, I'll take her for a walk around the house so she can work out the kinks and stuff, and then we'll join you guys inside. I'm sure your parents would like to see you and catch up without me being there."

Maeve rolled her eyes. "I hate to break it to you, but they're probably more interested in talking to you than me."

"All the more reason for me to take George on a long, slow walk."

Maeve laughed. "You're ridiculous."

"But you love me for it."

"Yeah." Maeve's smile softened as she nodded. "I do. So don't take too long hiding out with George so I can introduce you to my parents."

"Yes, ma'am." Joss winked at Maeve as she climbed out of the car. "Hello," she called toward Maeve's mother as she slammed her door shut.

Elizabeth smiled and waved. "How was the drive?"

"Long." Joss tilted her head at Maeve. "This one snored through half of it, though."

"Watch it, you," Maeve teased as she made her way past Joss' Jeep to the hook on the far wall with that had a collection of leases hanging from it.

Joss held her hands up in surrender. "Fine. She slept beautifully, never making a sound for half the drive."

"That's better," Maeve declared as she plucked a retractable leash with a big blue handle from the hook beside the door to George's run.

Elizabeth laughed. "And how about my granddog?"

"She really did snore through almost the entire drive," Joss reported as she peeked through the car window at George, who was trying to get to her feet. Joss took a deep breath caught Ben Dylan's eye. They needed to get moving. The last thing she wanted was George getting antsy in the small confines of the SUV and hurting herself. "You ready with that ramp? She's looking like she's ready to get out of there."

"Ready when you are," Ben confirmed.

"Here you go," Maeve said, handing Joss the leash.

Joss smiled. "Thanks."

"You're welcome." Maeve gave Joss' wrist a squeeze and then turned her attention to her dad. "Hi, Dad."

"Hey, pumpkin. How's your arm?"

"Still attached," Maeve quipped.

"Well, that's a good start," Ben replied. "Watch out now, I don't want you bumping your arm on anything."

"You sound like Joss," Maeve pointed out with a chuckle as she backed away.

"You make that sound like a bad thing," Joss retorted as she and Ben secured one end of the ramp on top of the rear bumper.

"Zip it, Perrault," Maeve sassed, slapping Joss on the ass as she walked by.

Joss blushed. "I..."

Ben laughed. "I'll pop the hatch if you think you can slow that beast of a dog down."

"Sounds good," Joss agreed. She knelt down to catch George's eye as the hatch lifted out of the way, pushing herself up with the rising door. "Wait..."

George froze and allowed Joss to clip the leash to her collar.

"Good girl." Joss slipped the handle of the lease as far onto her fingers as she could, and then folded the plastic cone closer to George's head so it wouldn't hit the frame while she was climbing out. "Okay, let's go. Slowly..."

George blinked and inched carefully toward the ramp, her eyes darting from the brown and beige plastic to Joss to Ben, whom she greeted with a wag of her tail. She looked stiff from the ride, but made it safely down the ramp, and let out a small bark of pride as she turned toward Joss.

"Good job, George," Joss said, scratching her head. "You wanna go for a walk?"

George turned, whacking Joss' leg with the side of her cone, and walked out of the garage.

"I guess that's a yes," Joss chuckled, looking at Maeve. "We'll be in in a minute, okay?"

Maeve nodded. "I'll unlock the back door for you guys."

"I could stand to stretch my legs a bit too," Ben announced. "I'll walk with you two."

"Okay," Joss agreed warily.

"Be good, Dad," Maeve said.

"Who, me?" Ben asked with a laugh.

"Yes, you, Benjamin," Elizabeth retorted, wagging a warning finger at her husband. She laughed and looped an affectionate arm around Maeve's waist.

Joss groaned silently. She was going to get The Talk. The only good thing so far as she could tell was that neither Maeve nor her mother looked all that concerned. George saved her having to figure out how to politely segue into leaving by tugging her toward the driveway, and Joss shot one last worried look at Maeve, who was being led inside by her mother, as she followed her.

It was cold, but not uncomfortably so, though Joss was glad the hoodie she wore was one of her thicker ones. She took a deep breath as she heard Ben jog to catch up to them, and looked up at the sky, hoping that she could distract herself from what was coming by pinpointing familiar constellations.

It did not work, however, and all she could think about was how she would respond to whatever he said. She had never done the whole meet-the-parents thing—and she could not help but feel that it was particularly unfair that she had to traverse this minefield when she was running on fumes, physically and emotionally exhausted from the events of the last week.

However, Ben seemed content to just walk with them, hands shoved in the front pockets of his 501s, whistling softly under his breath. The waiting was driving her nuts, but she would be damned if she broke the silence first. Maybe if she just kept quiet long enough they could make it inside without anything happening.

That, of course, failed to happen as Ben nudged her with his elbow just as they stepped off the driveway and onto the back lawn and asked, "Are you waiting for me to launch into the whole overprotective father spiel?"

Joss' heart leapt into her throat and she glanced at him. "Maybe?"

Ben chuckled and shook his head. "Sorry to disappoint you, but I really did just want to stretch my legs a bit. Never mind the fact that Maeve would kill me if I did anything like that."

Joss dared a small smile as she looked over at him. "Really?"

He shrugged. "I know that she loves you, and I'm assuming you love her?" He smiled when Joss nodded. "Well then, that's all I need to know." He grew silent, his smile fading into a pensive line. "Thank you for taking care of her. And George. God, I don't know what she would have done if she'd lost that stupid dog."

"It would have been hard," Joss agreed, her throat tightening as her mind drifted to those dark hours after the attack, when both Maeve and George were in surgery and she had no idea what was happening to them.

Ben nodded. "Yeah. That's one way to put it." He blew out a loud breath and stared into the night. After a minute or so, he spoke again. "How are you holding up?" He shook his head. "I would have been beside myself if I had been in your shoes."

"I'm okay," Joss said as she paused to let George relieve herself. "Tired. But good. They're home and they'll heal, and that's really all I can ask for. Right?"

"Right," Ben agreed as they started walking again. "Having your family home safe with you is absolutely what's most important."

They finished the walk in comfortable silence, and Joss unclipped George's leash as Ben pulled open the sliding glass door to the kitchen. She watched George make her way over to her water bowl before looking up to see what Maeve and her mother were doing at the island. Her stomach growled as she spied Maeve picking at a piece of bread and Elizabeth sliding large pieces of lasagna onto plates. "You survived," Maeve greeted with a smile.

"Of course she did," Ben said waving Joss inside and closing the door after them. "We had a nice talk, George went potty, and now we want dinner, damn it. It's late and we're hungry."

"Oh you do, do you?" Elizabeth laughed. "Well then, get your butts in here so we can eat."

Ben grinned. "Yes, ma'am. Oh." He snapped his fingers and looked at Maeve, who was making her way toward them. "We also picked up a few dog beds for George when we were at the pet store this afternoon. Figured she probably shouldn't be climbing onto the couch like she usually does for a while."

"I didn't even think of that," Joss murmured, shaking her head. "Thank you."

"Eh, it was nothing." He smiled. "You girls had your hands full enough. Besides, that's what family's for, right?"

"It is," Maeve agreed as she wrapped her good arm around Joss' waist and leaned into her. "Thanks, Dad."

"My pleasure, pumpkin."

"Who wants food?" Elizabeth called out as she carried two plates to the round dining table in the nook.

George stopped halfway to the family room and turned to look at them.

Joss laughed. "You want dinner too, George?"

George gave her a look full of *duh* and went to stand sentry at her empty bowl.

Maeve chuckled kissed Joss' cheek as she let her arm fall. "I think that's a yes."

"Me too." Joss stepped in front of Maeve and shook her head. "Sit down and rest. I'll do it."

Maeve shook her head and smiled, her eyes conveying so much more emotion than the quiet "Okay" that fell from her lips.

"Thank you," Joss murmured, hoping that her eyes said just as much. She took a deep breath as she looked away, and hurried to retrieve George's empty bowl from her stand. By the time she set George's bowl back in place with her food, the Dylans were all gathered around the table waiting for her. "Sorry."

"No reason to apologize," Elizabeth said kindly.

Joss smiled her thanks as she took her seat beside Maeve. "This looks wonderful."

"Thank you, Joss." Elizabeth smiled. "Now, let's eat so I can get these dishes cleaned up and get some of the prep work done for tomorrow."

"Mom…" Maeve started to protest, but her mother was not having it.

"We are taking care of Thanksgiving, and you two are going to relax and do nothing."

Ben froze with his fork halfway to his mouth. "We?"

"Please, like you weren't planning on deep frying the turkey anyway." Elizabeth arched a brow at Joss. "Joss, dear, I know what Maeve likes for sides, but are there any dishes you would like me to make?"

Joss shook her head. "No, thank you. I don't need anything special."

"Oh, but you do," Elizabeth argued with a kind look.

Joss blushed and looked at Maeve. "I've got Maeve, that's all I need."

George *aroo-ed* in protest.

"And you, too, George," Joss amended with a self-conscious laugh as she glanced back at Maeve's parents, who were regarding her with identical pleased expressions. A soft hand on her arm drew her eyes to Maeve, and she blushed as she leaned in and whispered, "Sorry. Too much?"

"Shut up, Perrault," Maeve murmured as she captured Joss' lips in a sweet kiss. She smiled and ran a gentle hand over Joss' cheek when she pulled away. "I love you."

"Love you too," Joss breathed.

"Yeah, yeah, yeah," Ben grumbled. "Knock it off. You're making me look bad over here."

Maeve laughed and waggled her eyebrows at her dad as she picked up her fork. "Then step up your game, old man."

"Who you calling an old man?"

"That's enough, you two," Elizabeth said, rolling her eyes. She shook her head and added, "I swear, Joss, we can't take them anywhere."

George burped loudly, proving Elizabeth's point, and everybody laughed.

"Ben"—Elizabeth looked pointedly at her husband—"can you go grab one of the beds for George from the living room and bring it in here?"

"I can do it," Joss protested, pushing her chair back.

"Enjoy your dinner," Ben said, shaking his head. "I got it."

"If you're sure…" Joss pulled her chair back to the table and picked up her fork. "Thank you."

"Try the lasagna," Maeve said as she speared a particularly large bite with her fork. "It's better than DiAmico's."

Joss arched a disbelieving brow. Nobody made better lasagna than DiAmico's. "Seriously?"

"Seriously."

And it was. By a mile.

Joss let the Dylans catch up with each other as she ate, only answering questions that were directed specifically at her, and groaned when she finally pushed her plate away, too full to even think of taking another bite. "That was the best lasagna I have ever had in my life."

"I'm glad you liked it," Elizabeth said, pleased. She stood and took Joss and Maeve's plates. "Now, scoot. We can talk more tomorrow."

Joss looked at George, who was snoring on the large round dog bed beside the table. "She probably shouldn't do the stairs."

"We put a bed for her in the guest room," Ben said as he gathered the remaining plates. "She can camp out with us, and I can take her out during the night if she needs it."

"Thanks, Dad," Maeve said, smiling at her father.

Joss was in the middle of trying to hide a yawn when Maeve turned to her, and she smiled guiltily. "Sorry."

Maeve shook her head. "It's been a long few days." She held out her hand. "Come on. Let's go upstairs."

"See you girls in the morning," Elizabeth called after them.

After placing the vacuum at the foot of the stairs so that George would not try to join them, they retreated to the master bedroom. Nighttime routines were completed quickly, and Joss sighed as she slipped beneath the covers of their bed.

"Comfy?" Maeve teased as she walked around the bed and squeezed herself in on what was usually Joss' side so that her good arm was in-between them.

Joss nodded as she sat up to capture Maeve's lips in a tender kiss as she scooted over to make more room. "Yes."

Maeve smiled as she pulled away and laid down, wiggling slightly to make herself comfortable on Joss' pillow. "Hold me?"

Like there's a universe where I would ever say no. "Always." Joss carefully stretched out beside Maeve and inched closer until she was pressed against her side. She let her right arm drape low over Maeve's hips, holding her lightly. "Is this okay?"

"It's perfect," Maeve confirmed through a yawn. "I love you, Joss Perrault."

"I love you, Maeve Dylan," Joss whispered as she closed her eyes.

Forty-Two

"How're they doing?"

Joss looked up at Maeve's dad and smiled. She was stretched out on the sofa facing the fireplace with her back pressed snugly into the cushions and Maeve cuddled up against her front, sleeping peacefully while George did the same on the dog bed she had pulled next to them. The Panthers were silently clashing with the Cowboys on the television that she had muted when Maeve had fallen asleep back in the first quarter, but she was not really paying attention to the game. It was just a distraction, something to pretend to focus on when in reality she was aware of very little beyond the woman snuggled up against her. "Good," she whispered. "They both needed the rest, so..."

"I meant the Cowboys," Ben said as he sat down on the empty sofa and turned to face the television.

Joss arched a brow in surprise. "I would've figured you for a Bears fan."

"I am," Ben confirmed. "But I really hate the Cowboys."

"Well, in that case, you'll be glad to know that they're down going into the fourth."

"Excellent." Ben folded his hands behind his head and stretched his legs out in front of himself, crossing his ankles and making himself comfortable. "Elizabeth says we've got like forty minutes until dinner."

"Are you sure I can't help with anything?" Joss offered for what seemed like the thousandth time that day. Elizabeth and Ben had been in the kitchen all day, and while she appreciated the time to just relax with Maeve and George, she felt guilty that Maeve's parents were doing so much work.

"Like you could get up now even if I said yes." Ben shook his head. "She's 'working her magic'"—he pulled his hands out from behind his head to emphasize the phrase with air quotes before returning them to their previous position and making himself comfortable once again— "and told me to get out of her kitchen."

Joss laughed softly and shook her head. "Still, I feel bad that I haven't done anything to help…"

"You're taking care of our girl there." Ben tipped his head at Maeve. "Believe me, you're doing plenty."

Joss blushed and looked down at Maeve. "Yeah, well…"

"Besides," Ben continued, changing the subject, "watching the game is the best part of Thanksgiving anyway. Am I right?"

"I guess so," Joss agreed. "This is the first Thanksgiving in ages where I haven't been working."

"At the bookstore?"

"No. Atramentum is closed for the holiday, but we have very restricted hours anyway right now because it's the off-season. I was a public accountant until May of this year."

"That's right. I remember Maeve saying something about that. How's running a bookstore compare to being an accountant?"

"I still do quite a bit of accounting, but just for myself. The hours are pretty comparable during the busy seasons, but it's nice having these handful of weeks every few months where I can just take a step back and relax." She rubbed her thumb over Maeve's hip. "And it gives me some quality time to spend with this one."

Ben's phone rang, the sound shrill despite the fact that it was in his pocket, and Maeve startled awake, blinking as she tried to get her bearings. "What?"

"You fell asleep," Joss informed her with a smile.

"Sorry about that, pumpkin," Ben apologized as he pulled his phone from his pocket. "It's your brother. Walker and them are all at Liam's for the day, and we told them we could FaceTime whenever the kids were ready."

"Of course." Maeve sat up and ran a hand through her hair. She looked down at Joss and whispered, "Do I need to go comb my hair or anything?"

"No." Joss shook her head as she angled herself to a sitting position beside Maeve. "You look beautiful."

"Good answer," Ben quipped as he pressed his thumb to his screen. A few seconds later, he grinned. "Hey, Hunter! How's it going, buddy?"

"Hey, Grandpa!" a tiny voice replied enthusiastically. "The Cowboys are losing!"

"I know!" Ben chortled. "Isn't it great?"

"So great," Hunter replied. "How's Auntie Maeve?"

"She's doing okay. You want to say hi?"

"Yes, sir."

Ben held the phone out toward Maeve. "Take this. I'll go tell your mom that the kids are on the phone."

Joss smiled and took the phone. "I'll hold it for you," she told Maeve as she angled the camera at her. An adorable little boy with messy brown hair pointed in Joss' direction.

"Who's that?"

Maeve grinned and patted Joss' leg. "Hunter, this is Joss."

A little girl with blond hair pulled back into braids pushed Hunter out of the way and peered at the screen. "Is she your girlfriend?"

"Hello to you too, Sam. And yes, she is," Maeve confirmed.

Sam waved. "Hi Aunt Maeve. Hi Joss."

Joss leaned her head into the shot and smiled. "Hey, Sam. It's nice to meet you."

"I wanna talk to Auntie Maeve!" a young voice called out.

Joss had to bite her cheek to keep from laughing when a little boy of about four popped in front of Sam and waved. "Hiii Auntie Maeve!"

"Hi Bobby." Maeve waved back. "You being a good boy?"

Bobby nodded. "Sometimes."

Joss snorted a laugh. "Sorry," she apologized.

Maeve rolled her eyes.

"You have a cast?" Bobby asked, looking at Maeve's arm.

"I do. You wanna see it?"

"Yeah!" Bobby turned around and yelled, "GUYS! AUNTIE MAEVE IS GOING TO SHOW US HER CAST!"

"Wow," Joss muttered.

"Oh, just wait until you get the full experience in person," Maeve said, dropping a quick kiss to Joss' cheek.

"Is that your girlfriend?" a new little girl asked, poking her head into the screen. She looked older than the others, though her hair was in the same tight braids as the other little girl.

"Yes. Heather, can you get everybody together and have one of your dads hold the phone so we can do this all at once?" Maeve suggested with a smile.

"DAD, HOLD THE PHONE FOR US, PLEASE!" Heather bellowed as the rest of the kids began jockeying for position on the coffee table.

The picture jostled as it changed hands, and Maeve laughed when a younger adult version of Ben turned the camera on himself and stuck out his tongue. "Hey, Sis. How you feeling?"

"Good. Liam," Maeve said, waving her good hand at Joss, "I'd like you to meet Joss."

"She's Auntie Maeve's girlfriend," a helpful voice chimed in from somewhere behind Liam.

Liam laughed. "I know. Hello, Joss. It's nice to finally meet you."

"Likewise," Joss murmured.

"Maeve!" another booming voice called out.

Maeve rolled her eyes. "Hey, Walker."

"Has Dad scared Joss off yet?" he teased.

"Nope. We figure we'll keep her around for a while," Ben said, winking at Joss as he and Elizabeth bent over the back of the couch so they could get in the shot too. "Now get your ugly mugs outta the way so we can see our grandkids."

Joss did her best to try and fade into the background as the Dylans caught up with each other. It did not take the kids long to get tired of talking on the phone after they had met her, seen Maeve's cast, and got to see that George really was okay—a fact George proved for them by sitting up and wagging her tail as she tried to lick the screen—and before long it was just the adults crouched around the screen.

"So, seriously, how're you feeling?" Liam asked Maeve.

"Like I have a broken elbow." Maeve smirked. "It's actually not that bad now. Just annoying."

"When are they going to take the pins out?"

"In three weeks."

"Joss," Walker butted in. Where Liam looked like their father, Walker was more like Maeve and took after their mother with his blond hair and fair complexion. The eldest of the three, he looked like he could have been Maeve's twin, except he had brown eyes like his mom and brother. "Take a picture of those suckers before they pull them out? I wanna see what they look like."

"Sure thing." Joss nodded. Honestly, she was a pretty curious too—especially since the surgeon said that it would be done in-office without any kind of anesthesia or anything. "I can do that."

"Awesome."

"DAD!" a chorus of distraught voices rang through the line.

"Sounds like you two are up," Ben chuckled. "Have fun with that. We'll be relaxing here and enjoying your mother's excellent cooking in peace and quiet."

"Way to rub it in, Dad. Thanks."

Ben smirked. "No problem."

"We'll be home Saturday," Elizabeth said as it looked like the boys were about to hang up. "Dinner at our house Sunday night?"

"Sounds good, Mom," Liam said with a grin. "Nice to meet you, Joss."

"You too," Joss said.

"Yeah. Take care of our sister for us," Walker said.

"Will do," Joss promised.

"And don't forget those pictures!" Walked added just before the screen went black.

"Wow," Joss breathed.

"Ben, come help me with this turkey," Elizabeth said.

"You got it," Ben said as he followed her back into the kitchen.

Maeve smiled and wrapped her good arm around Joss' waist. "You officially survived your first foray into the Dylan Clan. Congratulations."

"Thanks." Joss laughed and looked over at her. Maeve's smile was so sweet that she had to taste it, and she hummed softly when Maeve's tongue slipped past her lips to dance lightly with her own. The kiss was slow and deep and perfect, and she prayed that Ben and Elizabeth said in the kitchen a bit longer as she tenderly cupped Maeve's face in her hands and poured every ounce of love she felt for her into her kiss.

After a week of quick pecks and kisses that lingered not much longer than that, this kiss was pure heaven, and she let herself drift freely in the wonderful feelings it created. Warmth swept through her when Maeve's fingers landed lightly on her cheek, the simple touch radiating love and affection, making her heart flutter and her stomach tighten.

God, how I love this woman.

"Dinner!" Ben's voice boomed from the kitchen.

Maeve giggled as she pulled away, her eyes dancing with happiness and simmering with ardor as she nuzzled Joss' cheek. "At least he didn't walk in on us."

"Oh, he did," Ben called out, laughter ringing in his tone. "But he walked out and yelled instead of embarrassing you."

Joss' eyes went wide as a furious blush erupted across her cheeks. "Oh my God."

Maeve laughed. "Welcome to the family, babe. It's all downhill from here."

"You better not be making out again!" Ben hollered.

"And if we are?" Maeve retorted, arching a brow at Joss, playfully asking if she were willing.

Joss bit her lip and sucked in a deep breath, because goddamn it was tempting. She would do anything in her power to make Maeve look that happy for the rest of her life.

"Then I get all the pie!"

"Shit, he's playing hardball." Maeve groaned and stole one last quick kiss. "We better get in there."

"Okay." Joss nodded as she pushed herself to her feet and held a hand out to help Maeve up. She threaded their fingers together and lifted Maeve's hand to her lips, kissing it softly as a maelstrom of thoughts swirled in her mind, spinning faster and faster until they converged into a single life-altering decision that was simultaneously exhilarating and terrifying.

Maeve smiled and tilted her head inquiringly. "You okay?"

"Yeah." Joss nodded. "Yeah." She cleared her throat softly. "Just…thinking about something."

"Good thoughts, I hope?"

"Yeah." Joss looked down at George, a plan already forming in her mind. "Good thoughts." She smiled and pecked Maeve's lips one last time. "Come on. Dinner."

"You're not going to tell me?" Maeve asked sounding more amused than anything else.

"I will," Joss confessed. "Just not now."

"Soon?"

Joss looked from Maeve to Elizabeth and Ben, who were standing beside the table waiting for them with kind, accepting smiles, and nodded. There was no way she was going to be able to wait too long. "Yeah. Soon."

The trick was going to be figuring out how to do it right.

Forty-Three

Joss stood at the window next to the modest eight-foot decorated tree in the living room overlooking the backyard, scratching George's head as the two of them watched the snow fall through the faint reflection of colored lights. The flakes were fluffy and fat, perfect for making a snowman, and the sky was that strange, dull yellow hue that always accompanied a storm—the perfect backdrop to help little ones try to catch a peek of Santa flying overhead en route to deliver a stash of presents beneath their trees. A blazing fire crackled in the large fireplace behind her, the shadows of the flames flickering over the modest collection of presents beneath the tree, and the Christmas playlist Maeve had put together poured from the speakers mounted around the room, adding that perfect final dash of holiday ambiance.

Joss bit her lip as she ran her hand over her front pocket to make sure that the most important present she had for Maeve had not suddenly disappeared, and her stomach fluttered as she traced the distinctive shape with her fingertips.

As it turned out, gathering all the pieces needed to create the perfect a proposal was exceedingly difficult when one spent the majority of their time with the person they were planning on proposing to. The actual planning part was easy enough to manage—she had plenty of time to daydream about what she would like to do while they were laying about on the couch all day—but finding the time to go shopping for the perfect ring was a little more difficult. Thankfully, though, as Maeve healed enough to get back to work, typing away one-handed at her laptop in the office, Joss was able to sneak out under the guise of making sure Atramentum was ready for the winter season to look for one. Nothing that was already in the display cases was quite right, however she was able to collaborate with one jewelry designer to create the perfect ring.

It took several sessions for them to come up with a design she loved, and then several weeks for the jeweler to craft the piece. She had gotten a call that it was finally finished the night before, and she had ducked out to pick up earlier that morning before the snow really started falling.

Her plan had revolved around a Christmas morning proposal, but as she toyed with the loose ring in her pocket through fabric of her jeans, she was leaning toward revising her plan.

She looked down at George and shook her head. "What do you think we should do?"

"What does she think you should do about what?" Maeve asked, her tone light and amused as she wrapped her arm around Joss' waist and leaned against her side. She still had another week to go until she was completely cast-free, but she had healed more than enough to reach over and tickle Joss' stomach with her left hand.

Joss laughed and grabbed Maeve's hand, grasping her fingers lightly. Maeve looked like an angel in her thigh-length cream cashmere sweater and jeans, her hair still tousled from the time they spent in bed earlier that afternoon, and Joss sucked in a deep breath as she looked into soulful emerald eyes that sparkled with joy. *Please let her say yes.* "I was debating giving you one of your presents tonight. But since you're being all nosy and eavesdropping on mine and George's private conversation..."

"Oh." Maeve pressed a breathy, heart-stoppingly soft kiss to Joss' ear, nuzzling her cheek as she whispered, "We can do a present tonight if you want."

Joss' stomach erupted in butterflies as she nodded. "Okay. But I have to go get yours."

Maeve grinned. "Okay. I finished wrapping yours earlier this afternoon, so I'll go get it and meet you back here?"

Joss nodded again. "Sure."

Maeve chuckled and wrapped her fingers in the collar of Joss' charcoal gray cable-knit sweater, using that hold to pull her into a deep, searing kiss. "I love you."

"Love you too," Joss murmured. She smiled and dropped a playful kiss to the tip of Maeve's nose. "Now, stop distracting me. I have to go get your present, and you're holding things up."

"Oh, well, in that case, I apologize." Maeve's eyes twinkled with mirth as she captured Joss' lips in kiss that was deeper and hotter than the one before.

Joss swayed on her feet when the hold on her sweater disappeared, and blinked her eyes open when the kiss eventually broke. "Wow…"

"Indeed." Maeve winked as she turned on her heel and sashayed out of the room, putting an extra sway in her hips because she knew that Joss would be looking.

"Fuck me," Joss muttered when Maeve had finally disappeared down the hall toward her office.

George head butted her leg and looked up at her with wide eyes.

Joss nodded. "Right. It's show time, George. You ready?"

George sneezed.

"Good enough," Joss chuckled, grateful for the comic relief as she gave her thigh a couple quick pats. "Let's go."

George followed at her out of the living room and up the stairs, and sat down to wait beside the fireplace that divided the master bedroom and sitting area while Joss rifled through her sock drawer for the satiny red ribbon she had bought for the occasion. She lifted her head when Joss knelt in front of her, and held perfectly still as the length of ribbon was slipped through the metal loop that held her tags on her collar.

"Good girl," Joss murmured as she fished the ring from her pocket. She held it up for George's inspection. "Do you think she'll like it?"

George leaned in and gave the ring a quick sniff before daintily licking the point of Joss' chin.

"Good. Me too." Joss looped the ribbon around the diamond studded platinum band that had a stunning, single carat princess-cut diamond as its focal point, before tying it in a bow. George looked quite dapper with the bow on her collar, and Joss smiled as she straightened it out.

"You look good, George. The bow tie suits you."

George cocked her head and gave Joss a big doggy grin.

"Right." Joss rubbed George's head. "Do you remember our plan?"

George chuffed softly.

"All right then, buddy. Let's go." Joss pushed herself to her feet and brushed her hands off on the seat of her jeans.

They made their way back down the stairs, and Joss double-checked her reflection in the mirror in the foyer before they turned toward the living room. Maeve had pulled the quilt they snuggled under at night while watching television off the couch and spread it out beside the tree, creating a cozy little sitting area.

Joss smiled. *Okay. Yeah. That will work quite nicely.*

Maeve eyed Joss' empty hands and arched a brow in surprise. "I thought you were going to go get my present?"

"Who says I didn't?" Joss retorted as she sat on the blanket beside Maeve. She glanced at George and pointed at the ground, which was their signal for her to lie down, and was pleased when the Dane did it immediately. The last thing she needed was Maeve noticing the ring before she was ready for her to. Joss ran a hand through her hair as she looked back at Maeve, who had a shirt box wrapped in glossy red and white paper on the ground beside her, and quickly considered her options. It seemed weird to propose first and then sit back and open whatever Maeve had gotten for her—never mind the fact that the only thing she wanted for Christmas this year was to see the ring she had picked out on Maeve's finger—so that meant she had to get Maeve to go first. "Is it okay if I go second? Please?"

Maeve's brow wrinkled in confusion, but she nodded. "Of course." She picked up the box and handed it to Joss. "This is for you."

"Thank you." Joss took the package, which was so light that it felt like it was completely empty, and arched a brow at Maeve as she gave it a shake. She could hear the faint sound of paper quietly rattling against the sides of the box, but that did nothing to help her guess what was inside, and she smiled as she slipped a finger beneath a flap of paper to rip it open.

"This isn't a present you can use right away," Maeve explained as Joss slipped the box free of its paper. "But I thought it'd be fun."

"I'm sure it will be," Joss agreed as she lifted the lid off the box and looked inside. There, nestled atop candy cane patterned tissue paper, she saw a picture of a catamaran that had the name *Veritas* emblazoned on its hull. She picked up the picture to look at it more closely, and that was when she noticed the plane tickets. "Maeve?"

Maeve smiled and pushed her glasses back into place. "The *Veritas* is a charter yacht that sails around the Virgin Islands. I booked us a weeklong vacation on it in April after the winter season is over. I thought it'd be a nice—"

Joss cut her off with a kiss, completely blown away by the gift. "That sounds amazing." She grinned and kissed her again. "Thank you."

"I'm glad you like it."

"I love it," Joss enthused, capturing her lips in a tender, lingering kiss. "I love you," she breathed when she finally pulled away.

"Love you, too," Maeve murmured.

"Good." Joss flashed what she hoped was a confident smile and took a deep breath. *My turn.* She looked at George, who was watching them through sleepy-looking eyes, and nodded. "Ready to help me out here?"

George scrambled to a sitting position, lifting her head up and puffing out her chest, just like they had practiced. Joss could not have been more proud of her if she tried, and she held her breath as she looked back at Maeve, waiting for the moment she noticed the sparkling platinum band hanging from the red bow on George's new green collar.

And then she did.

"Joss?"

"Well," Joss began as she reached for the end of the ribbon and gave it a tug, letting the treasure it held fall into her hand. She palmed the ring and smiled shakily. "I thought it would only be appropriate to have George help me with all of this since she's the reason we met."

Maeve let out a small gasp and covered her mouth with her hand as her eyes filled with tears.

"It's not a super-awesome vacation," Joss hedged as she tried to remember the speech she had planned out. But instead of those carefully crafted words, all she saw was Maeve smiling at her, shaking her head in disbelief, waiting for the question she knew would be coming. "I wrote a really good speech to do this right, but I can only remember the end…"

Maeve choked out a laugh and nodded as tears trickled down her cheeks to collect in the upturned corners of her lips. "I'm sure the end will be more than good enough."

"I hope so." Joss took Maeve's hands into her own and smiled as she smoothed her thumbs over the backs of Maeve's knuckles. The feeling of Maeve's hand in hers calmed the majority of her nerves, and she suddenly remembered the words she had planned.

So, even though Maeve seemed happy for her to jump right to the end, she went back to the beginning instead.

"Of all the places I might have reasonably expected my life to change, it was certainly not sitting in the dirt in front of the cottage looking up at this beast of a dog that was trying to lick me to death. But that's exactly what happened. Because then you showed up, looking all pink-cheeked and out-of-breath and beautiful, and I felt like

I had my legs knocked out from under me all over again." She smiled and shook her head at the memory. "I find myself continuously in awe of your strength, your humor, your passion, and your beauty, and I fall more and more in love with you with every day that passes. Heaven, for me, would be a lifetime spent loving you, because I honestly can't imagine my life without you by my side." She took a deep breath, trying to calm her racing heart for the finale of her speech as she stared into Maeve's eyes. The answer to the question she had yet to ask was written plainly in the watery smile that lit Maeve's entire face with happiness, and she blew out the breath she had been holding as she beamed back at her and placed the ring at the tip of the appropriate finger on Maeve's left hand. "Maeve Dylan, would you please make me the happiest woman in the world and say that you'll let me be your wife?"

Maeve nodded. "Yes."

"Thank you," Joss murmured as she slid the ring home.

"Oh, Joss," Maeve breathed, looking at the ring on her finger for only the briefest of moments before she leaned in and captured her lips in a sweet saltwater kiss. "I love you."

"I love you." Joss smoothed a hand over Maeve's cheek and guided their lips together once more, smiling into the kiss.

Not to be outdone, George took advantage of their being distracted and pounced, knocking them onto the ground and bathing both their faces with slobbery kisses. And, as Joss laughed and wrestled the dog away from Maeve, she had to admit that George barging in was the perfect end to her proposal.

After all, if it were not for her, who knows what would have happened.

Epilogue

Four years and five months later...

"What are you doing here?"

Joss looked up at Scott, who was trying to safely set his almost two-year-old daughter Nora on her feet despite the fact that she looked hell-bent on diving from his arms to the floor, and laughed. There were two weeks of peace and quiet left before the summer season revved up, so there was really no reason either of them should have been at Atramentum. "Forget me. What are you doing here?"

"We were going for a walk and saw the lights on in here." Scott ran a hand through his hair as Nora squealed and bolted toward the small coffee table in the sitting area at the store that was now perpetually covered with coloring books and crayons, her short auburn curls flopping with every step.

Joss smiled as she watched her own daughter Molly—a perfect mini-Maeve with striking green eyes that were more beautiful than her mother's—wave at her friend and offer her a blue crayon. George watched the toddlers from her spot in front of the fireplace, while Rosencrantz and Guildenstern—the British shorthairs she had adopted not long after Willy Shakes and Dickens finally joined Helen in the big bookstore in the sky—took off for the safety of the high ground. The cats were fine with George, who had mellowed considerably in the last few years, but they did not have the patience for the girls' not-so-gentle affections as the Dane did. "When did the girls get so big?"

"Hell if I know," Scott chuckled. "Seems like only yesterday we were both walking around here like zombies from being up all night with them. Oh, and before I forget, Michelle wanted me to see if you guys wanted to do a joint birthday party for them again this year."

Joss nodded. Nora had been born three days before Molly, so they were enrolled in all the same classes and had all the same little friends, and so it just made sense to save everybody's weekends and combine the two celebrations into one. "I'll have to check with the boss, but I think it'd be fun."

"Cool. No rush," Scott said and, in the same breath, continued, "Nora, we don't color on George."

George just closed her eyes and remained still, resigned to the blue Mohawk Nora was drawing on her head.

"I'm so sorry."

"You should see her toenails," Joss said, waving him off. "Maeve and Molly had a great time painting them bright pink last night."

"I swear to God, man, your dog is a fucking saint."

Across the room, the girls began chanting, "Futting… Futting…"

Joss laughed. "You are so lucky they don't that 'K' sound down yet."

"Tell me about it," Scott chuckled. "So, anyway, seriously—what are you doing here? Don't you and Maeve need to get going soon?"

Joss checked her watch. It was only four, and their flight was not until five thirty. She shook her head. "Nah. Our flight isn't until eight and her they've arranged a charter for us out of Sky Airport." Maeve had just won her third Gold Dagger award in a row, and her publisher was flying them to New York so Maeve could do the morning talk show circuit to promote her books. She could have made the trip on her own, but by Joss tagging along, the trip also netted them a nice little weekend away where they could celebrate both Maeve's success and their three-year anniversary in style. "Besides, she's busy putting some finishing touches on her comments to the scripted questions the talk shows'll be giving her, and her parents are still driving up from Denver, so me and Molly and George got out of the house for a bit so she could have some peace and quiet."

"Makes sense, but she loves spending time with her mini-me. Why couldn't she work on that kind of stuff on the plane?"

"Two words." Joss waggled her eyebrows. "Private. Charter. We have other plans for the flight to New York."

Scott grinned and held up his hand for a high five. "Nice."

"I know." Joss smacked his hand. "It's just going to be nice to get away for a few days. I'm gonna miss those little buggers"—she tilted her head at Molly and George—"but I am really looking forward to having Maeve all to myself for a bit."

"I hear ya on that one, sister," Scott commiserated.

Joss smiled as her phone that was laying facedown on the counter beside the register buzzed with an incoming text. *Mom and dad just got here and are demanding their grandchildren be brought home ASAP.* "Our presence has been requested back at home," she shared as she slipped her phone into her pocket.

Scott checked his watch and nodded. "Yeah. We should probably get going too. I'll come by while you guys are gone and take care of the cats."

"Thanks for that." Joss picked up Molly's green zip-up hoodie from the counter. "Molly. George. Time to go home and see Mommy."

George barked and Molly squealed excitedly as they took off for the front door.

"Coat, Molly-girl," Joss said, stepping in front of the toddler. She smiled as she helped her into the hoodie and then zipped it up. "All done."

"Thanks, Momma!" Molly beamed and kissed her cheek.

"You're welcome, sweet girl. You want to walk George to the car?" Joss asked as she clipped a short, nylon leash to George's collar.

"Yeah!" Molly cheered.

"I walk George too!" Nora said.

"We share!" Molly said, nodding.

"Looks like you guys are walking us to our car," Joss chuckled as she handed Molly and Nora the leash. "Wait on the sidewalk, girls, okay?"

"Otay," they chirruped.

George *aroo*-ed her understanding as well, and together the five of them exited the store. Scott kept an eye on the kids while Joss locked up, and then they all made their way slowly across the street. The sight of the girls walking George, a dog they very easily could have ridden tandem, never failed to make Joss smile. George had been great with Molly from the moment they brought her home from the hospital— they had a picture of the giant dog sleeping with Molly curled up beside her on the mantle that both her and Maeve swore would never be replaced—and she kept her head on a swivel as they crossed the street, looking for cars while her handlers chatted happily away beside her.

"Good girl, George," Joss said when they reached the far sidewalk. "Now, wait…"

George barked once and stopped to partake in the bouquet of scents on the fire hydrant.

"Thank you for helping, Nora," Joss said.

"You weltome," Nora said. "Bye, Molly!"

"Bye, Nora!" Molly waved, the extra leash dangling from her fist flapping in the air beside her.

"Later, Heitz," Joss chuckled.

"Get some, Perrault," Scott quipped. Joss laughed and shook her head as Scott smirked at her and took Nora's hand and started walking down the street. "You wanna go get Mommy some flowers?"

Nora nodded vigorously. "Yay!"

"We get Mommy flowers too?" Molly asked.

"Not today, baby girl," Joss said as she gave George's side a light tap and started for their car, knowing that the Dane would bring Molly along with her. "We gotta get home. Grandma and Grandpa are waiting to play with you!"

Molly cheered, and George looked at her excitedly. Joss laughed as she took the leash from Molly and let it drop to the ground so she could lift the toddler into her chair. "Yes, George. They're waiting to play with you, too."

George barked and danced in place next to Joss as she buckled Molly in, and then let out a thunderous *aroo* when Joss opened the passenger door for her. George still refused to ride anywhere but shotgun if the seat was available.

Joss shook her head as she slammed the door shut and hurried around the back of the car to get behind the wheel. "So, who's the most excited to go see Mommy, Grandma, and Grandpa?"

"Me!" Molly yelled.

George barked.

Joss grinned and turned to look at her daughter. "No, I am!"

"Are not!"

"I don't think you're right," Joss retorted with a laugh as she turned back around and started the car. Once they were on the main road headed for home, she called Maeve to let her know they were on their way back, so when they finally pulled up to the house, Maeve and her parents were sitting on the front porch waiting for them.

"There're my grandkids!" Elizabeth Dylan cheered when Joss let Molly and George out of the car.

"Nice to see you too, Elizabeth," Joss chuckled.

"Psht. We didn't come for you," Ben said as he swooped Molly into his arms and spun her around while Elizabeth rubbed George's sides in greeting. "Don't you have a flight to catch or something?"

Joss shook her head as she walked over to Maeve and pulled her into her arms. "At least we know where we stand," she said as she watched Maeve's parents with their kids.

"Right?" Maeve chuckled as she brushed their lips together. "The pilot called a couple minutes ago, he's at the airport and ready to go whenever we are," she whispered huskily.

Joss' stomach flip-flopped, and she smiled against Maeve's lips. "So do you want to go now?"

Maeve slipped her hands under the hem of Joss' untucked tee and grinned as she fluttered her fingers just below Joss' breasts. "Do you?" She teased Joss' lips with her tongue. "Because I'm all for getting on that plane and getting into your pants, but if you want—"

Joss groaned as her nipples went instantly hard and her stomach clenched with need. "Suitcase?" she asked as she tore herself away from Maeve and started for the house.

"Foyer," Maeve instructed with a laugh. She turned toward her parents and daughter and added, "Molly, me and Momma are going to go on our trip now so you can have a super-fun weekend with Grandma and Grandpa. Can I have a love goodbye?"

Joss watched Molly wriggle out of Ben's arms so she could run into Maeve's, and her heart swelled with love as she watched Maeve hold their child to her. Not wanting to be left out, George joined them, and Joss smiled as she picked up the suitcase.

I am so goddamn lucky.

She gave George a hug and Molly a kiss on the forehead as she passed, and smiled her thanks at Ben as he raced ahead of her to open the back hatch of the jeep for her.

"Have fun this weekend," Ben said as she hefted the suitcase into the car.

Joss nodded. "We will."

"It'll be late when we get into New York, so I'll call in the morning," Maeve said.

"Whatever," Elizabeth said, smiling. "We'll be here, so just have fun doing your shows and enjoy your weekend together."

Maeve looked at Joss, her eyes smoldering with lust and twinkling playfulness, and grinned. "Oh, we will."

Joss tried to hide the blush she felt burning her cheeks as she rushed back to steal one last kiss from Molly and to give George one last pat before she climbed behind the wheel of the car. "I can't believe you gave me that look with your parents right there," she muttered when Maeve joined her.

"What look?" Maeve asked, batting her lashes innocently as she buckled her seatbelt.

Joss waved at Elizabeth, Ben, Molly, and George, who had all retreated to the front porch for safety while they drove off, and started the car. "The I'm-going-to-make-you-come-so-hard-you-forget-your-own-name look."

Maeve laughed and waved at everyone on the porch. "That wasn't a look. That was a promise, sweetheart."

Joss huffed a quiet laugh and shook her head as she shifted the car into gear. "God, I love you."

Maeve smiled, took Joss' right hand into her own, and laced their fingers together. "I love you."

Acknowledgements

Many, many thanks to you, my amazing readers, without whom I would have to go get a "real" job and wouldn't be able to spend my days doing what I truly love. Thanks also go to my amazing Alpha readers Jade and Amy, who were once again right there with me from the very beginning, reading this thing in bits and pieces, and offering both editorial suggestions as well as the occasional (much needed) pat on the head. To KJ for finding time in your busy schedule to take this thing on a test run and give me some much-appreciated feedback. To Clom, for your medical prowess and suggestion that I add a prologue (you were right, by the way, it is much better now). And, lastly, to Wye, for squeezing me into your busy schedule and once again pointing out all the ways I could go about making this thing better.

Thank you.

Made in the USA
San Bernardino, CA
04 April 2016